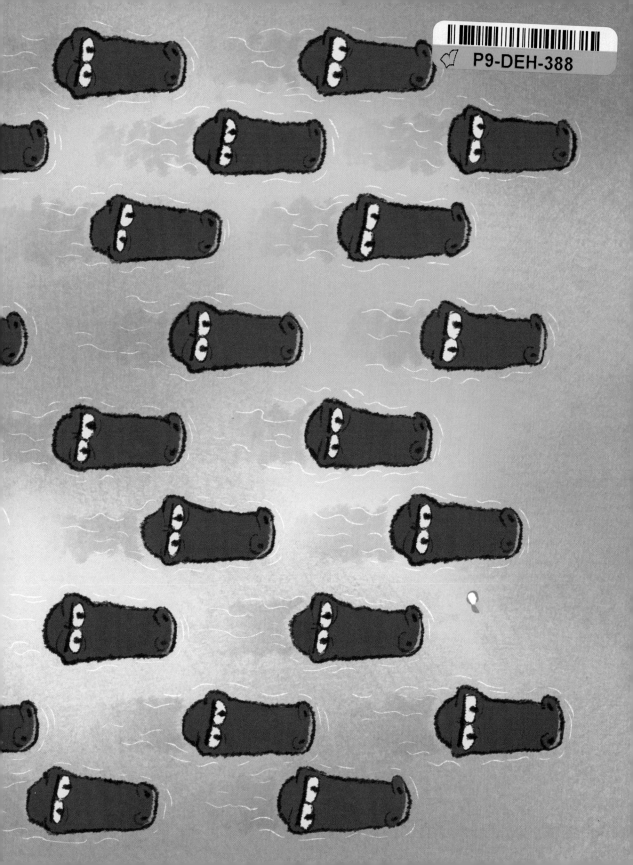

# PETER & ERNESTO
## the LOST SLOTHS

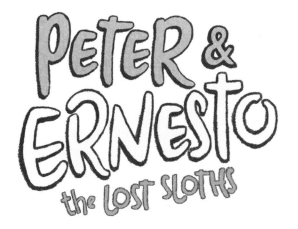

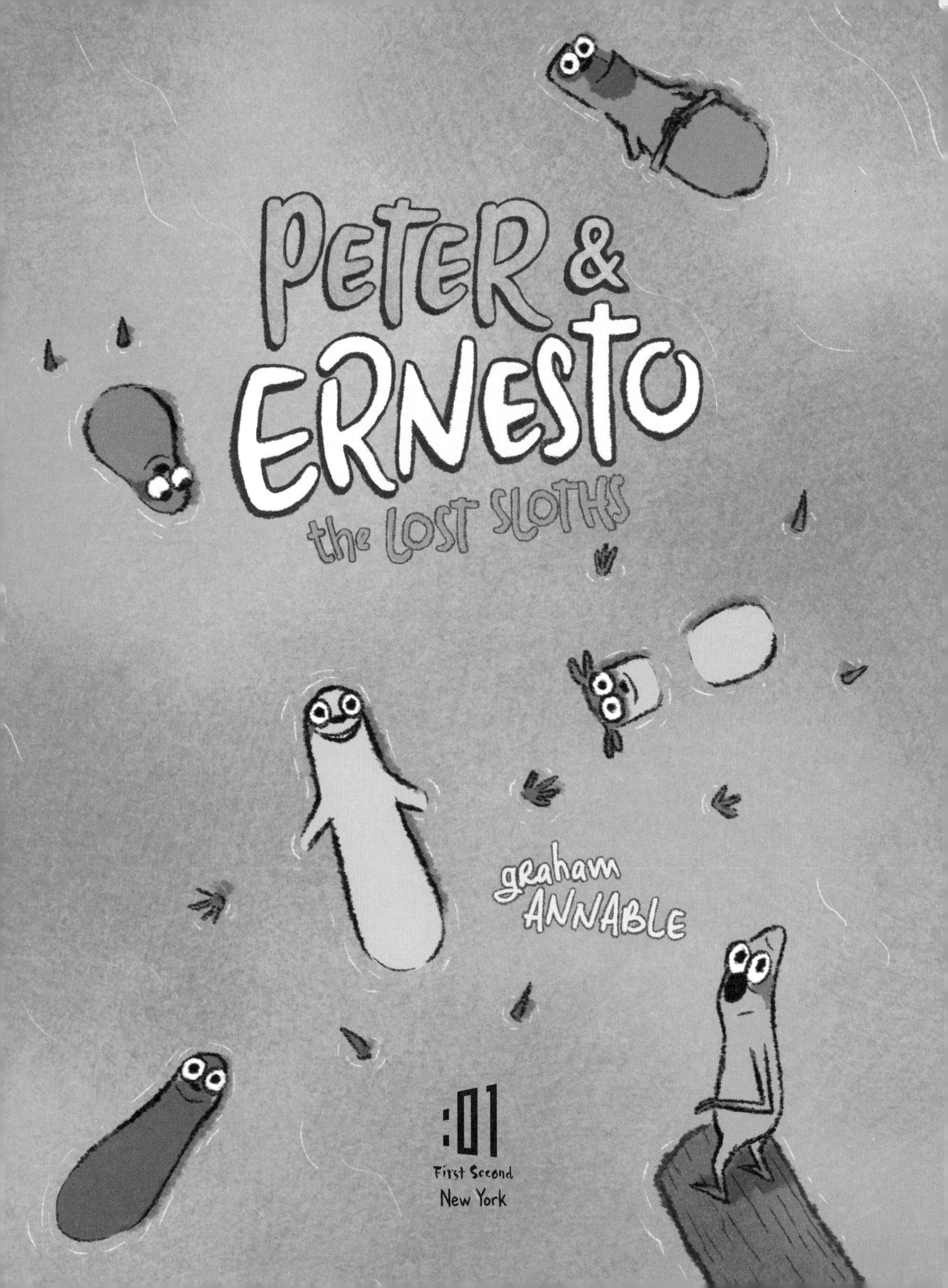
PETER &
ERNESTO
the LOST SLOTHS
graham ANNABLE
:01
First Second
New York

Dedicated to Malena
and my two boys,
James and Carson

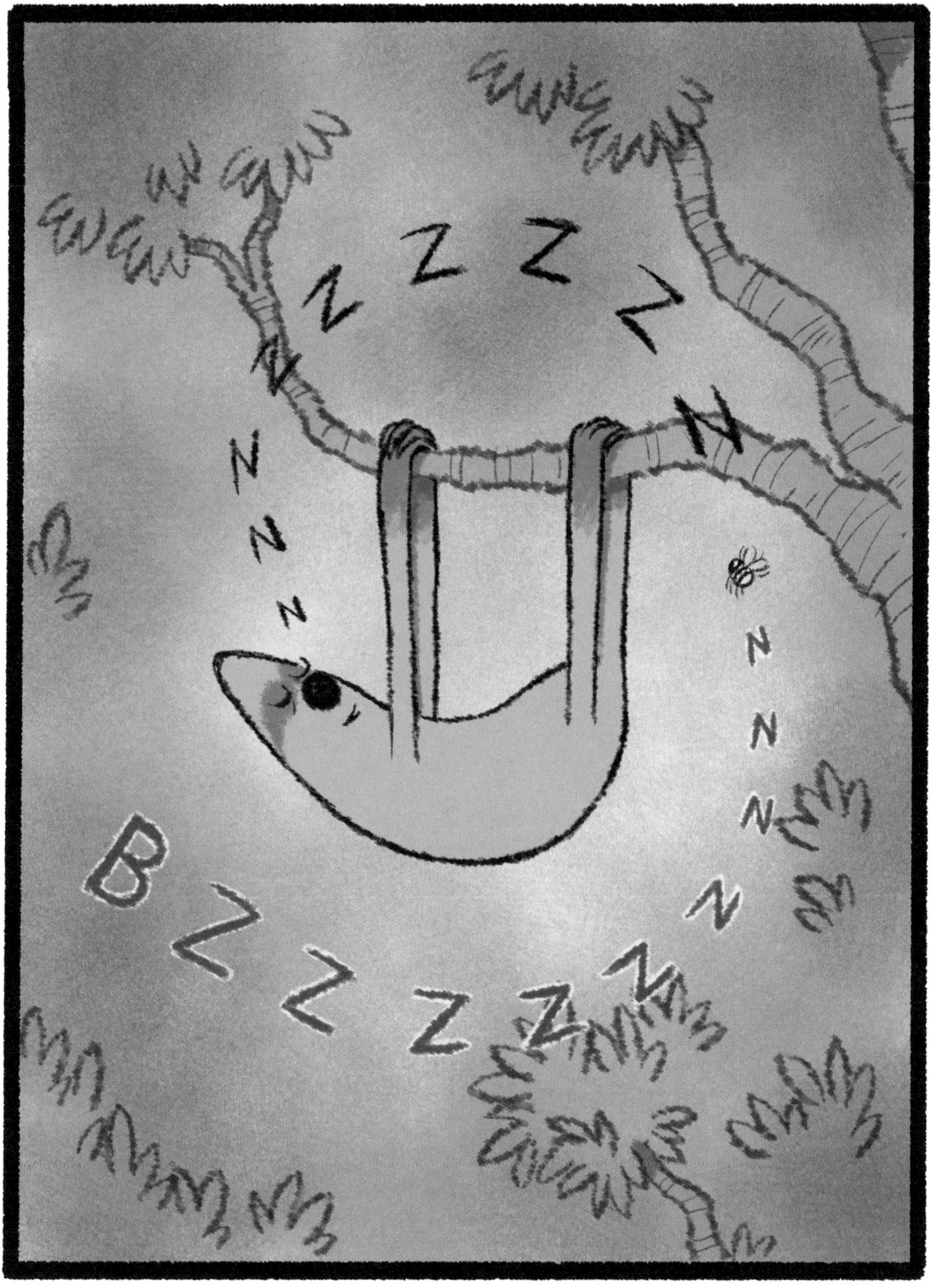
ZZZZZZ
ZZZ
BZZZZZZZZZ

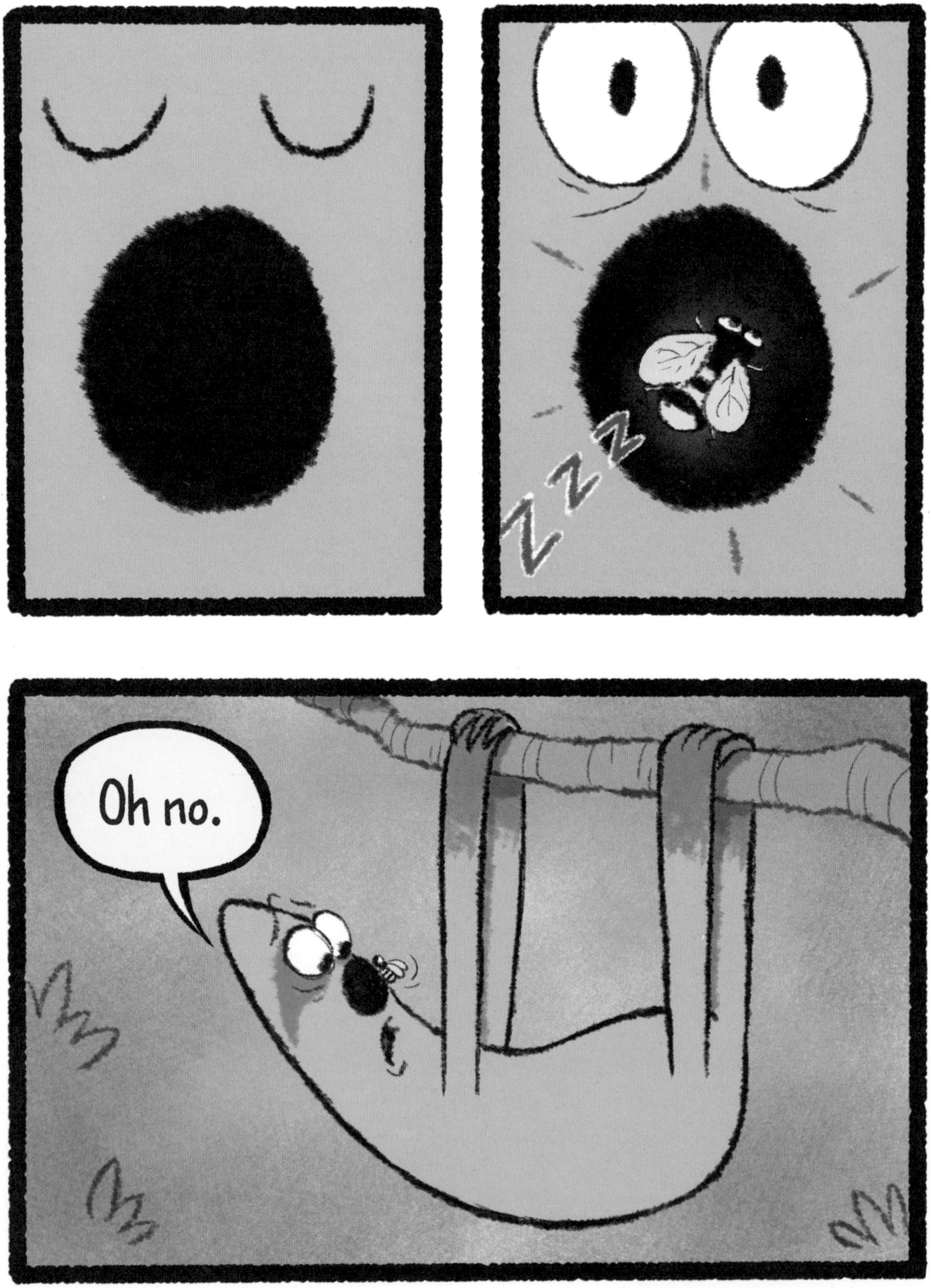
Z Z Z
Oh no.

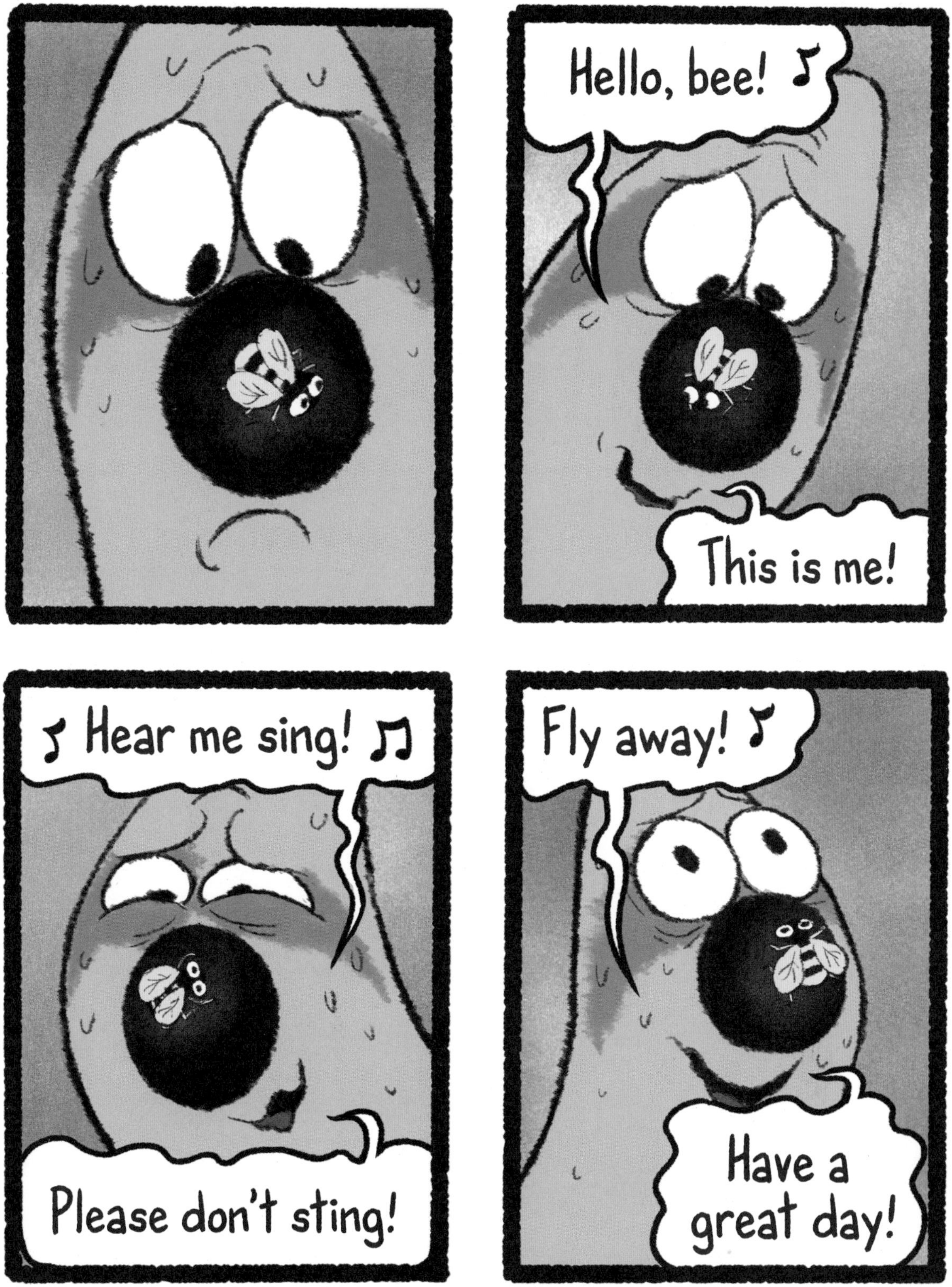
Hello, bee! ♪
This is me!
♪ Hear me sing! ♫
Please don't sting!
Fly away! ♪
Have a great day!

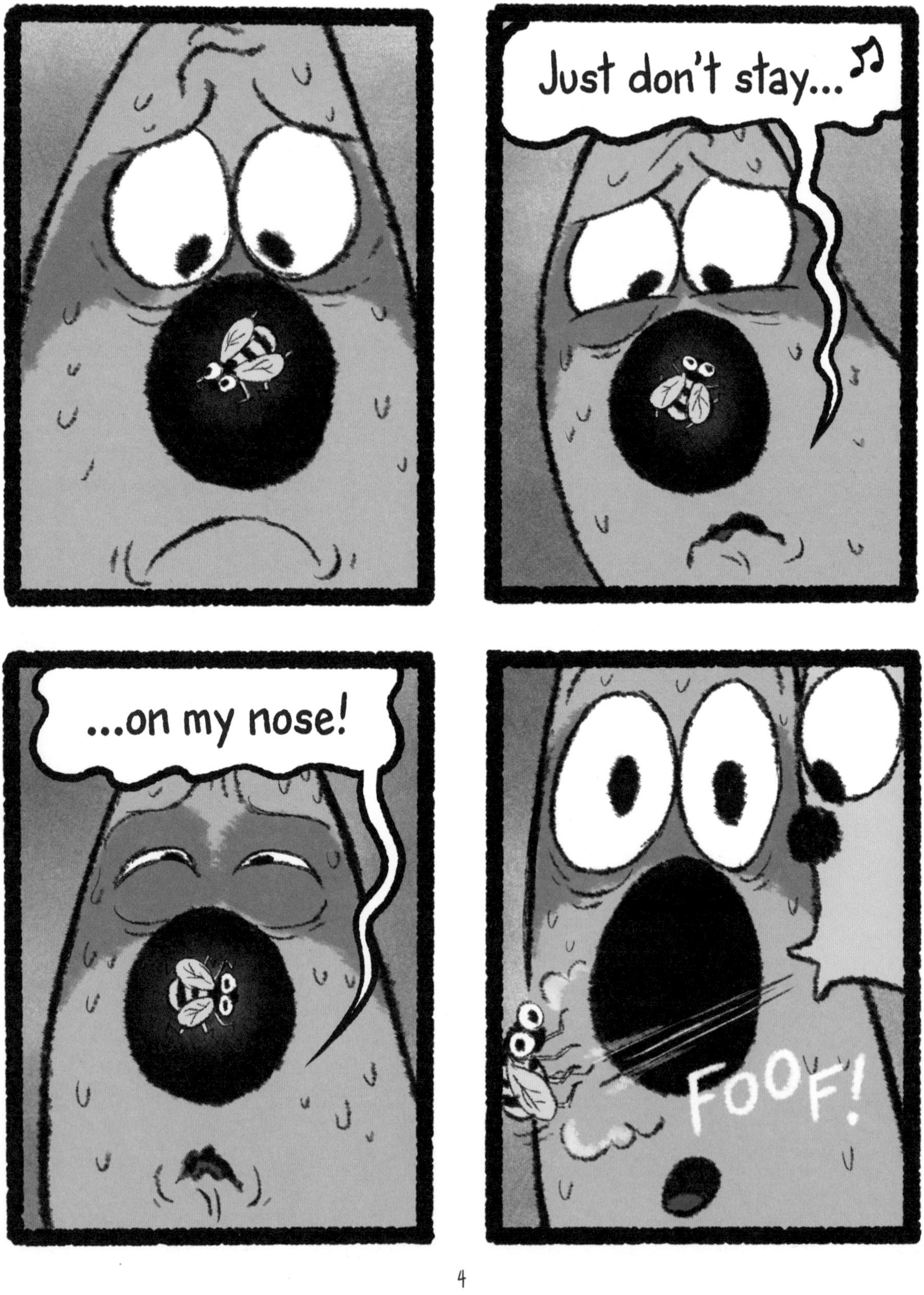
Just don't stay...♫
...on my nose!
FOOF!

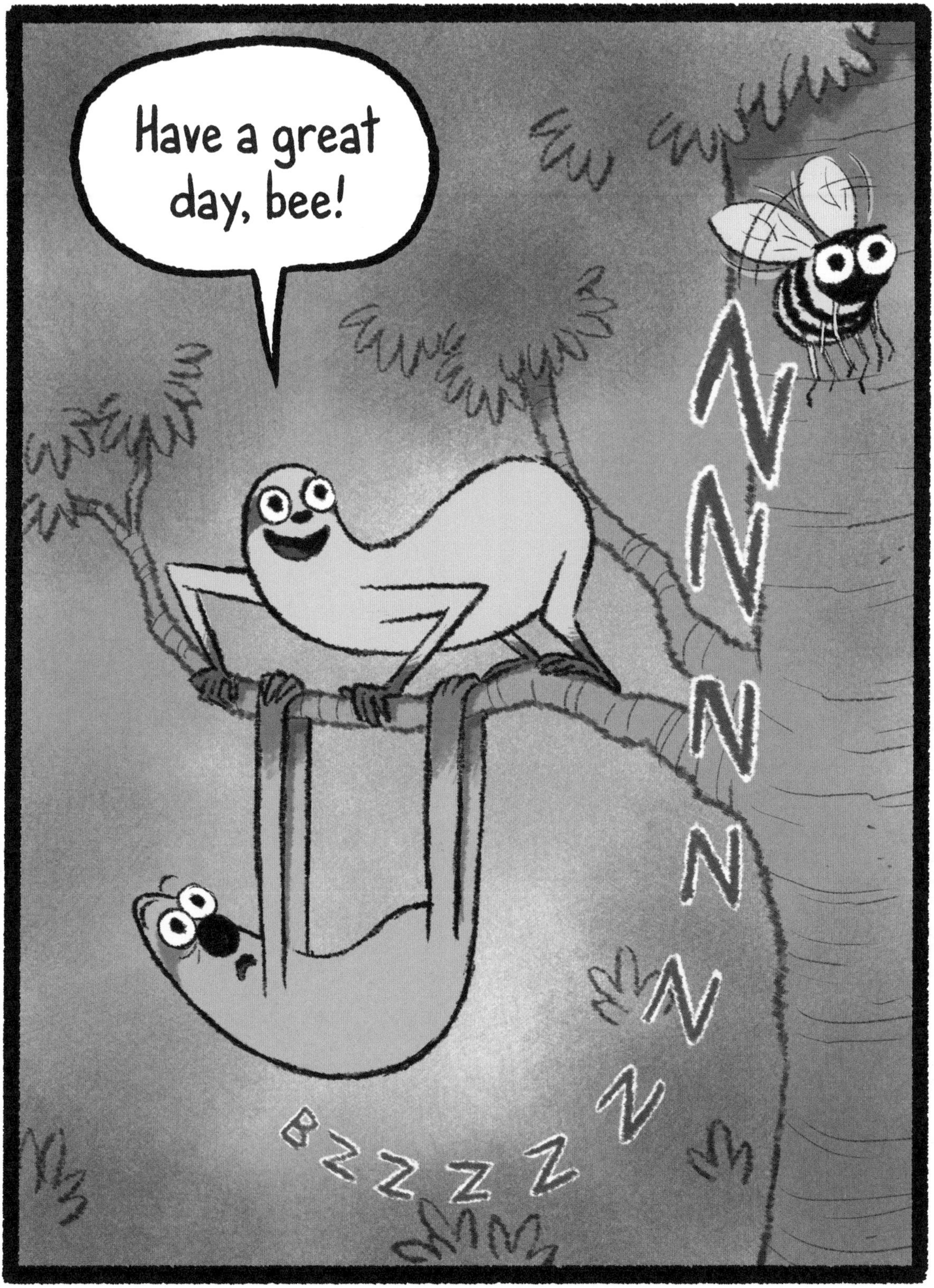
Have a great day, bee!
BZZZZZZZZZZZ

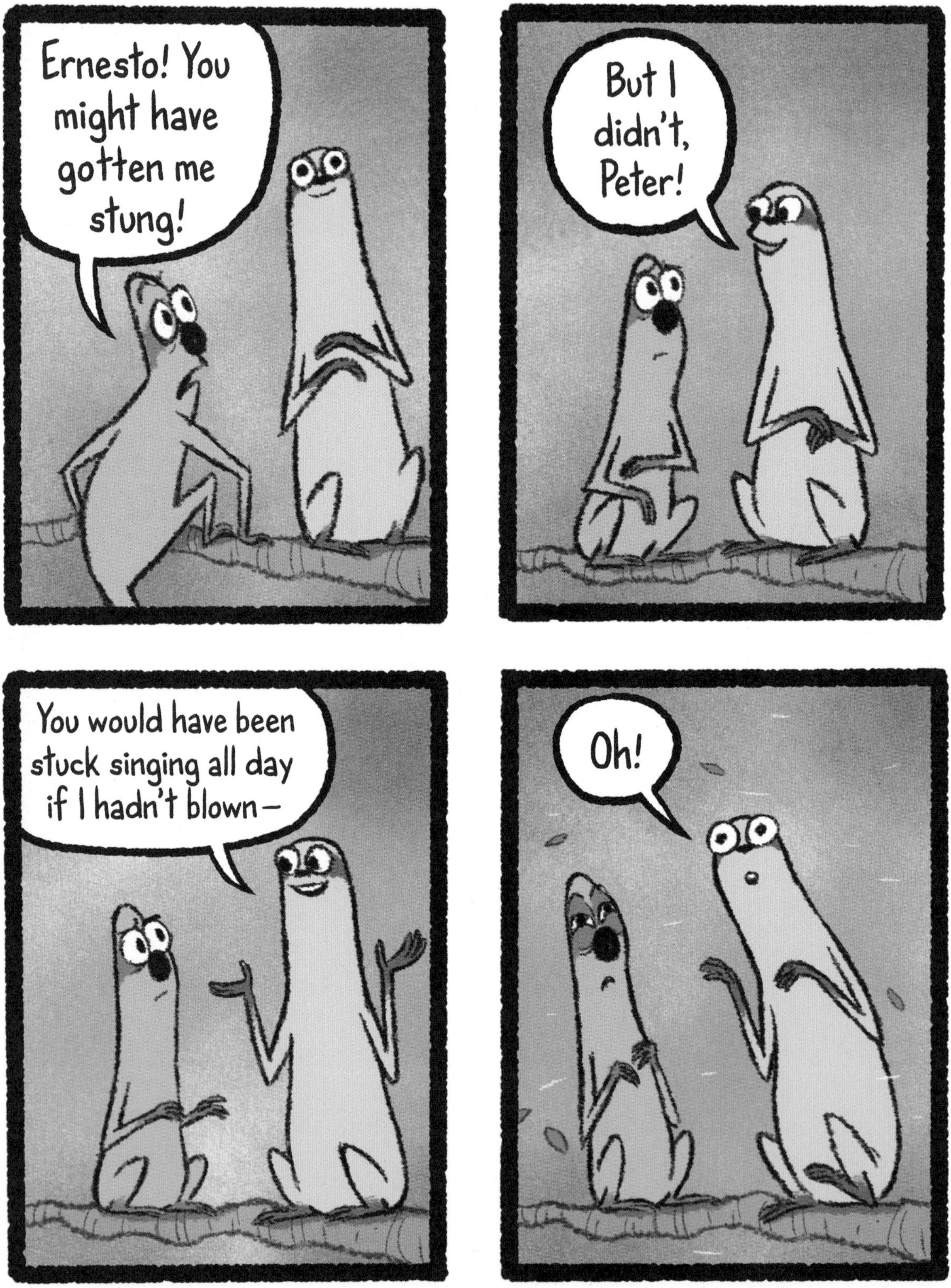
Ernesto! You might have gotten me stung!
But I didn't, Peter!
You would have been stuck singing all day if I hadn't blown—
Oh!

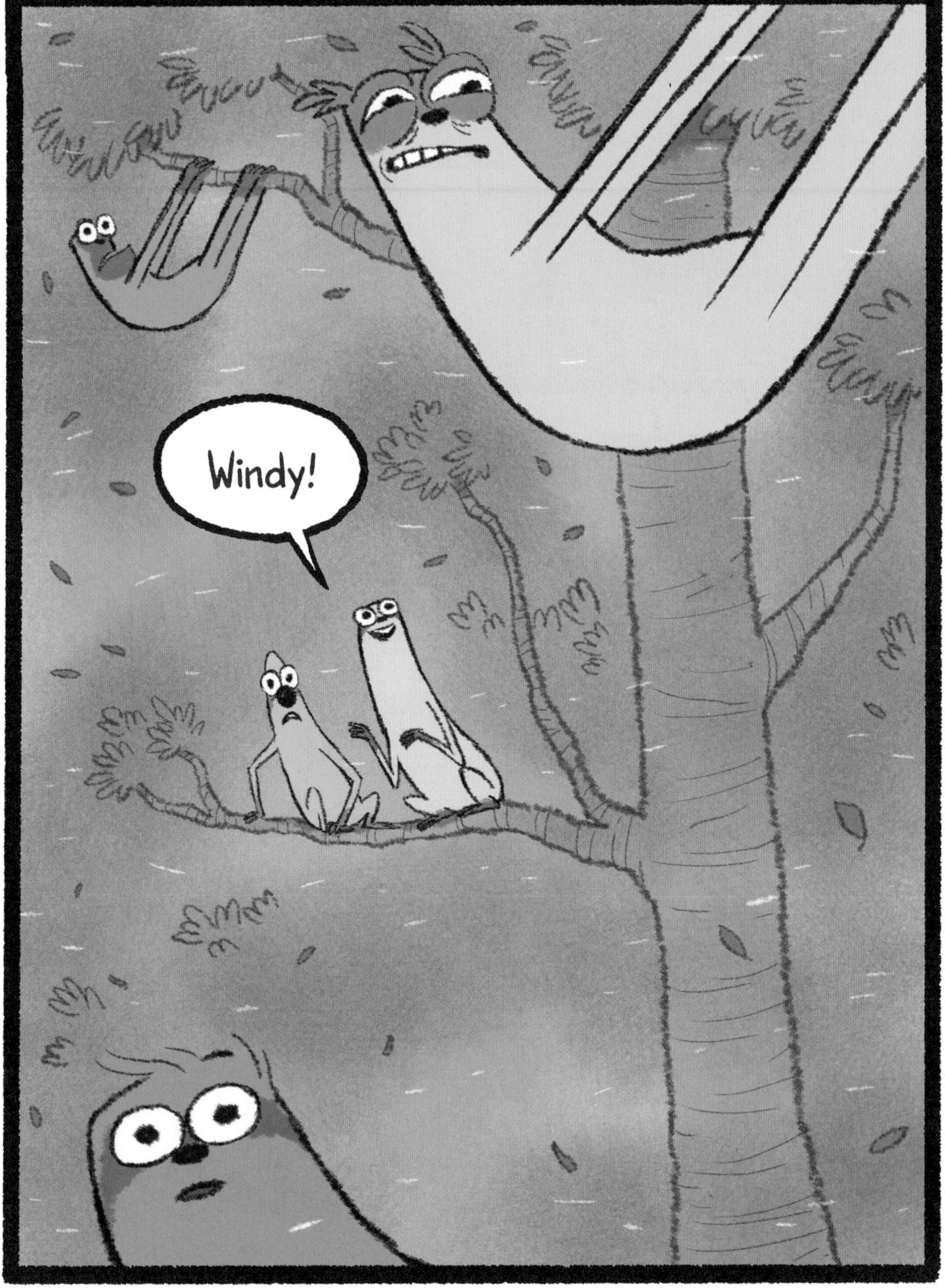
Windy!

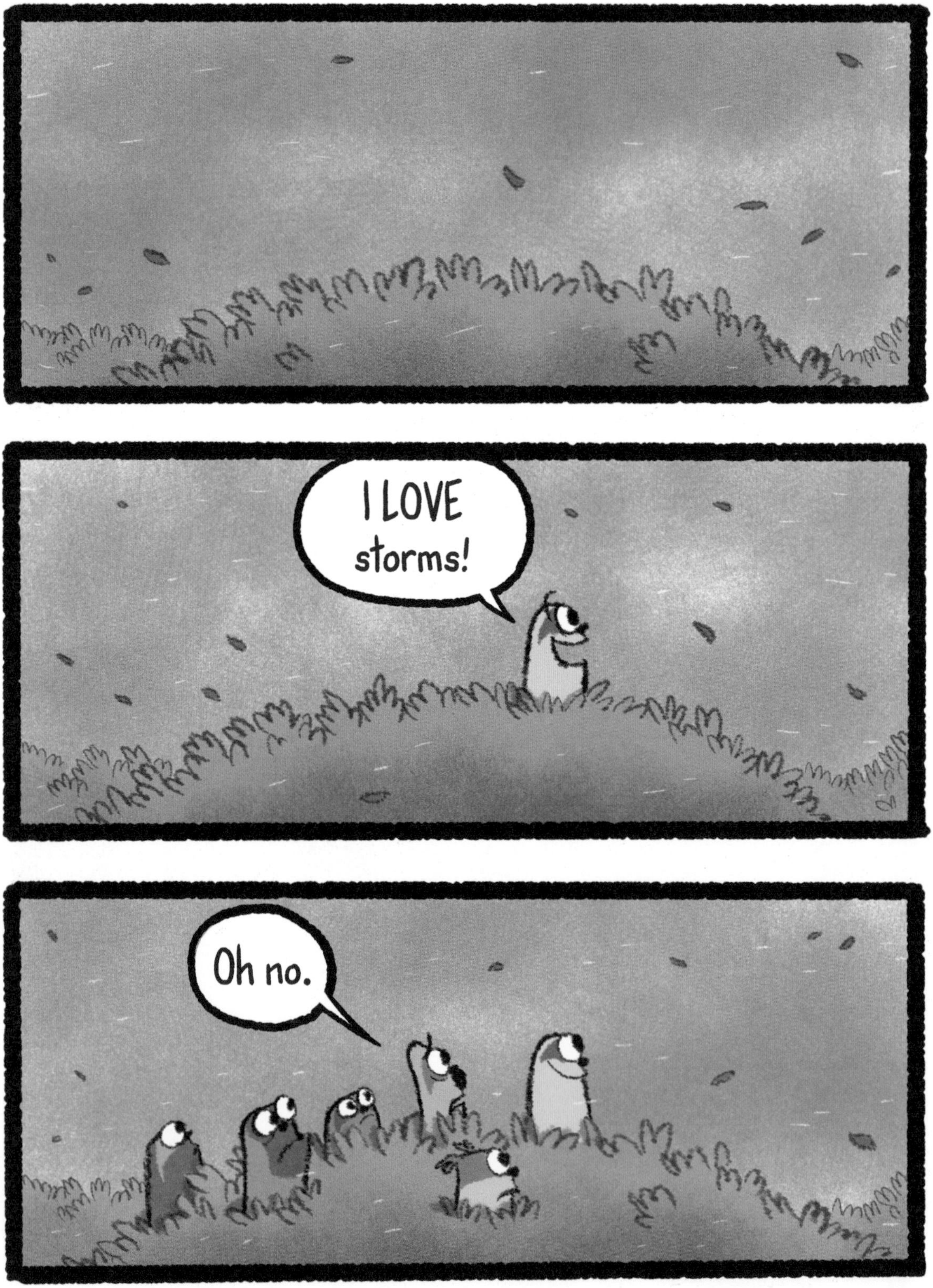
I LOVE storms!
Oh no.

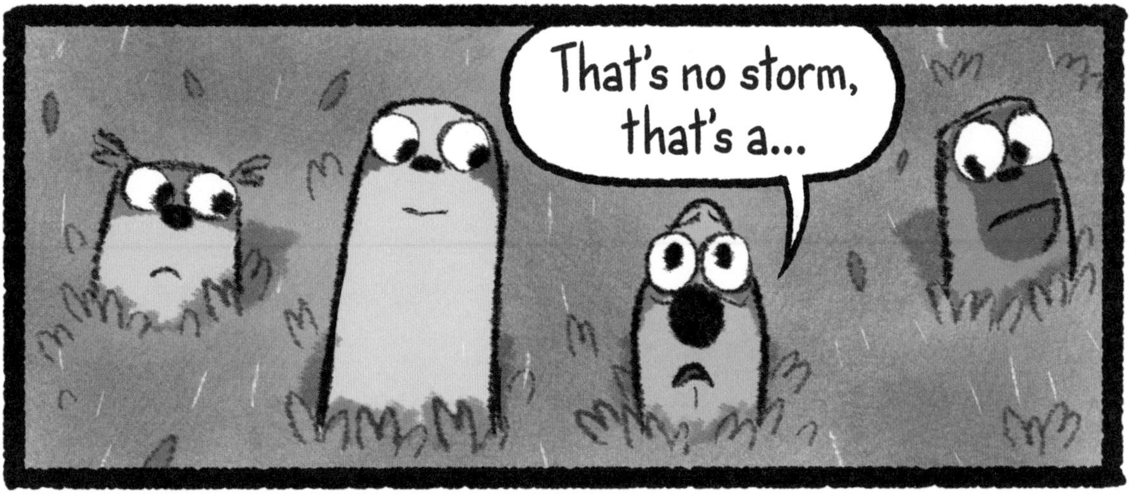
That's no storm, that's a...

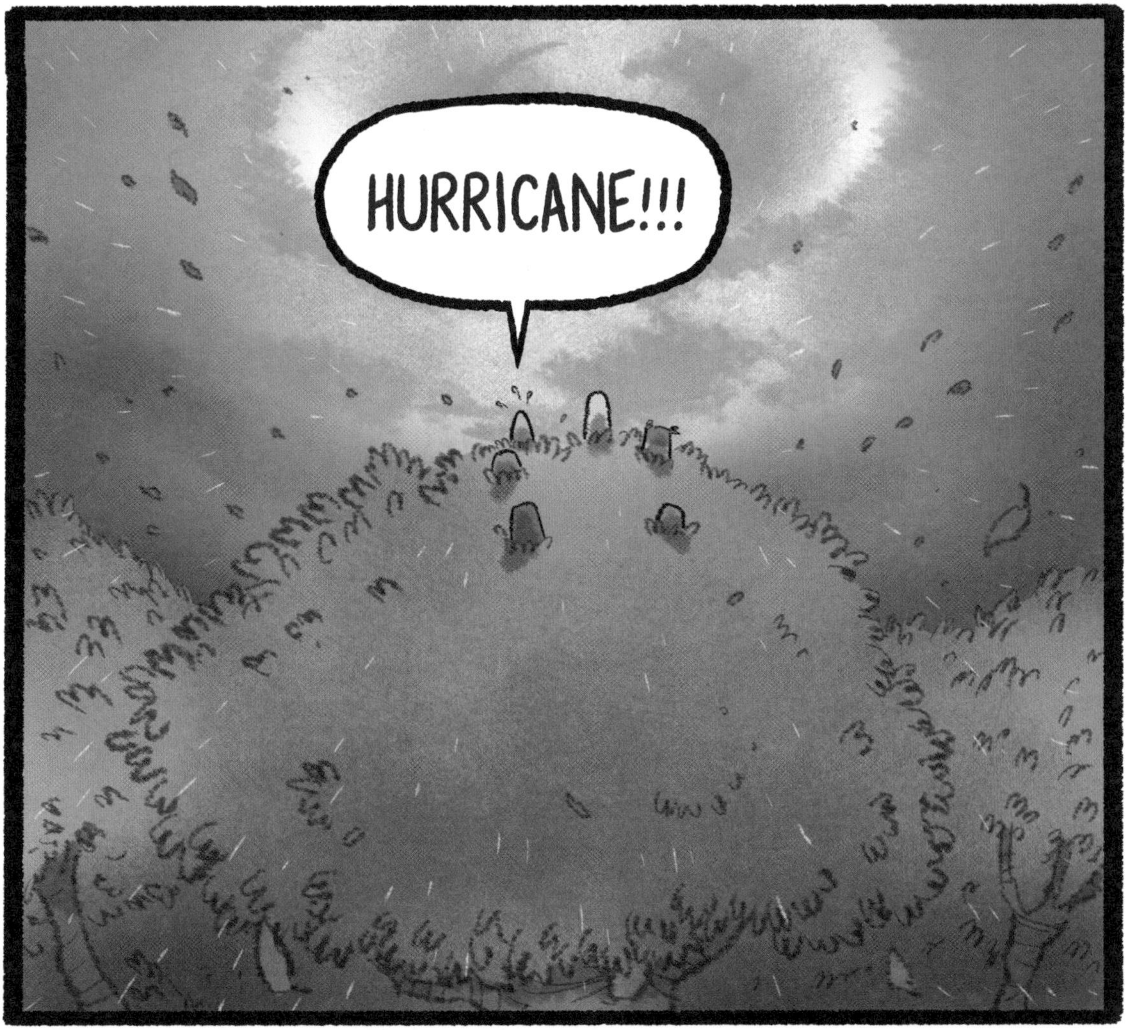
HURRICANE!!!

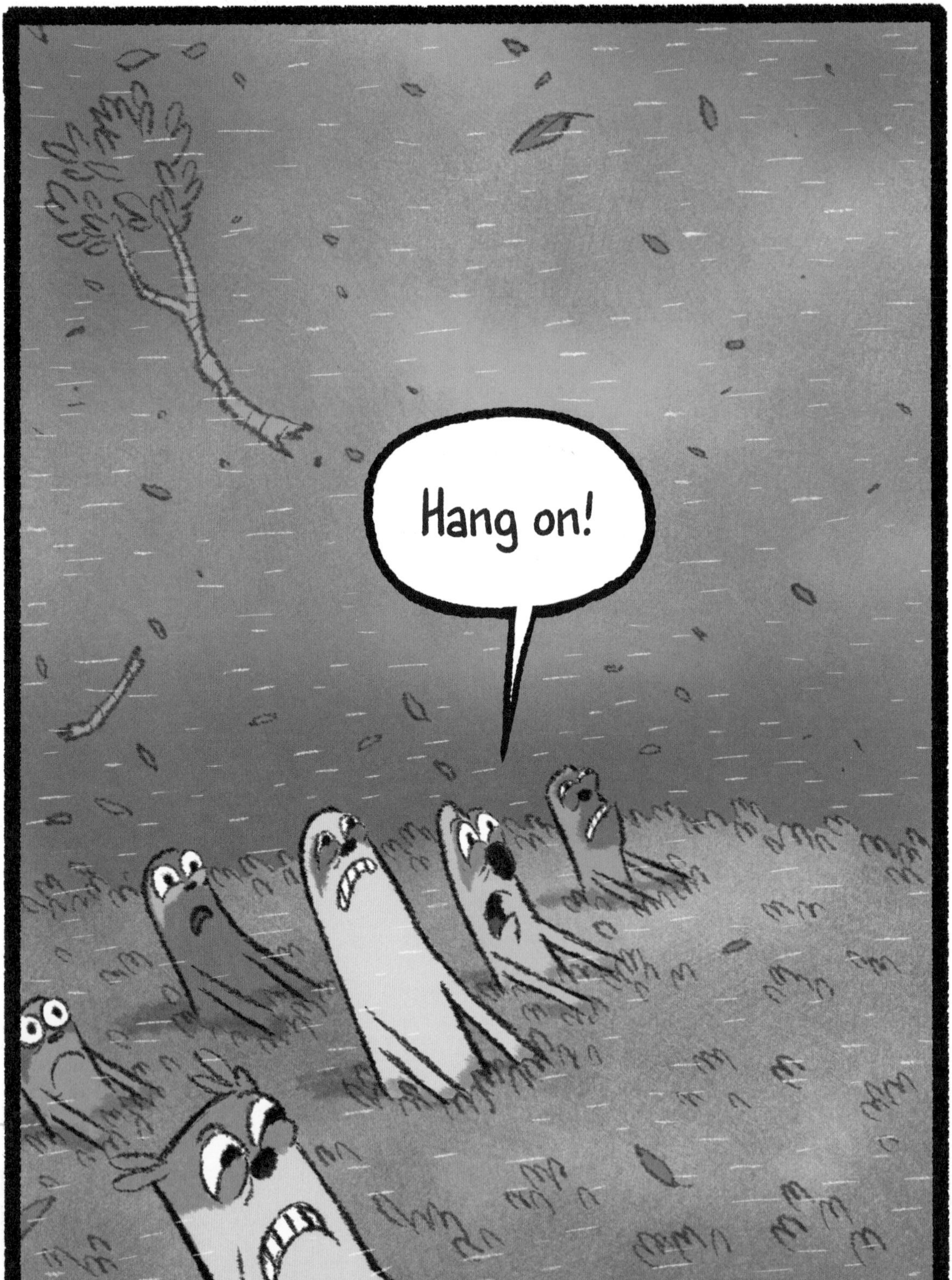
Hang on!

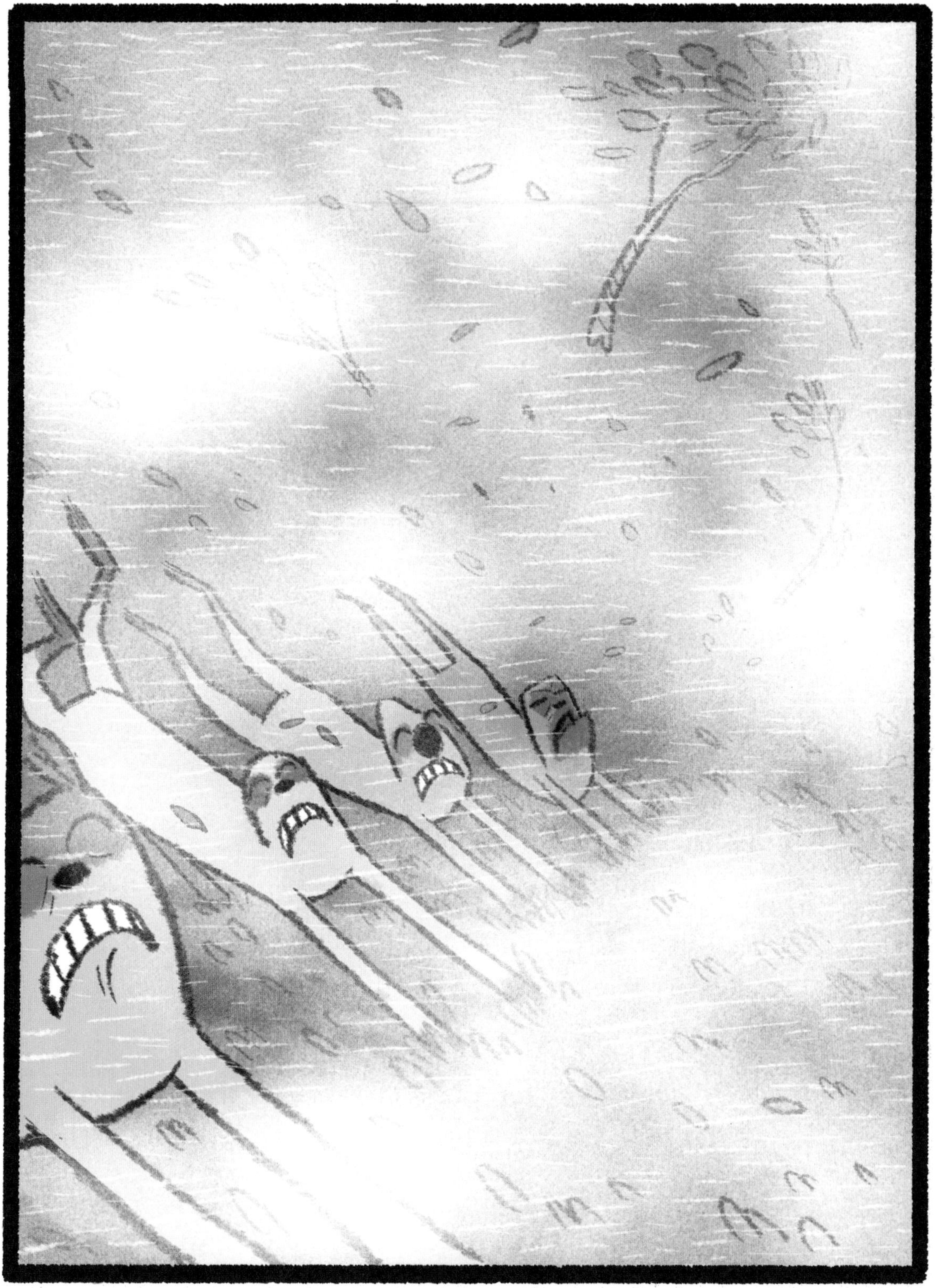

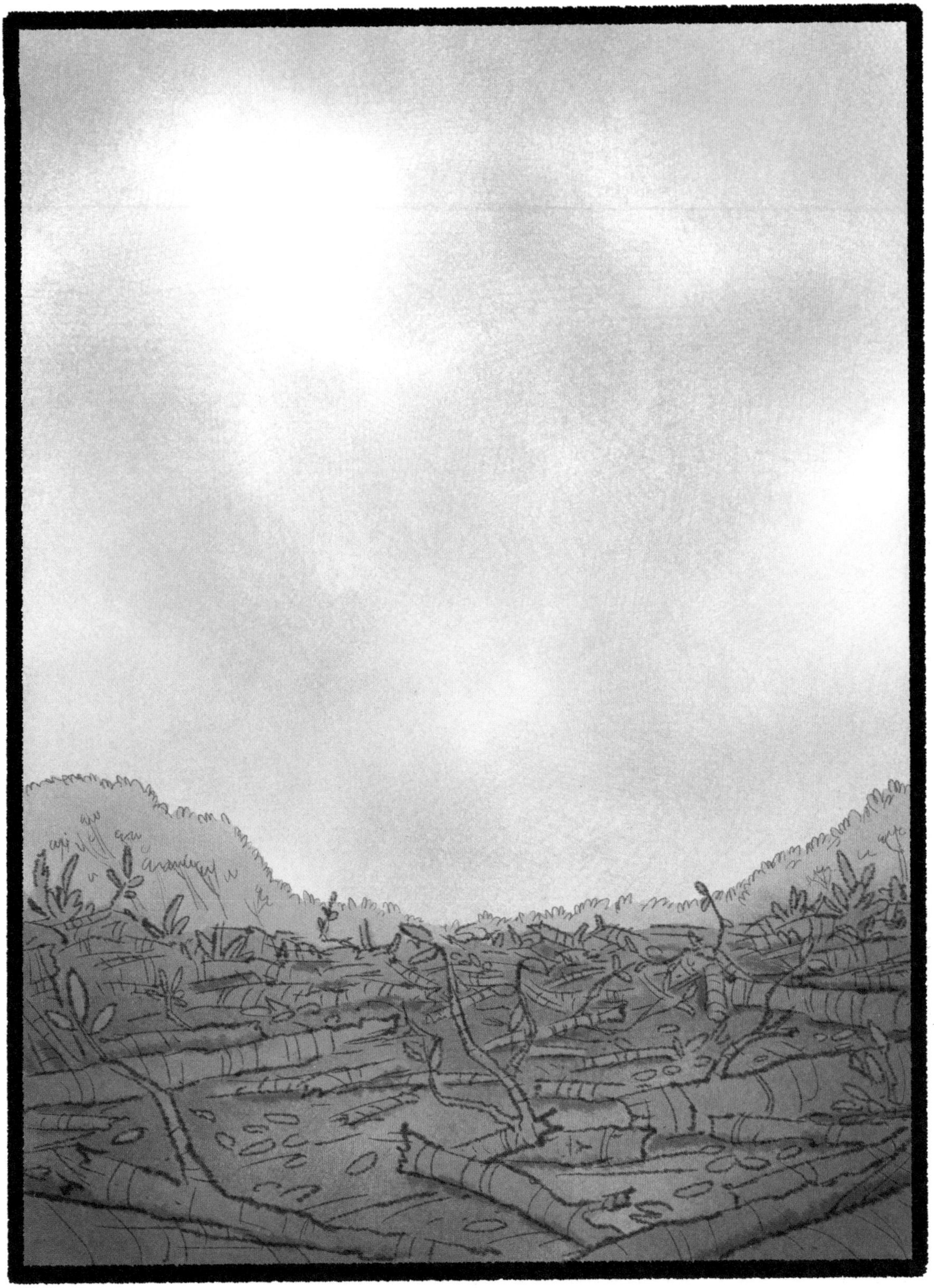

Gasp!
Hello?
Where is everyone?

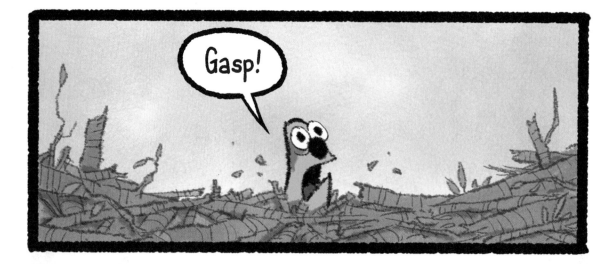

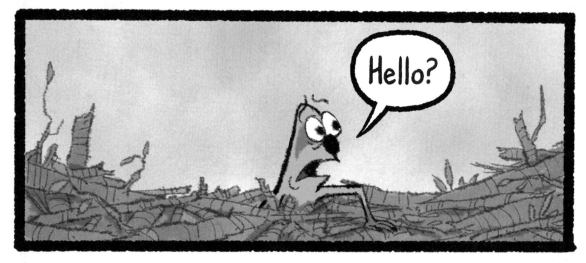

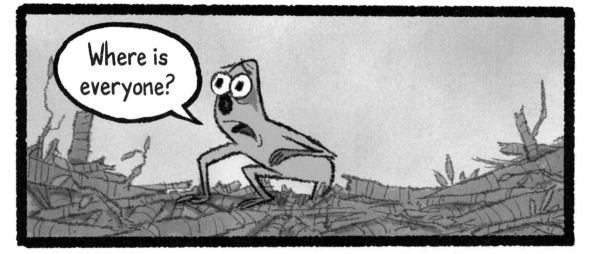

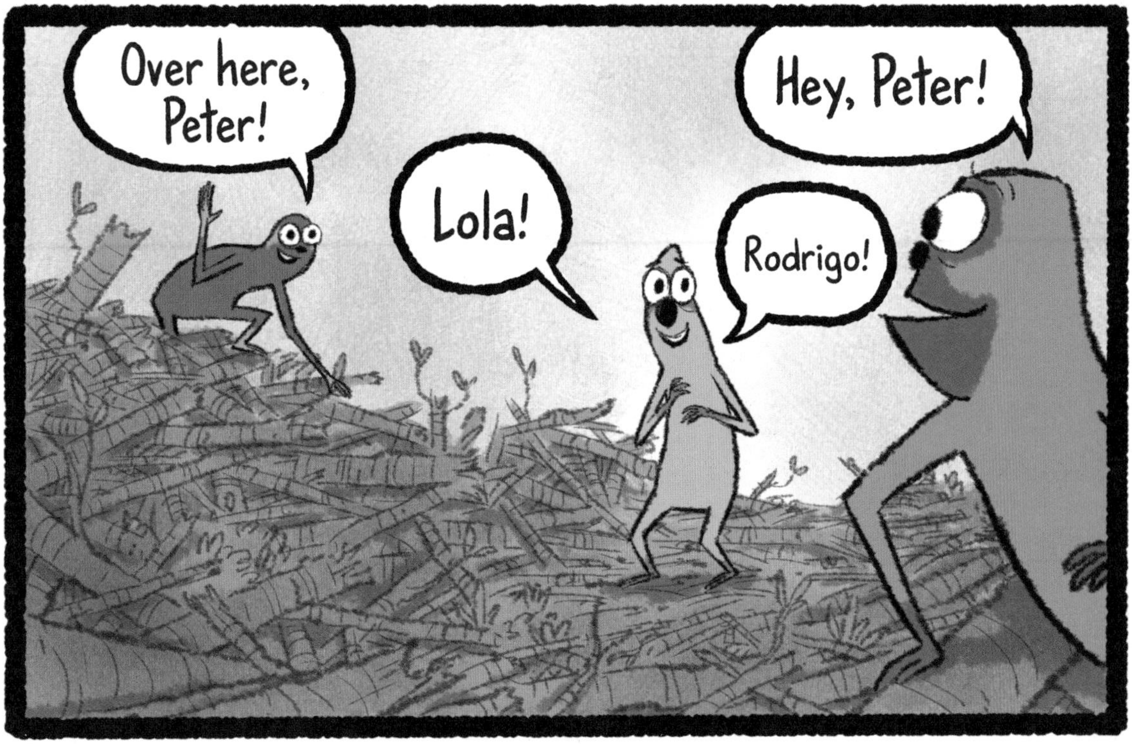
Over here, Peter!
Lola!
Rodrigo!
Hey, Peter!

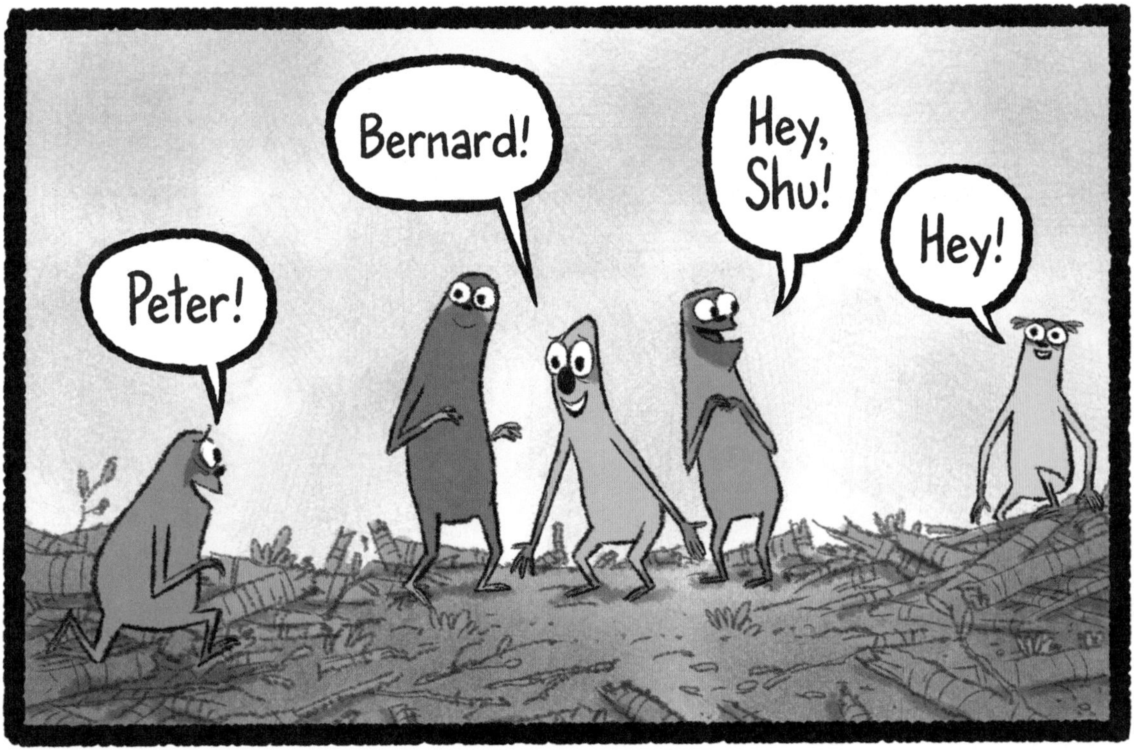
Peter!
Bernard!
Hey, Shu!
Hey!

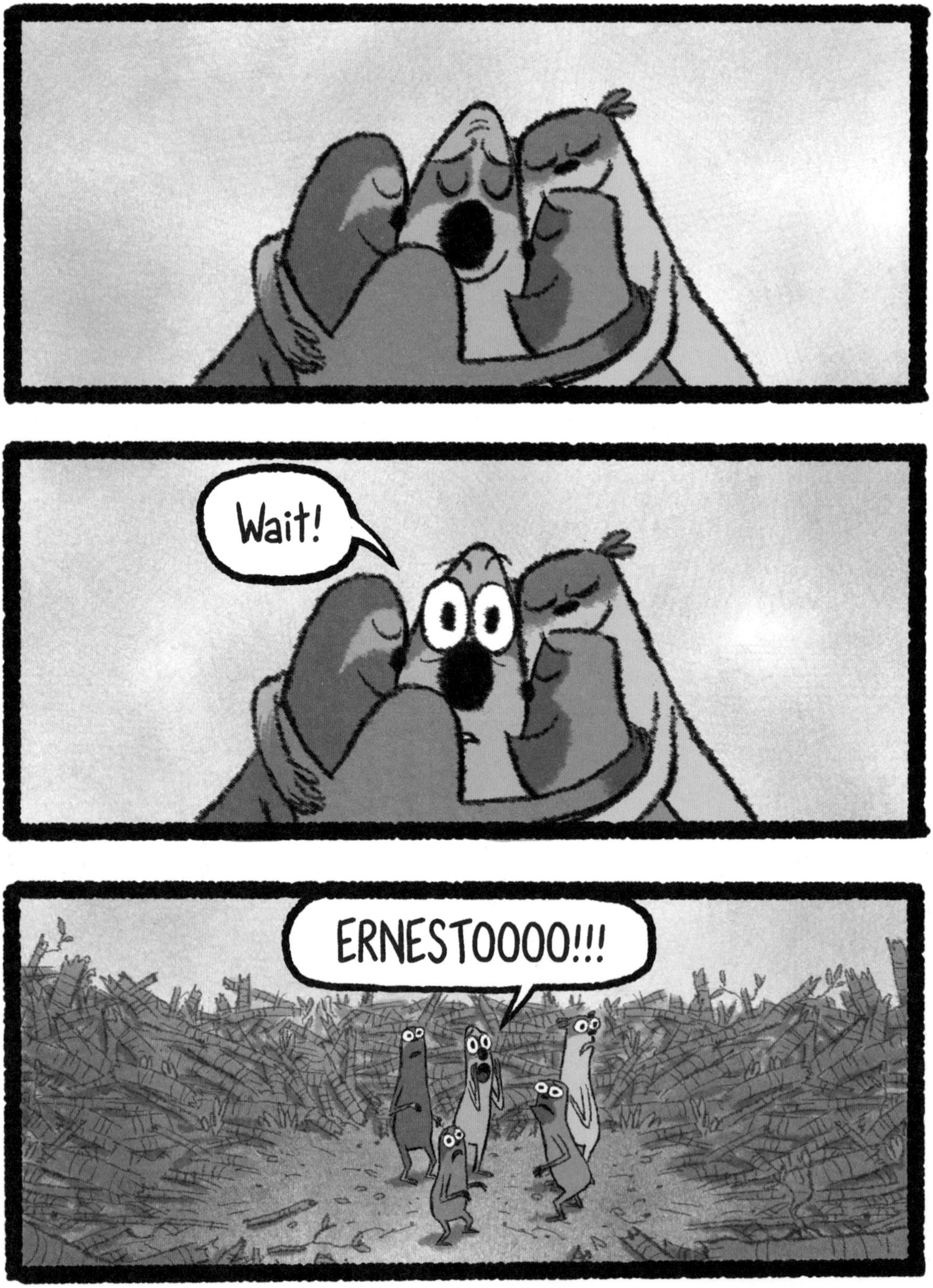
Wait!
ERNESTOOOO!!!

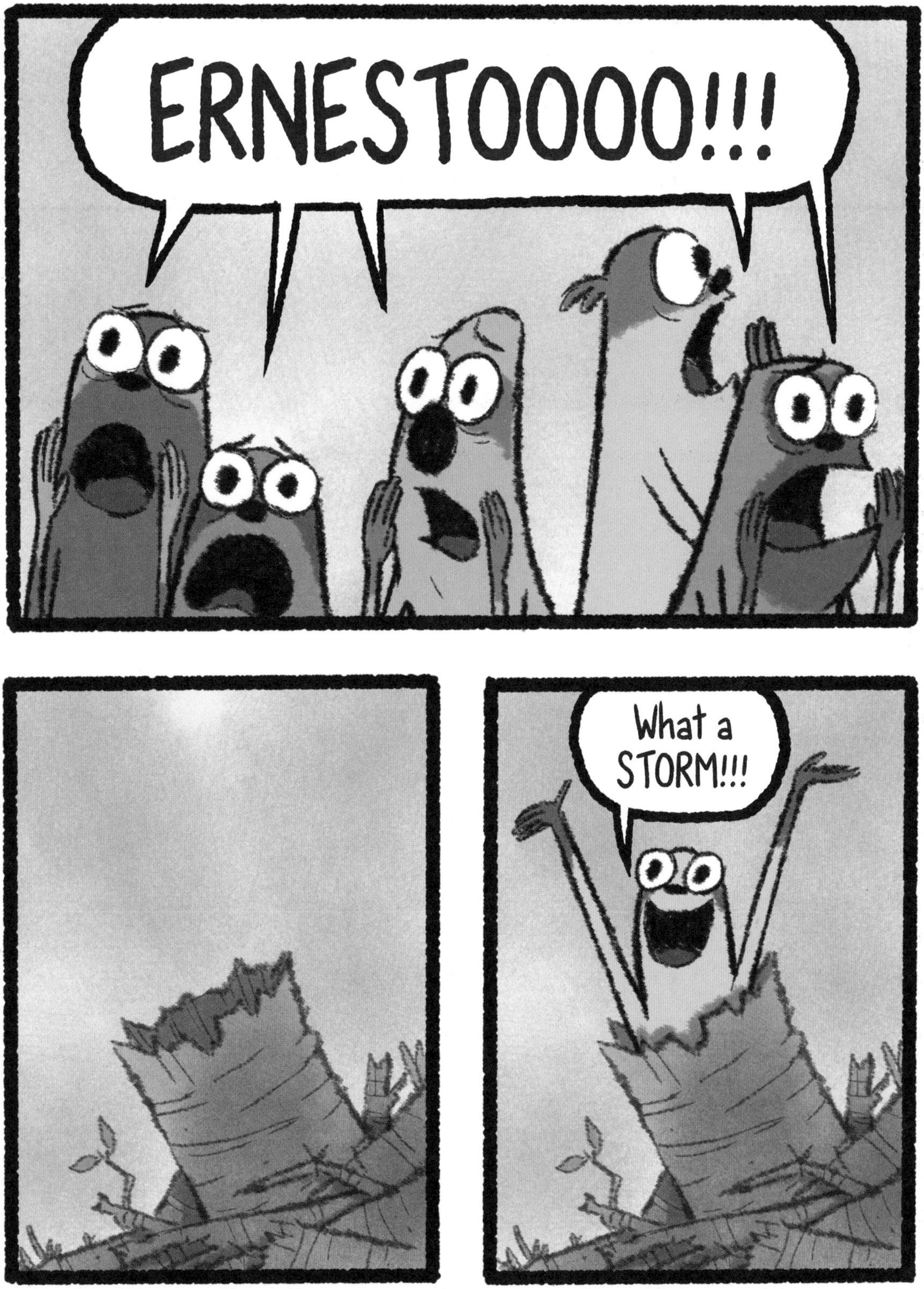
ERNESTOOOO!!!
What a STORM!!!

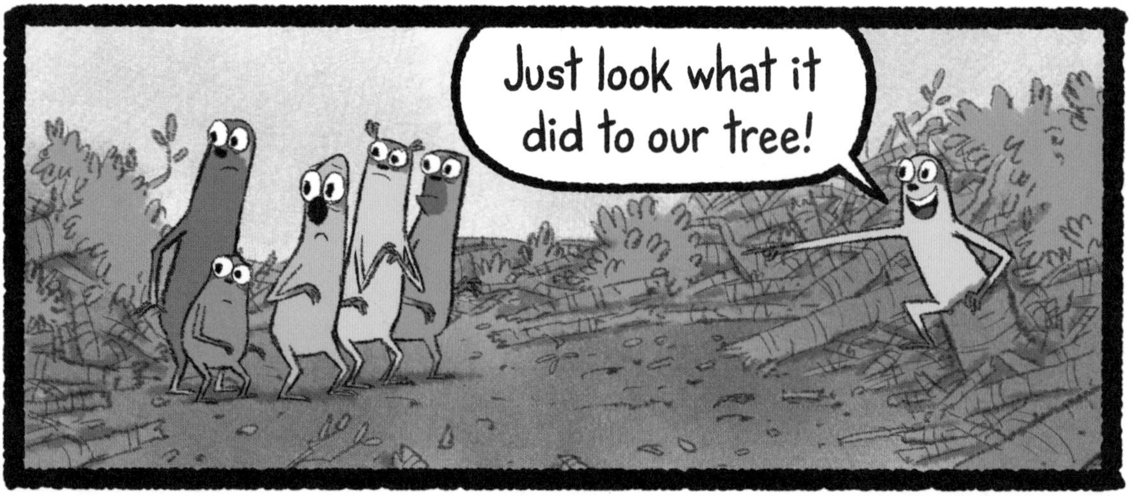
Just look what it did to our tree!

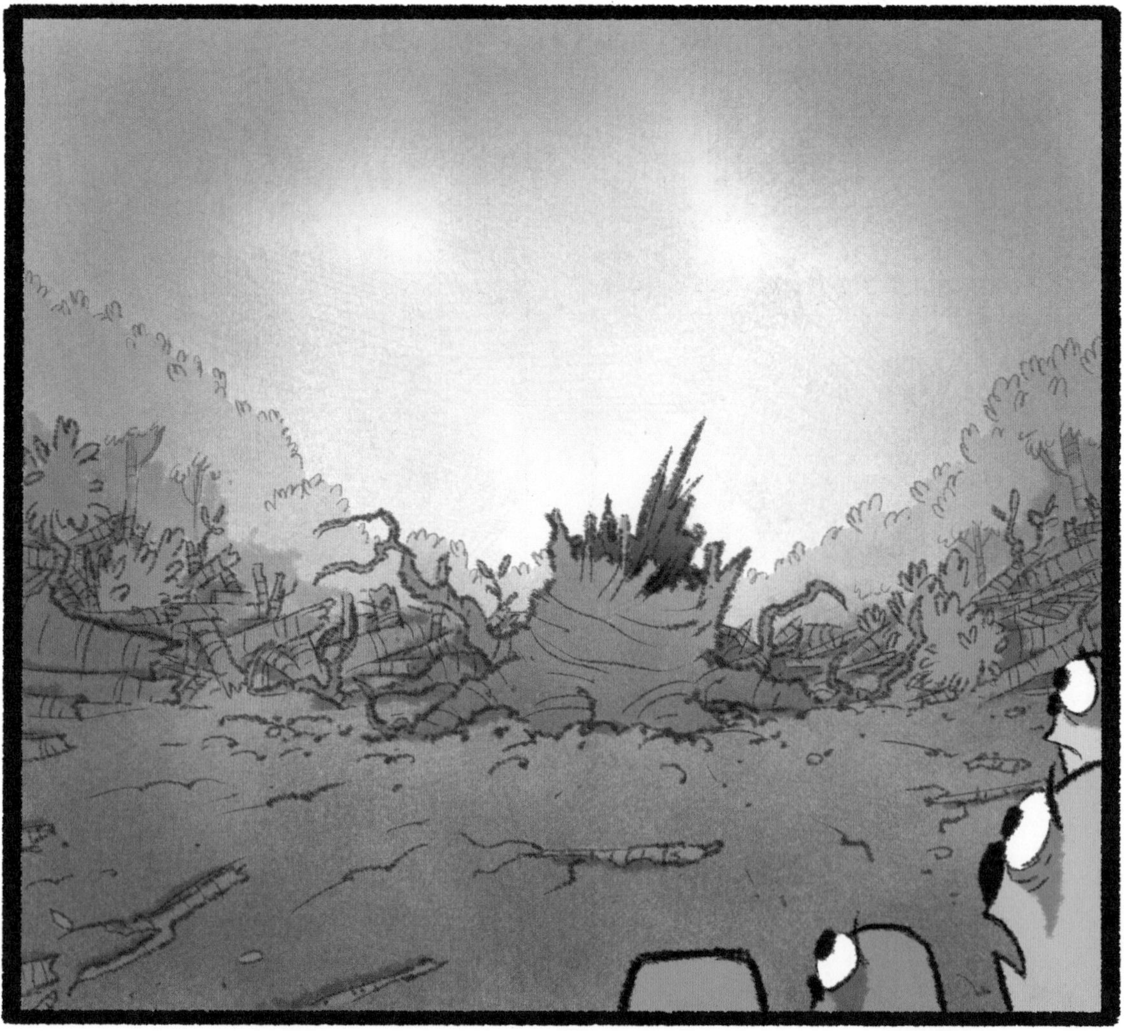

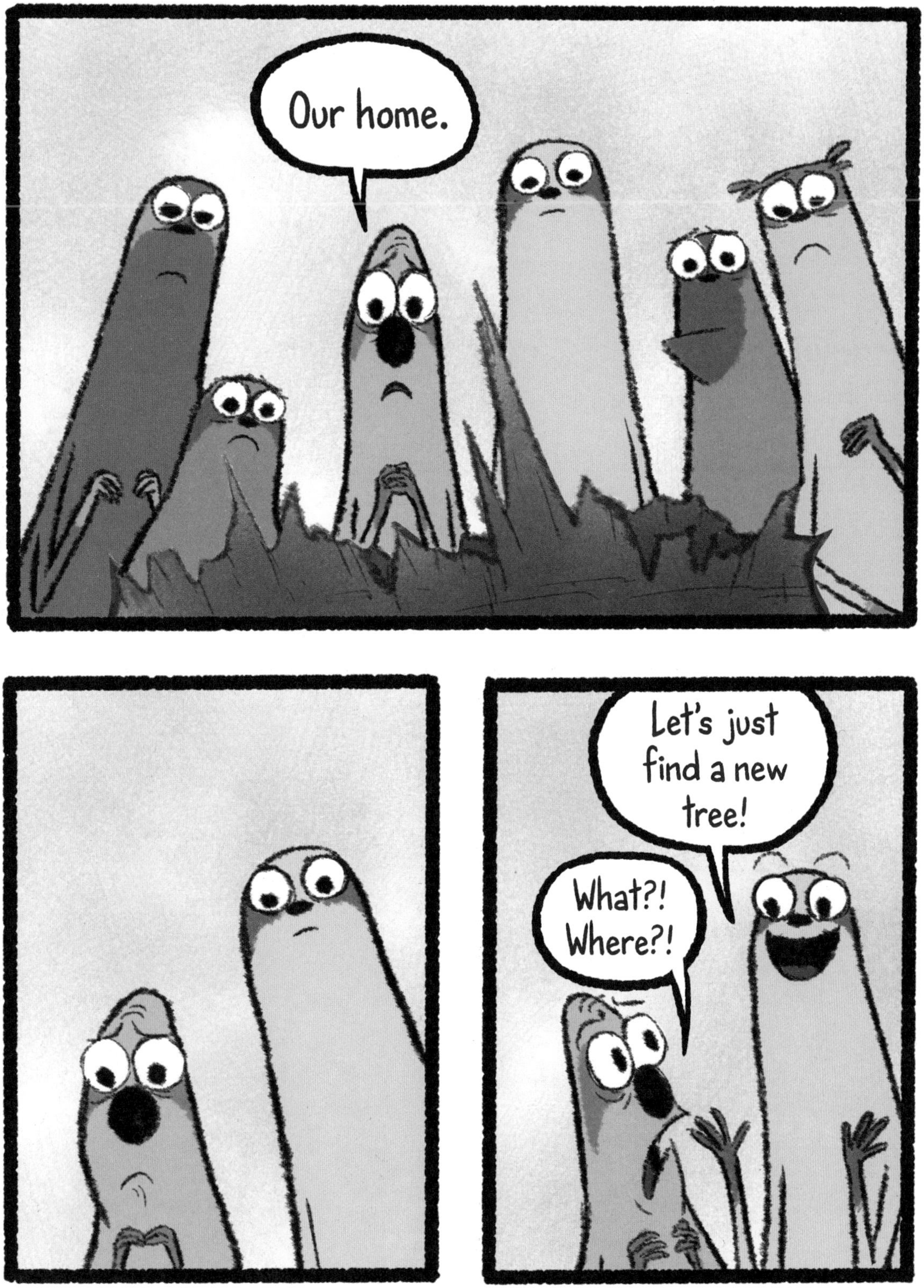

Our home.
Let's just find a new tree!
What?! Where?!

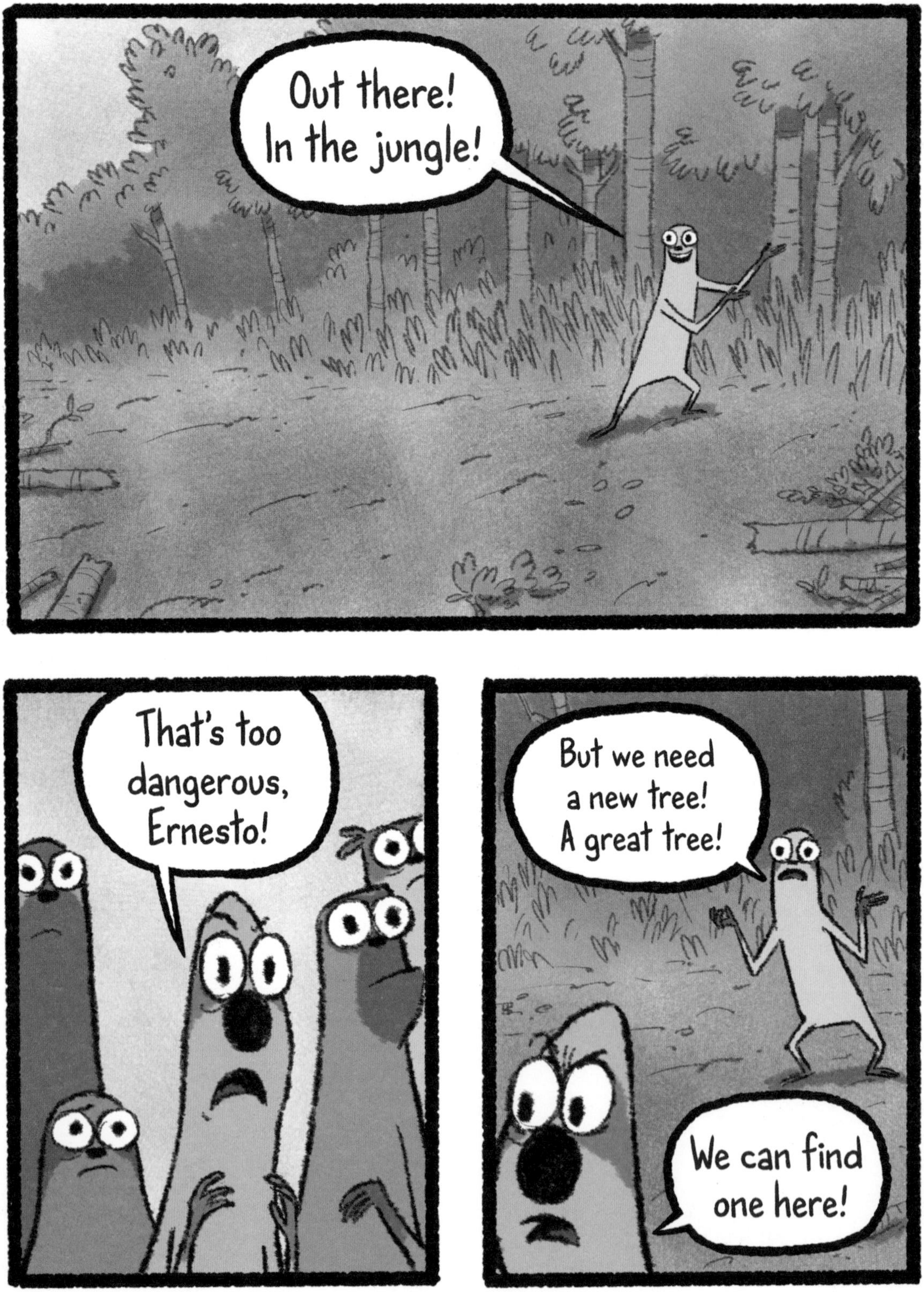
Out there! In the jungle!
That's too dangerous, Ernesto!
But we need a new tree! A great tree!
We can find one here!

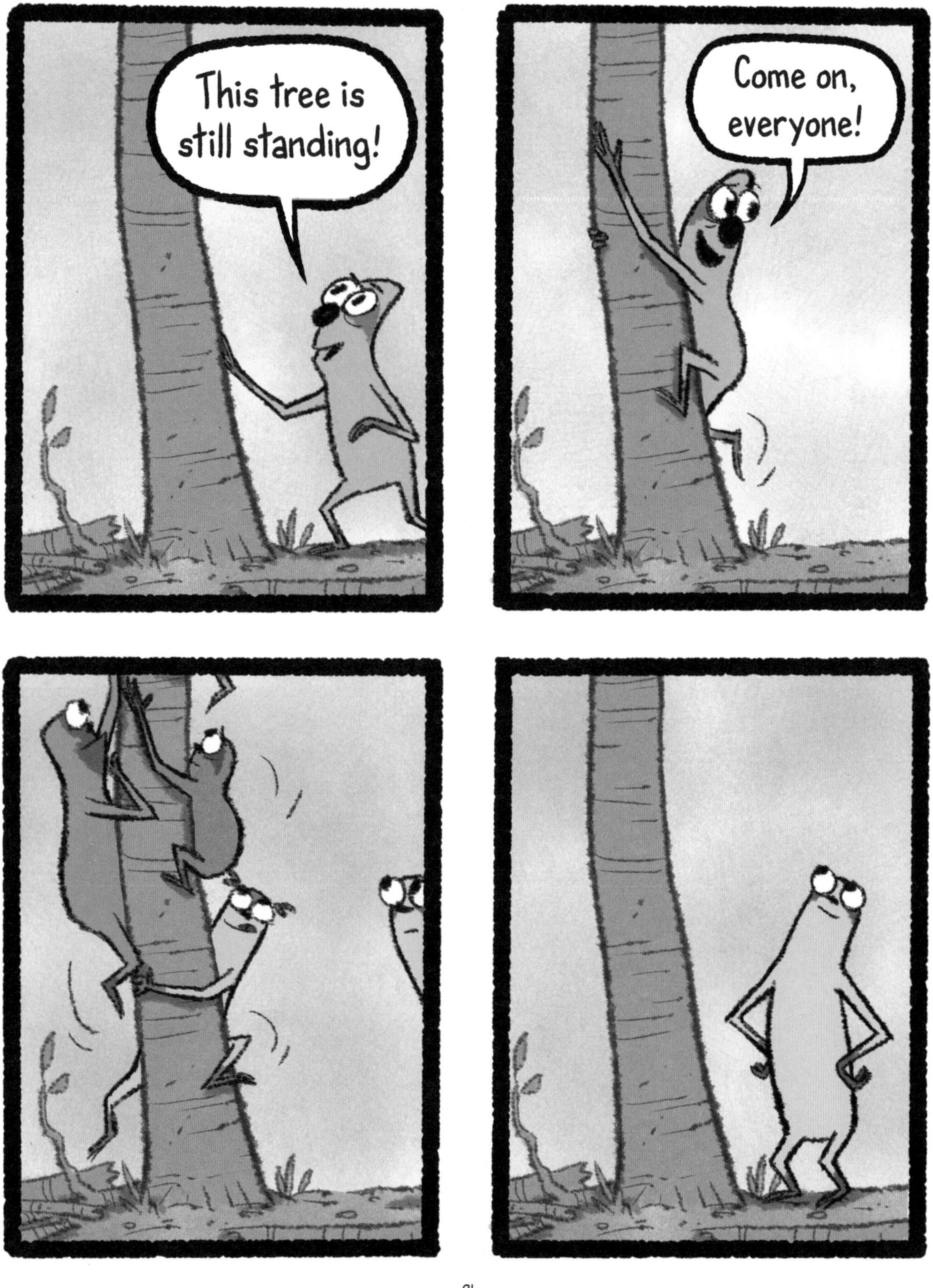
This tree is still standing!
Come on, everyone!

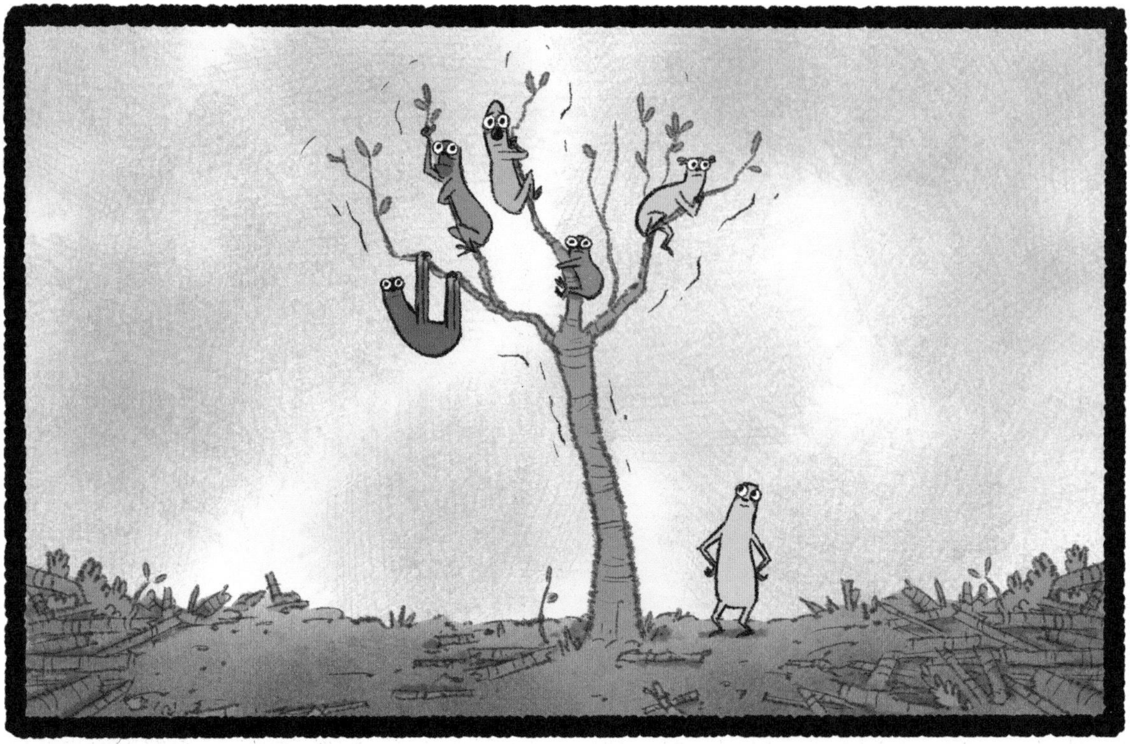

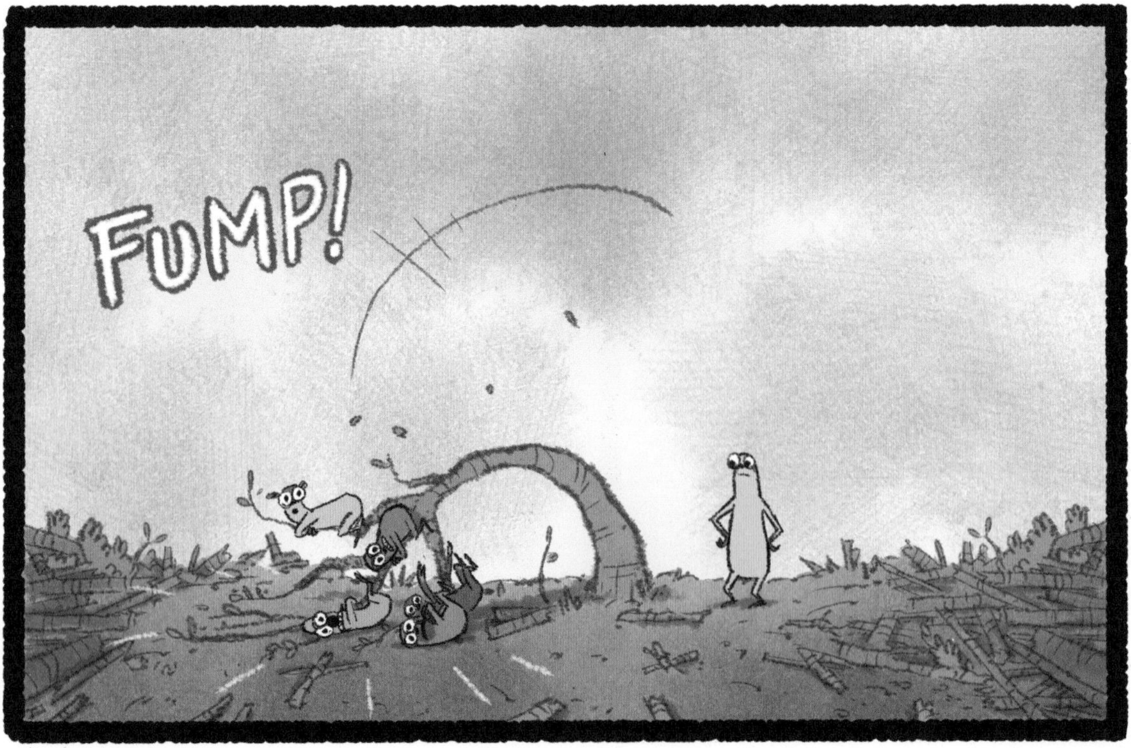
FUMP!

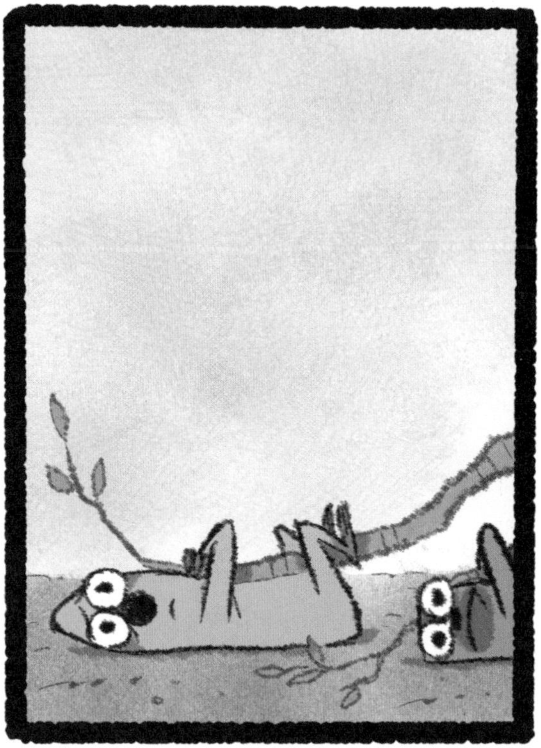

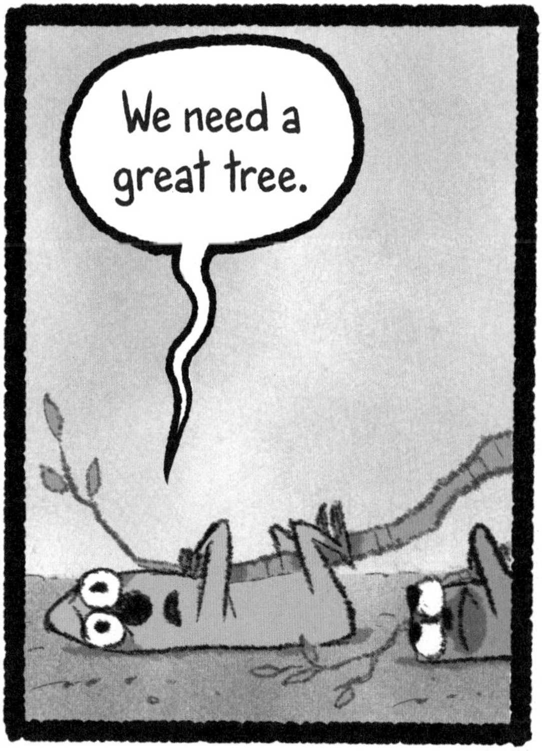
We need a great tree.

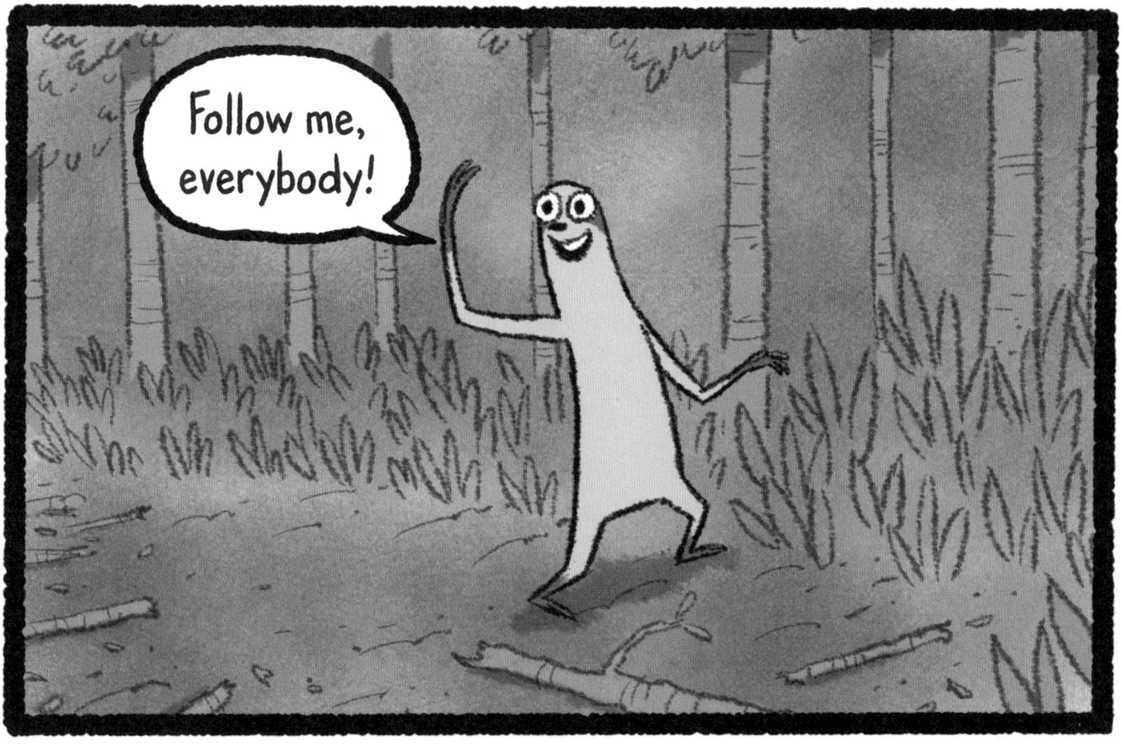
Follow me, everybody!

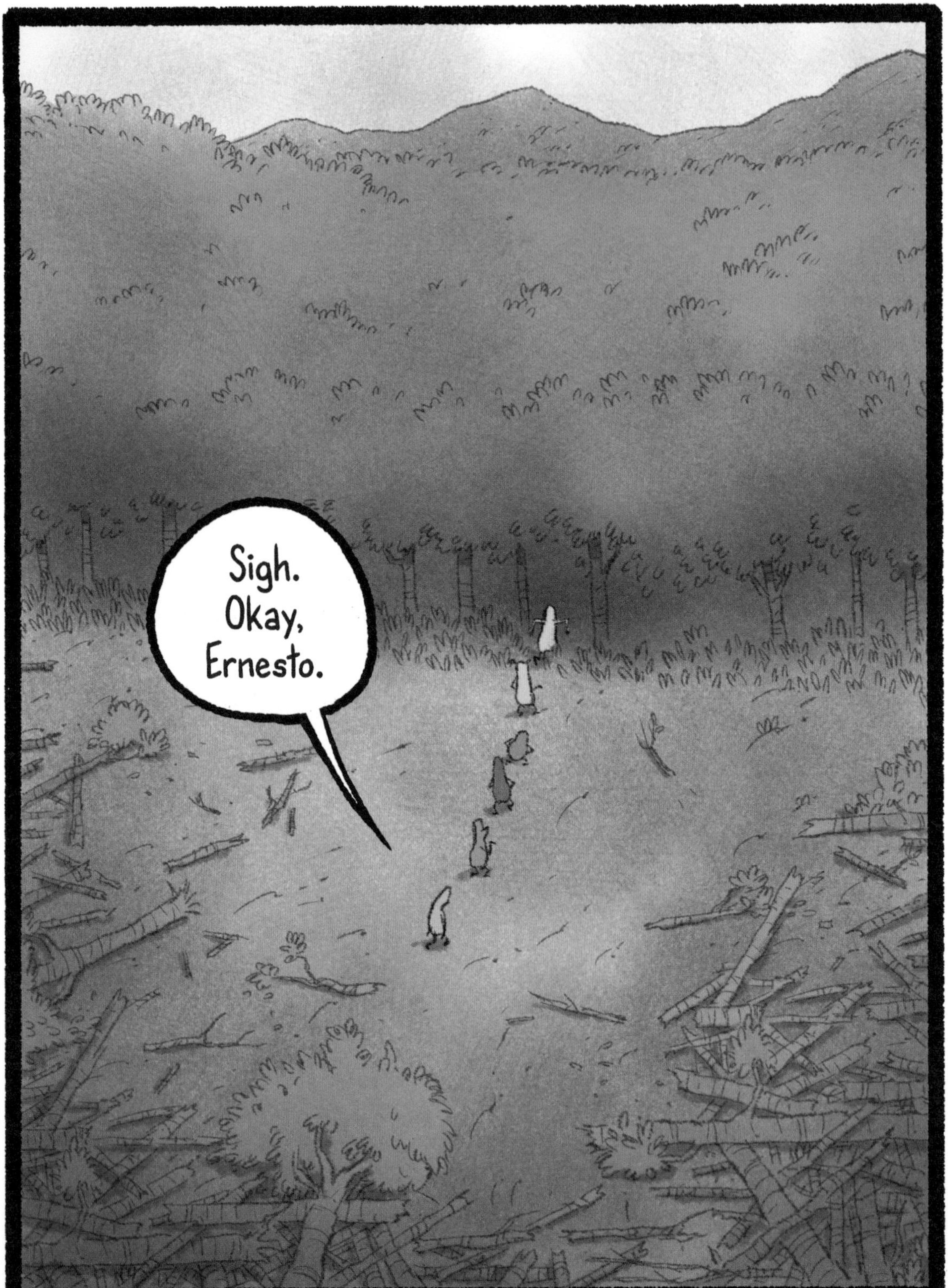
Sigh. Okay, Ernesto.

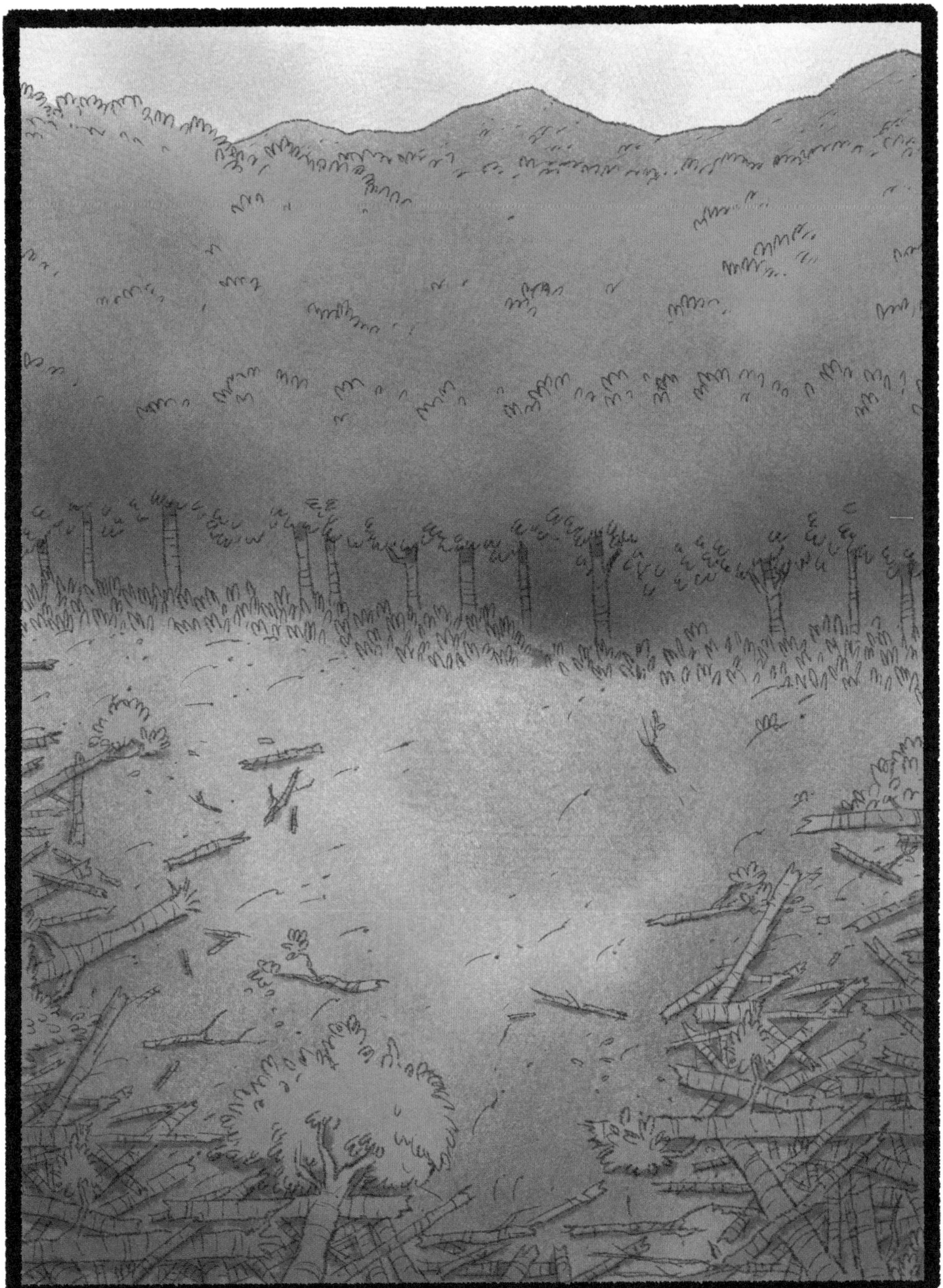

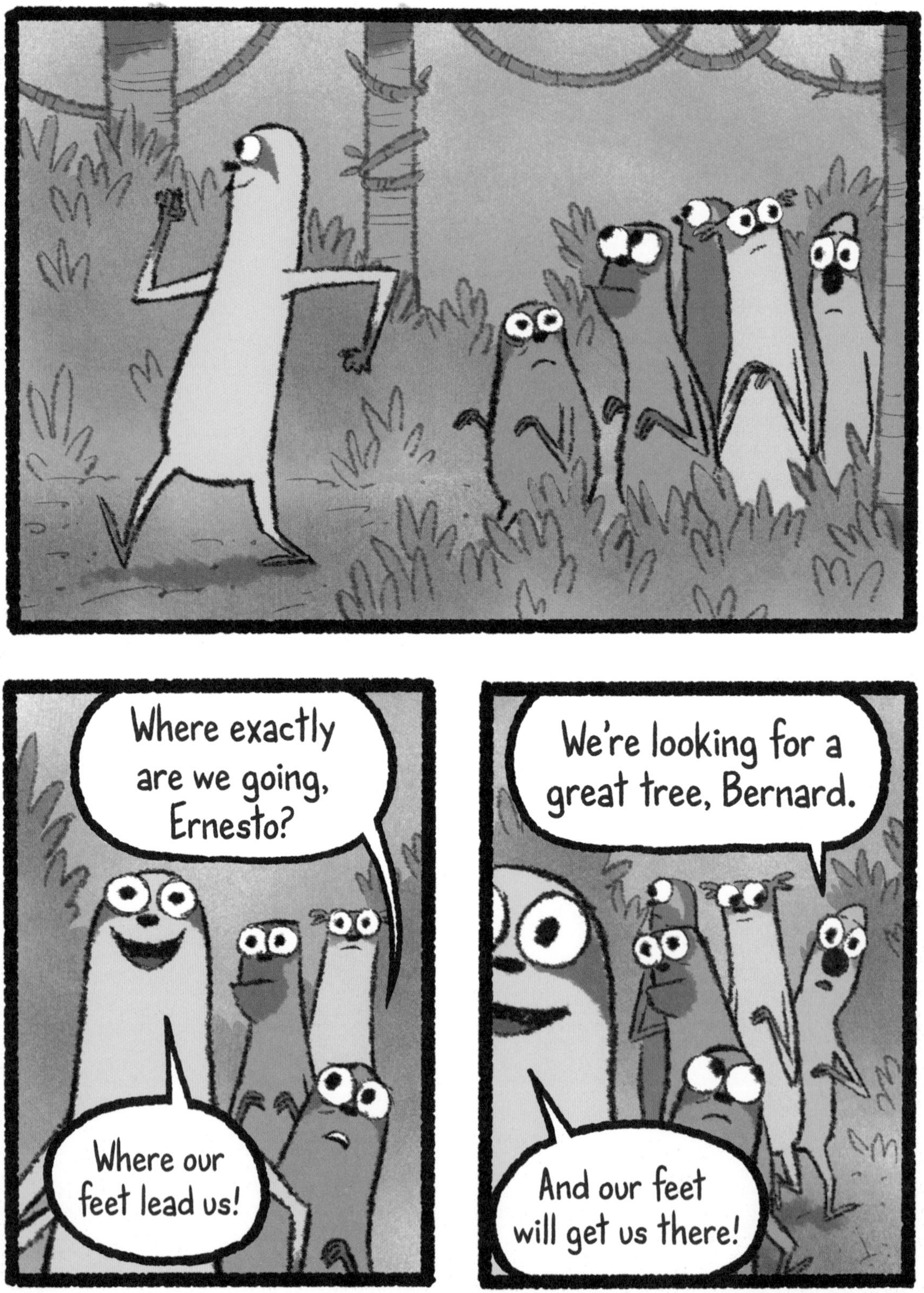
Where exactly are we going, Ernesto?
Where our feet lead us!
We're looking for a great tree, Bernard.
And our feet will get us there!

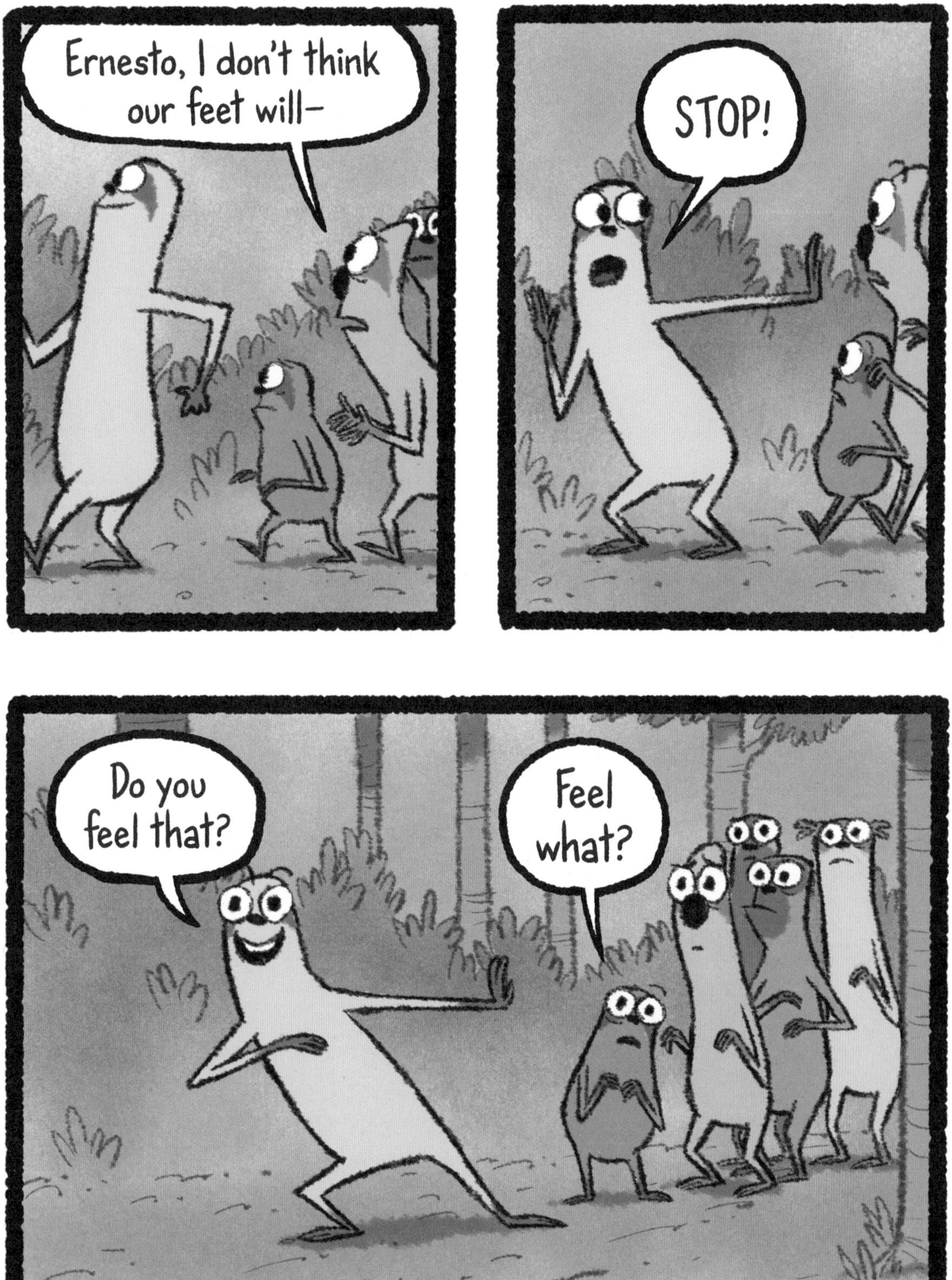
Ernesto, I don't think our feet will-
STOP!
Do you feel that?
Feel what?

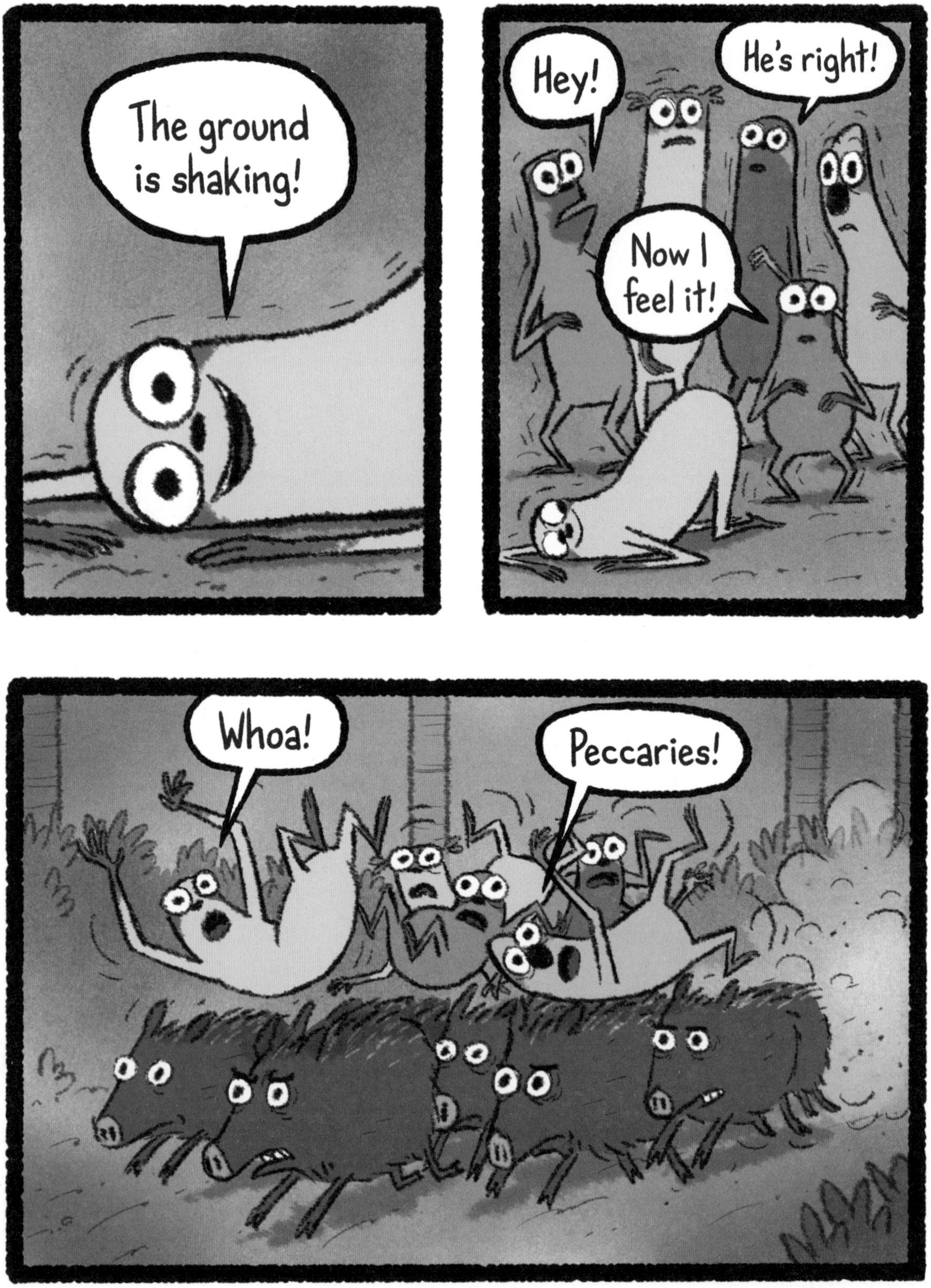
The ground is shaking!
Hey!
He's right!
Now I feel it!
Whoa!
Peccaries!

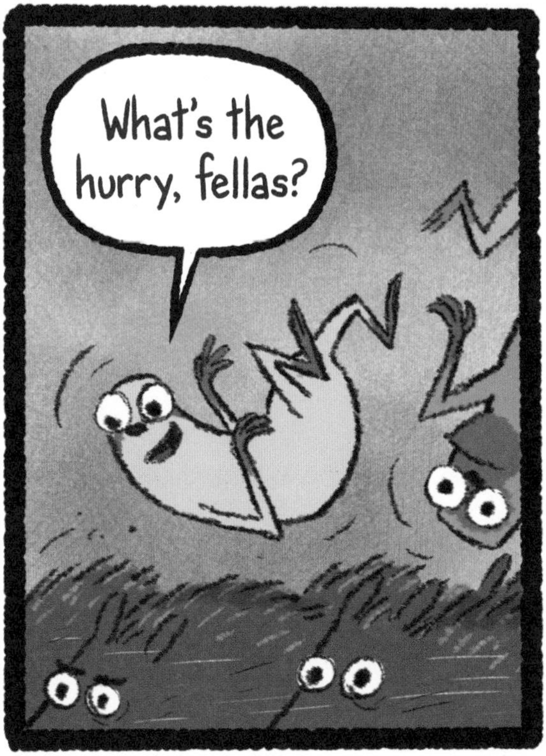
What's the hurry, fellas?

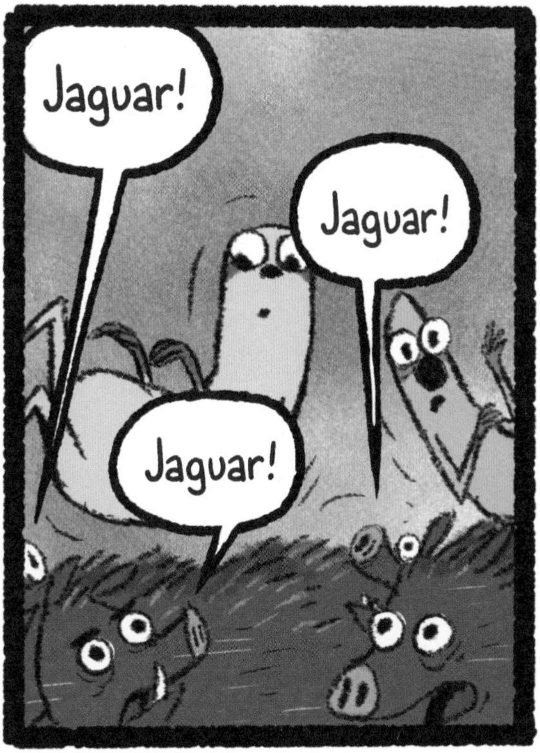
Jaguar!
Jaguar!
Jaguar!

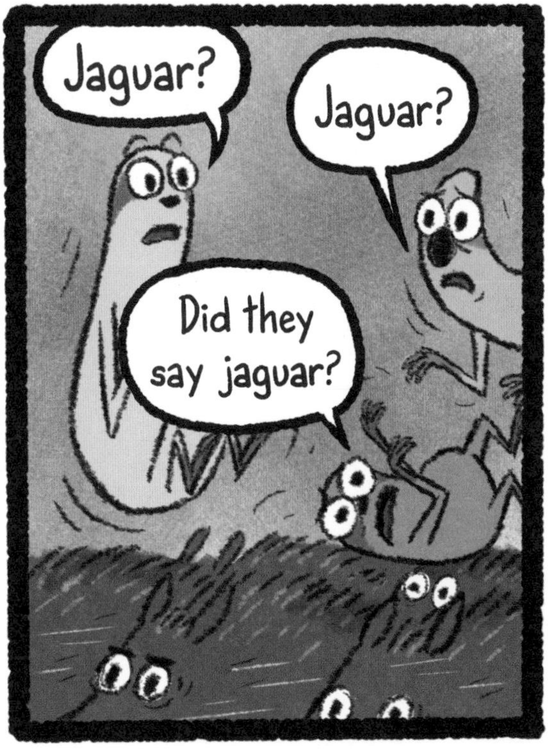
Jaguar?
Jaguar?
Did they say jaguar?

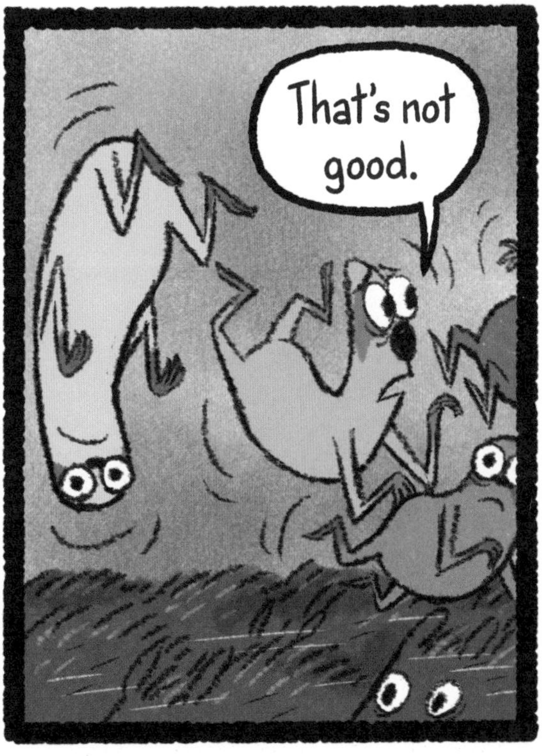
That's not good.

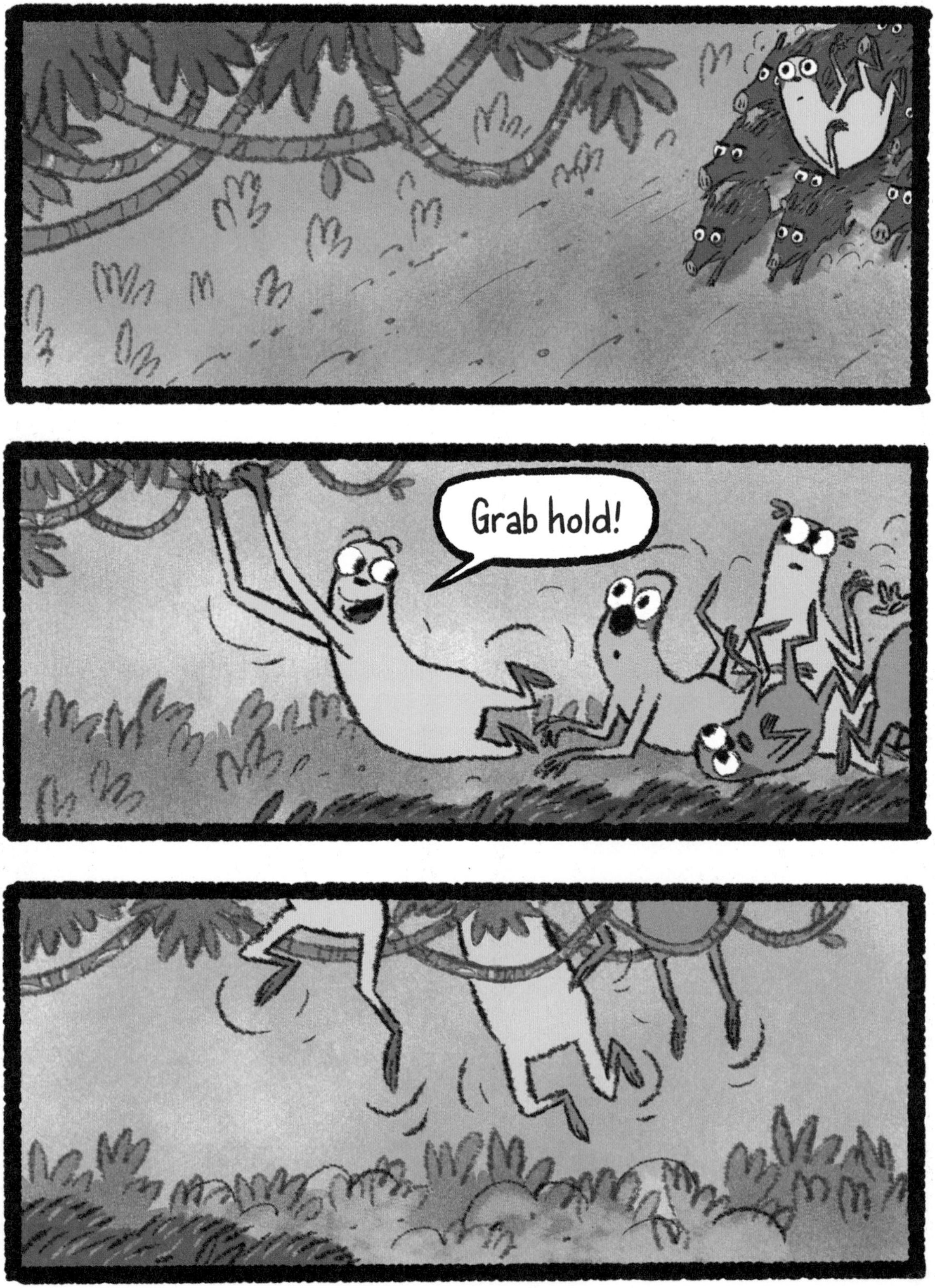
Grab hold!

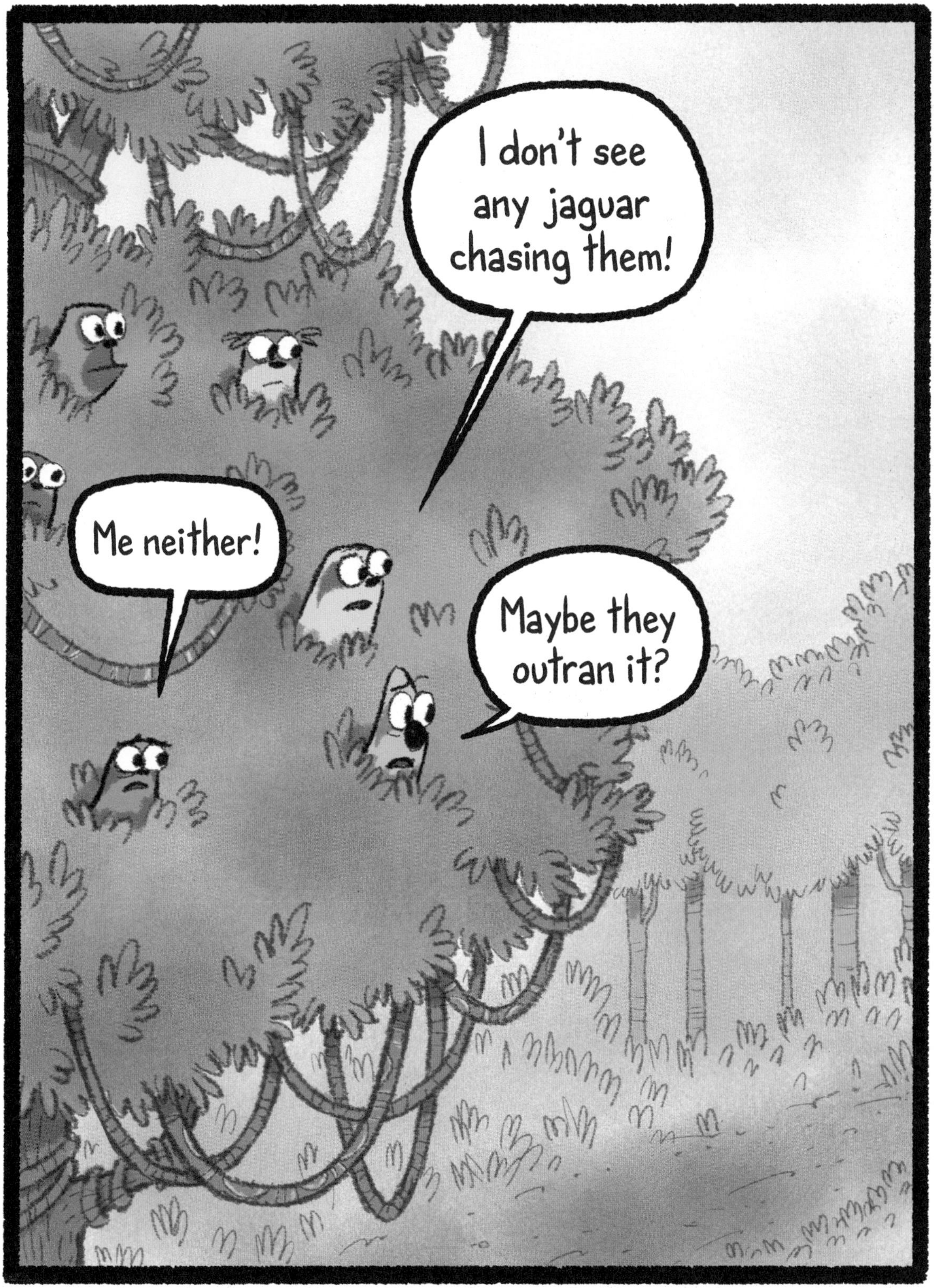
I don't see any jaguar chasing them!
Me neither!
Maybe they outran it?

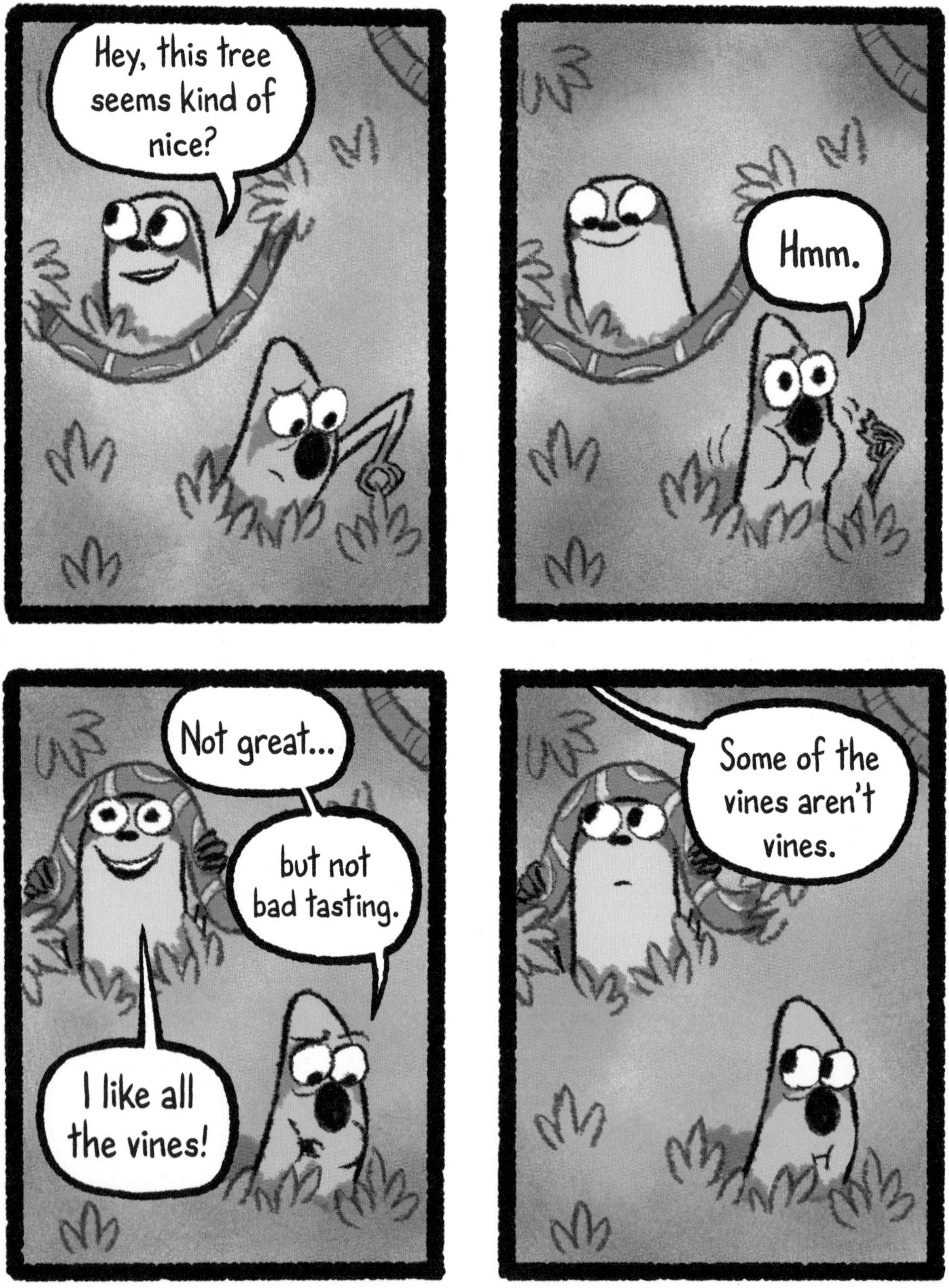
Hey, this tree seems kind of nice?
Hmm.
Not great...
but not bad tasting.
I like all the vines!
Some of the vines aren't vines.

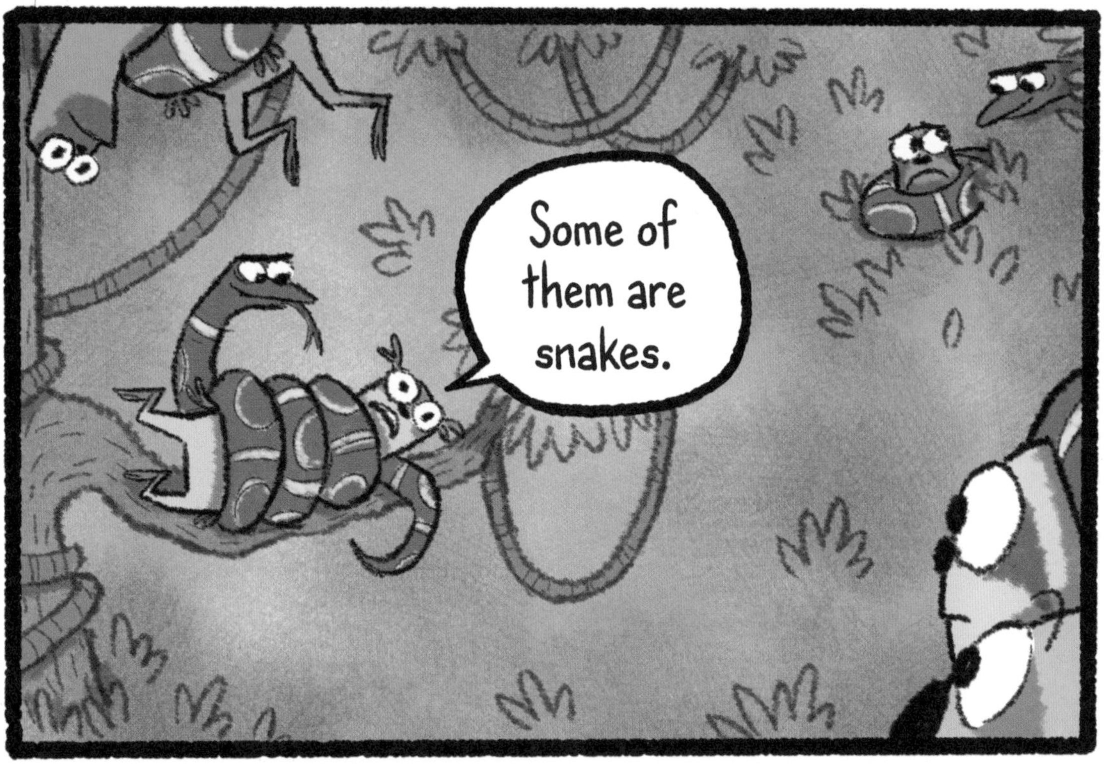
Some of them are snakes.

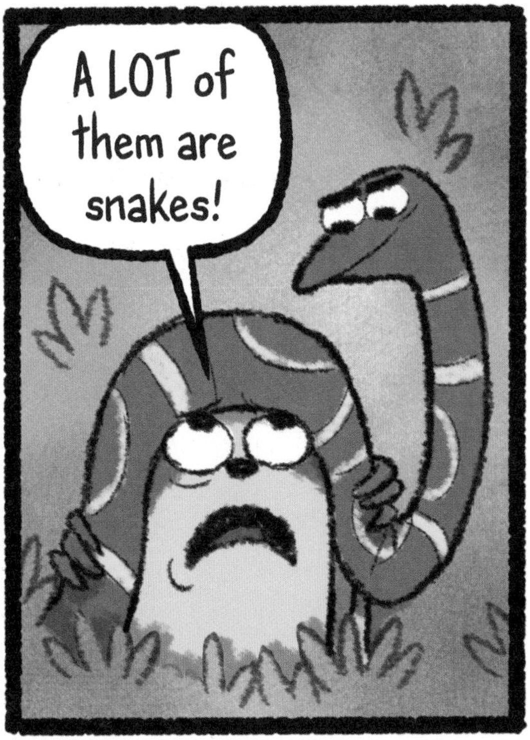
A LOT of them are snakes!

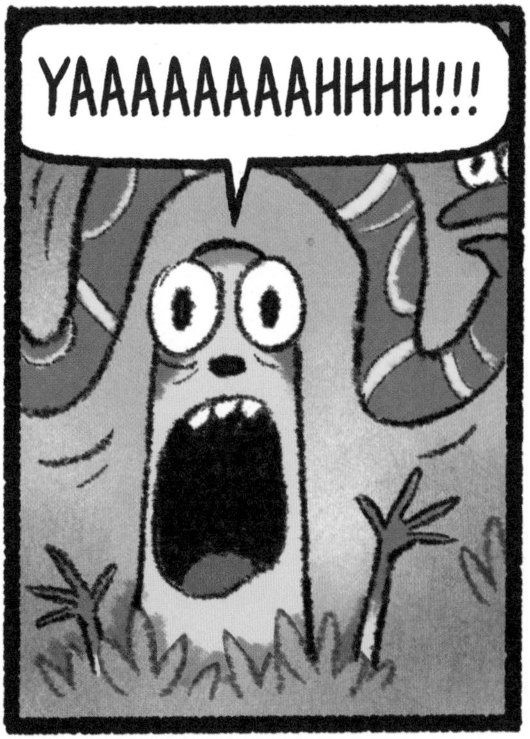
YAAAAAAAAHHHH!!!

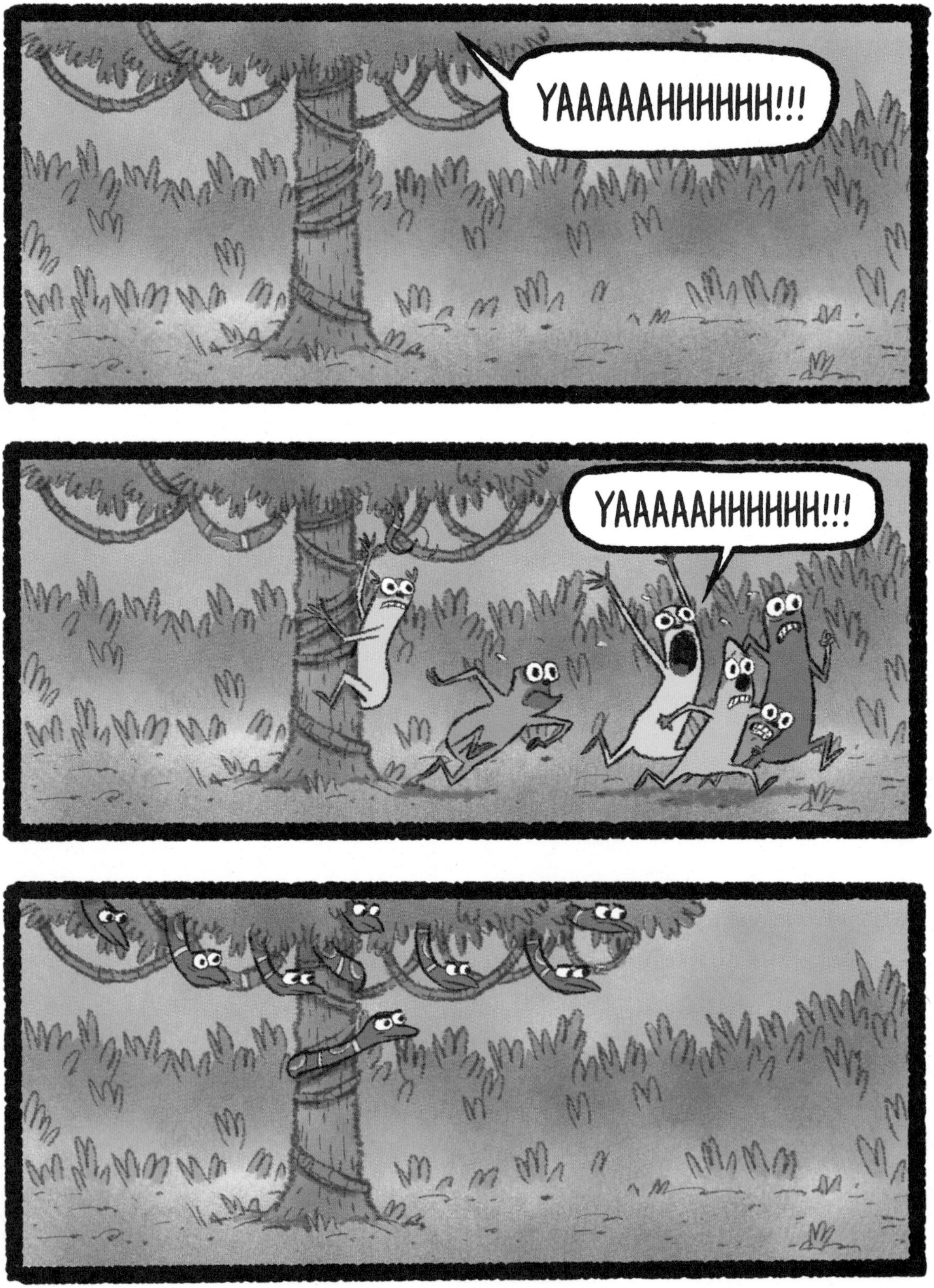
YAAAAAHHHHHH!!!
YAAAAAHHHHHH!!!

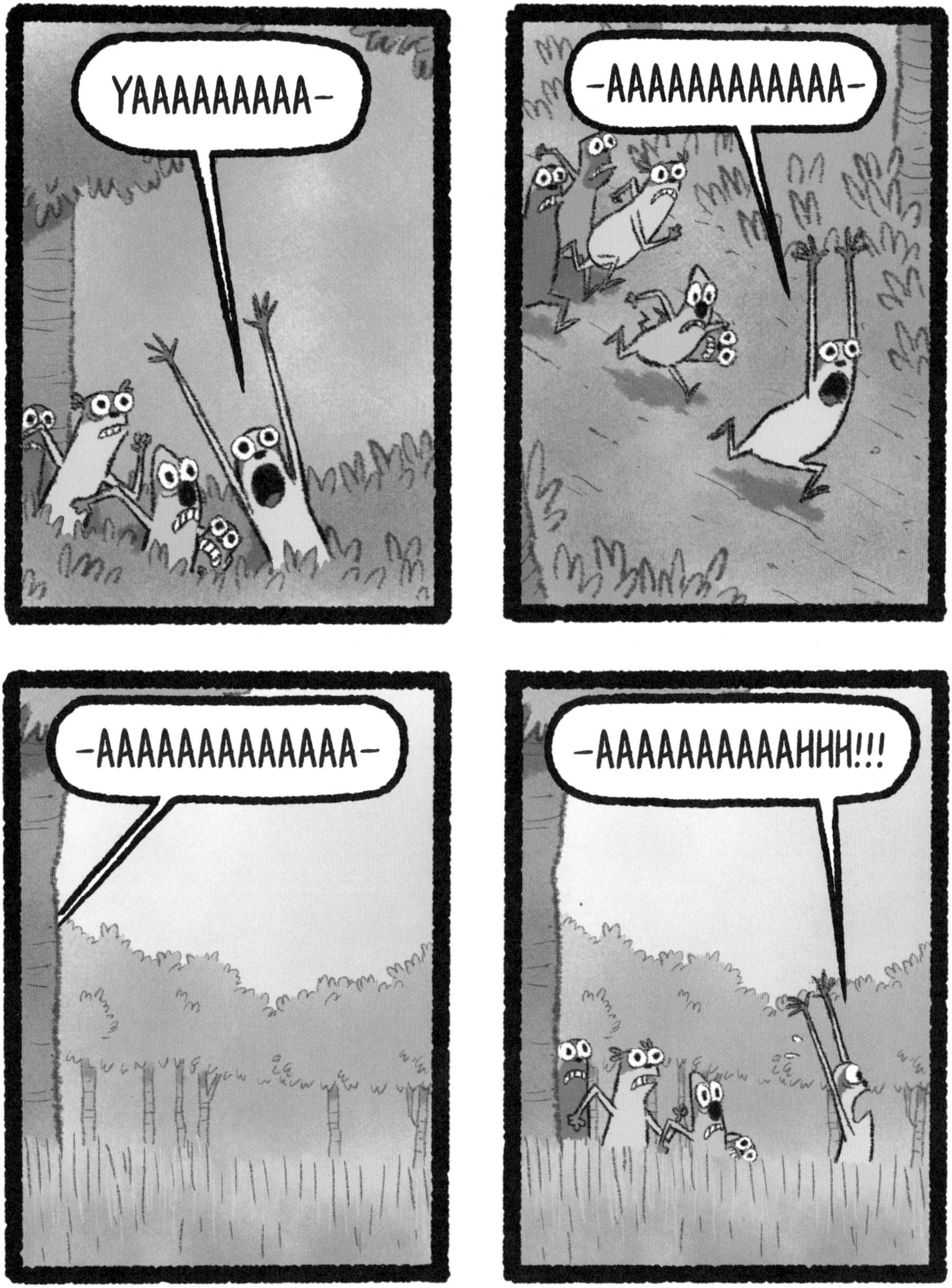
YAAAAAAAAA-
-AAAAAAAAAAAA-
-AAAAAAAAAAAAA-
-AAAAAAAAAAHHH!!!

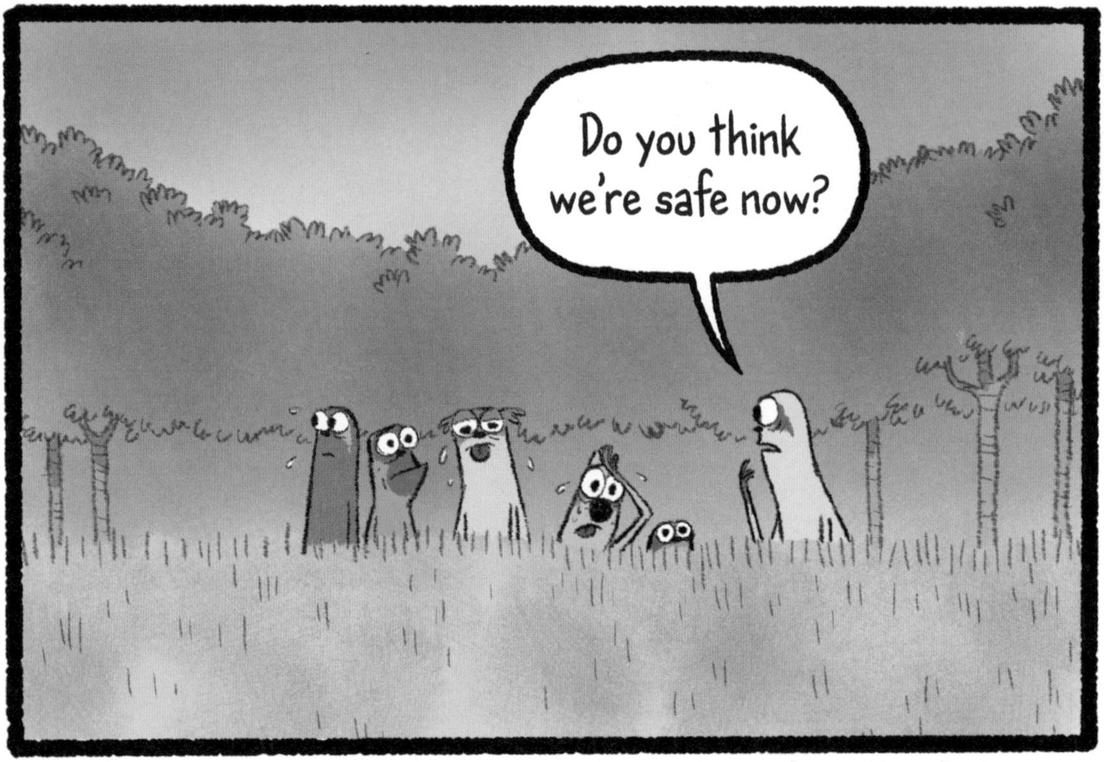
Do you think we're safe now?

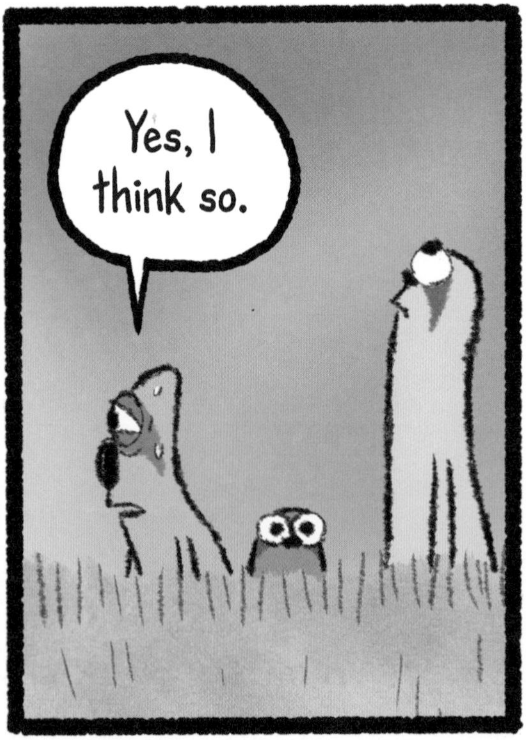
Yes, I think so.

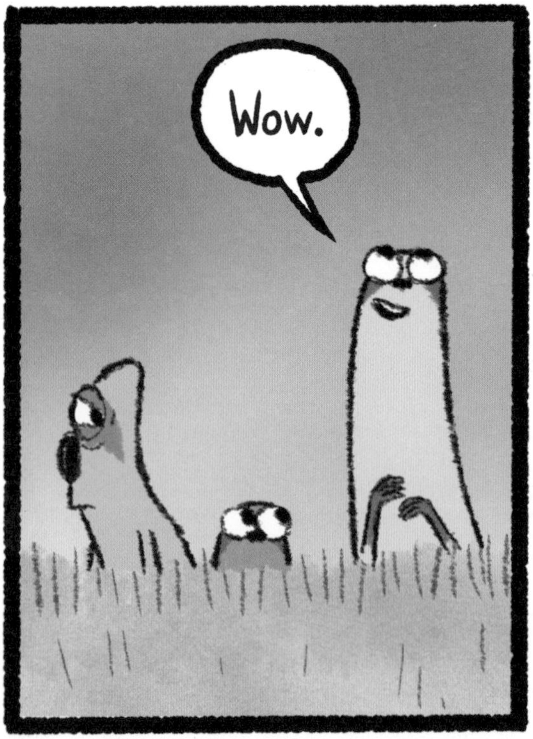
Wow.

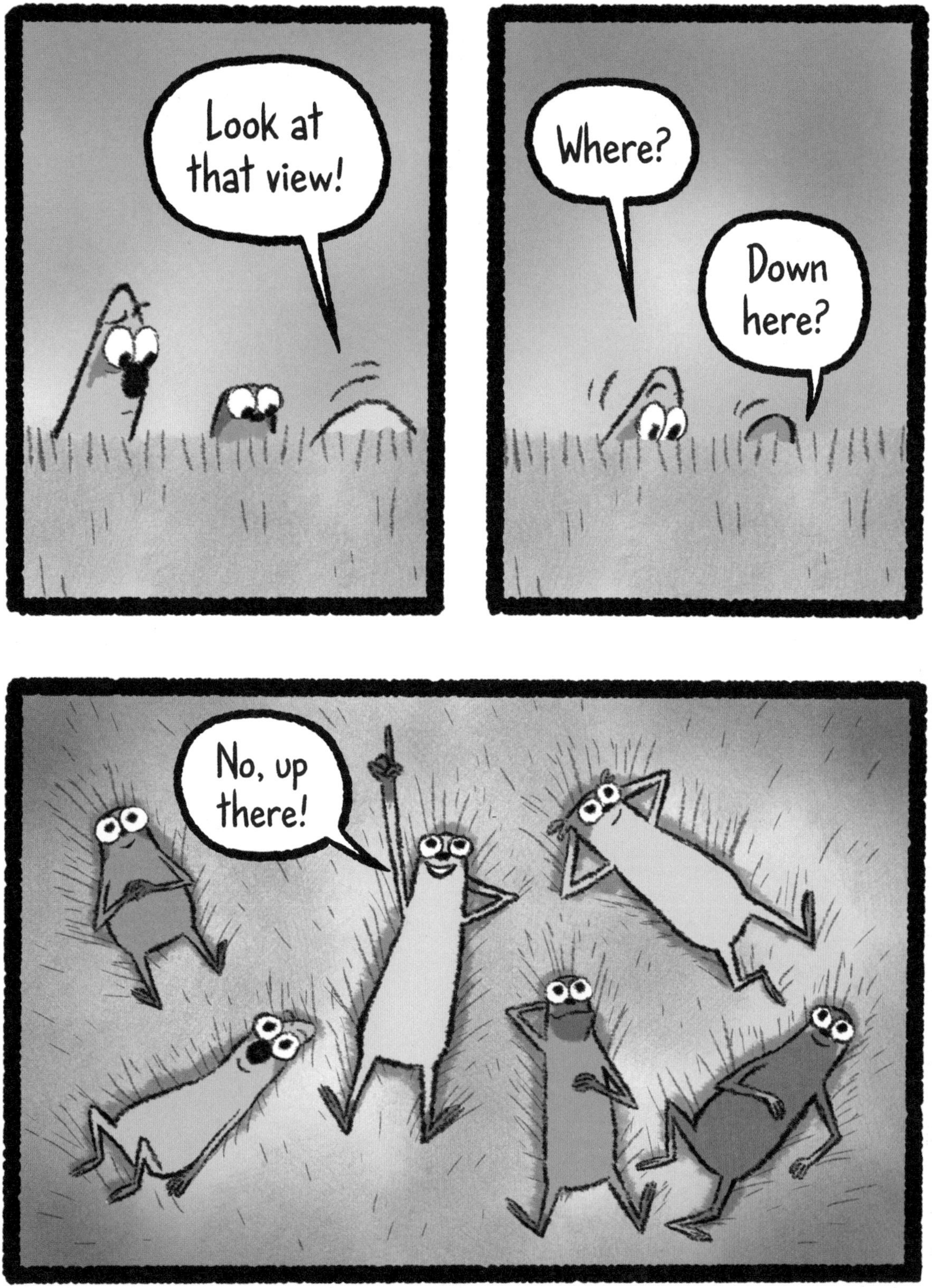
Look at that view!
Where?
Down here?
No, up there!

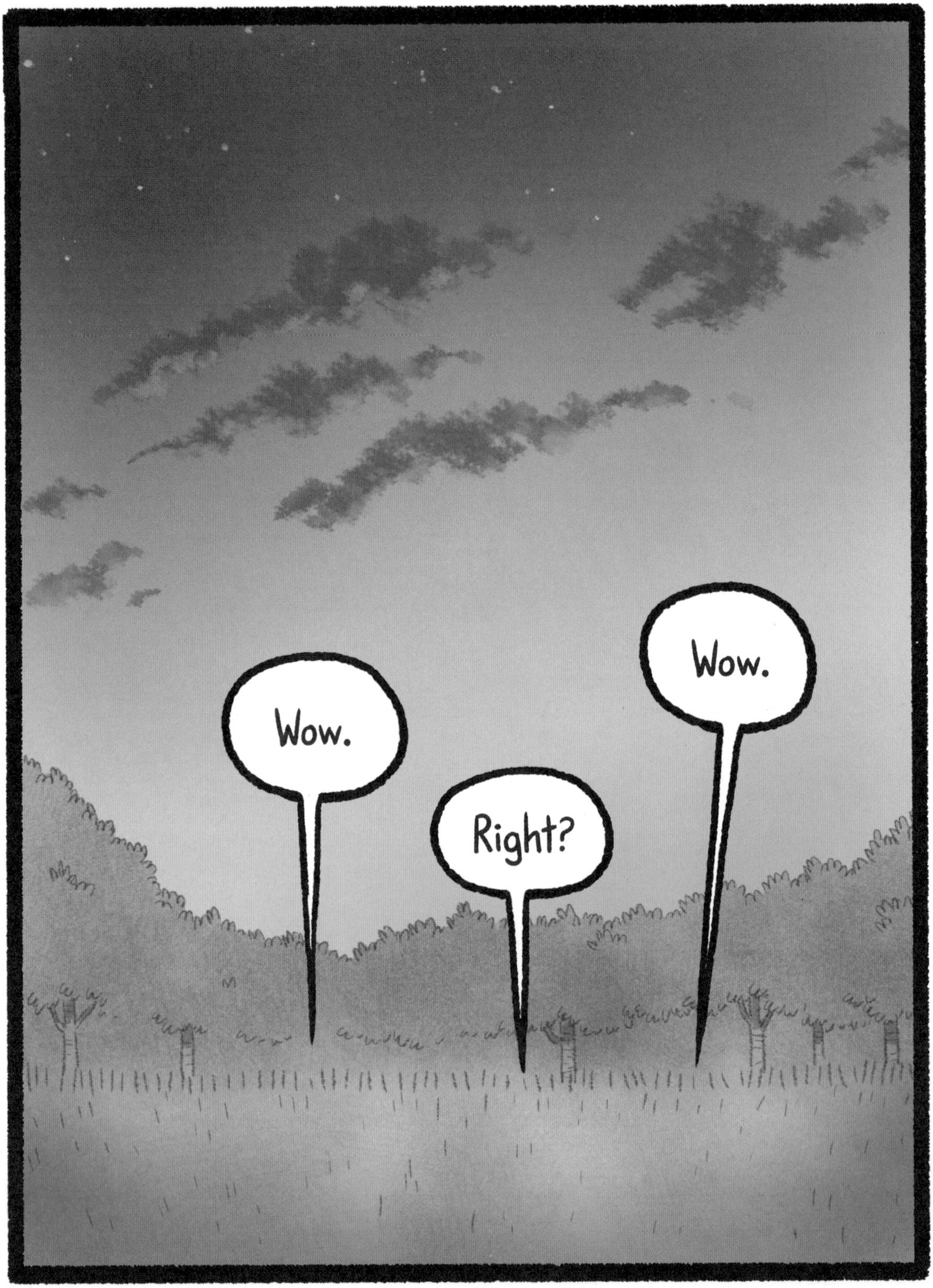
Wow.
Right?
Wow.

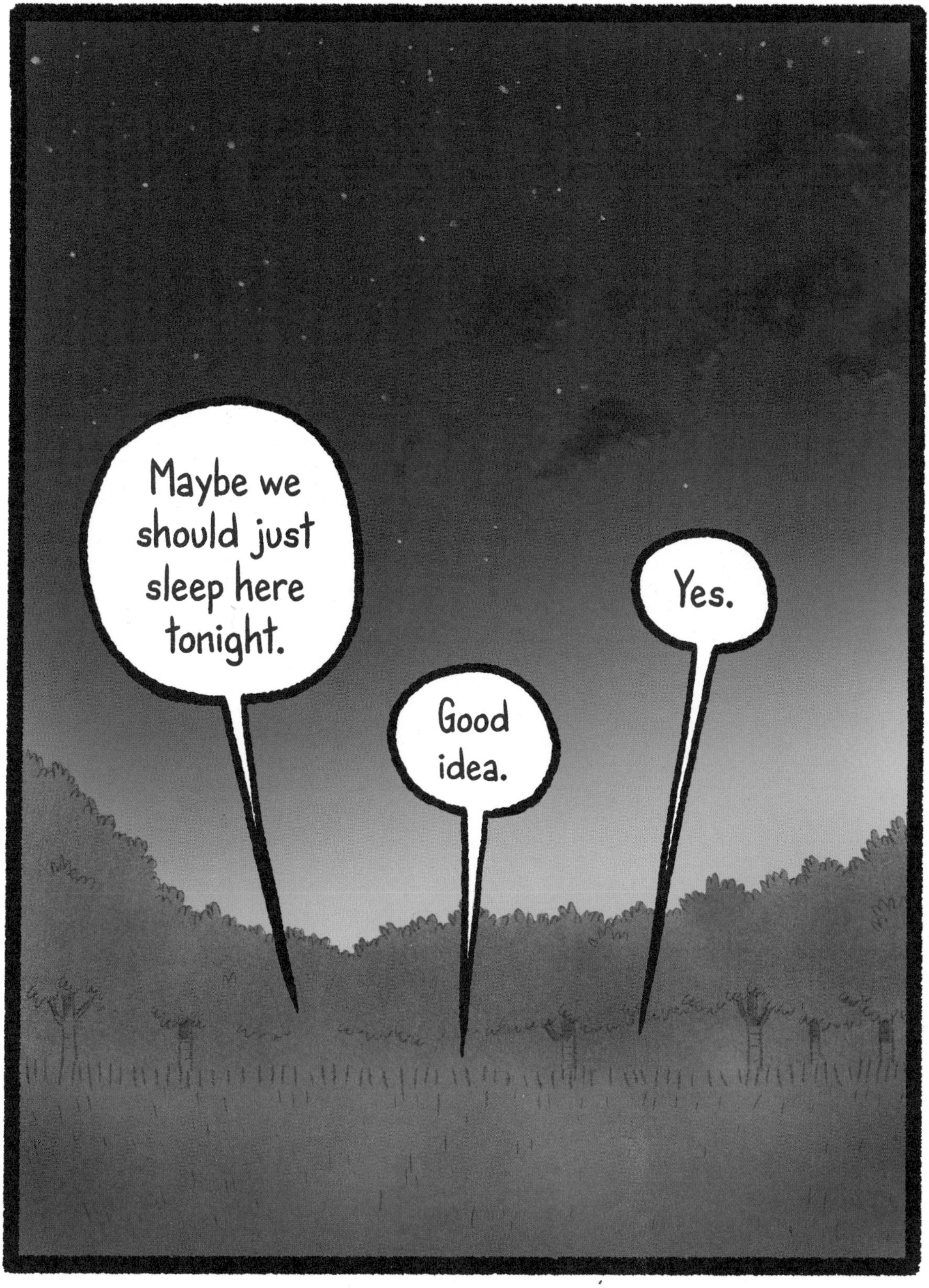
Maybe we should just sleep here tonight.
Good idea.
Yes.

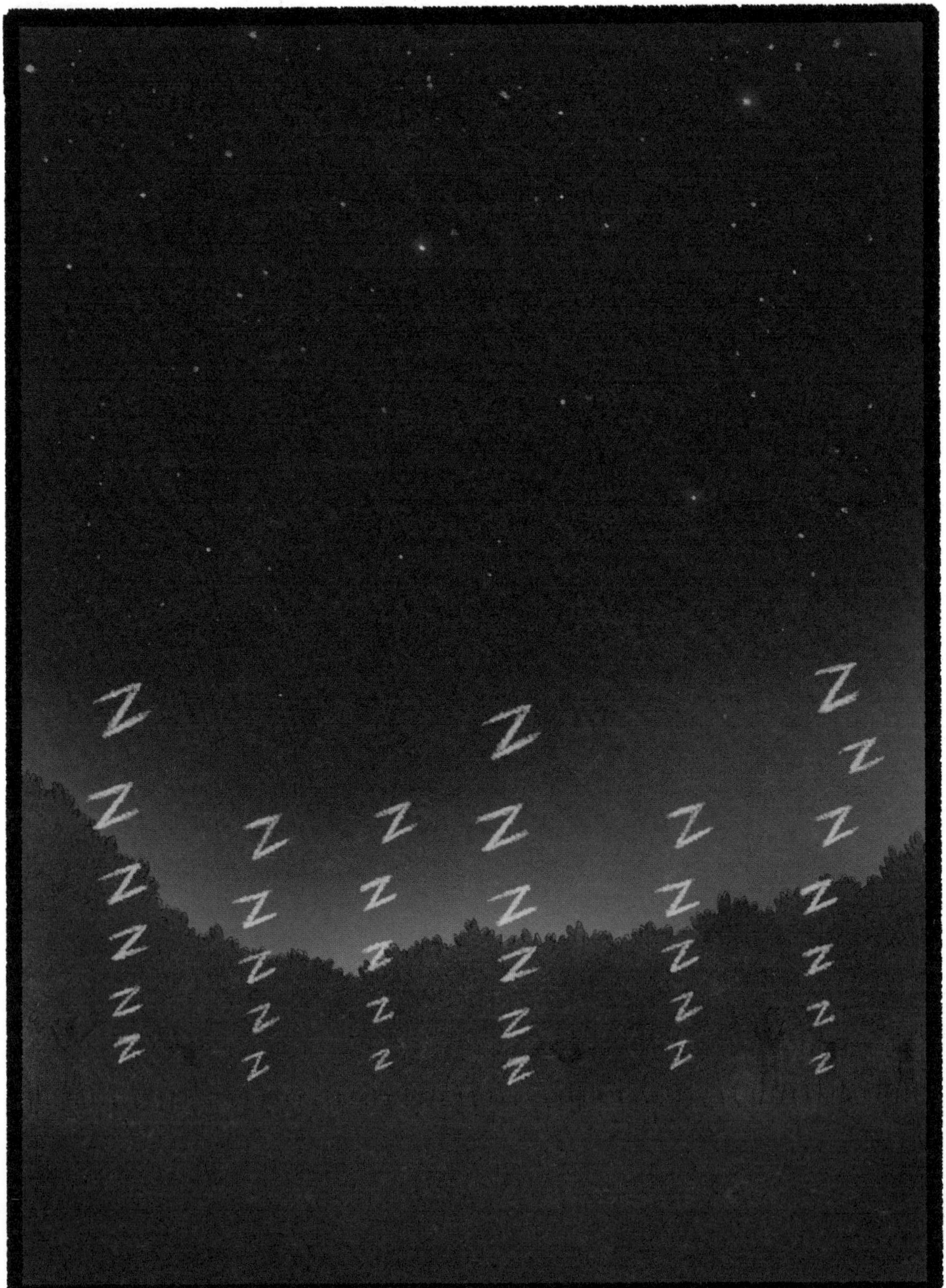

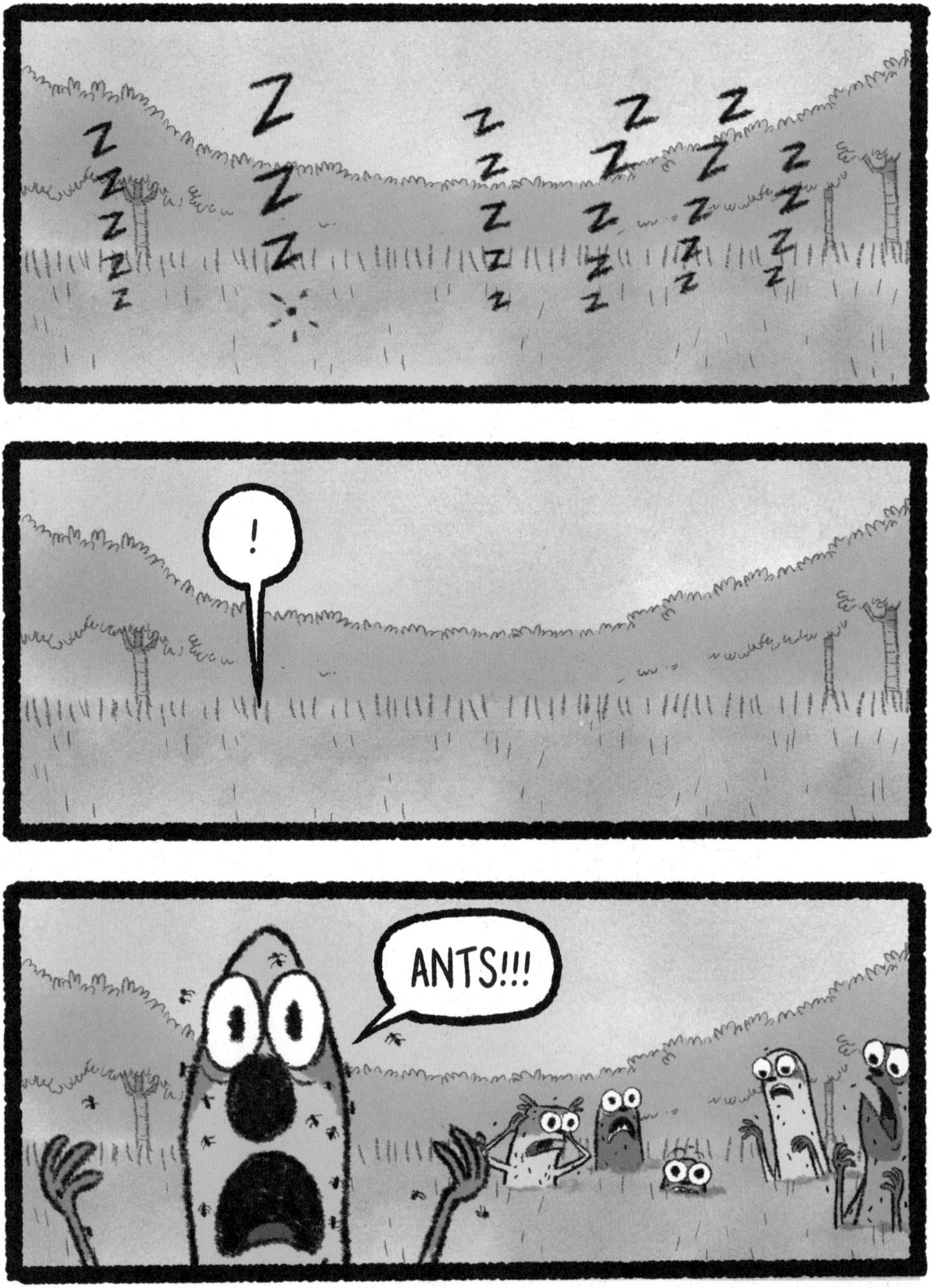
Z Z Z Z Z
Z Z Z
Z Z Z Z Z
Z Z Z Z Z
Z Z Z Z Z
Z Z Z Z
!
ANTS!!!

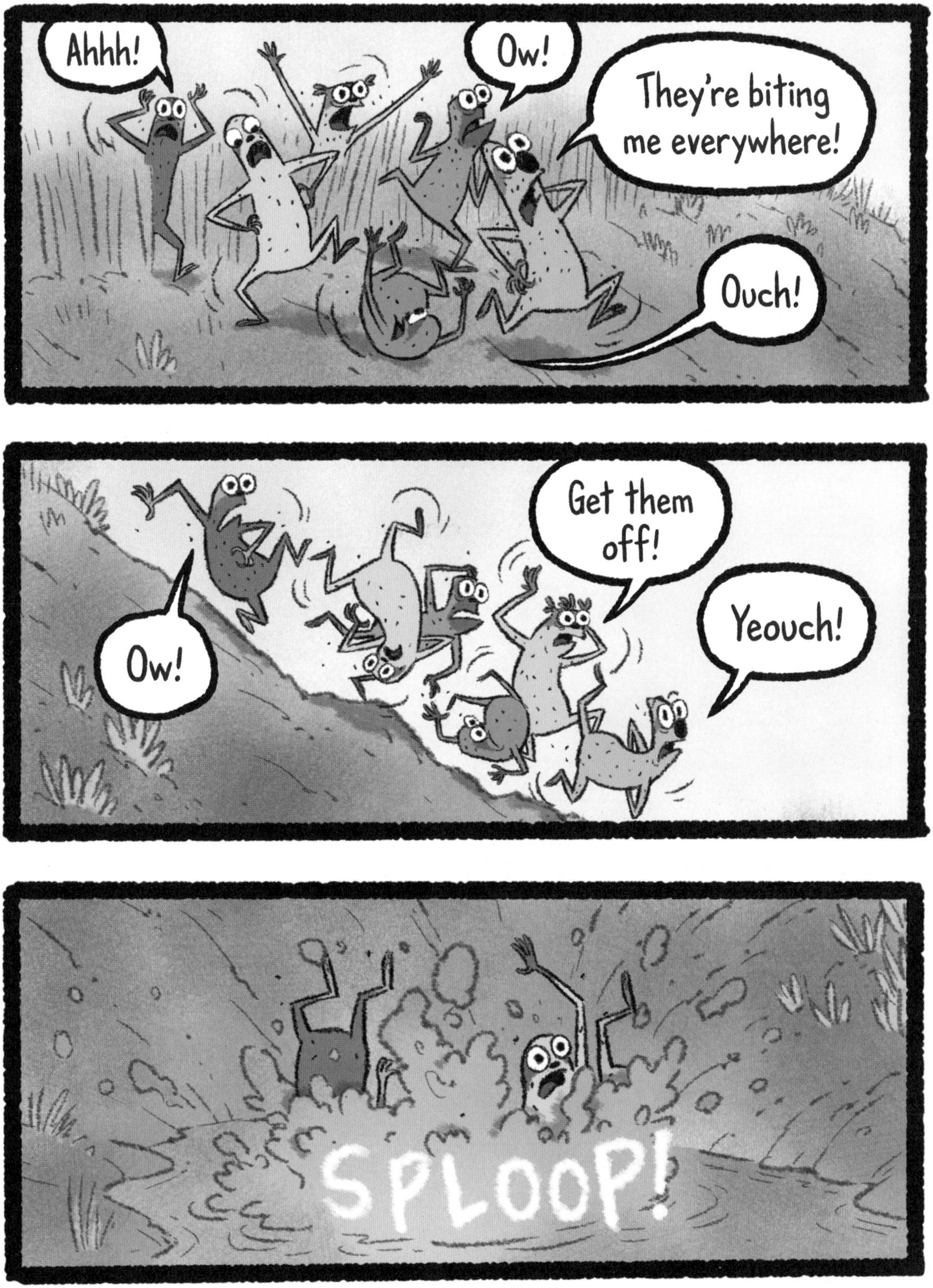
Ahhh!
Ow!
They're biting me everywhere!
Ouch!
Ow!
Get them off!
Yeouch!
SPLOOP!

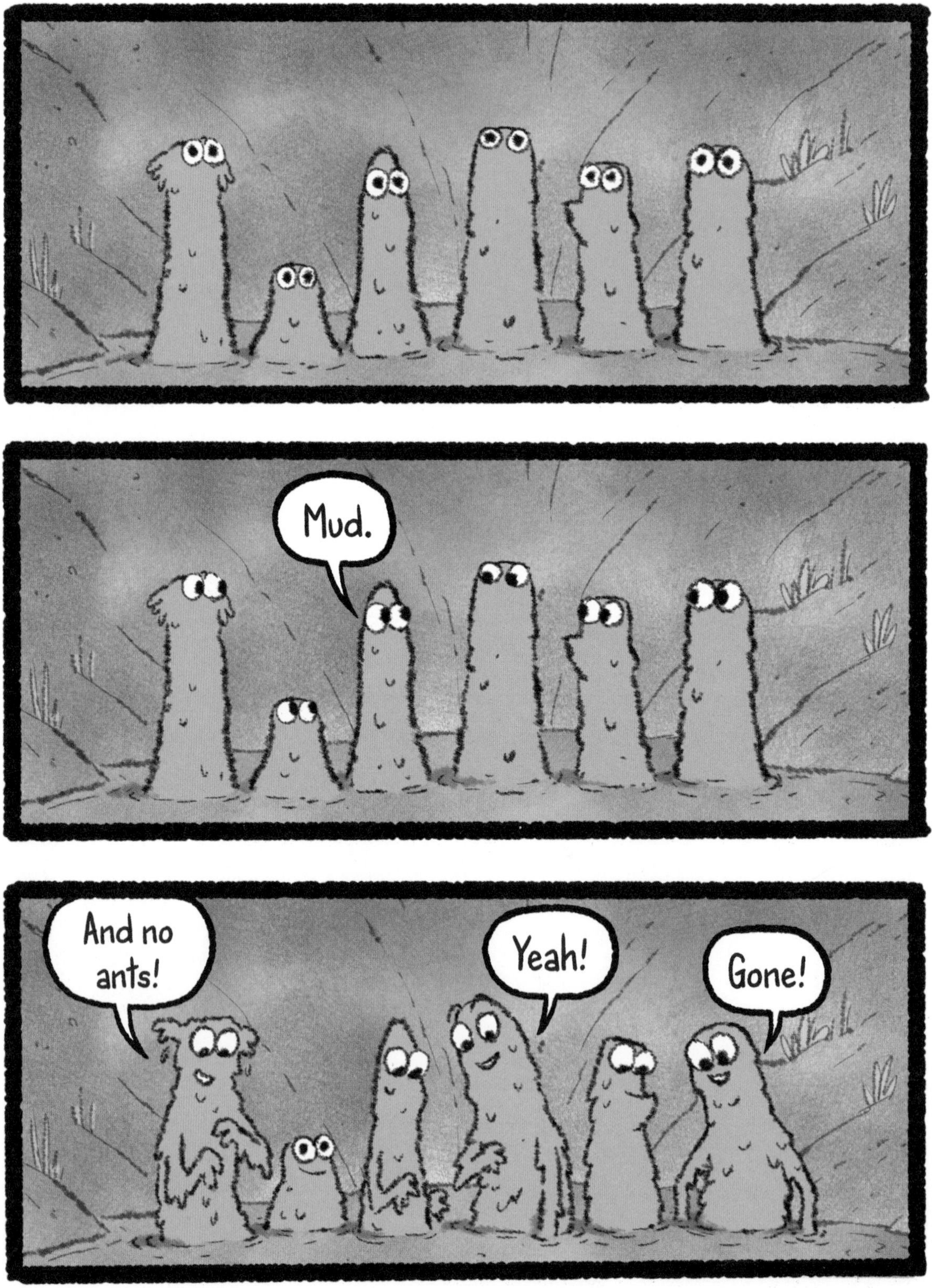
Mud.
And no ants!
Yeah!
Gone!

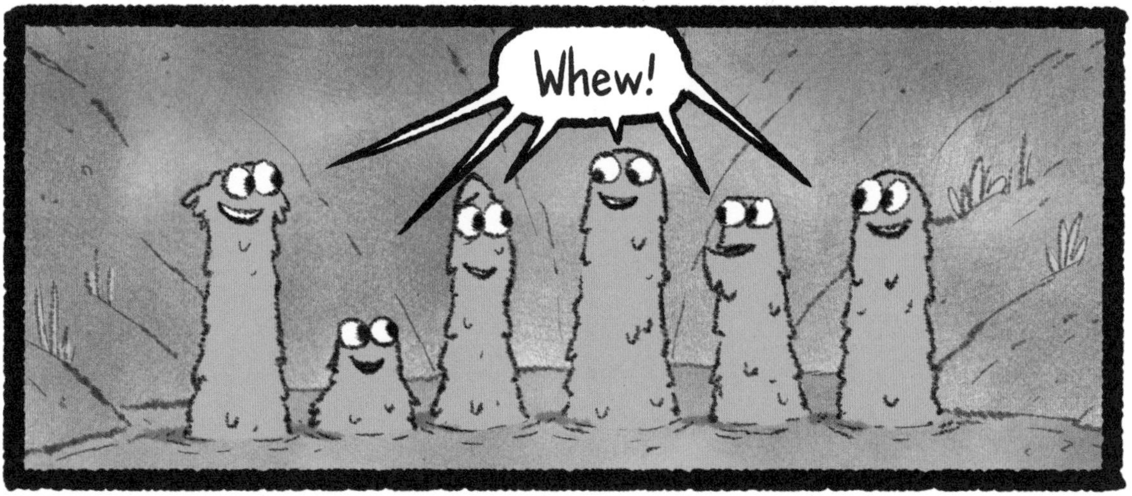
Whew!

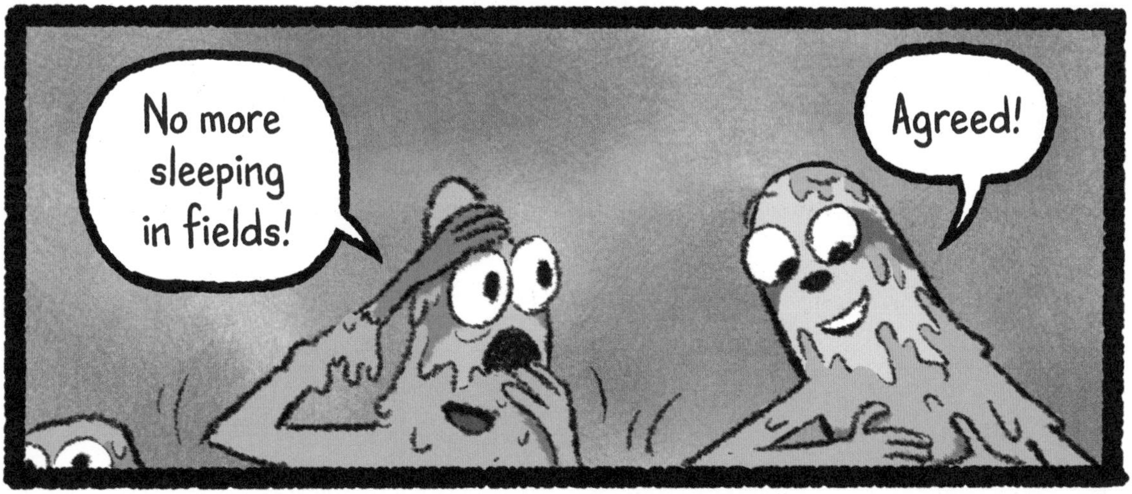
No more sleeping in fields!
Agreed!

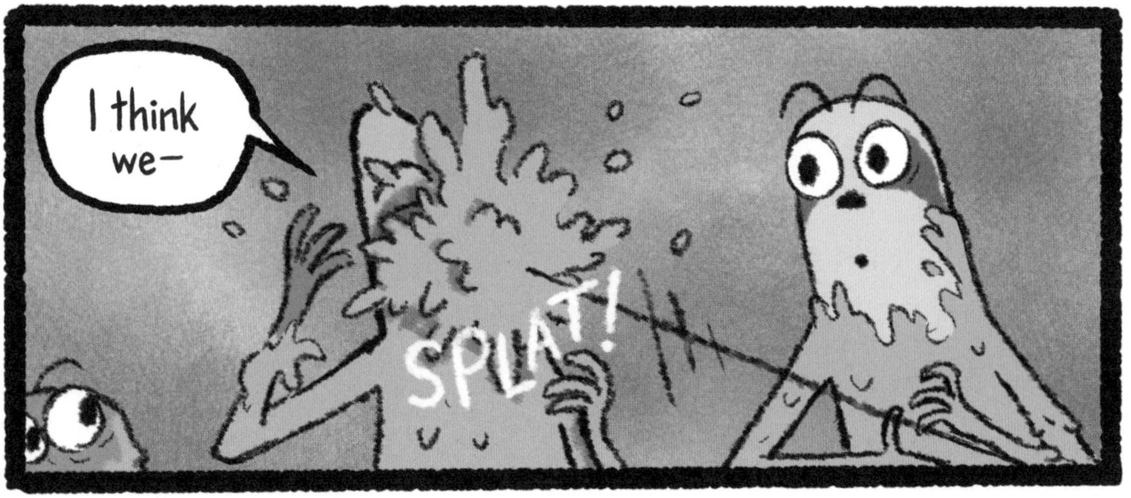
I think we–
SPLAT!

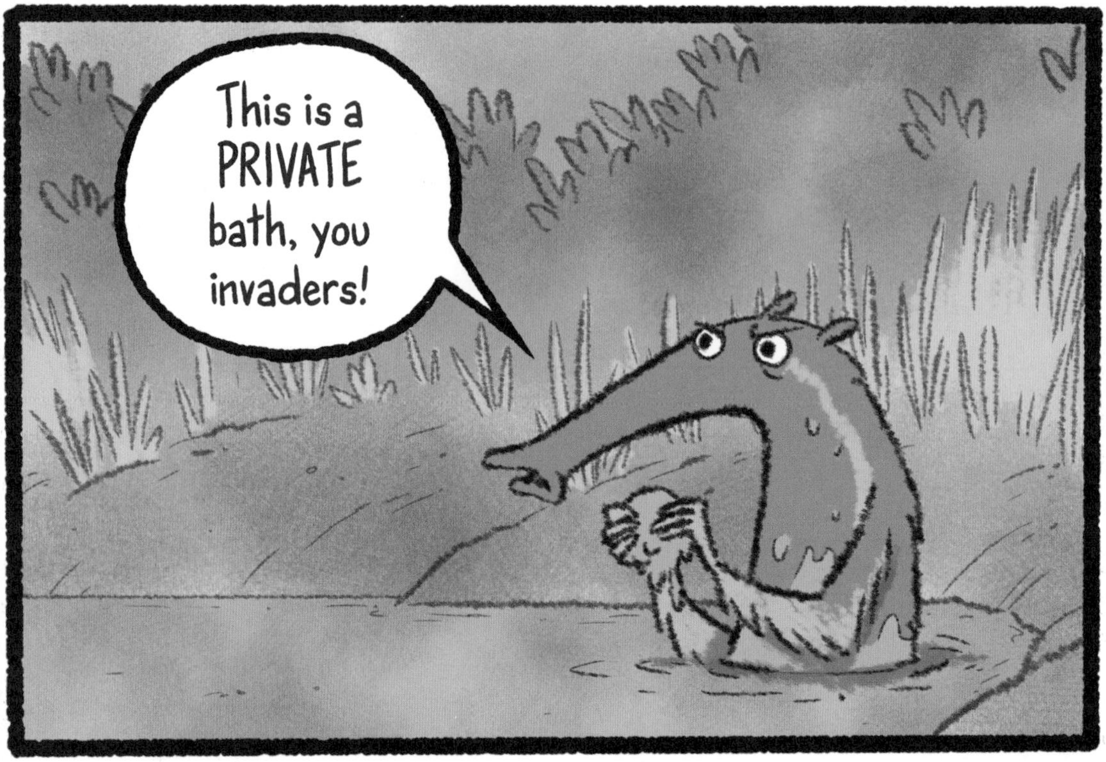
This is a PRIVATE bath, you invaders!

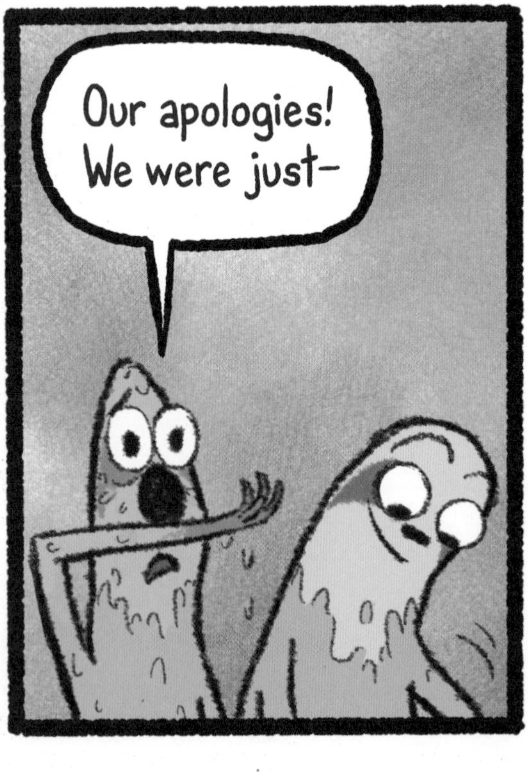
Our apologies! We were just-

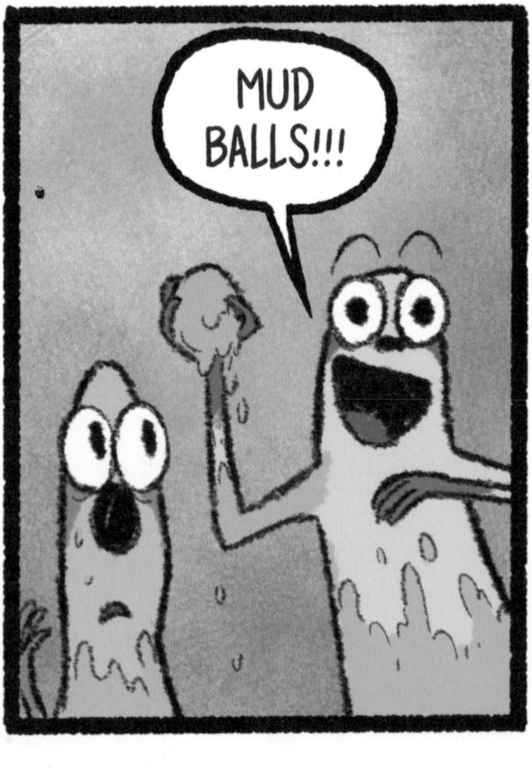
MUD BALLS!!!

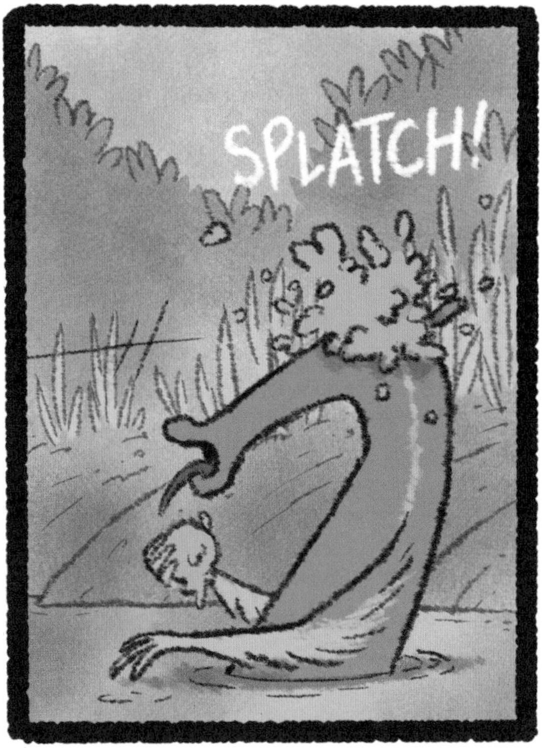
SPLATCH!

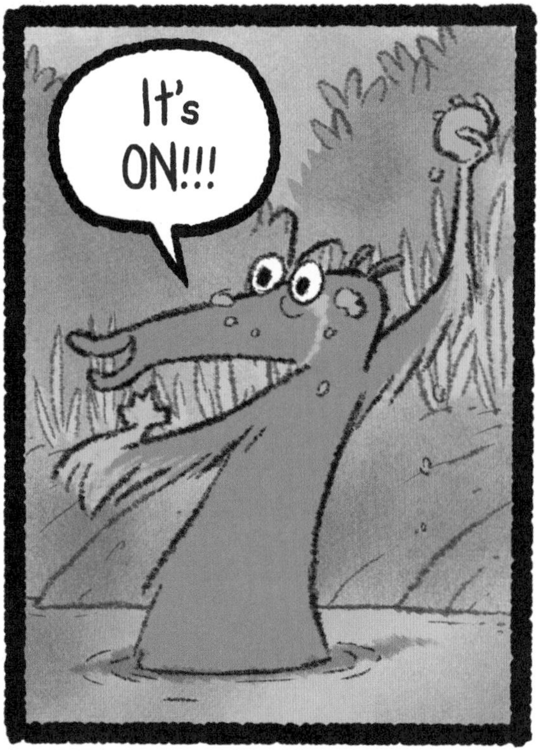
It's ON!!!

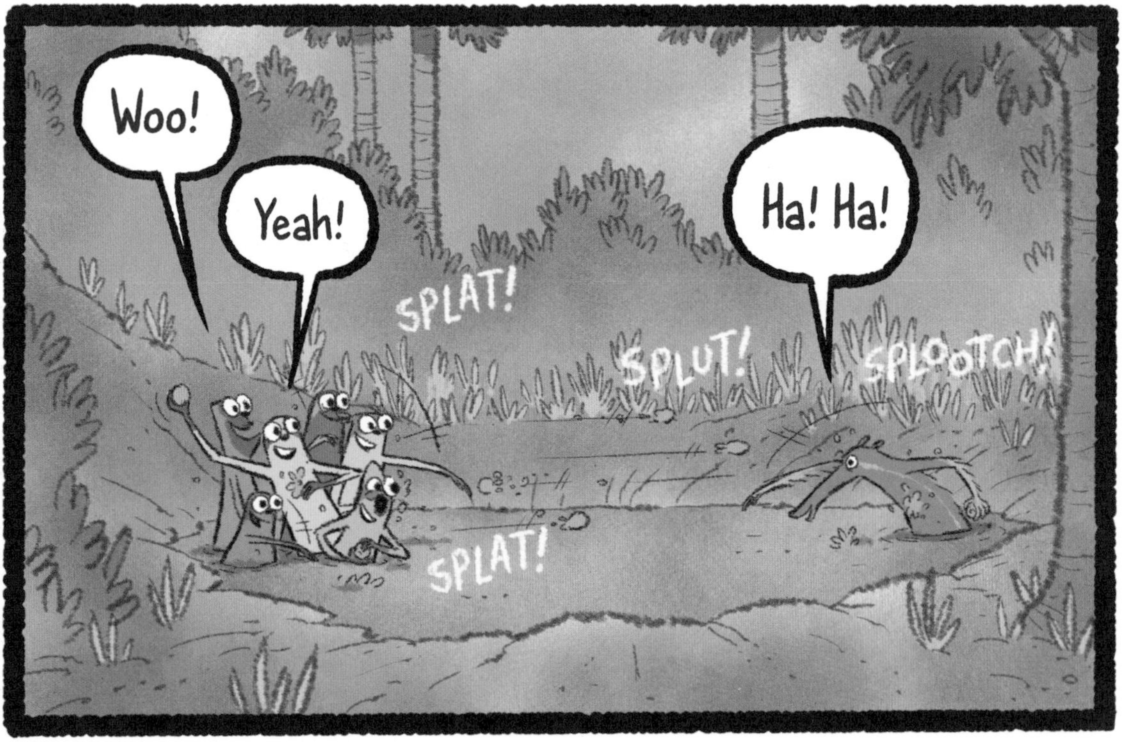
Woo!
Yeah!
SPLAT!
SPLUT!
Ha! Ha!
SPLOOTCH!
SPLAT!

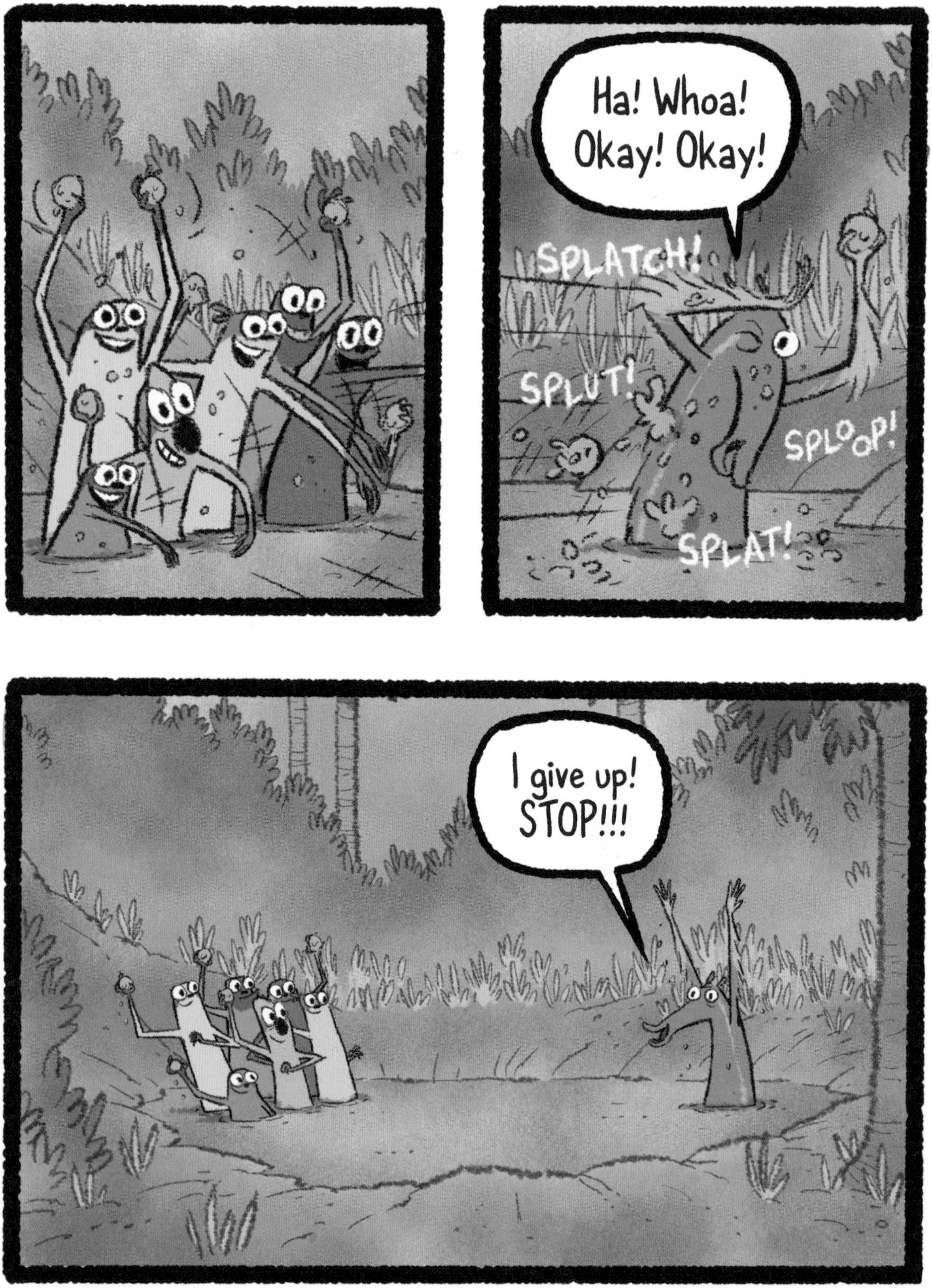
Ha! Whoa! Okay! Okay!
SPLATCH!
SPLUT!
SPLOOP!
SPLAT!
I give up! STOP!!!

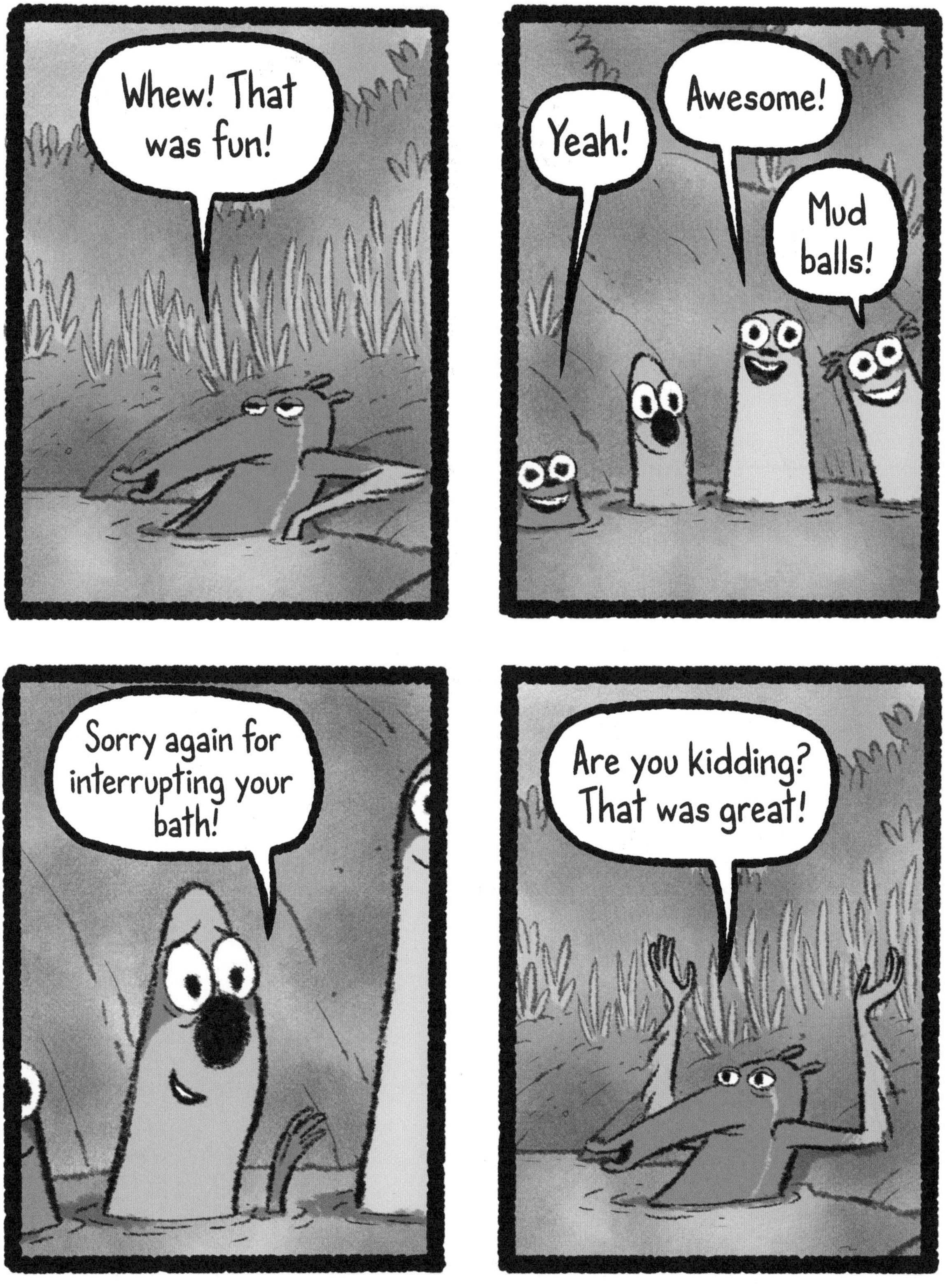
Whew! That was fun!
Yeah!
Awesome!
Mud balls!
Sorry again for interrupting your bath!
Are you kidding? That was great!

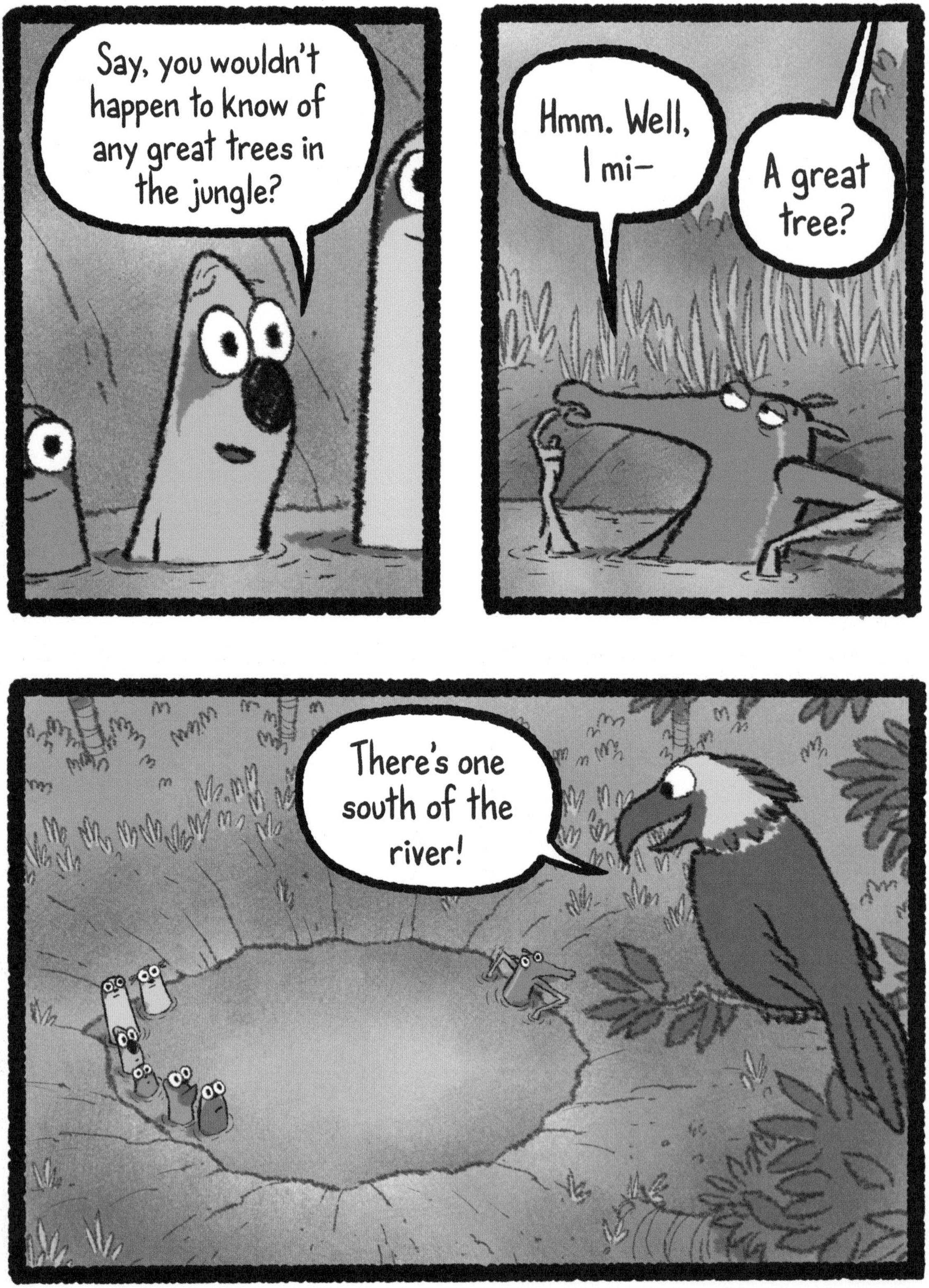
Say, you wouldn't happen to know of any great trees in the jungle?
Hmm. Well, I mi–
A great tree?
There's one south of the river!

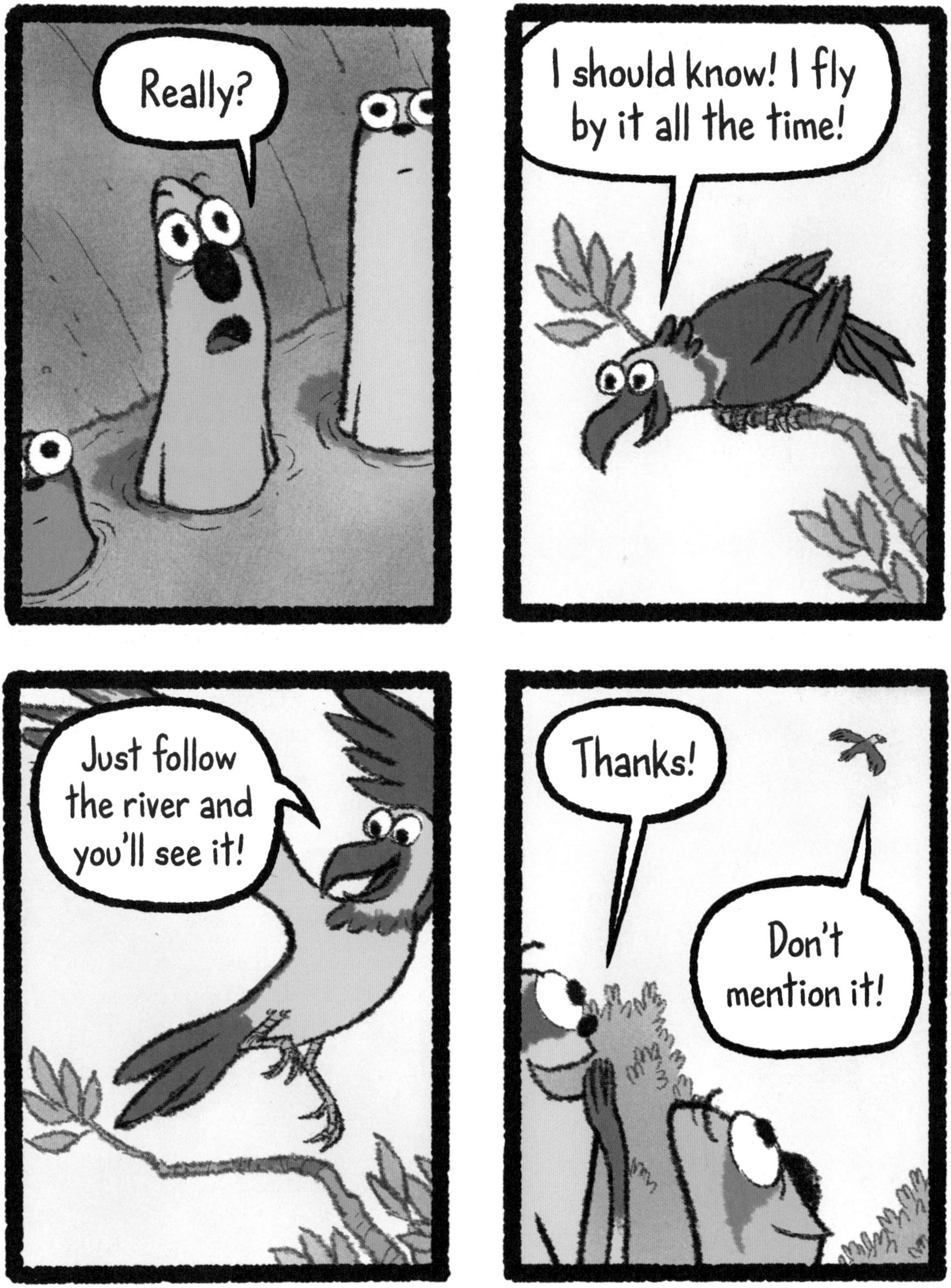
Really?
I should know! I fly by it all the time!
Just follow the river and you'll see it!
Thanks!
Don't mention it!

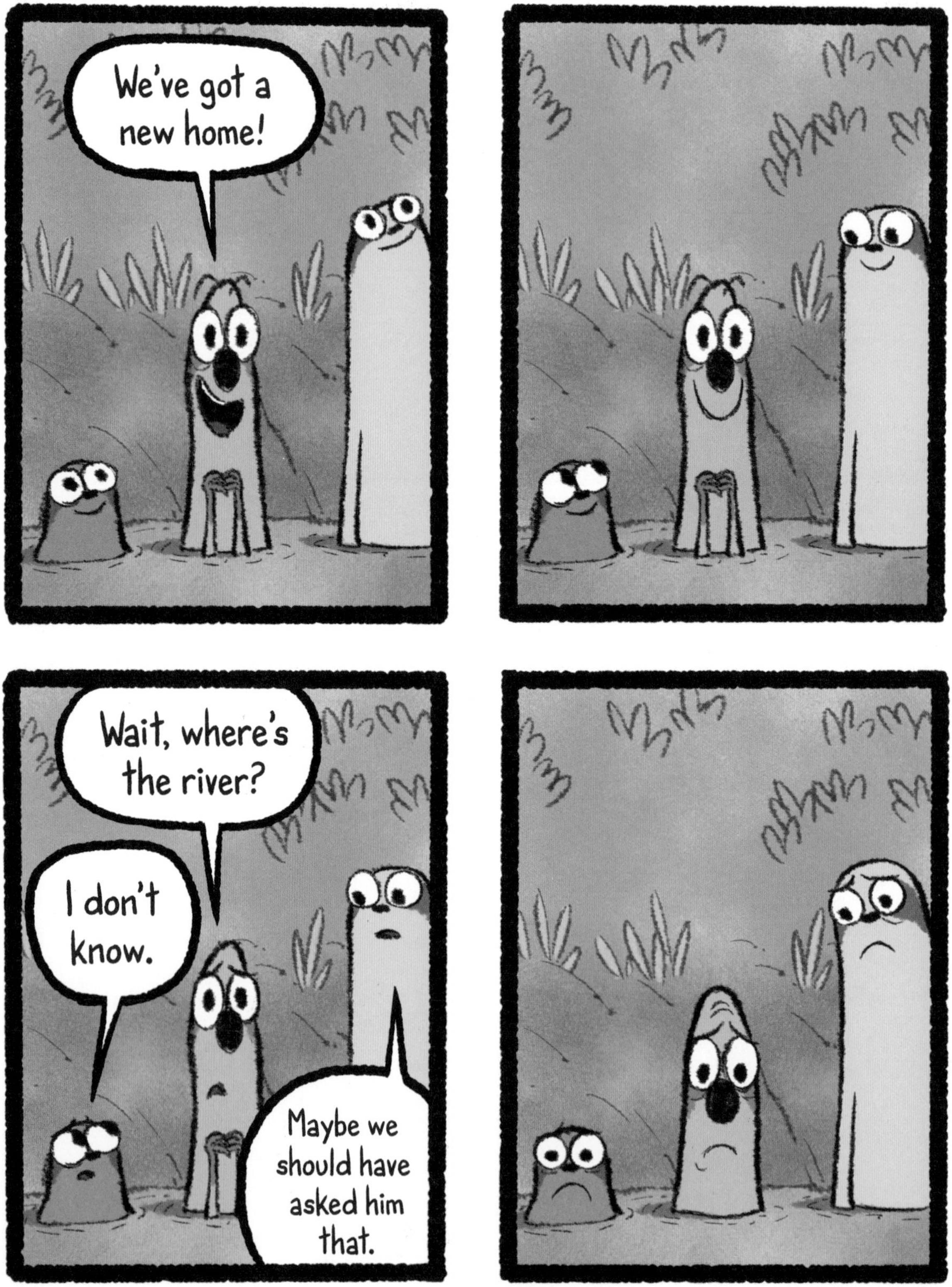
We've got a new home!
Wait, where's the river?
I don't know.
Maybe we should have asked him that.

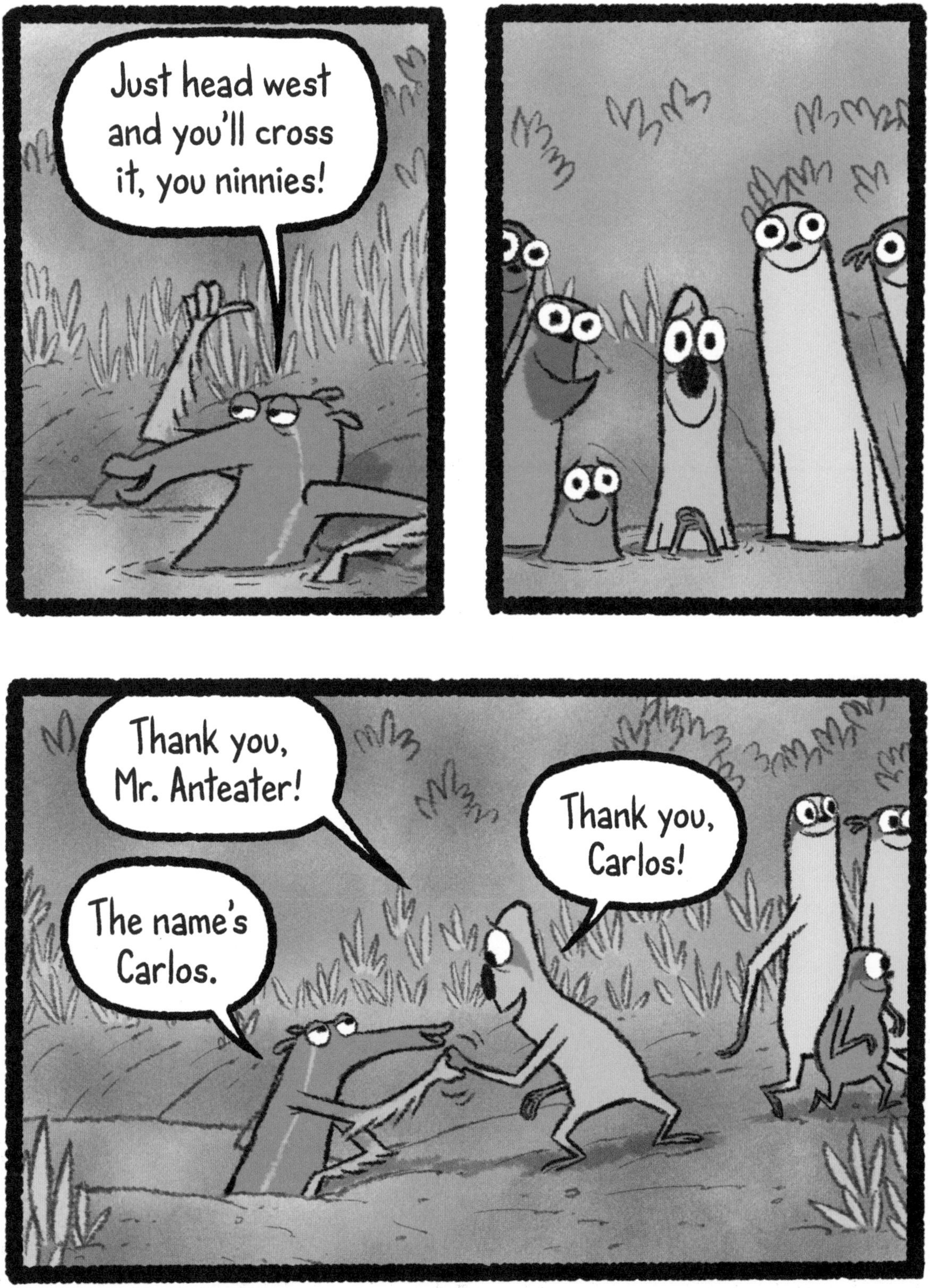
Just head west and you'll cross it, you ninnies!
Thank you, Mr. Anteater!
The name's Carlos.
Thank you, Carlos!

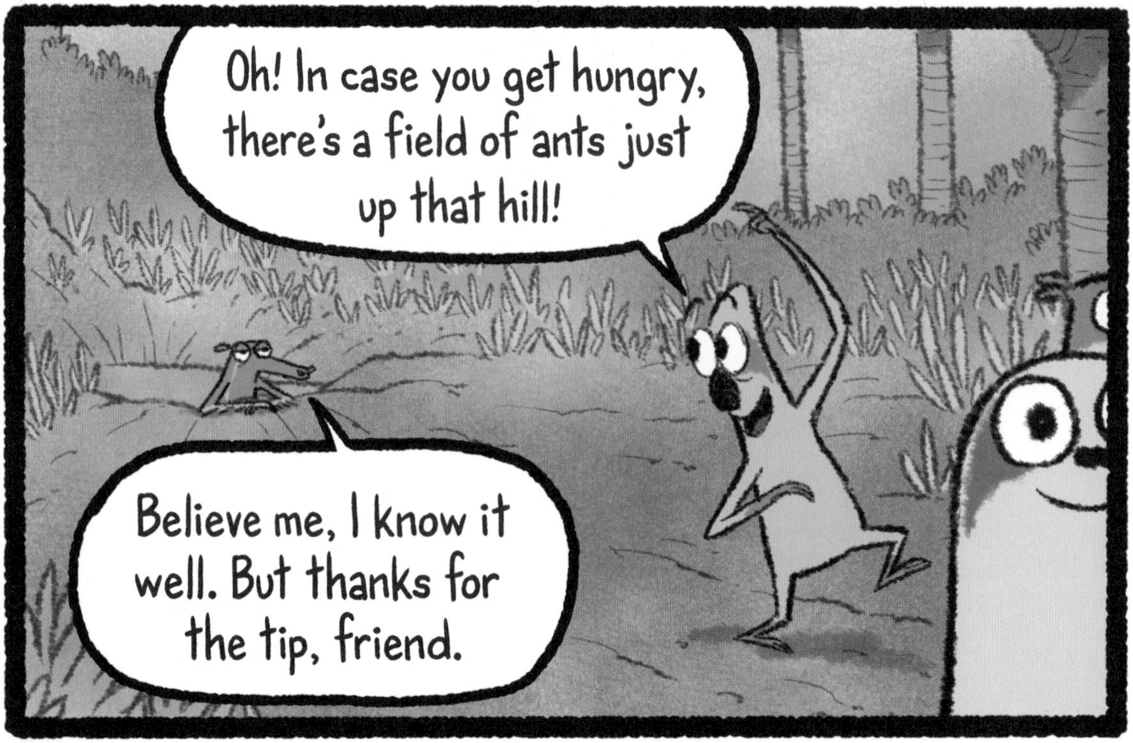
Oh! In case you get hungry, there's a field of ants just up that hill!
Believe me, I know it well. But thanks for the tip, friend.

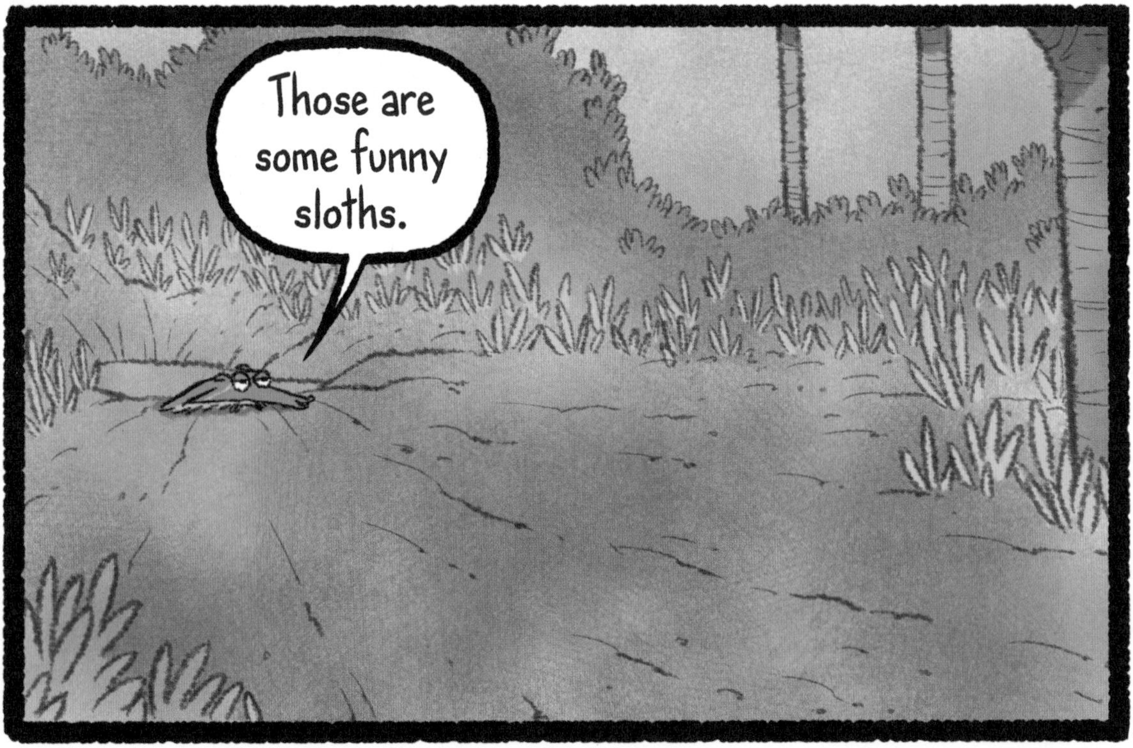
Those are some funny sloths.

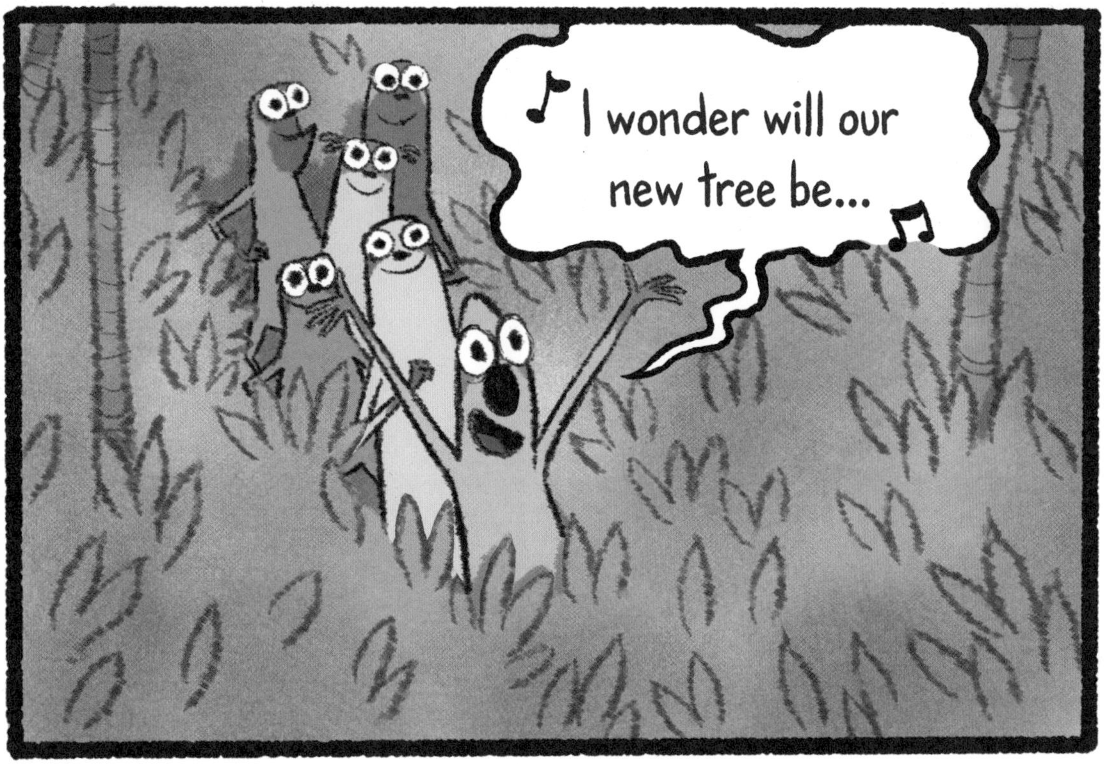
I wonder will our new tree be...

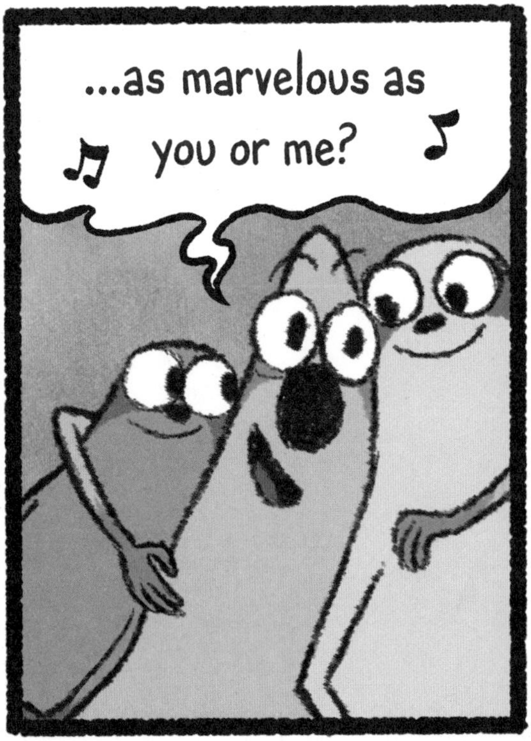
...as marvelous as you or me?

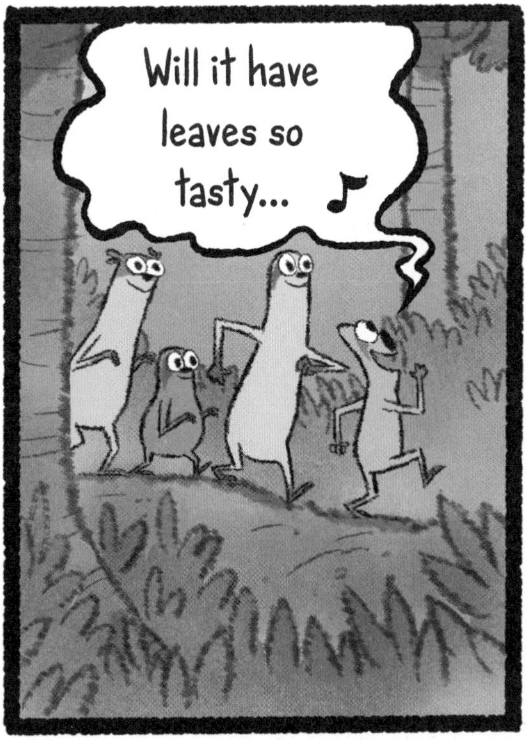
Will it have leaves so tasty...

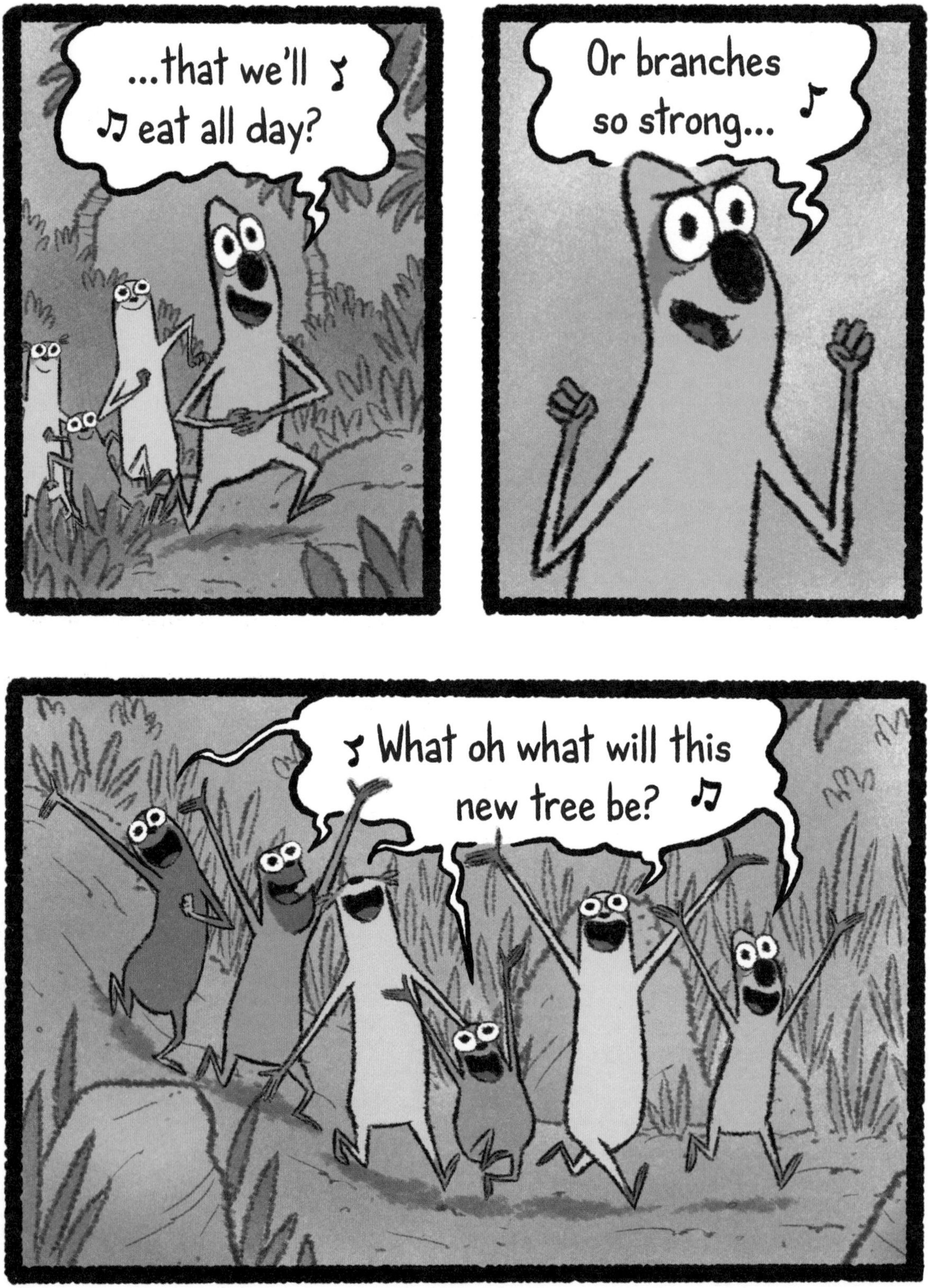
...that we'll ♪ eat all day?
Or branches so strong...
What oh what will this new tree be?

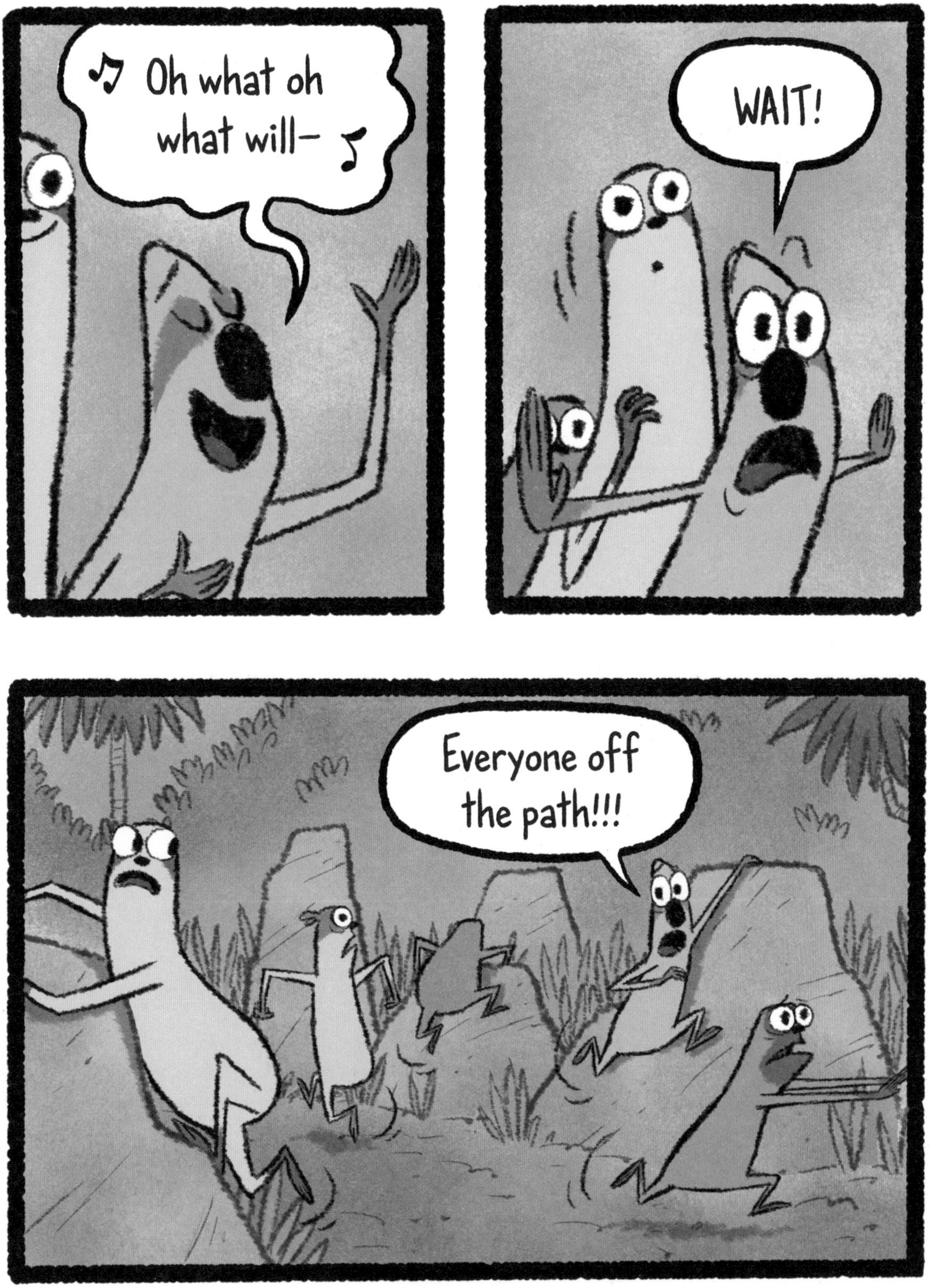
♫ Oh what oh what will– ♪
WAIT!
Everyone off the path!!!

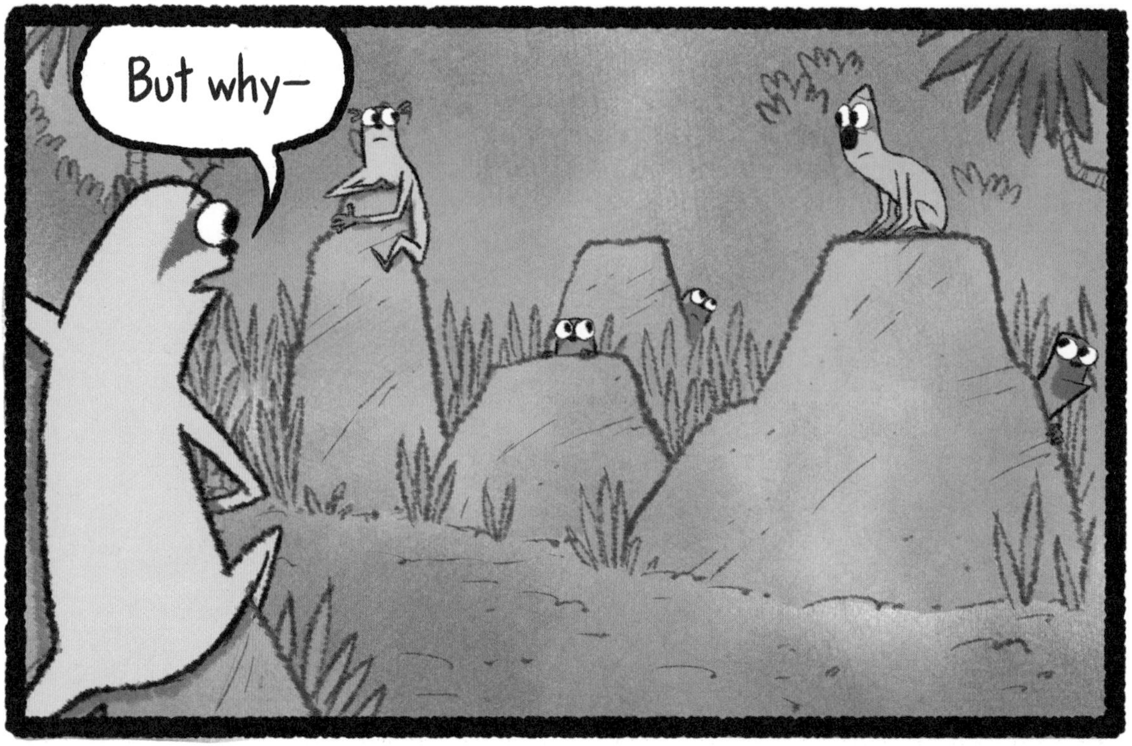
But why-

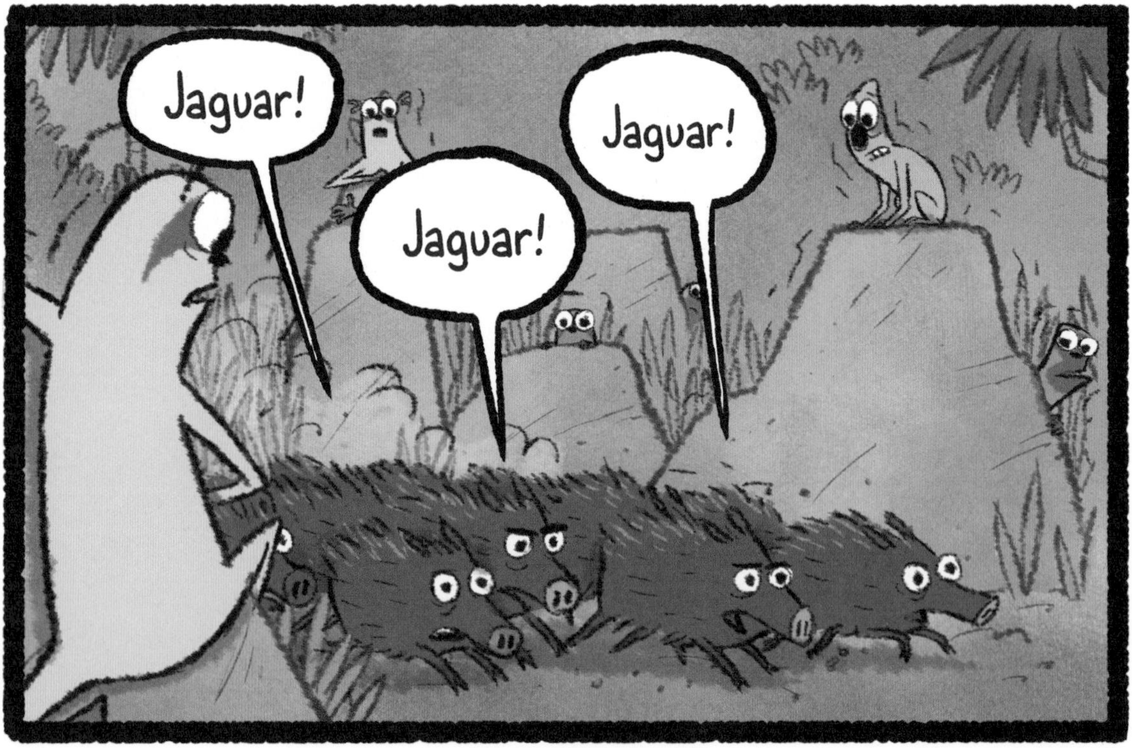
Jaguar!
Jaguar!
Jaguar!

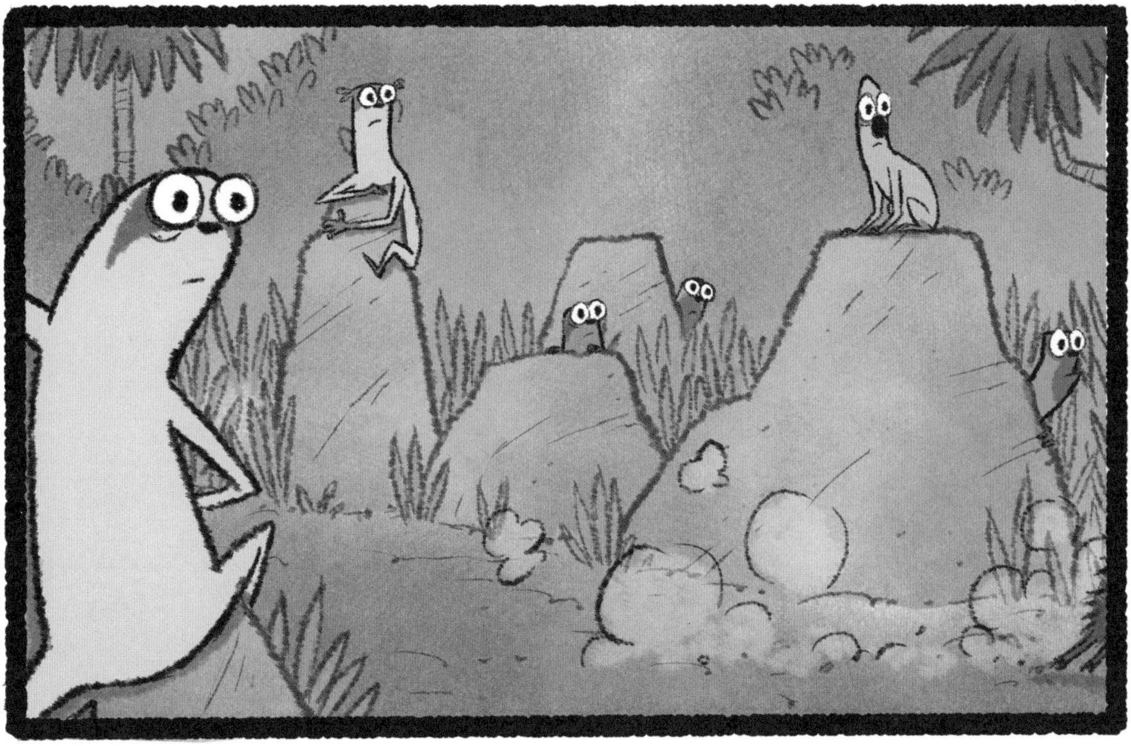

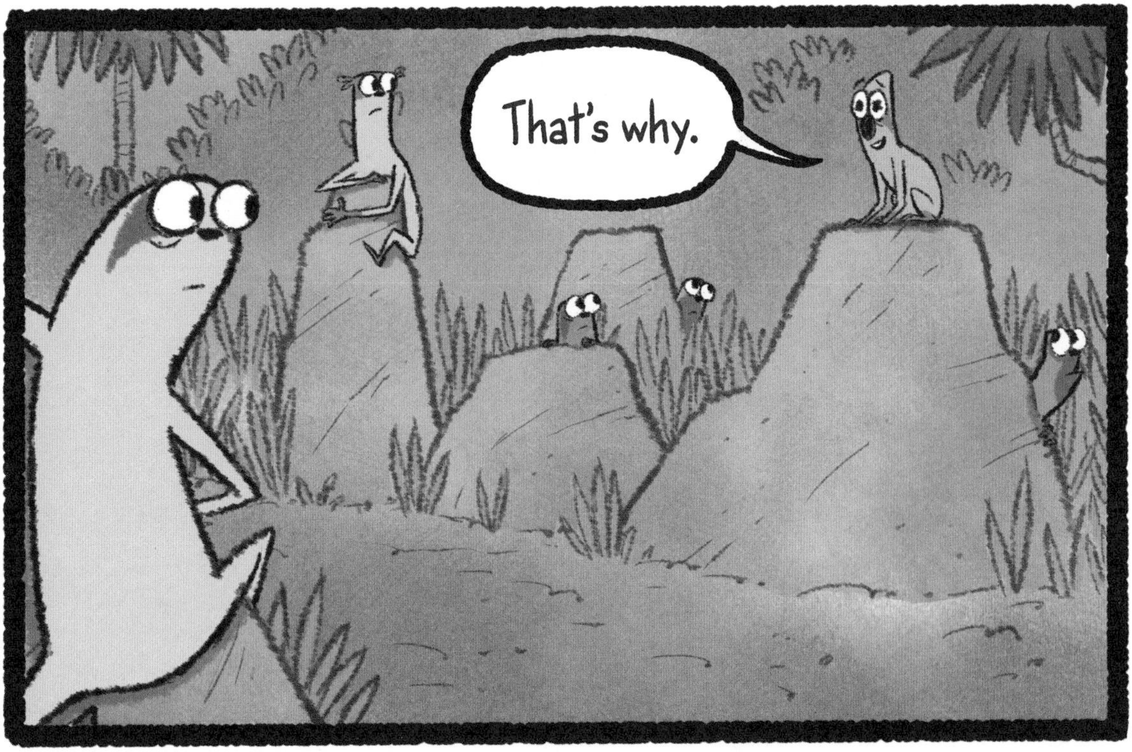
That's why.

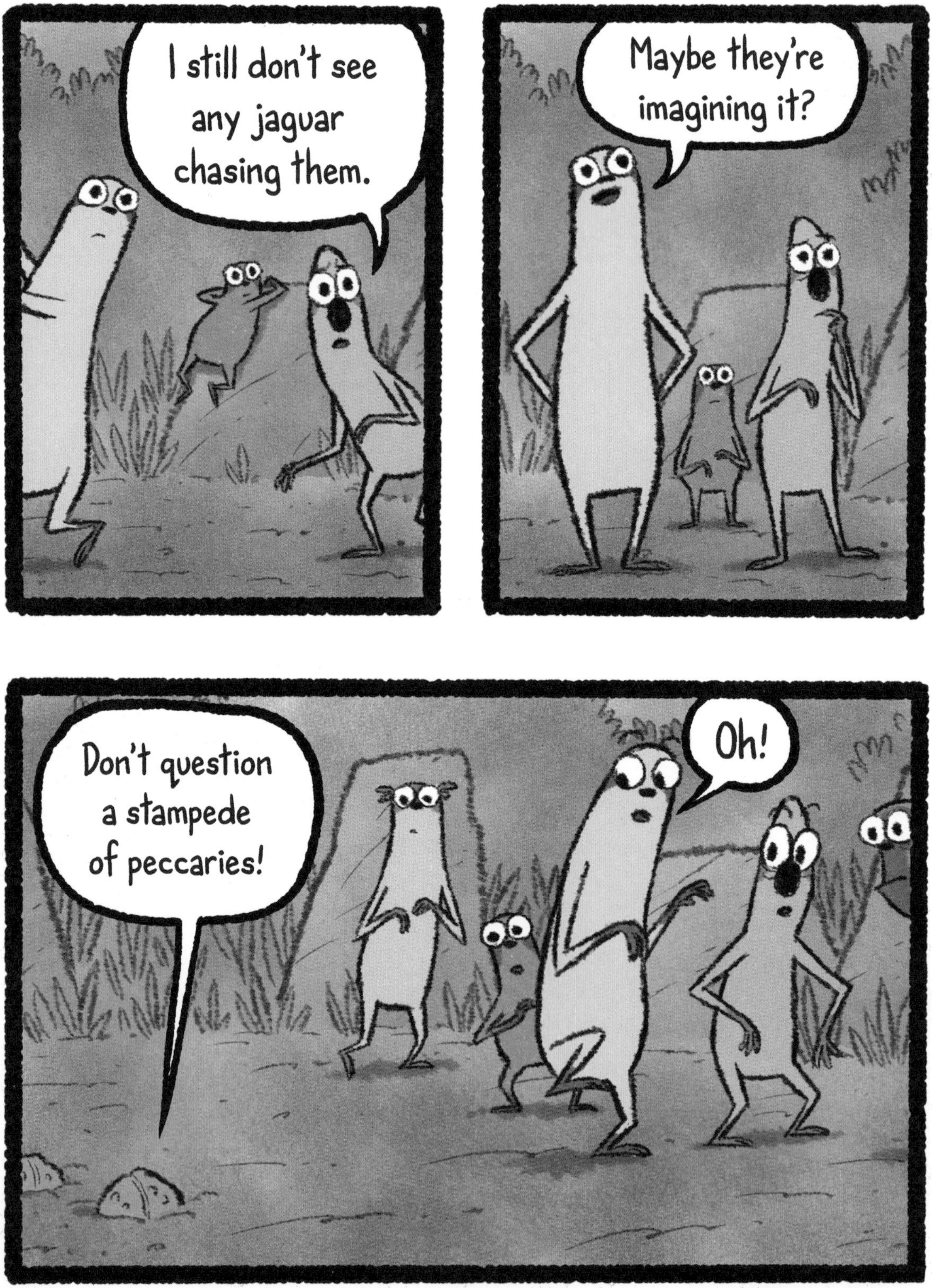
I still don't see any jaguar chasing them.
Maybe they're imagining it?
Don't question a stampede of peccaries!
Oh!

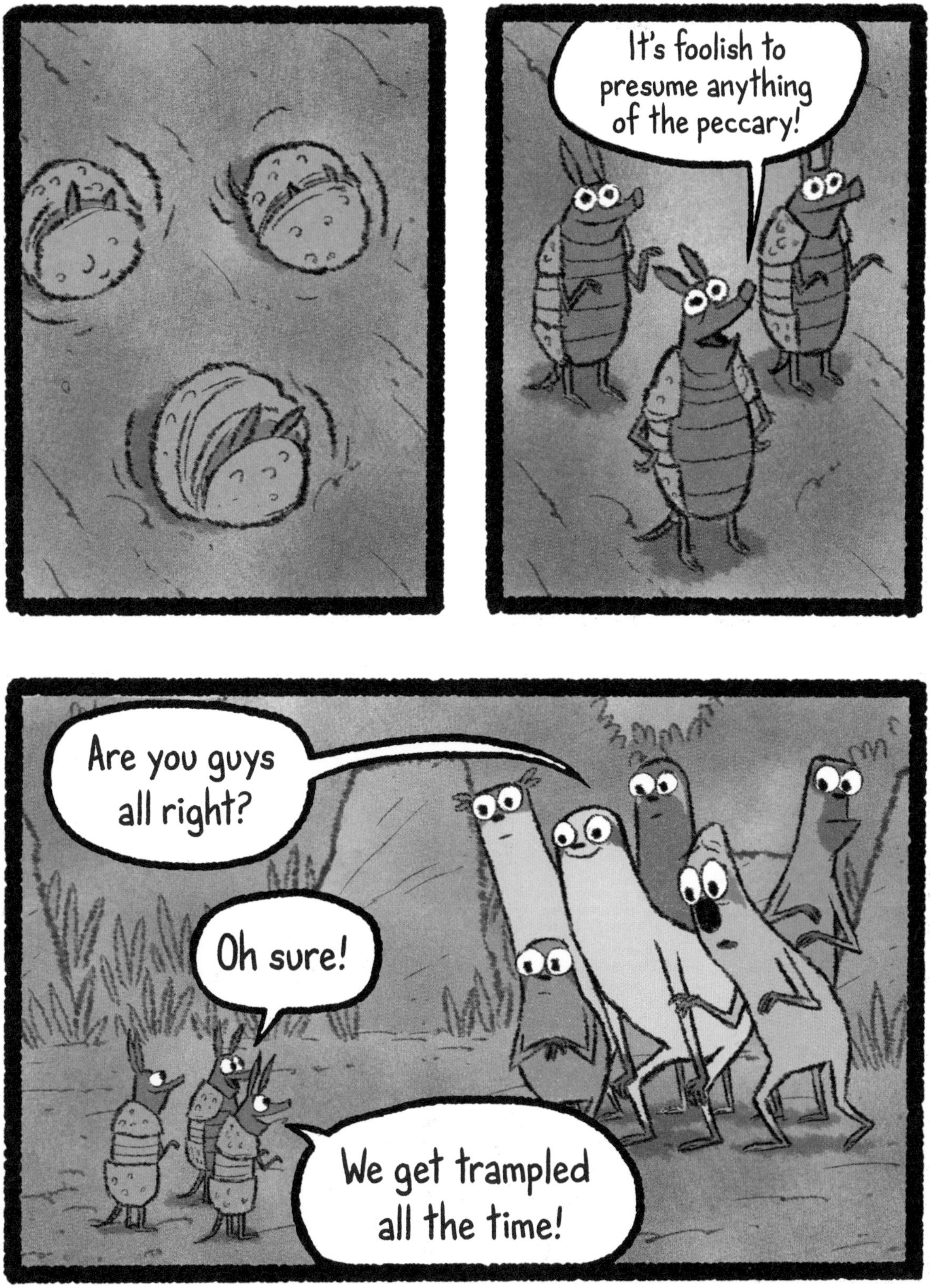
It's foolish to presume anything of the peccary!
Are you guys all right?
Oh sure!
We get trampled all the time!

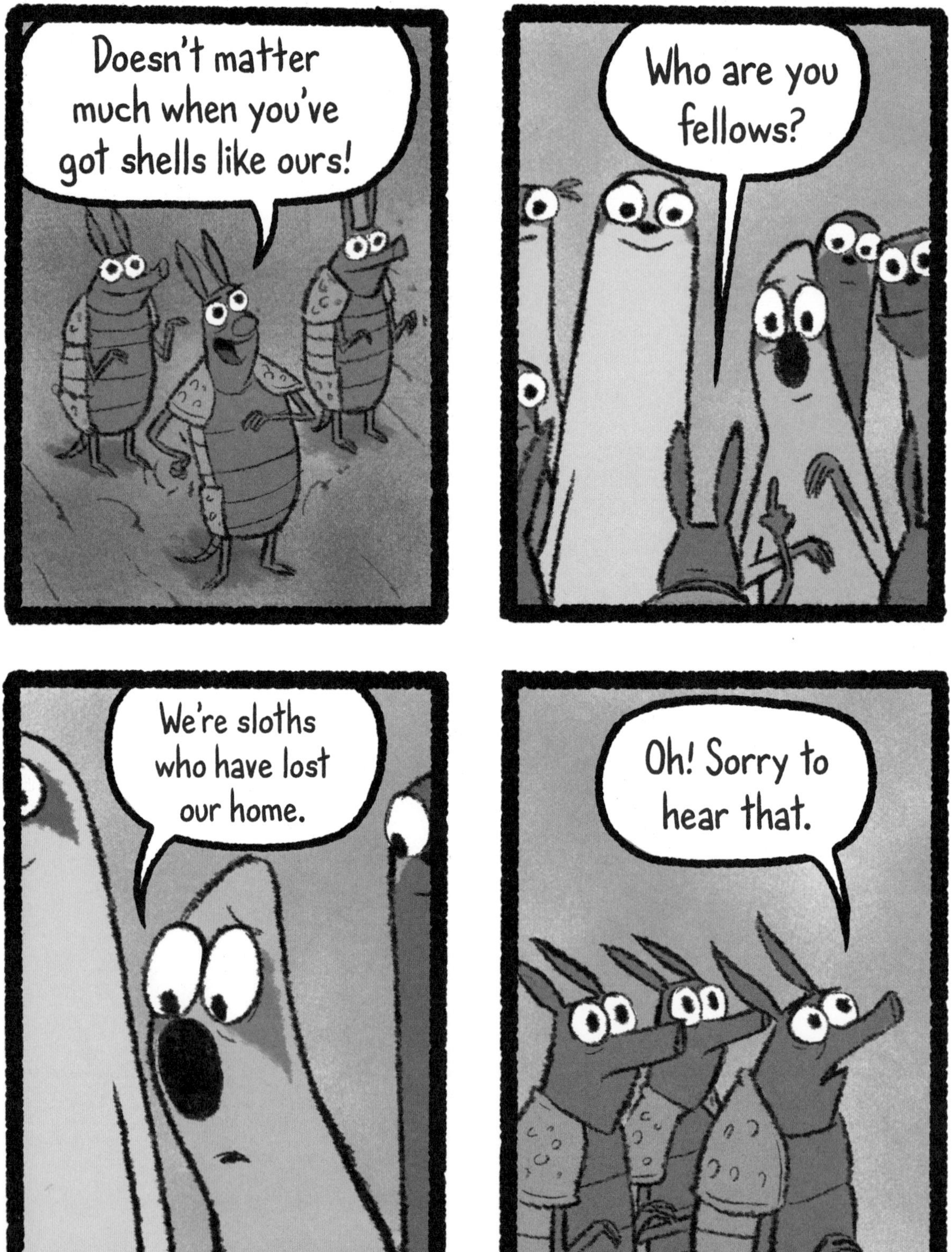
Doesn't matter much when you've got shells like ours!
Who are you fellows?
We're sloths who have lost our home.
Oh! Sorry to hear that.

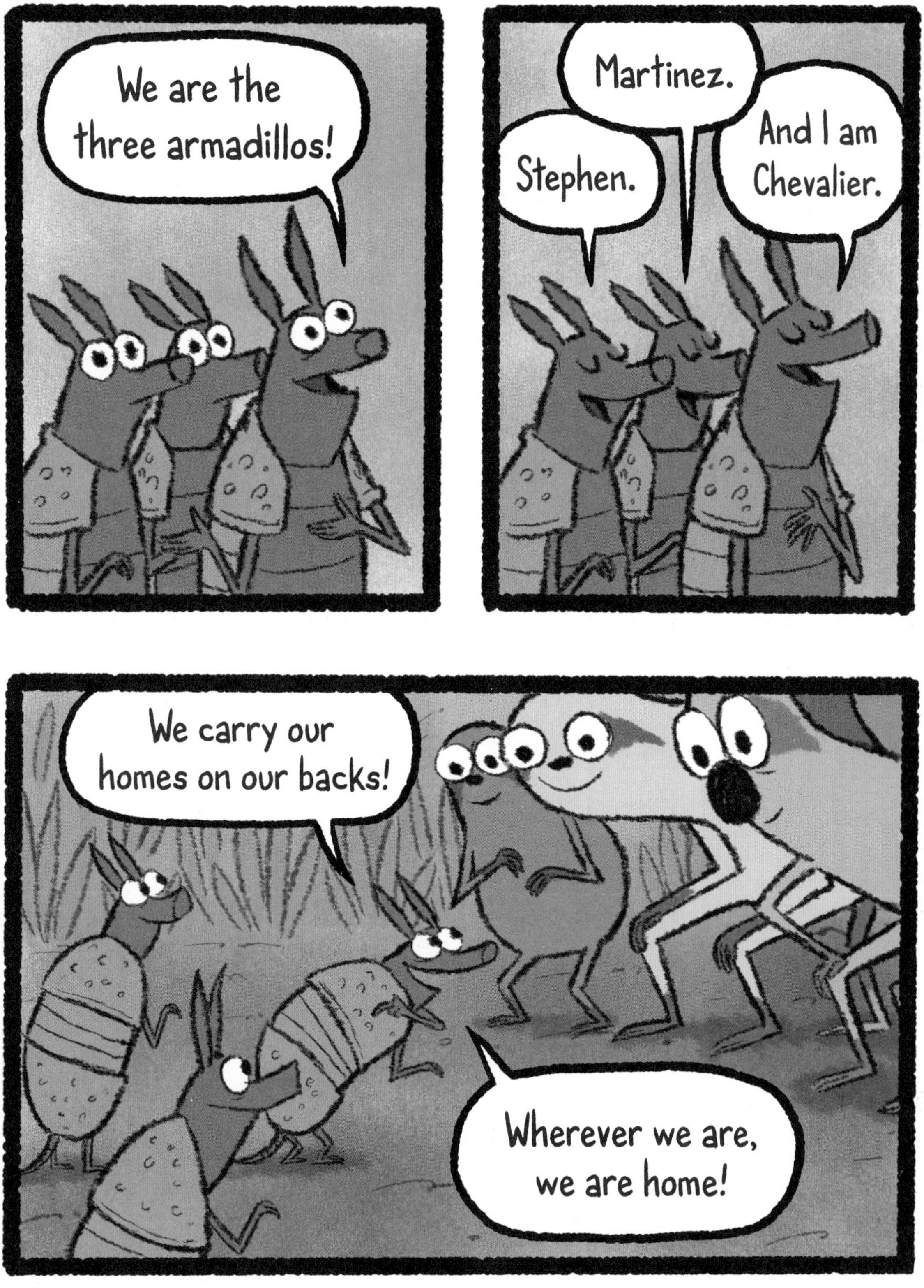
We are the three armadillos!
Stephen.
Martinez.
And I am Chevalier.
We carry our homes on our backs!
Wherever we are, we are home!

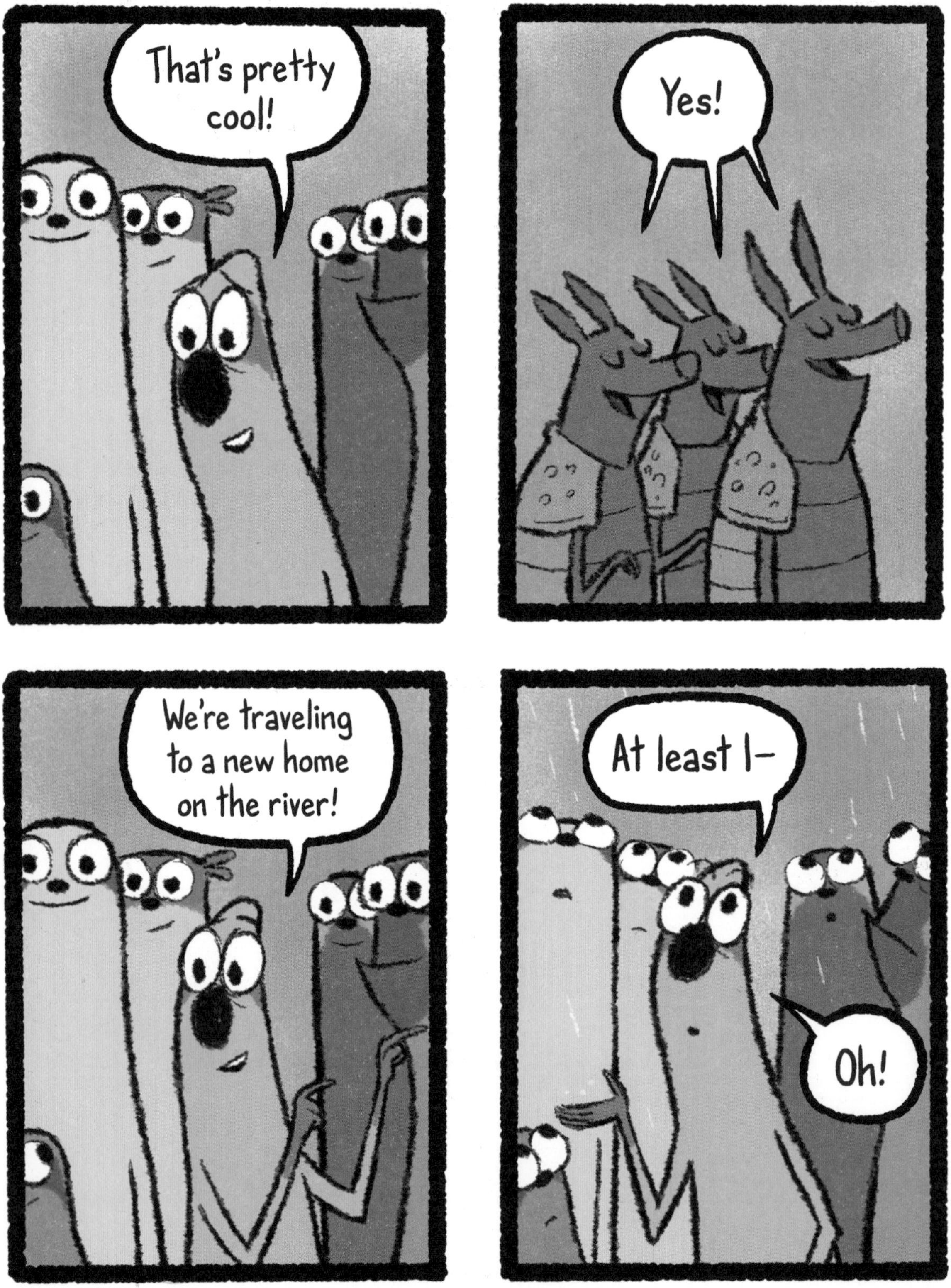
That's pretty cool!
Yes!
We're traveling to a new home on the river!
At least I-
Oh!

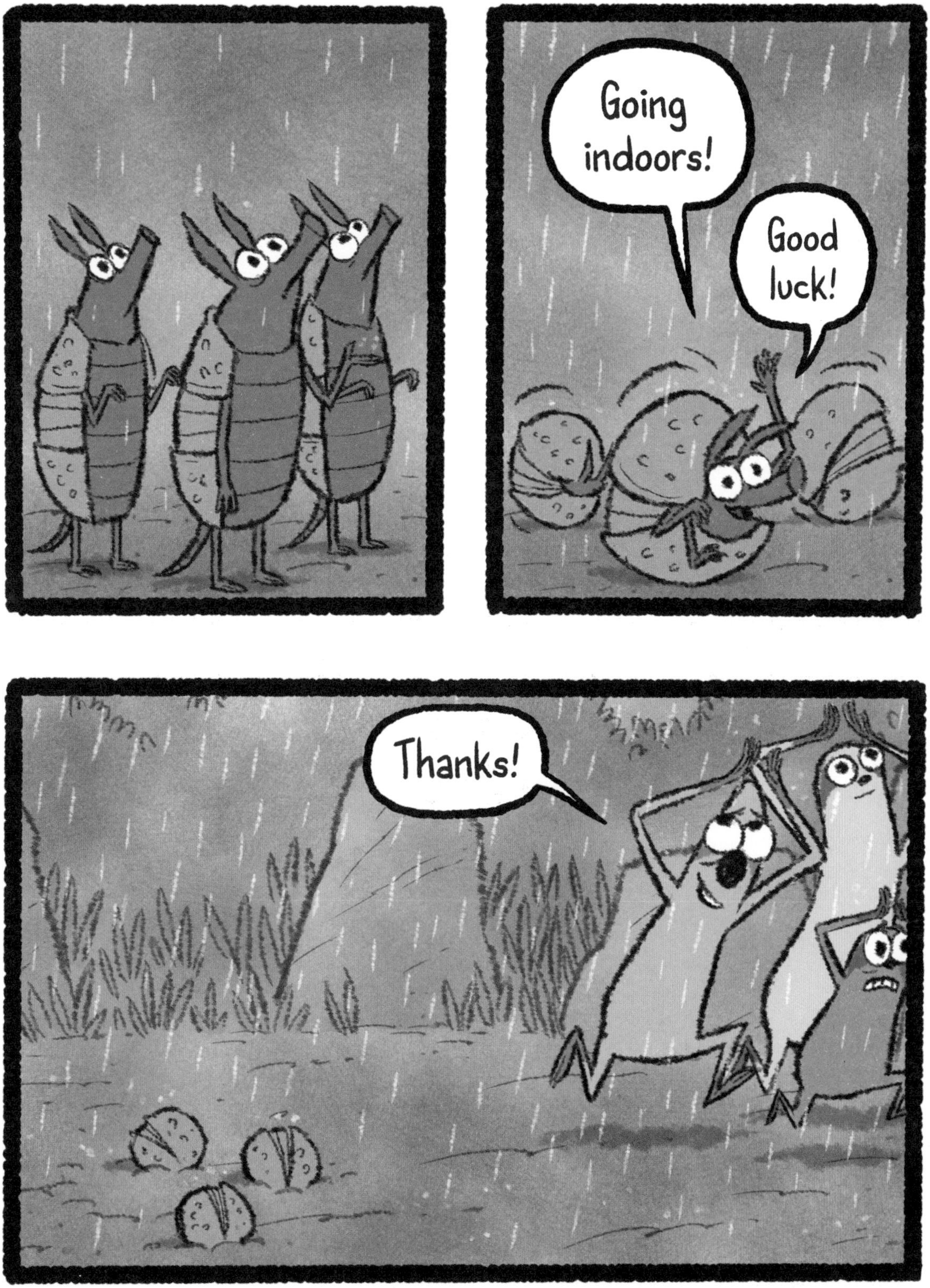
Going indoors!
Good luck!
Thanks!

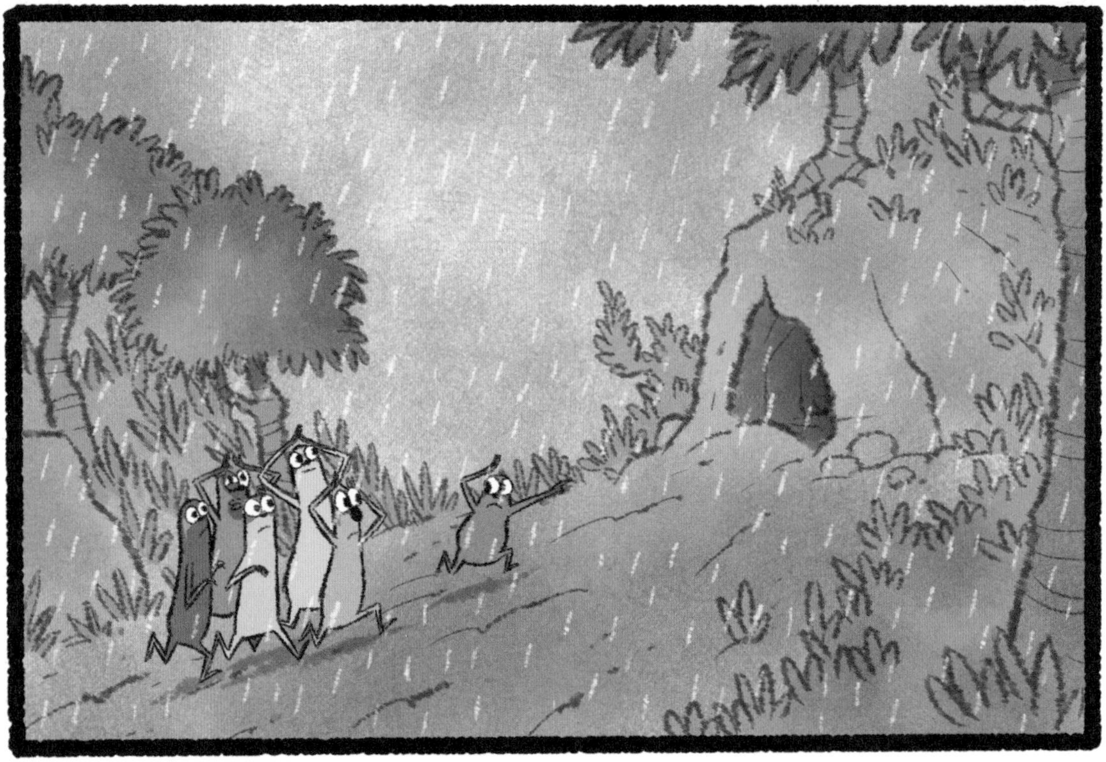

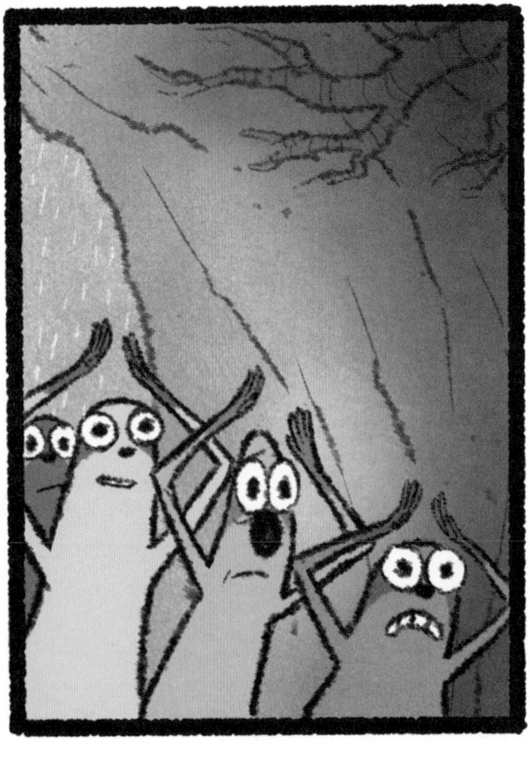

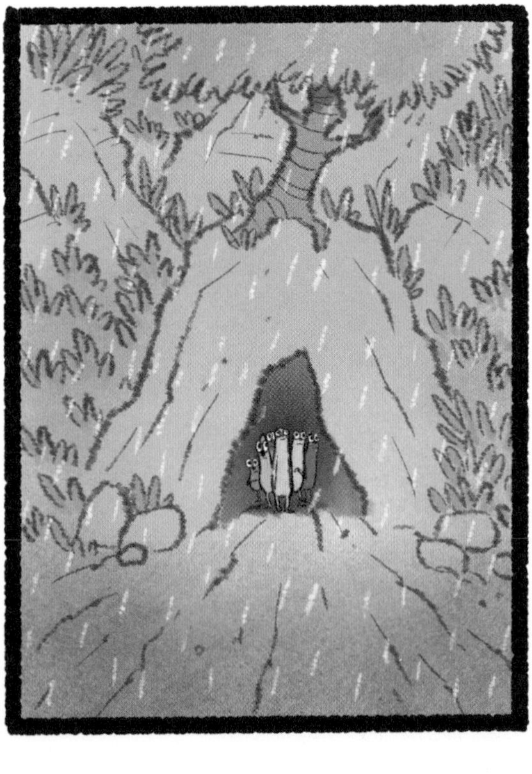

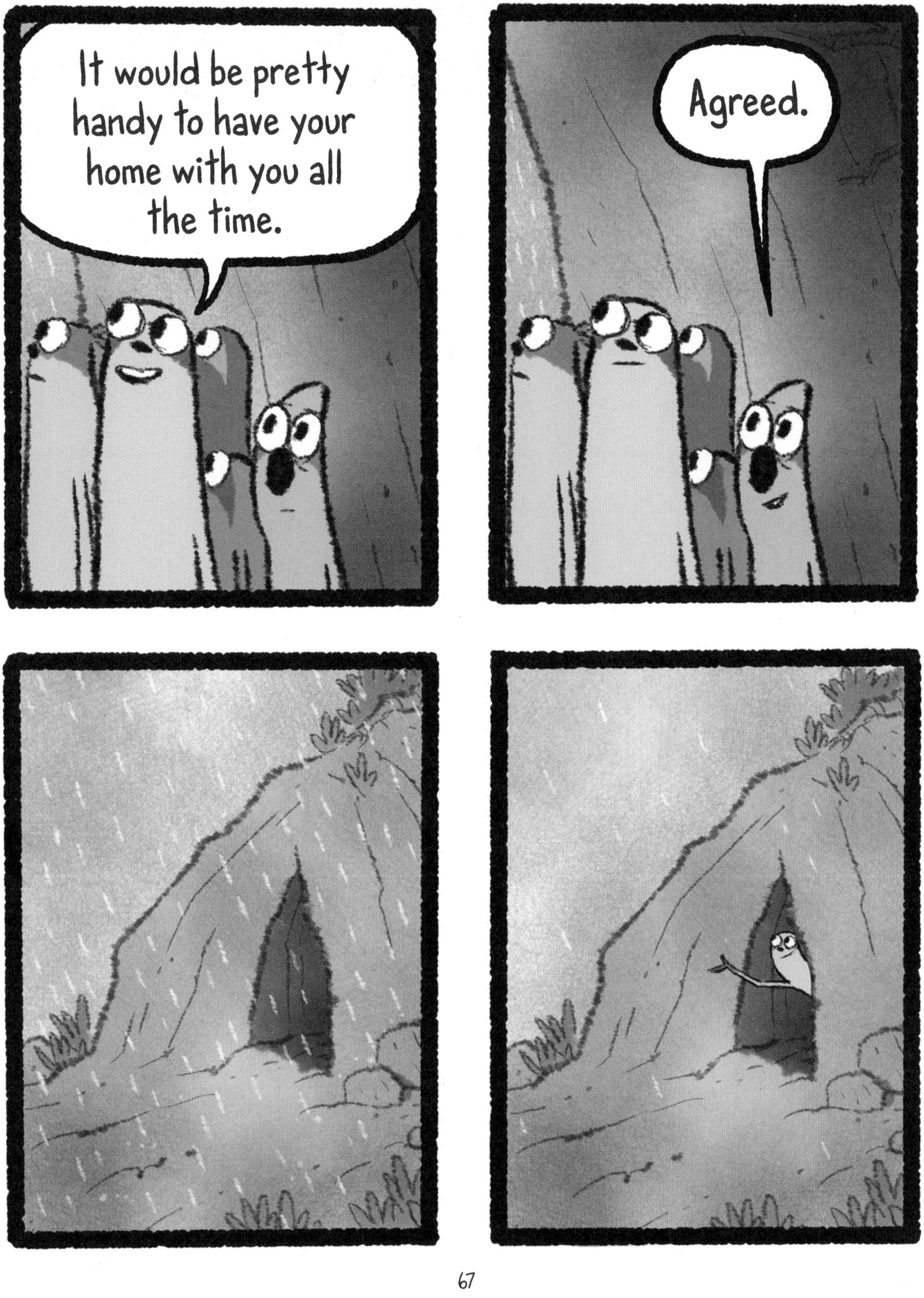
It would be pretty handy to have your home with you all the time.
Agreed.

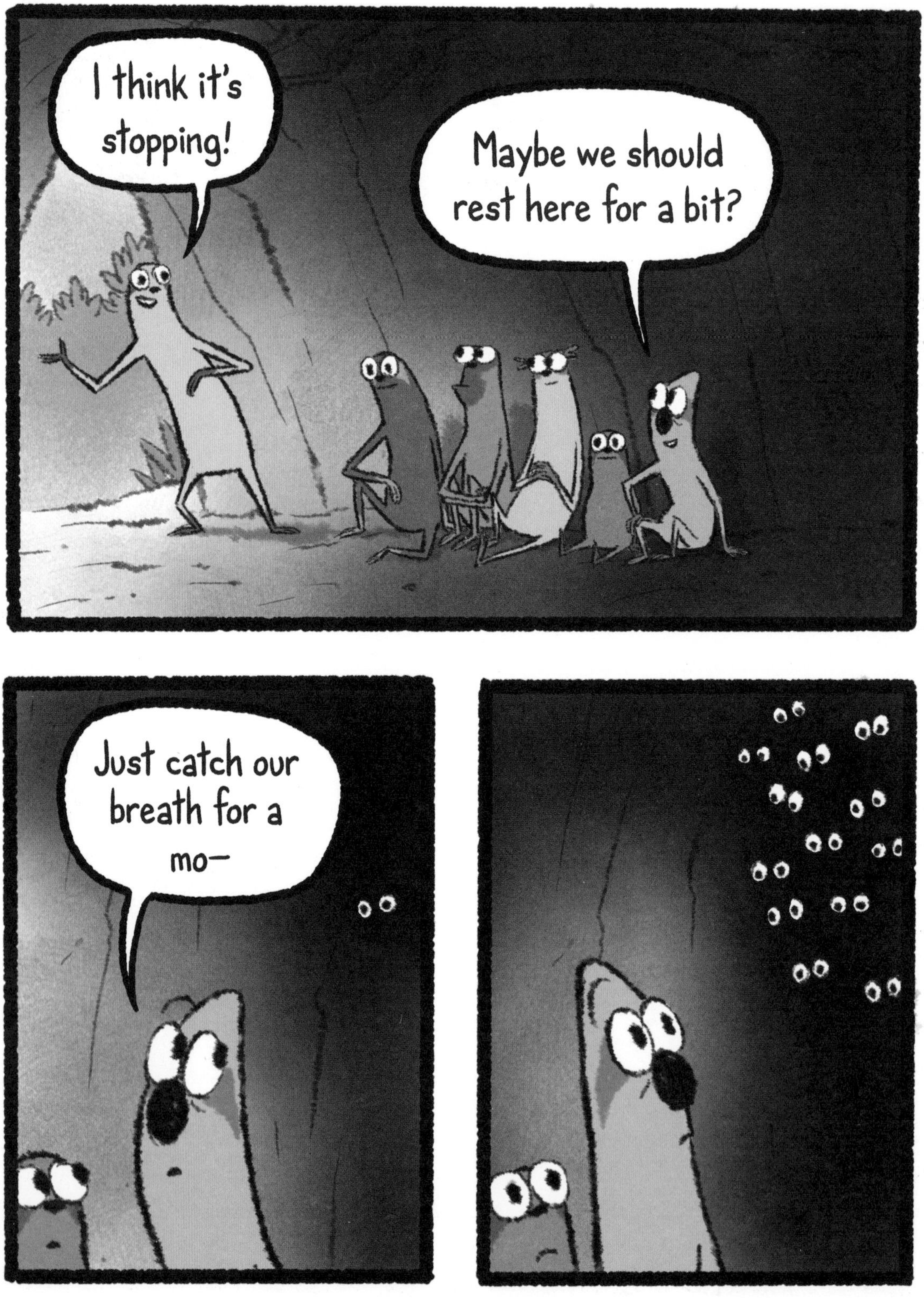
I think it's stopping!
Maybe we should rest here for a bit?
Just catch our breath for a mo–

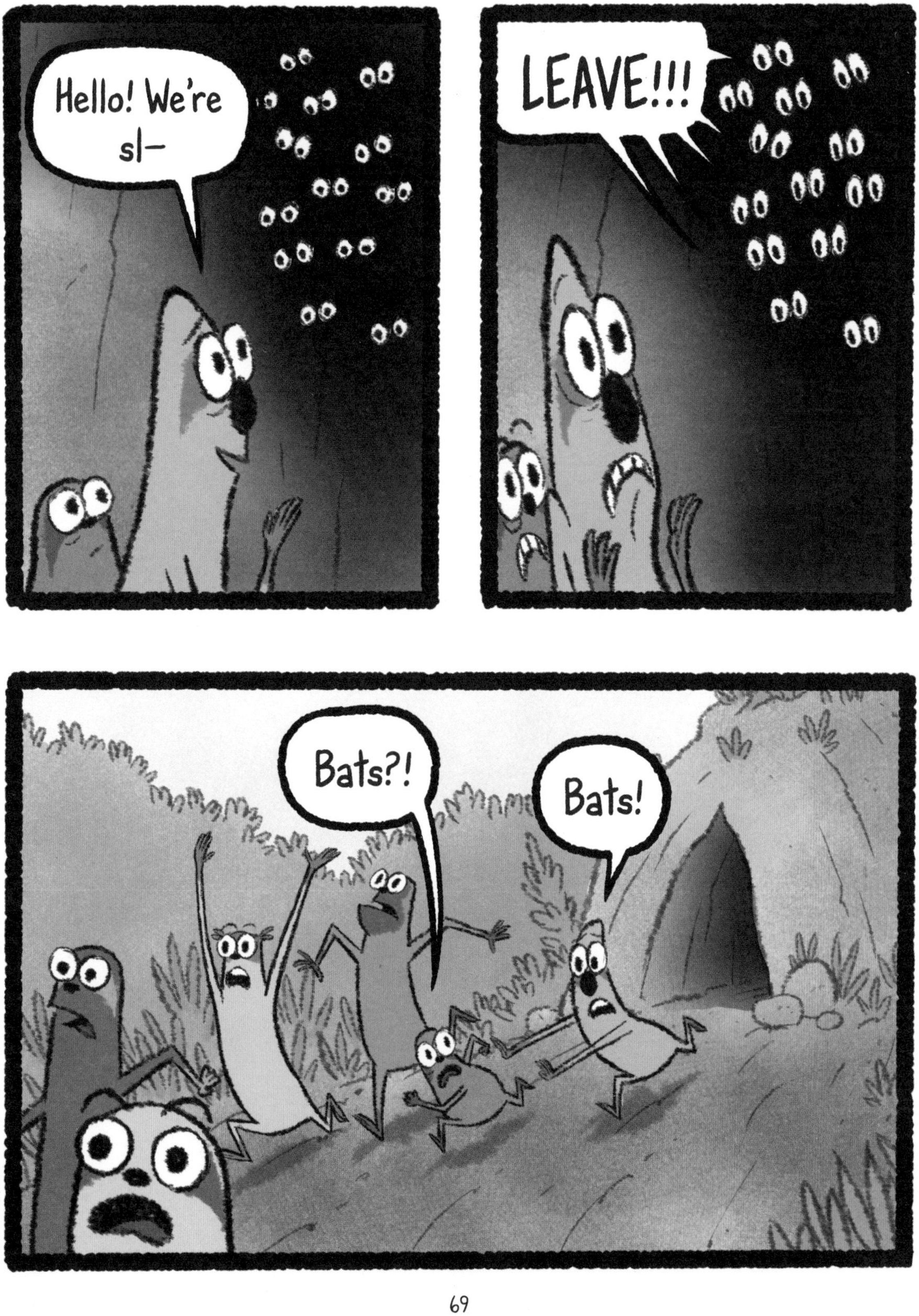
Hello! We're sl—
LEAVE!!!
Bats?!
Bats!

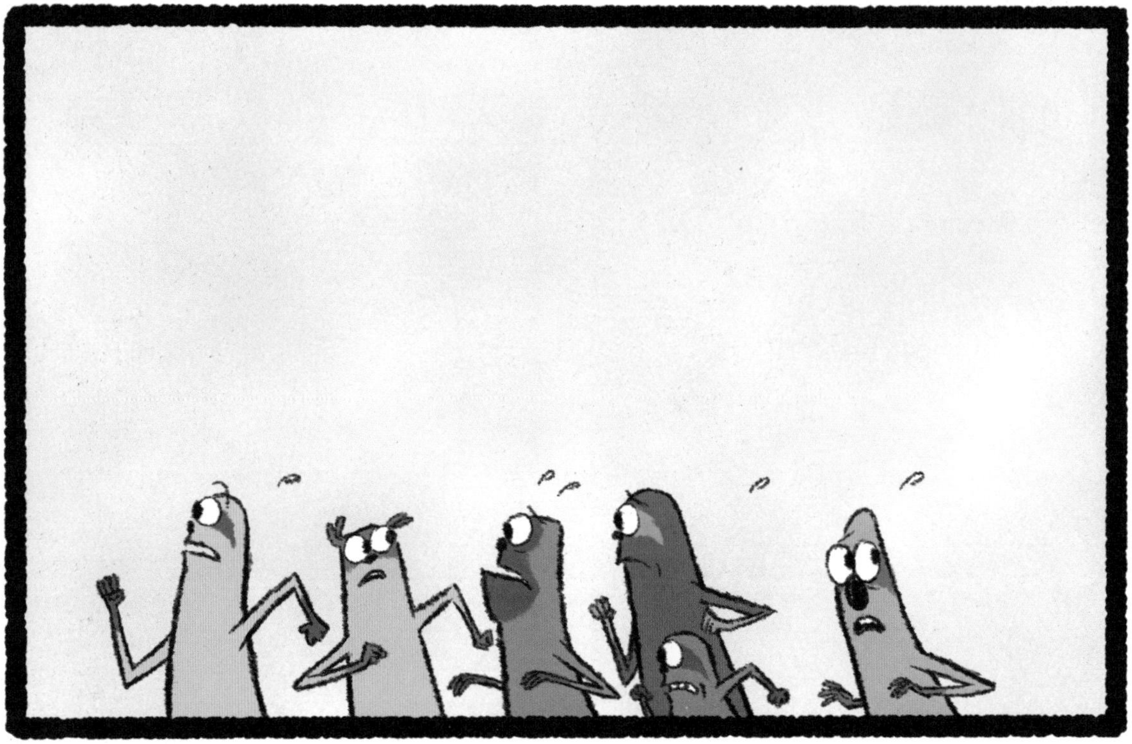

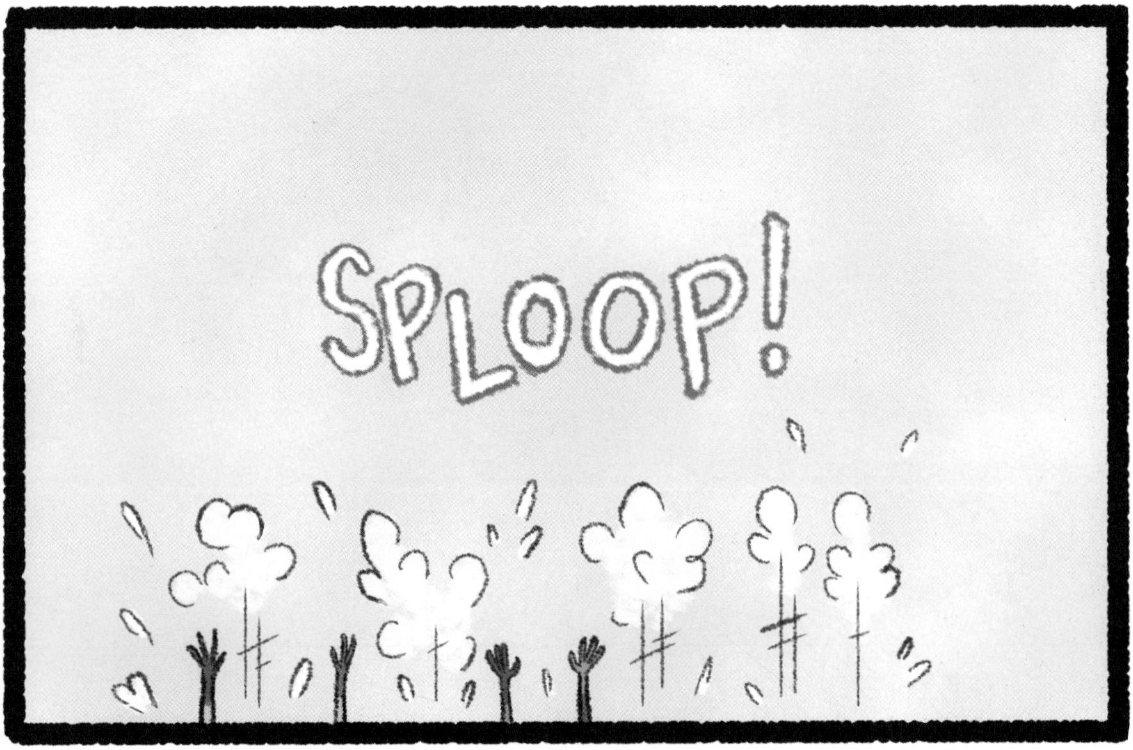
SPLOOP!

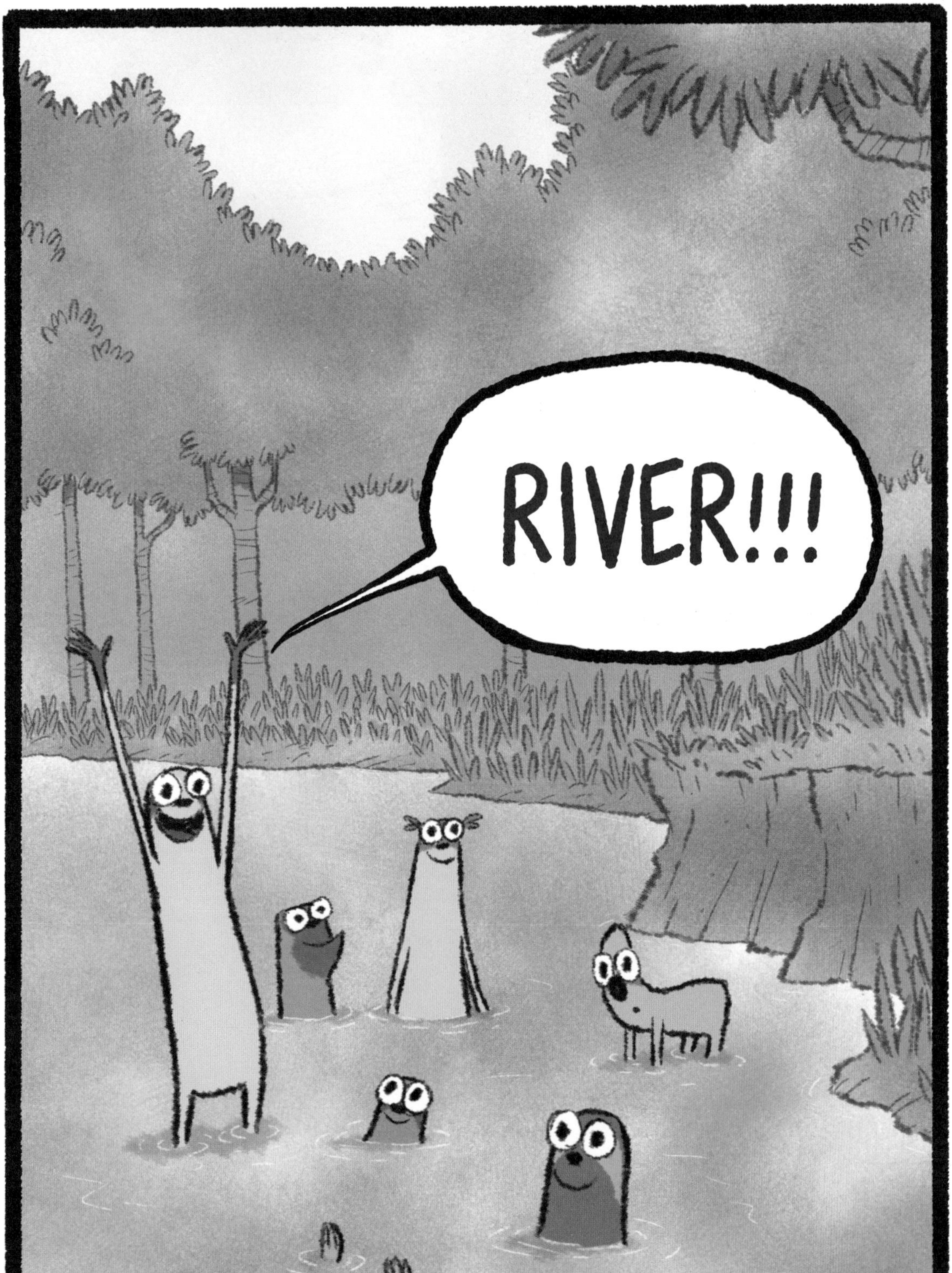
RIVER!!!

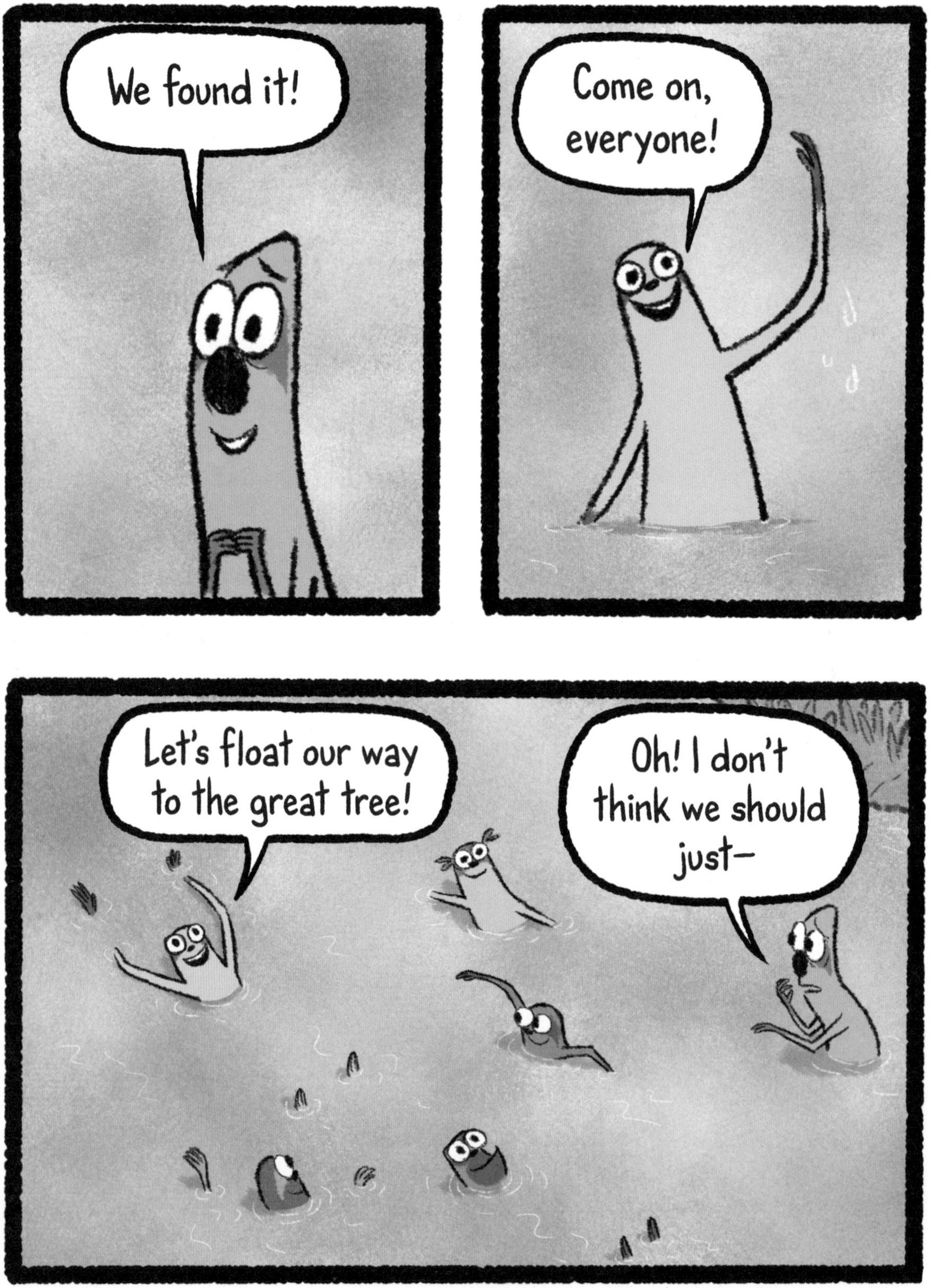
We found it!
Come on, everyone!
Let's float our way to the great tree!
Oh! I don't think we should just–

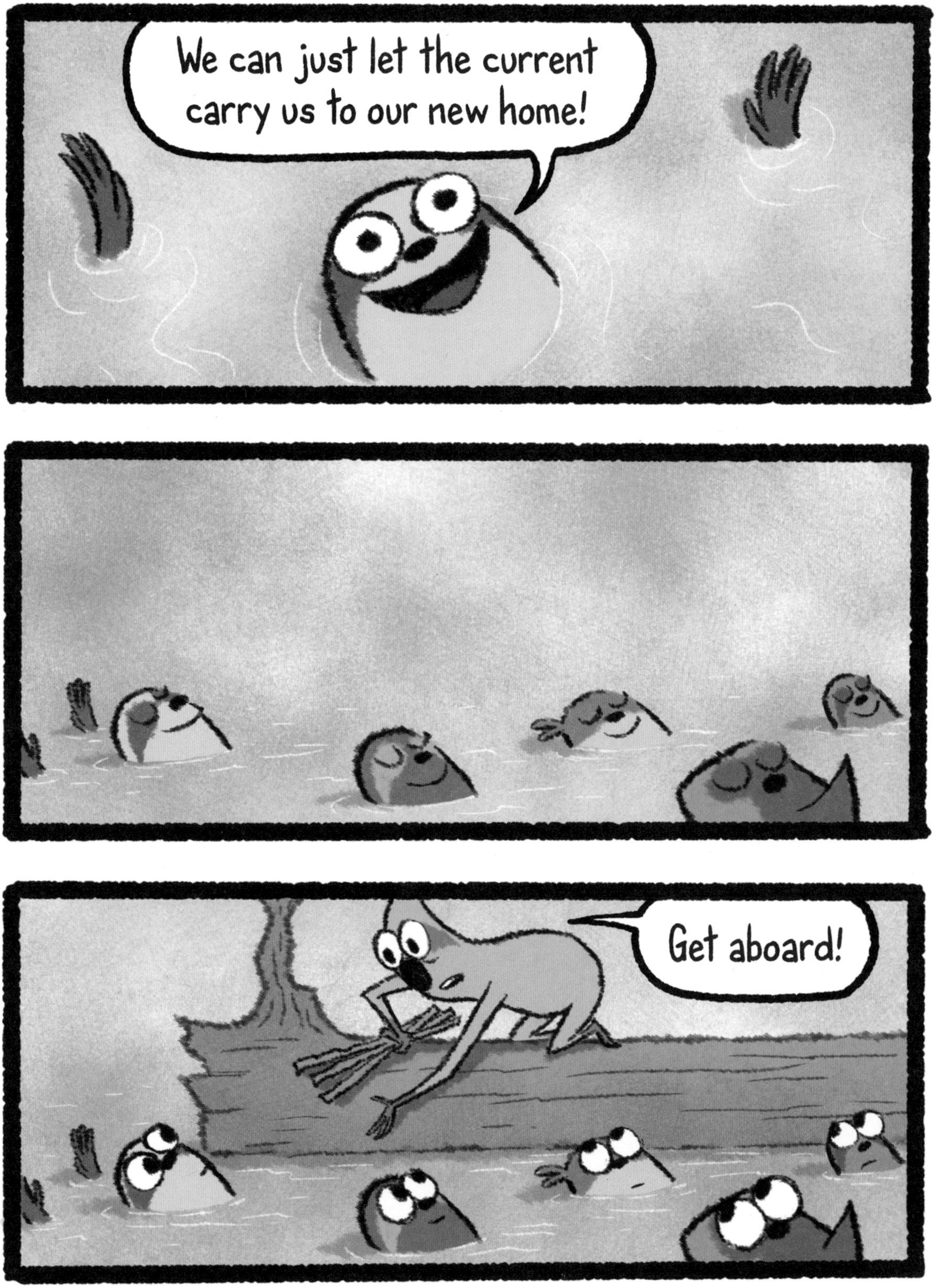
We can just let the current carry us to our new home!
Get aboard!

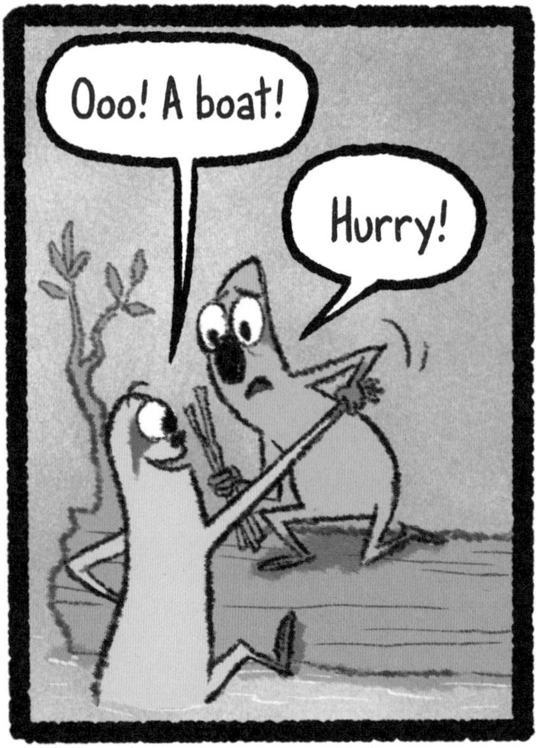
Ooo! A boat!
Hurry!

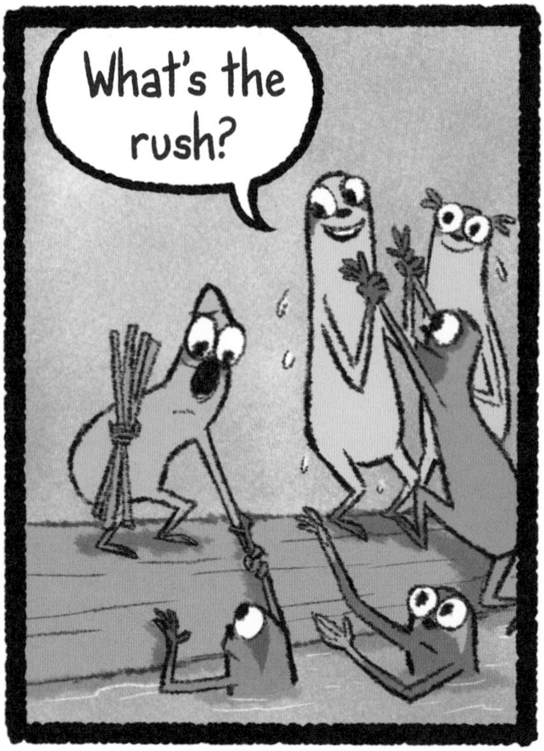
What's the rush?

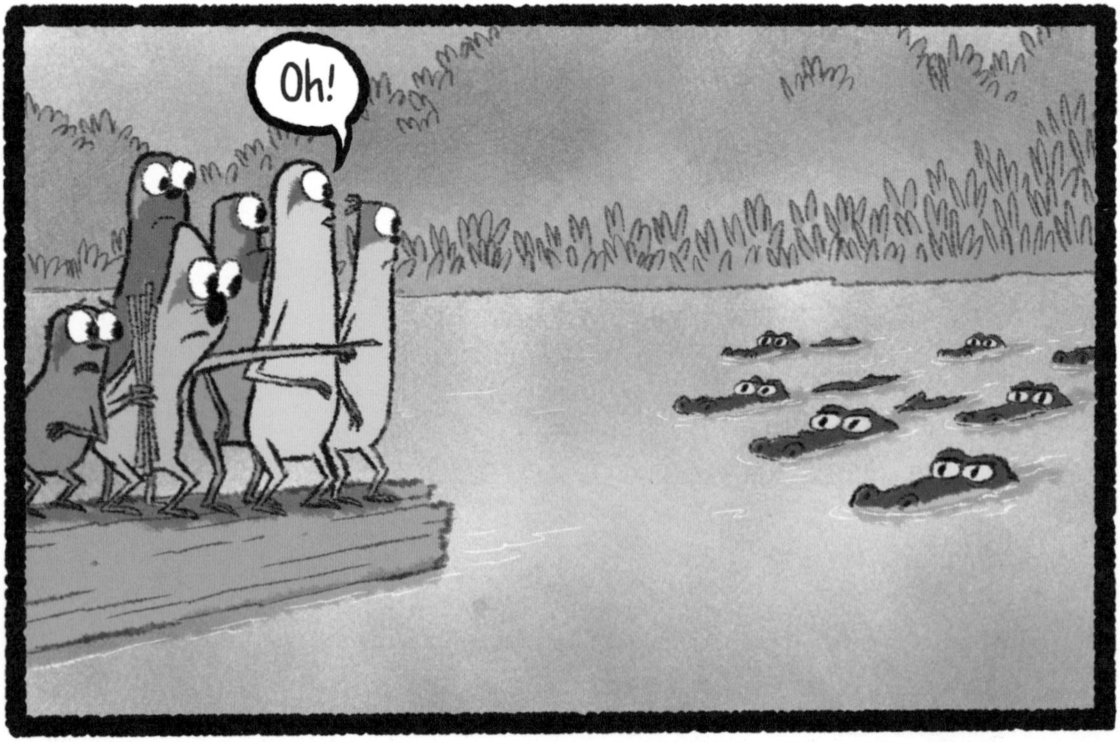
Oh!

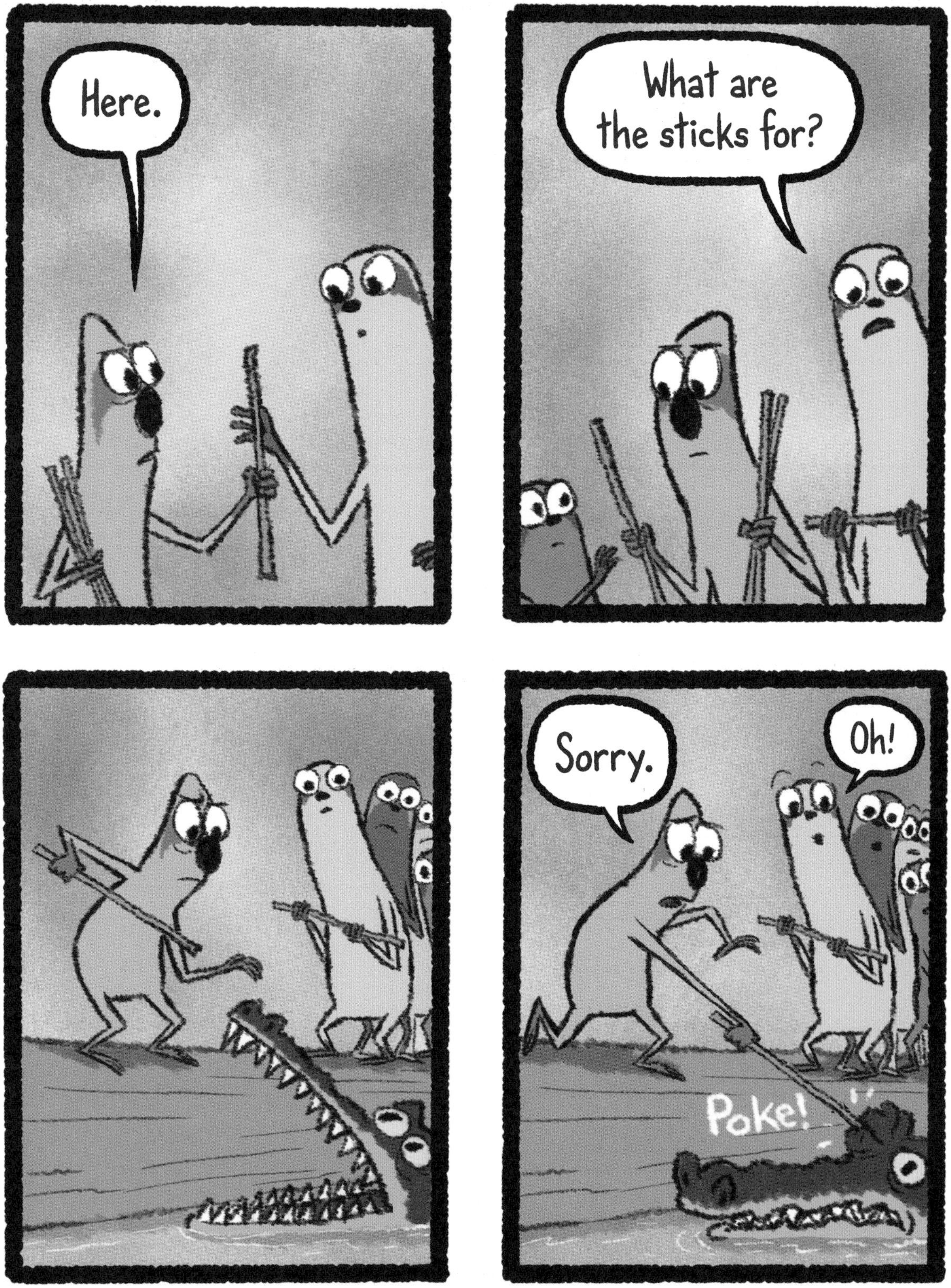
Here.
What are the sticks for?
Sorry.
Oh!
Poke!

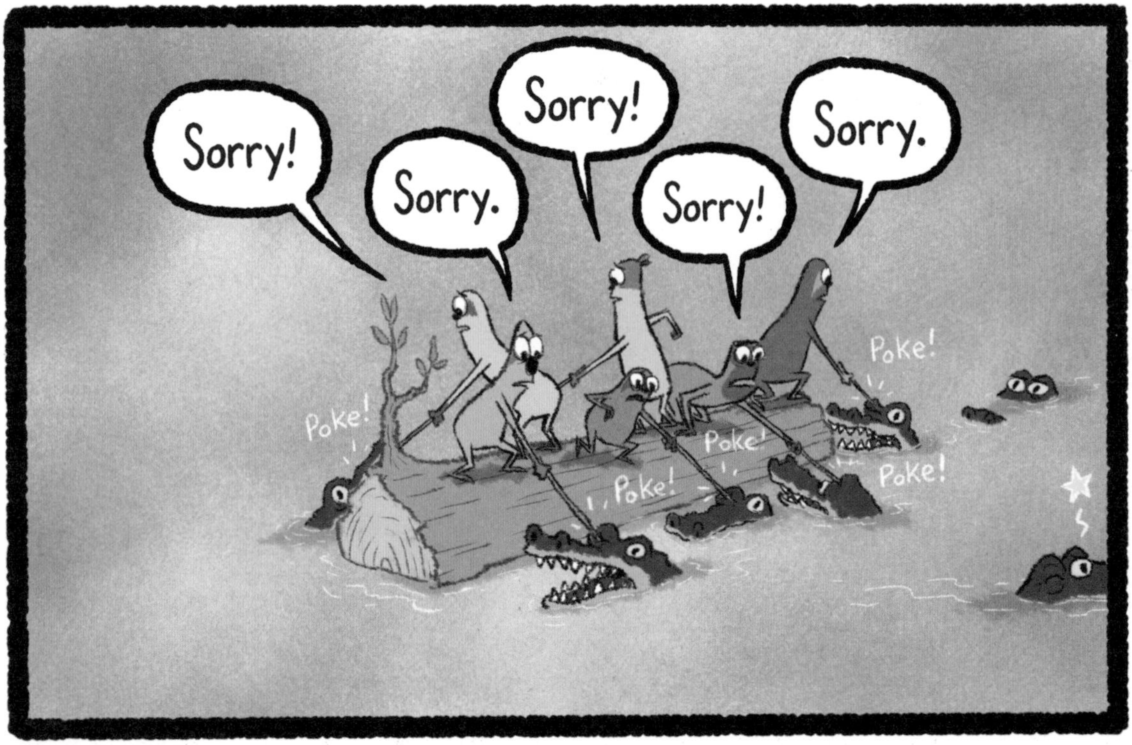

Sorry!
Sorry.
Sorry!
Sorry!
Sorry.
Poke!
Poke!
Poke!
Poke!
Poke!


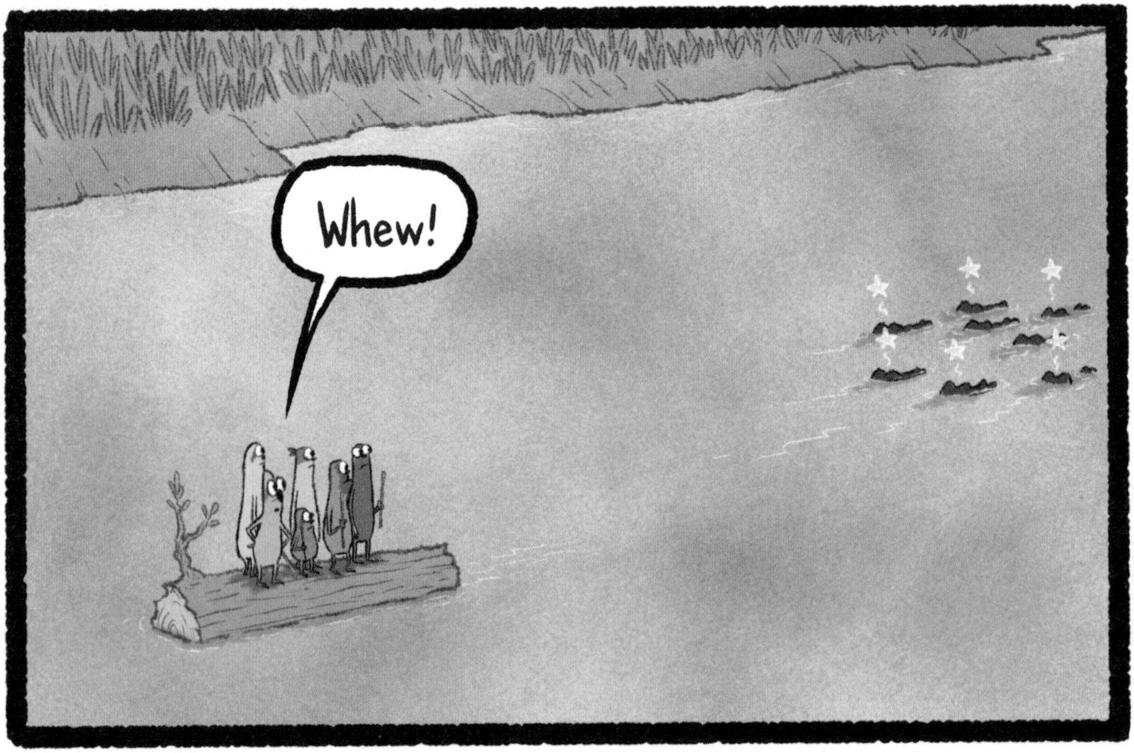

Whew!

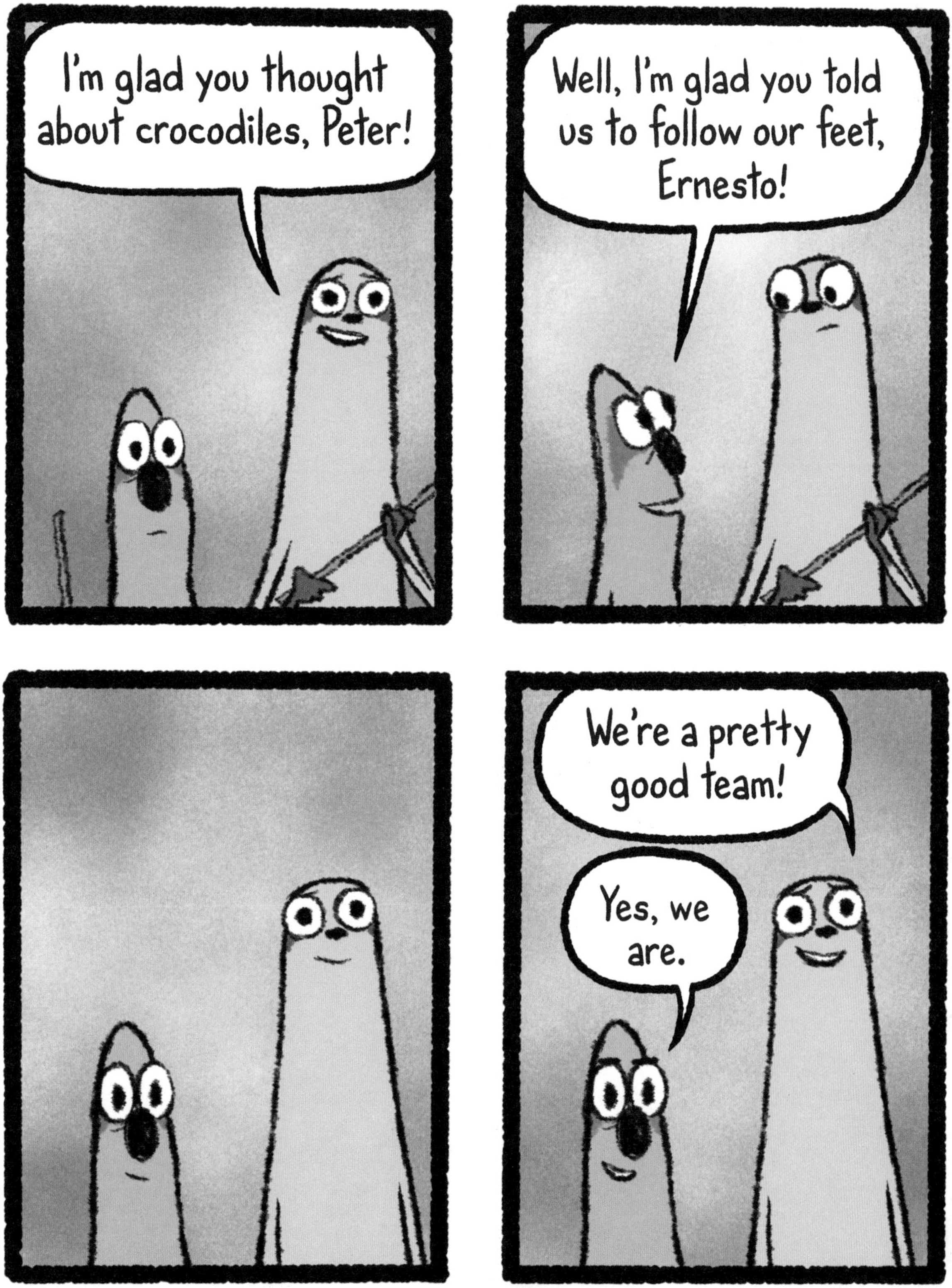
I'm glad you thought about crocodiles, Peter!
Well, I'm glad you told us to follow our feet, Ernesto!
We're a pretty good team!
Yes, we are.

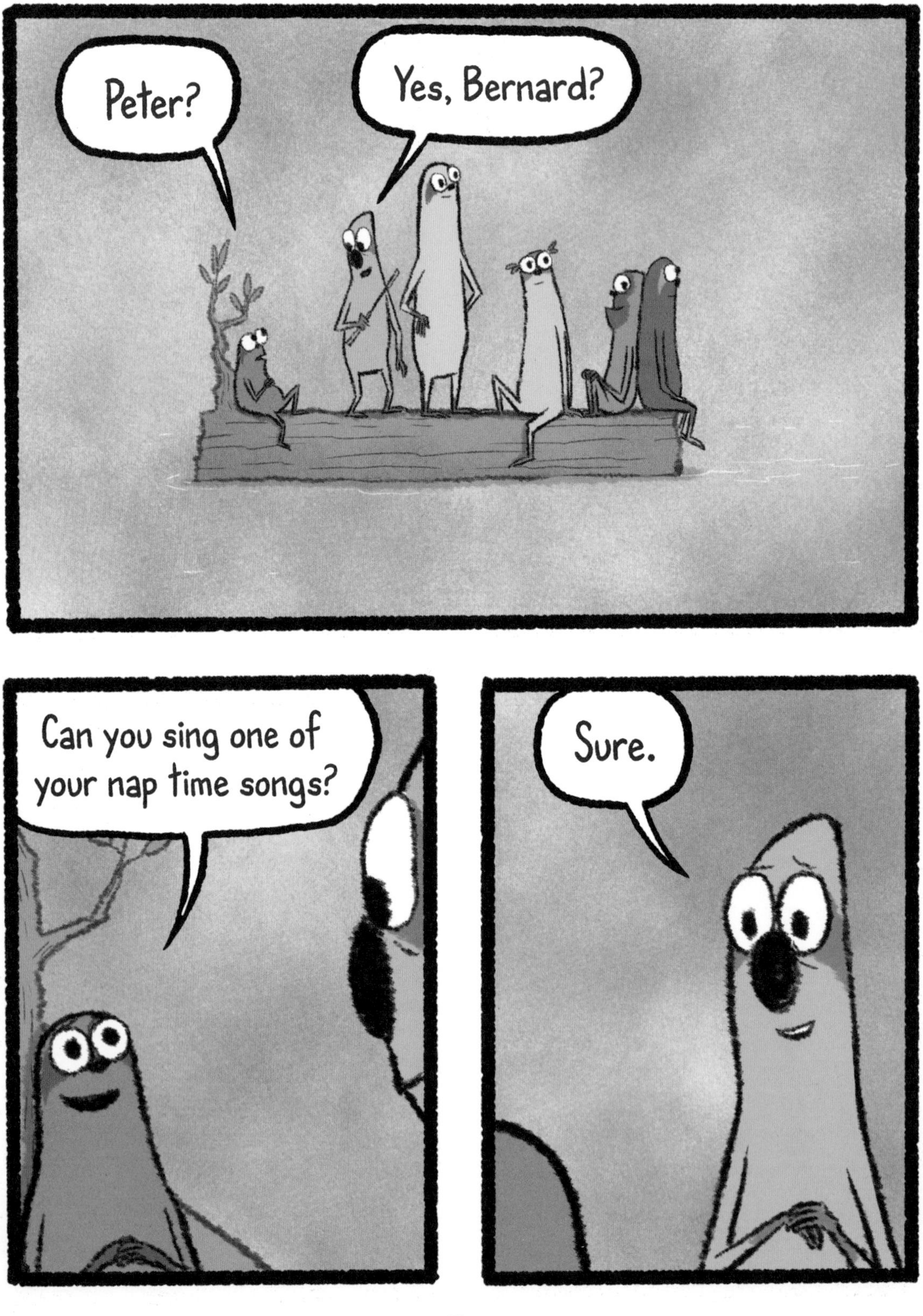
Peter?
Yes, Bernard?
Can you sing one of your nap time songs?
Sure.

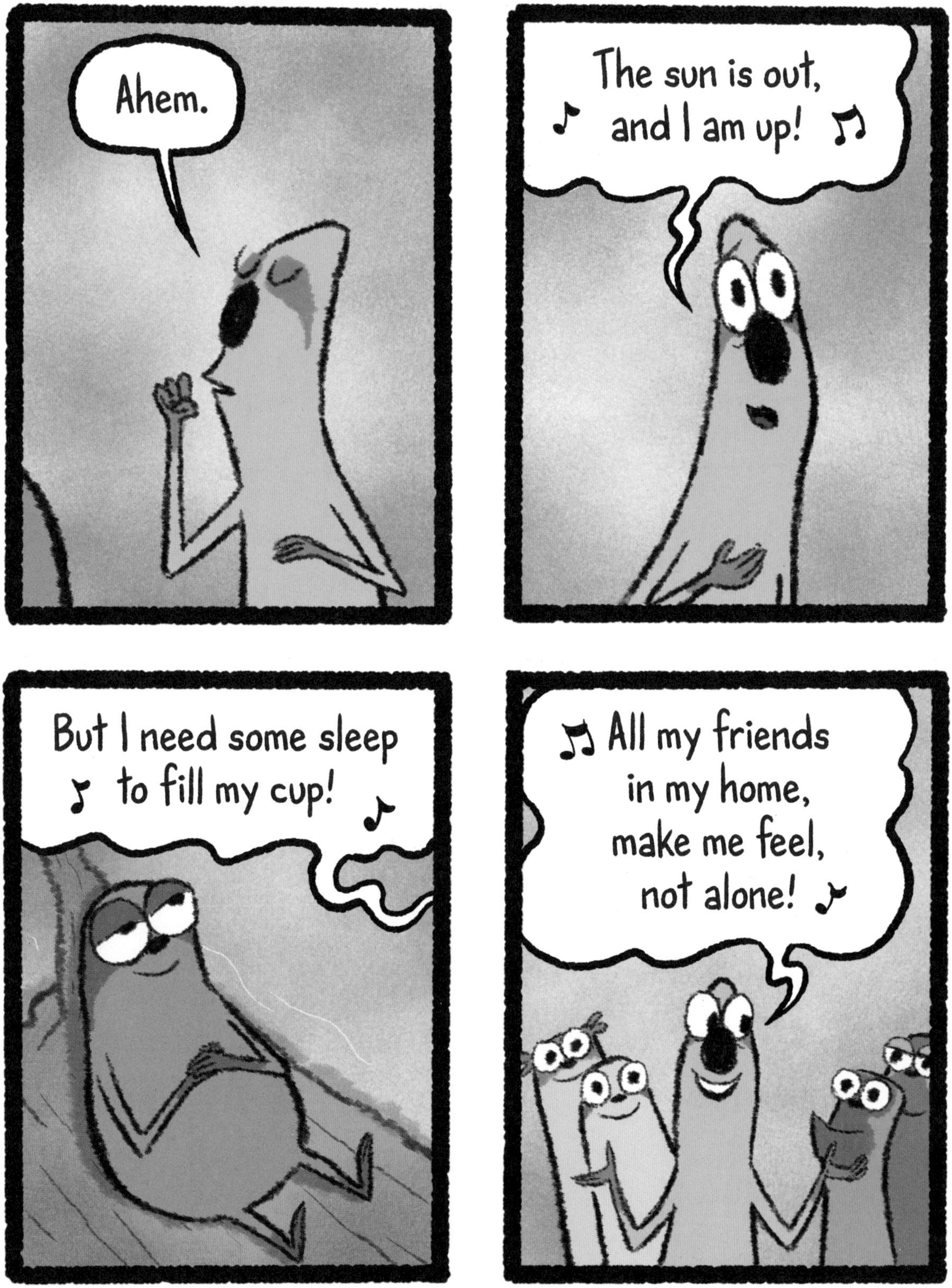
Ahem.
The sun is out, and I am up!
But I need some sleep to fill my cup!
All my friends in my home, make me feel, not alone!

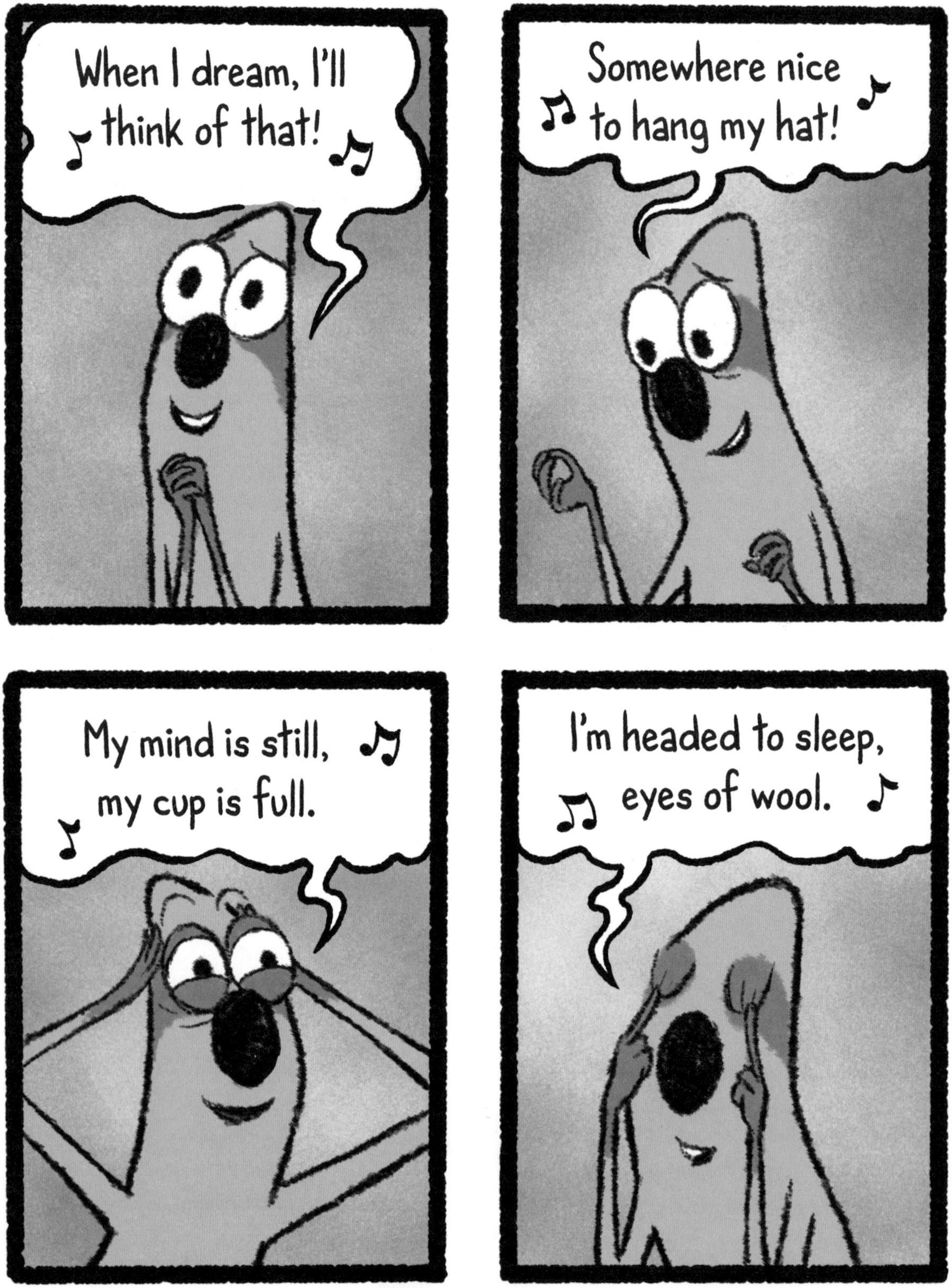
When I dream, I'll think of that!
Somewhere nice to hang my hat!
My mind is still, my cup is full.
I'm headed to sleep, eyes of wool.

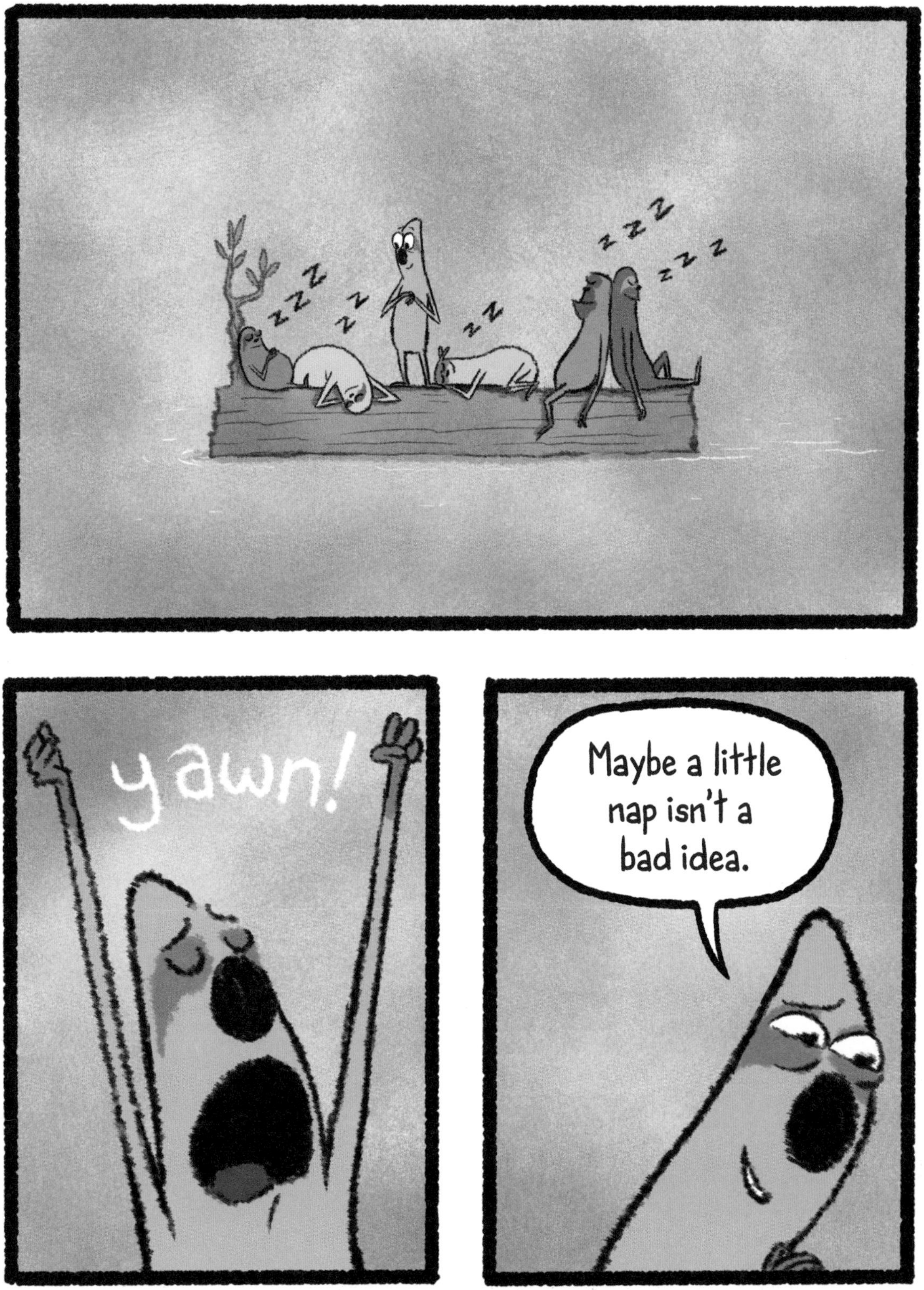
yawn!
Maybe a little nap isn't a bad idea.

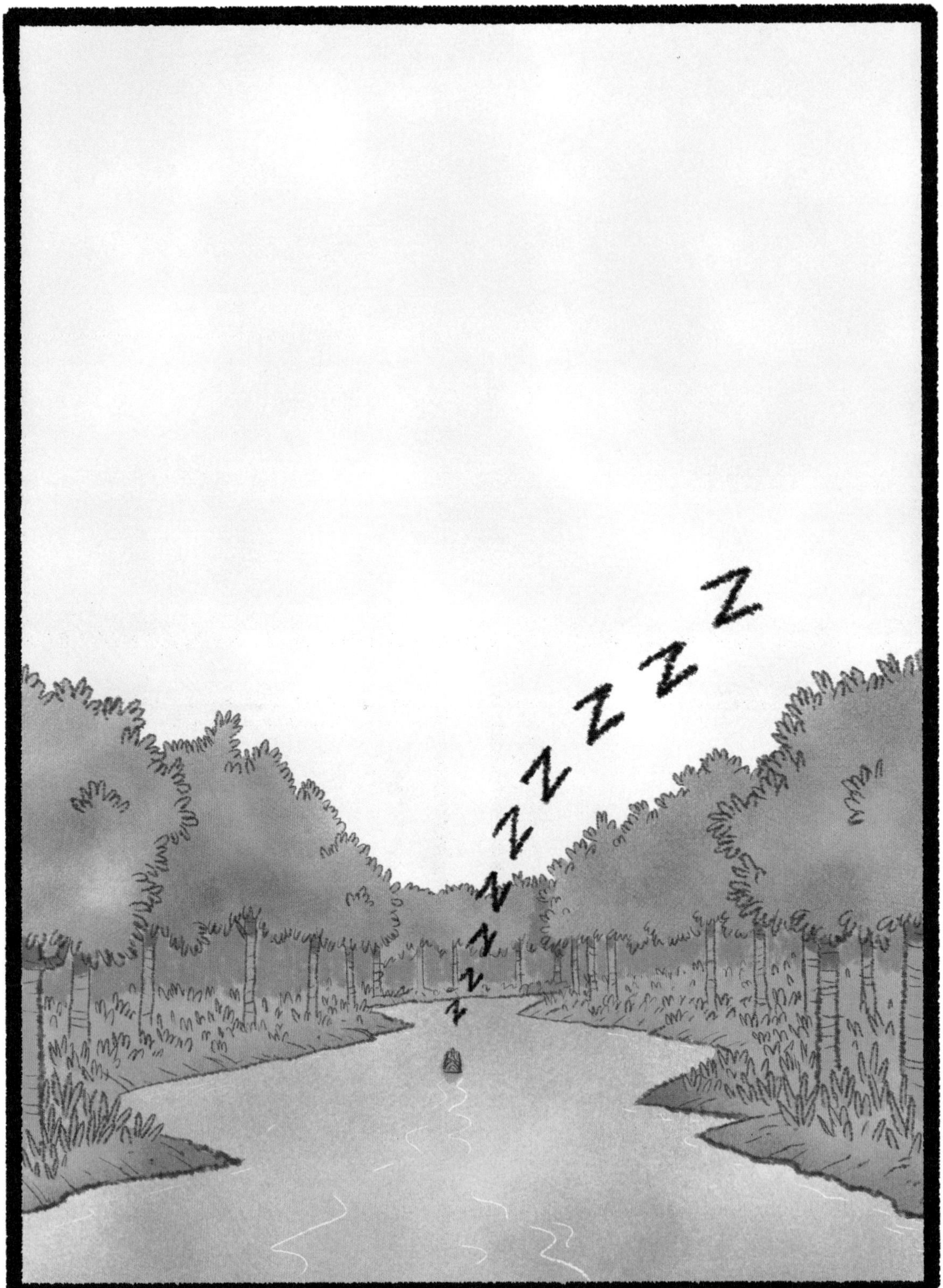
ZZZZZZZZ

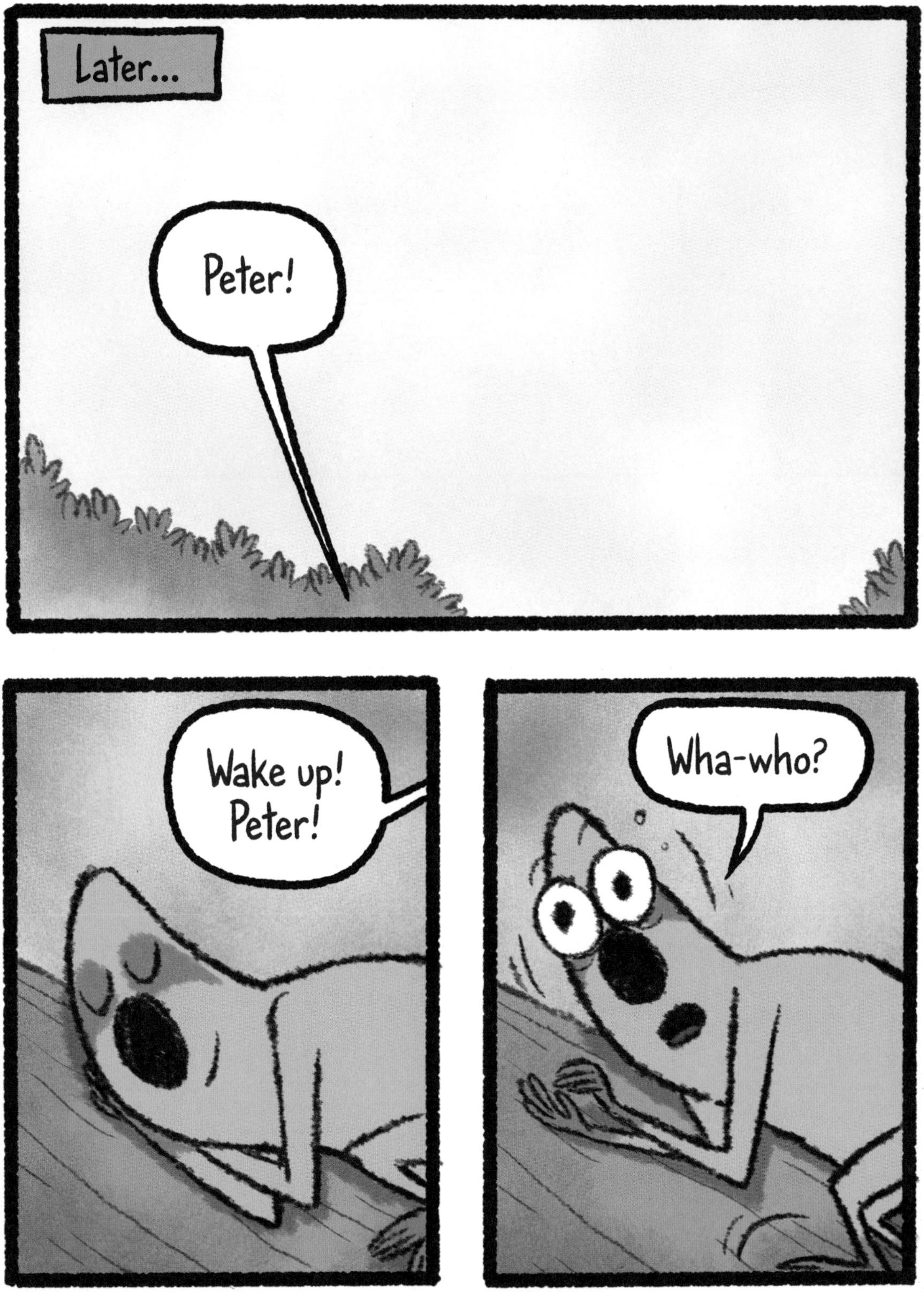
Later...
Peter!
Wake up! Peter!
Wha-who?

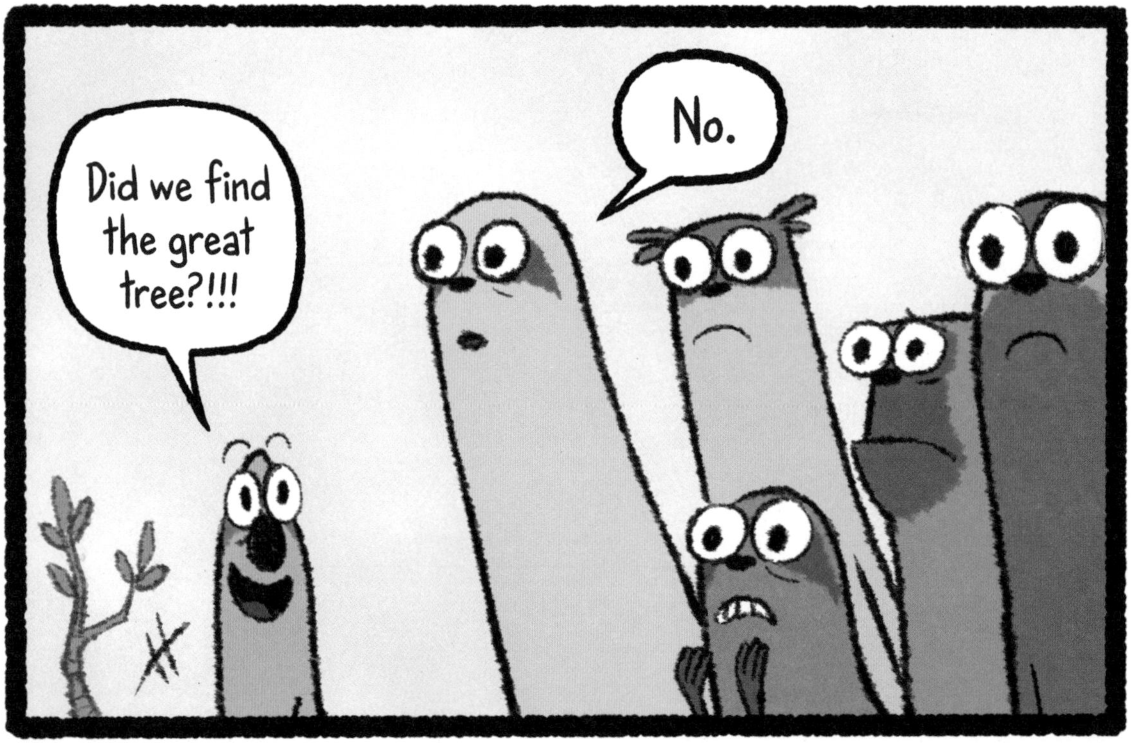
Did we find the great tree?!!!
No.

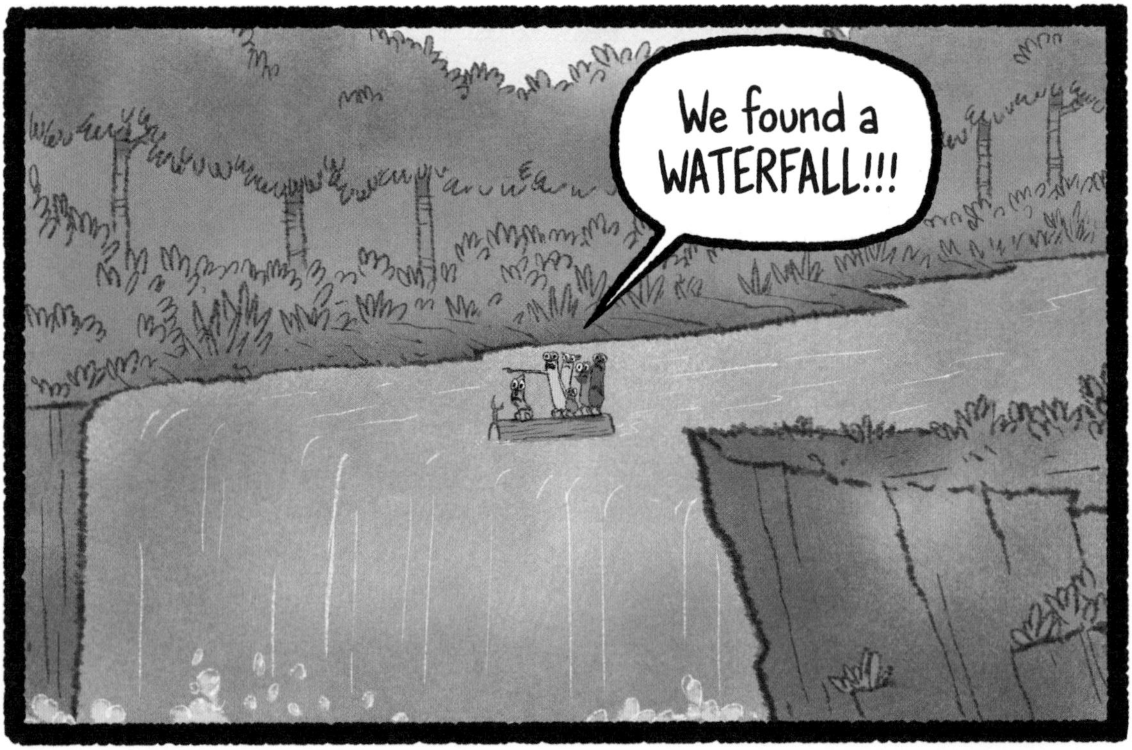
We found a WATERFALL!!!

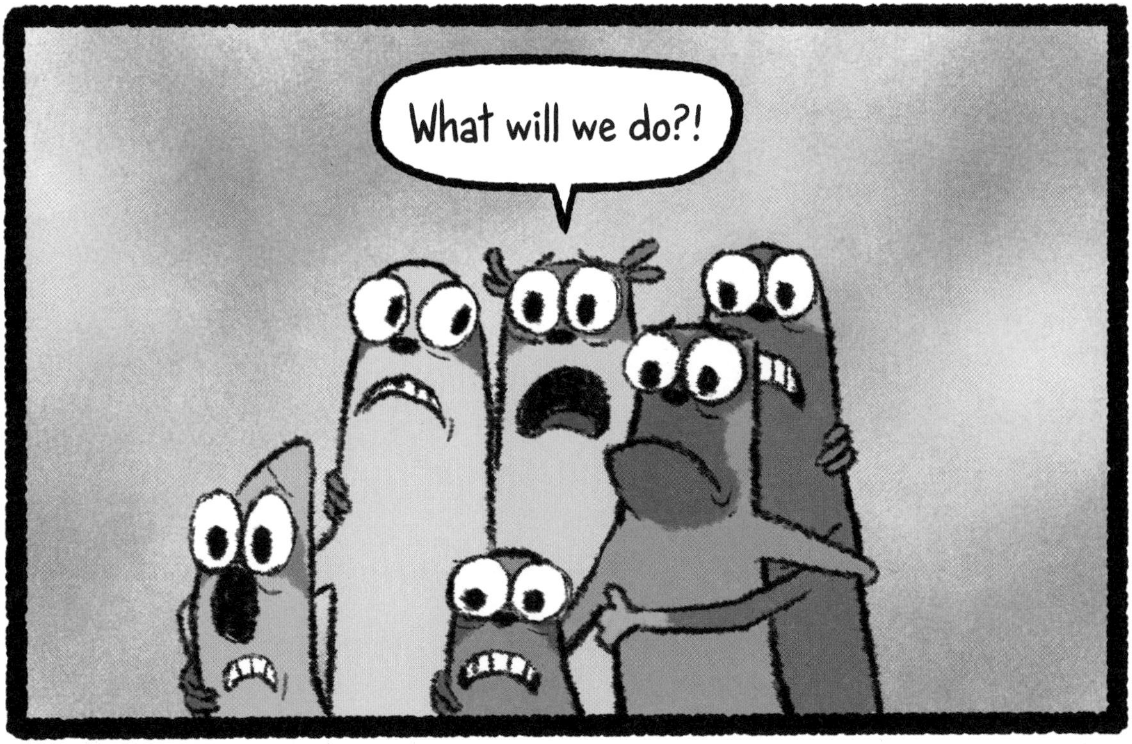
What will we do?!

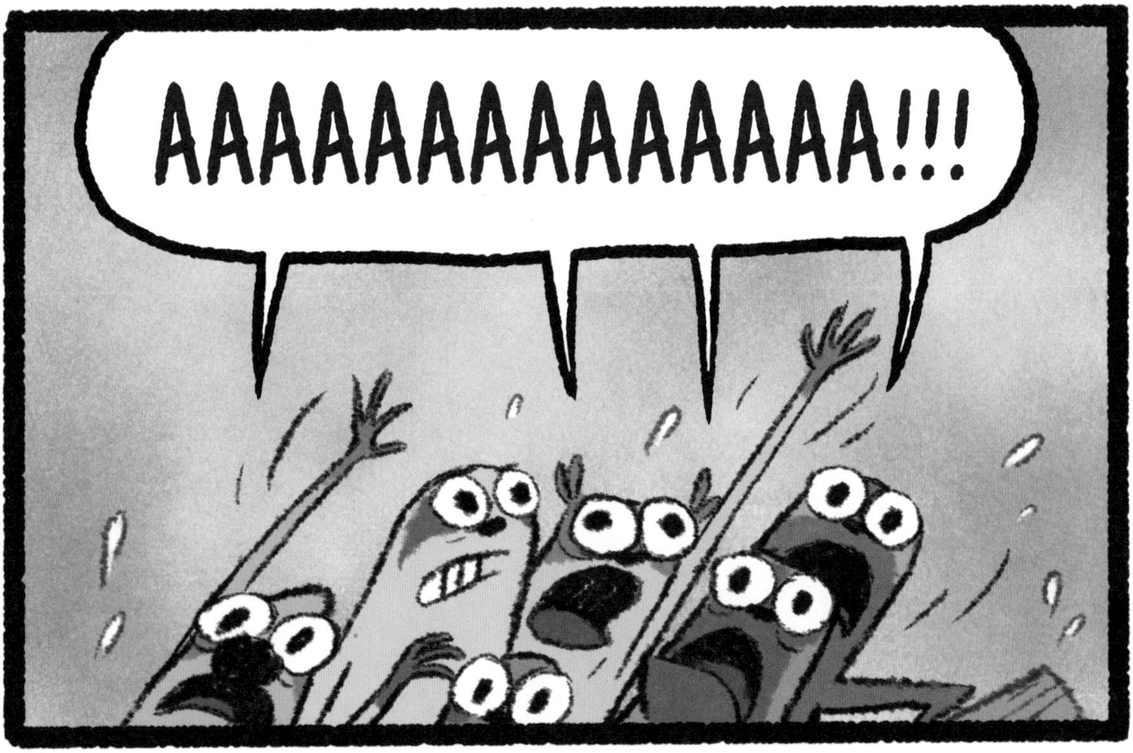
AAAAAAAAAAAAAAA!!!

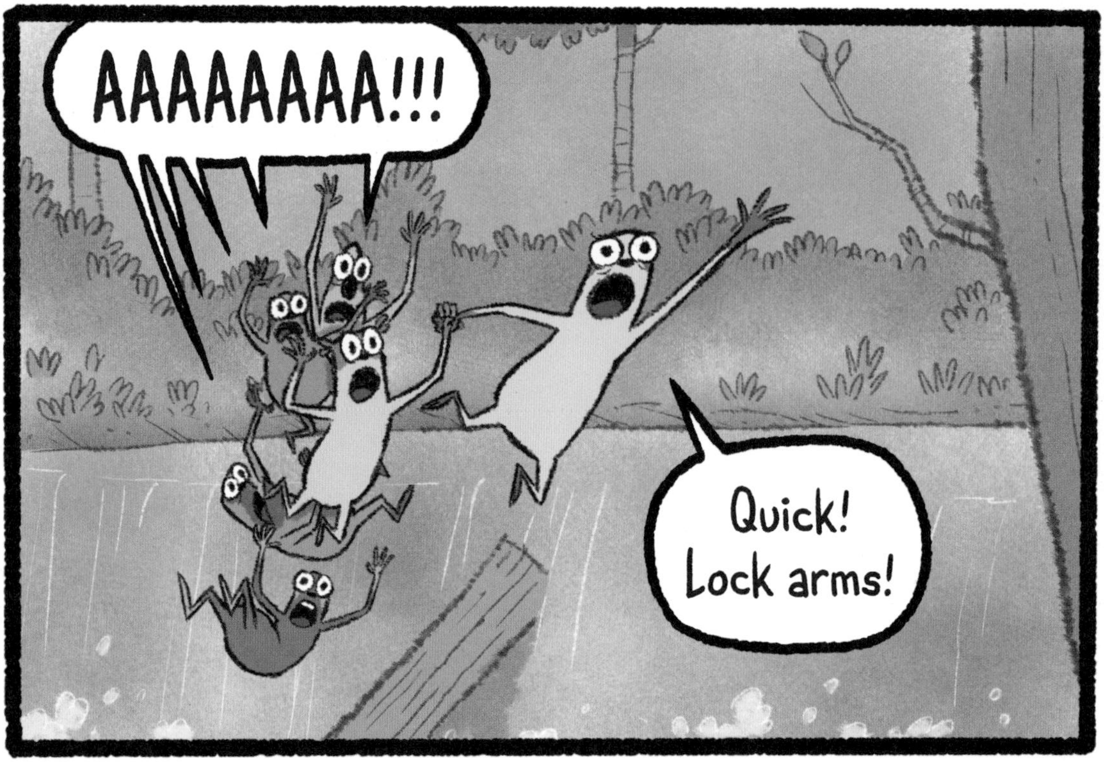
AAAAAAAA!!!
Quick! Lock arms!

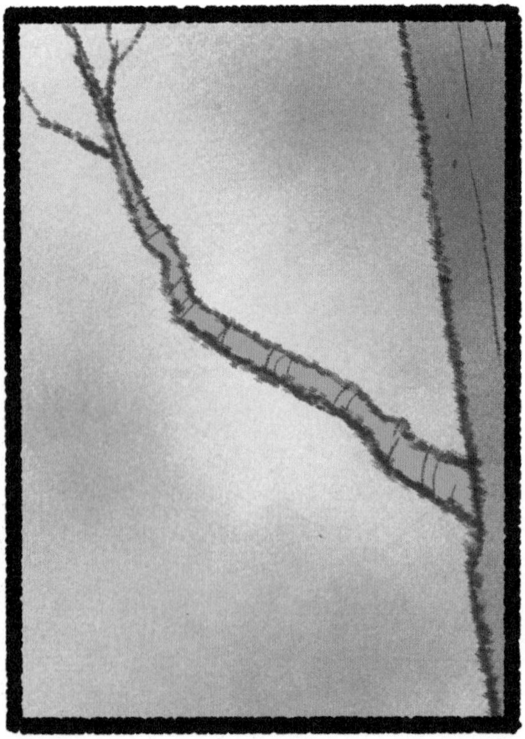

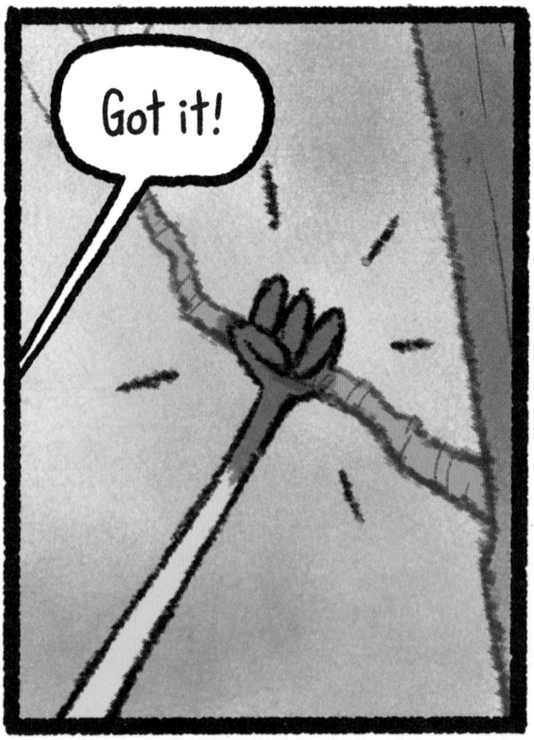
Got it!

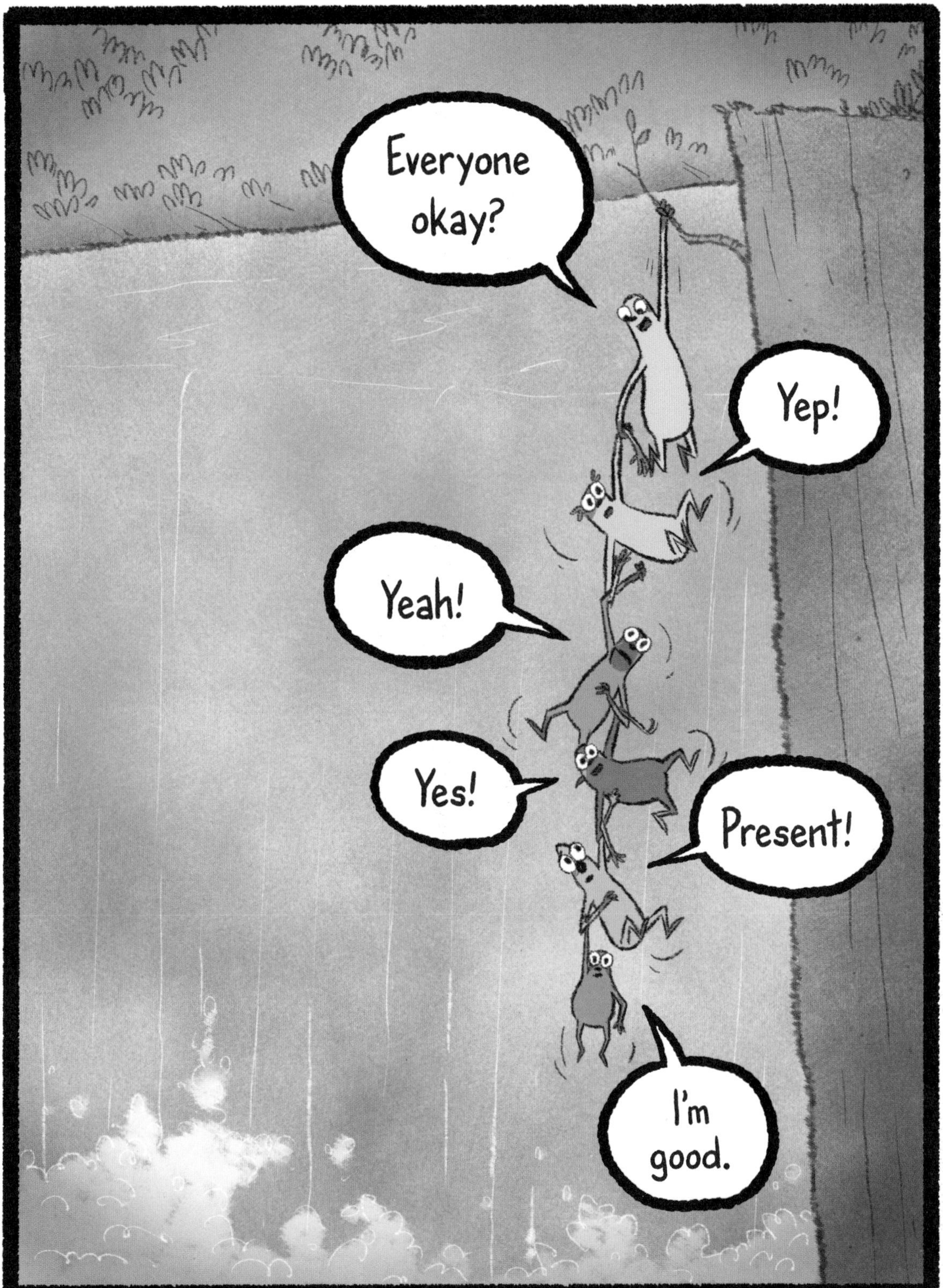
Everyone okay?
Yep!
Yeah!
Yes!
Present!
I'm good.

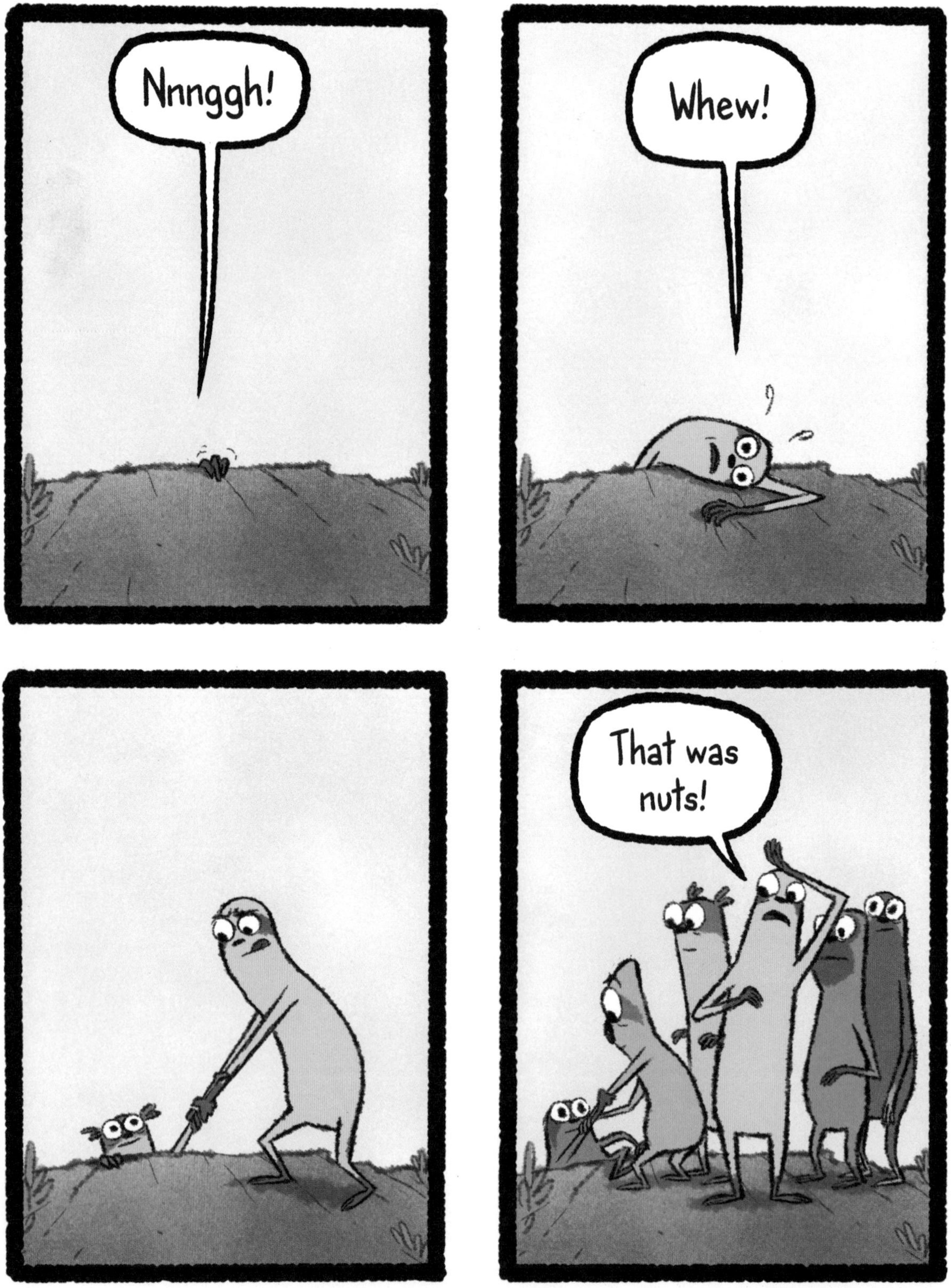
Nnnggh!
Whew!
That was nuts!

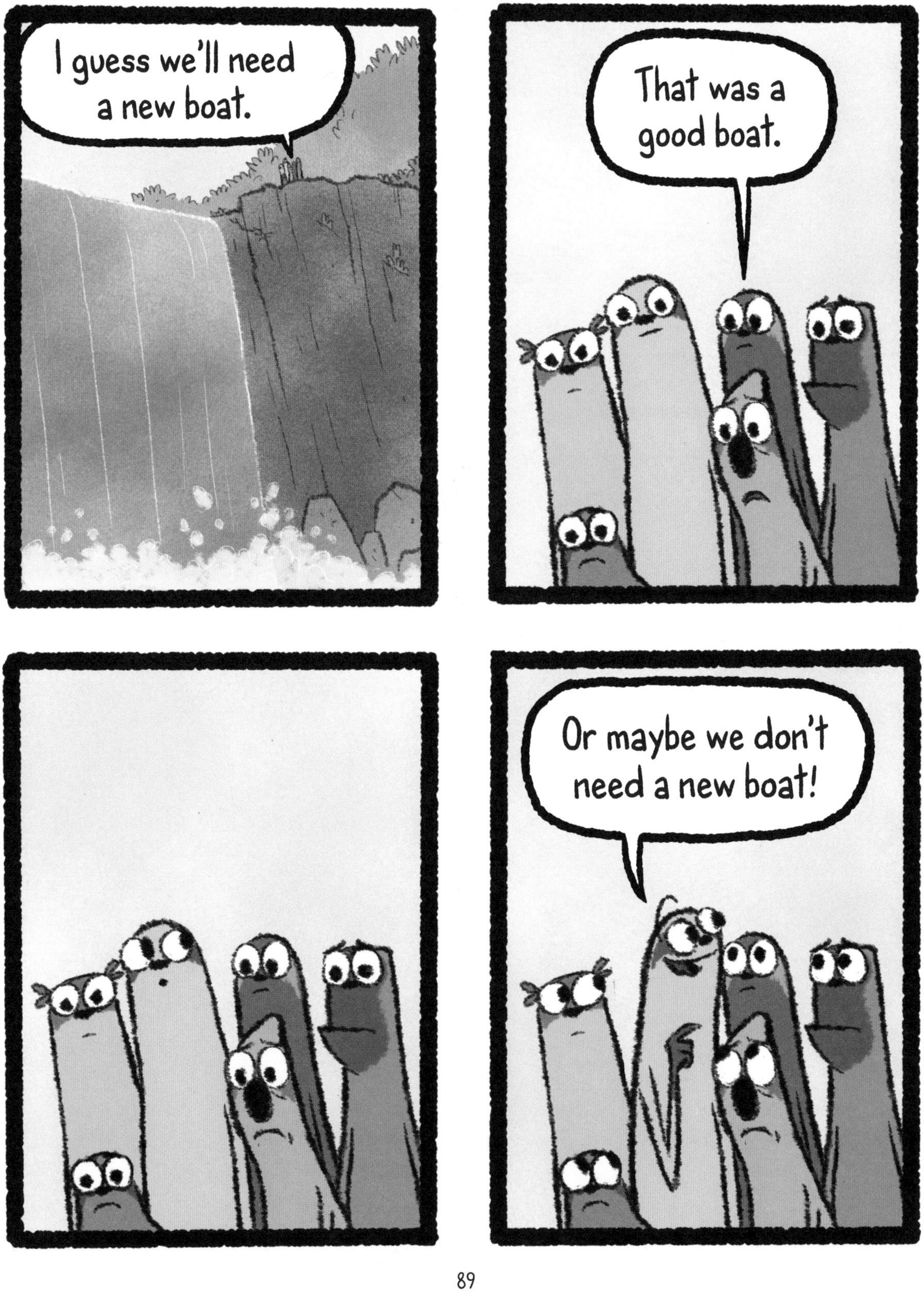
I guess we'll need a new boat.
That was a good boat.
Or maybe we don't need a new boat!

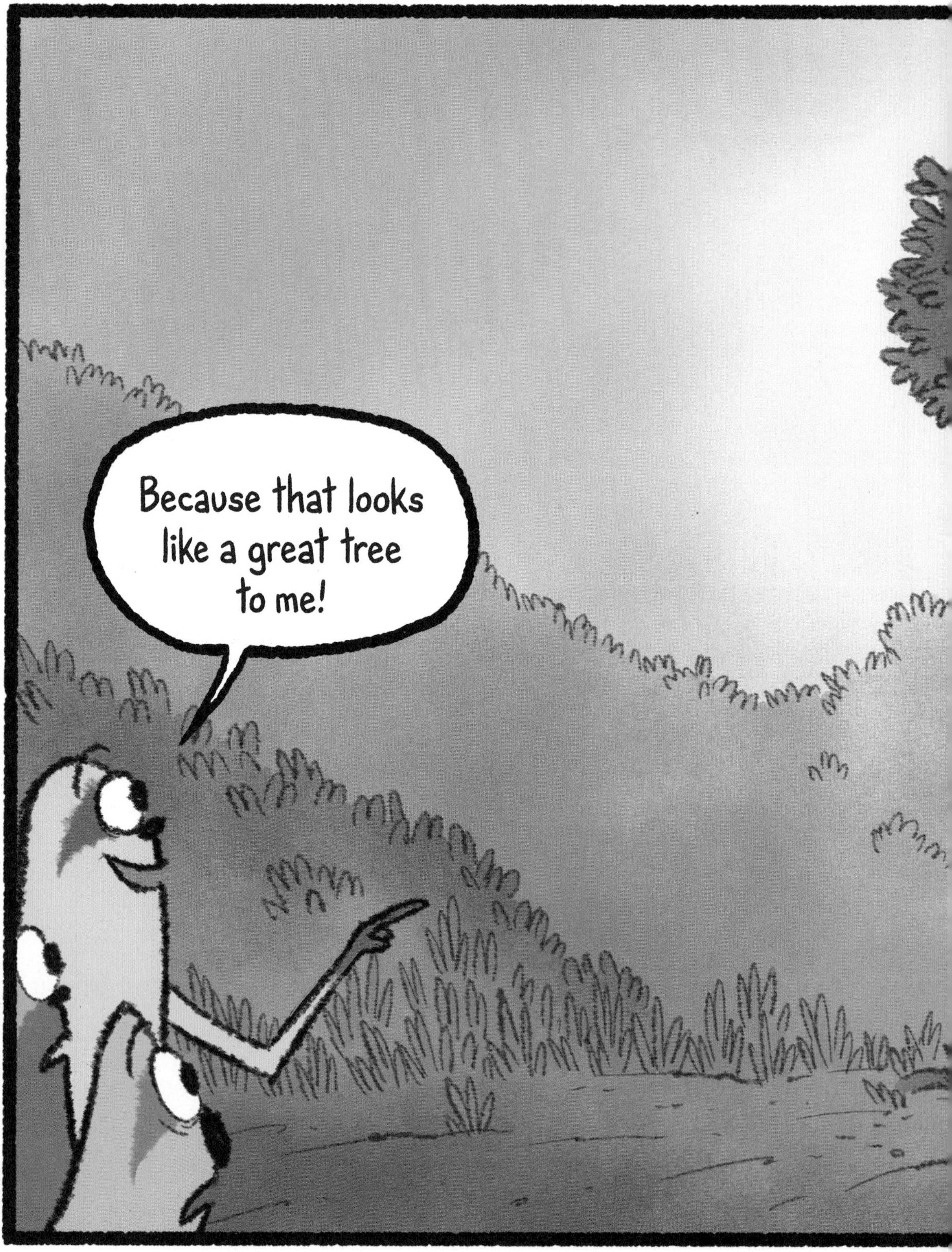
Because that looks like a great tree to me!

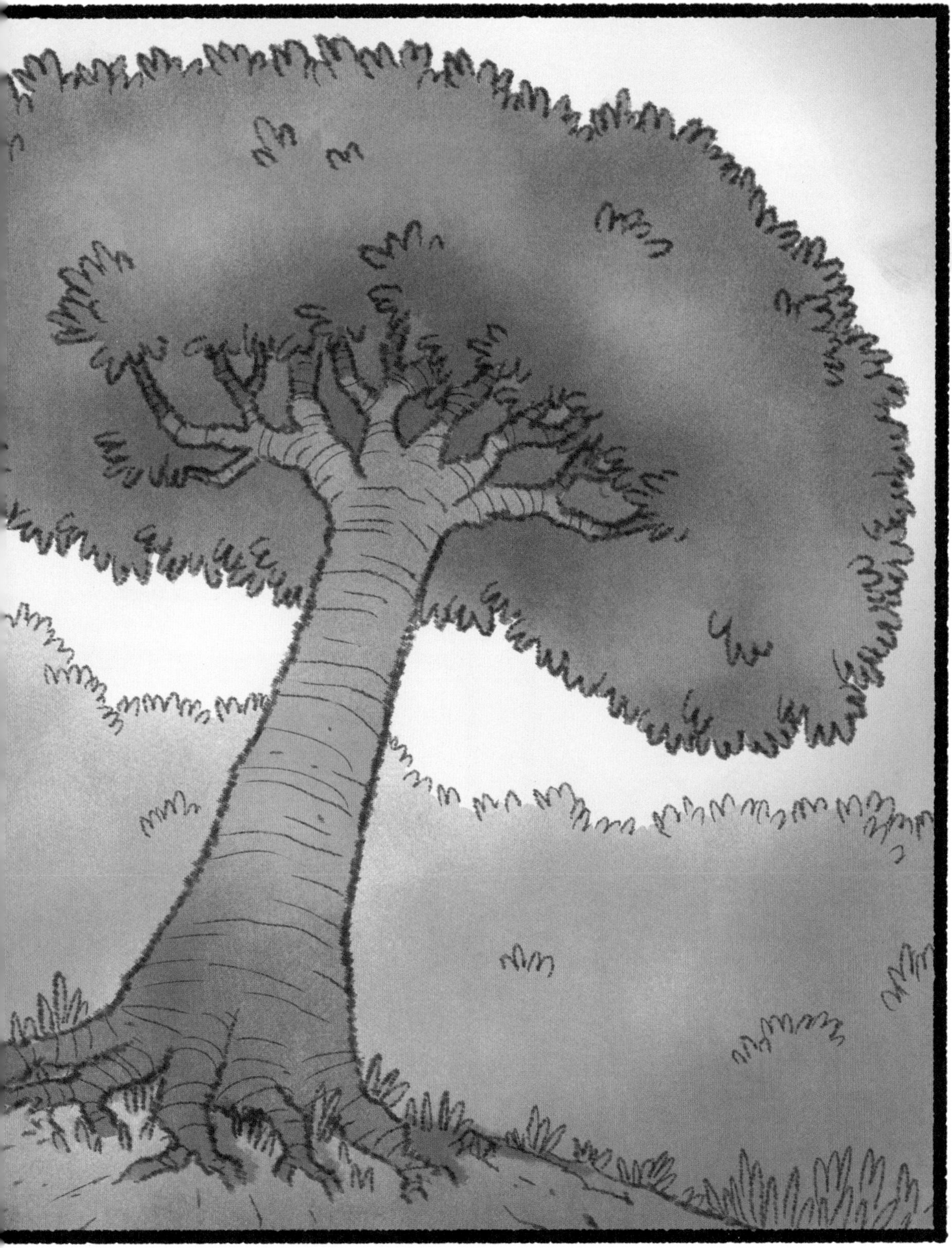

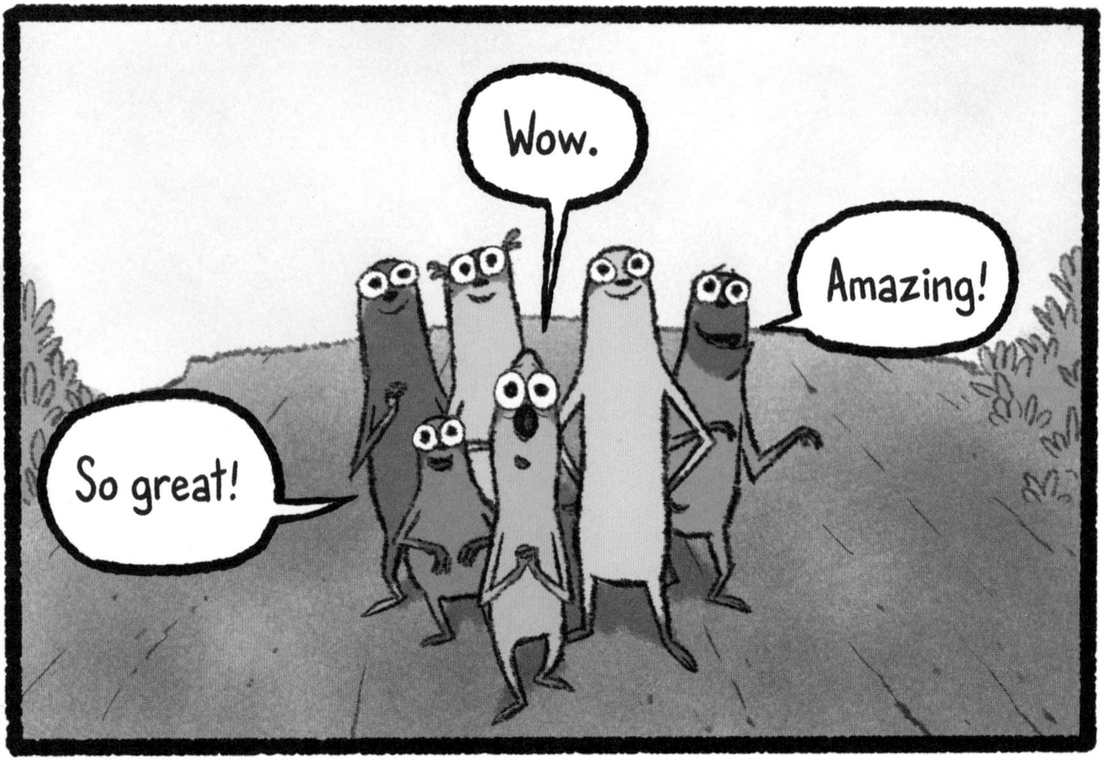
Wow.
Amazing!
So great!

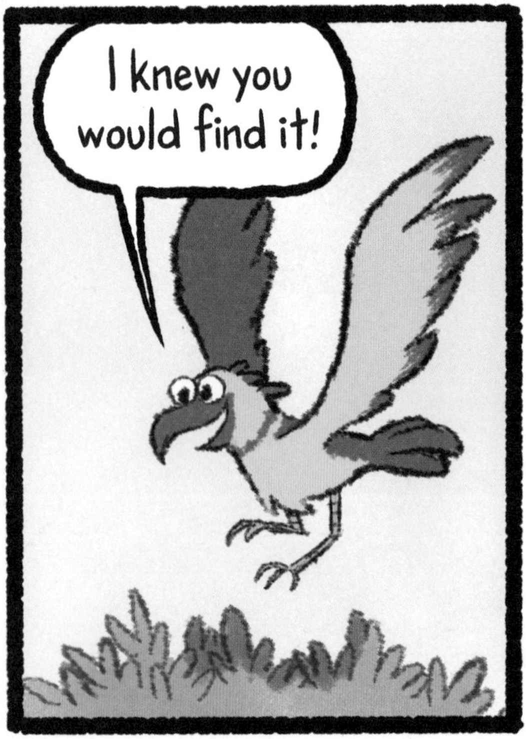
I knew you would find it!

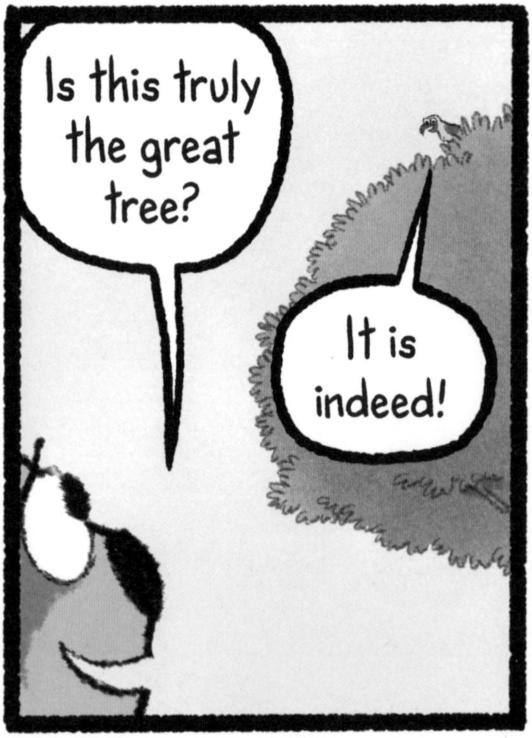
Is this truly the great tree?
It is indeed!

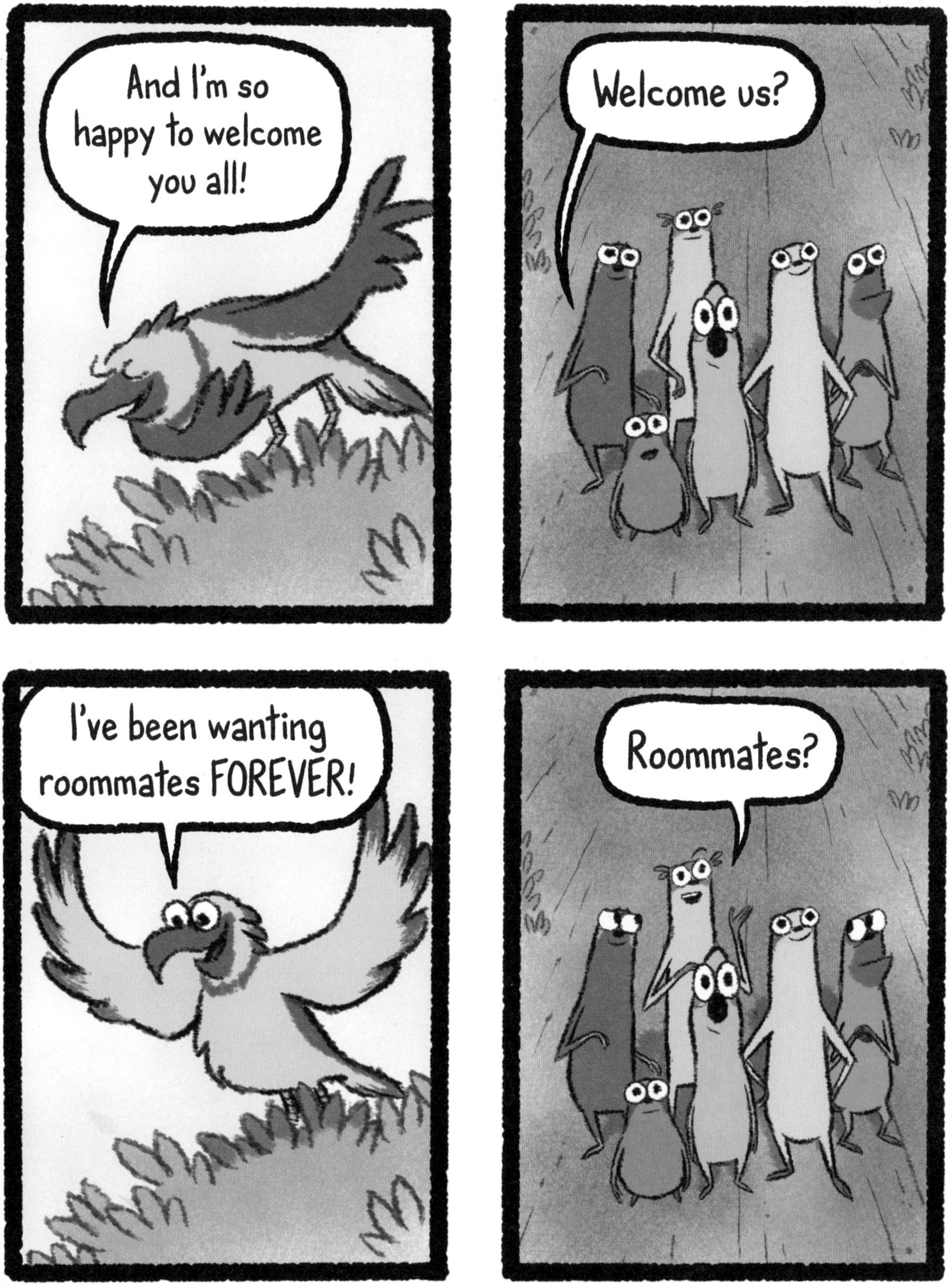
And I'm so happy to welcome you all!
Welcome us?
I've been wanting roommates FOREVER!
Roommates?

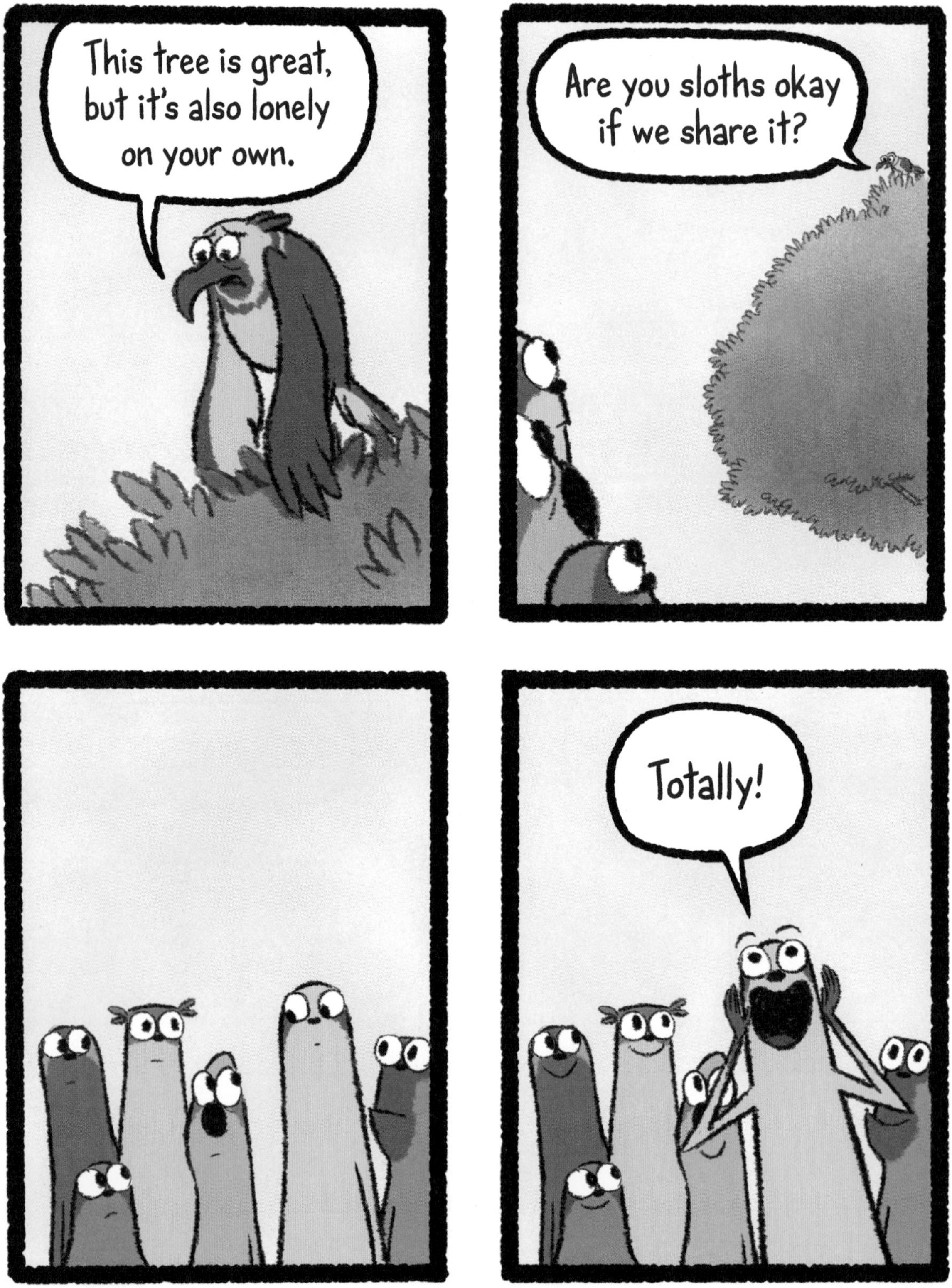
This tree is great, but it's also lonely on your own.
Are you sloths okay if we share it?
Totally!

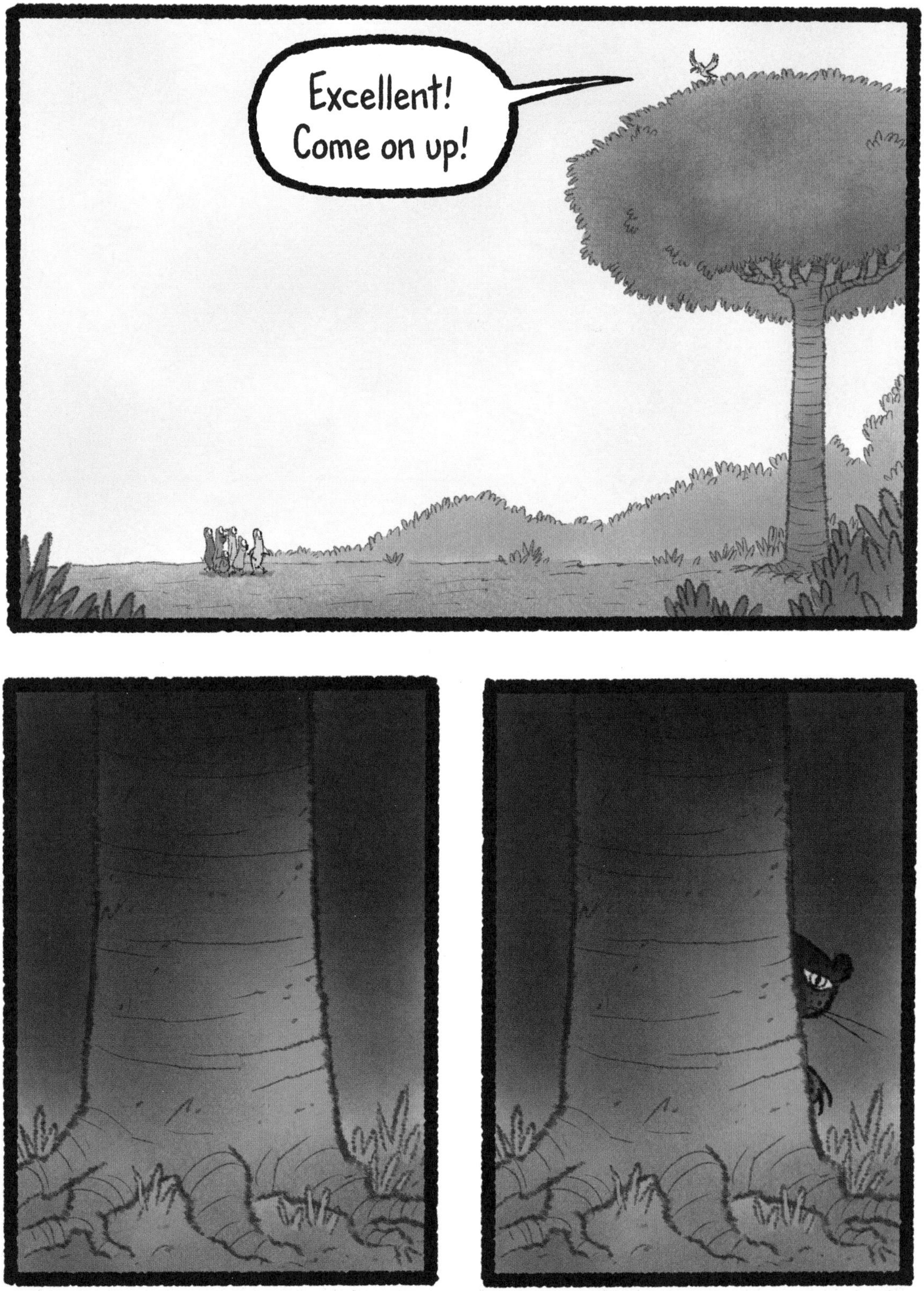
Excellent! Come on up!

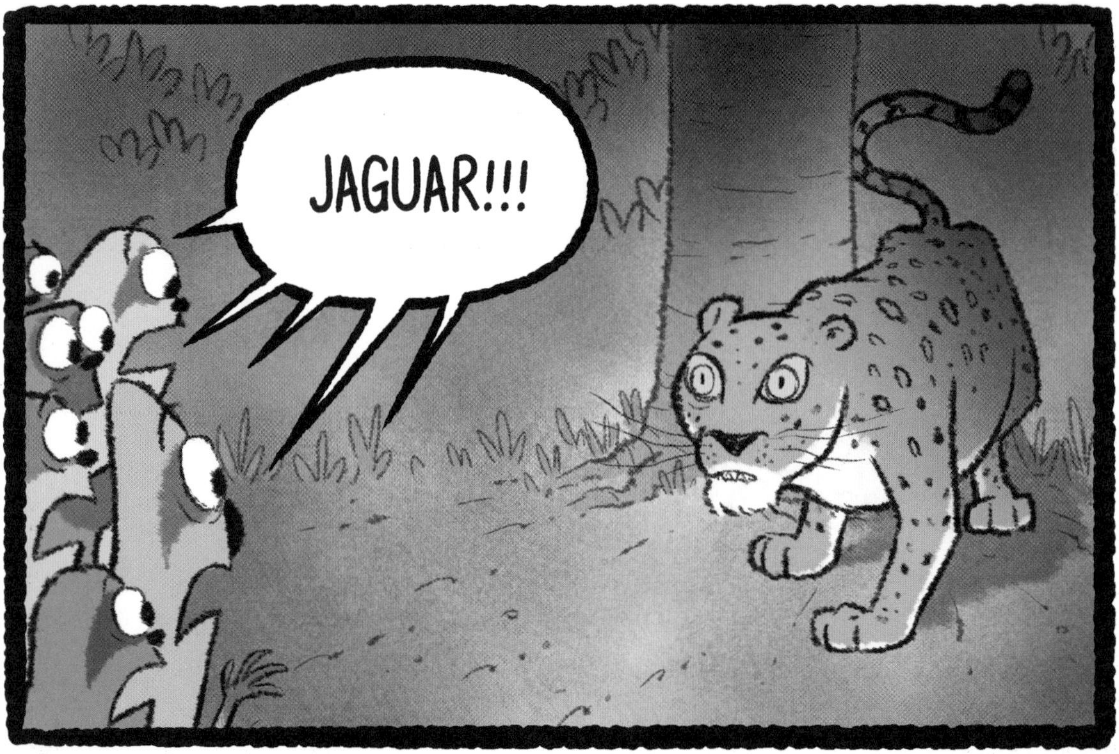
JAGUAR!!!

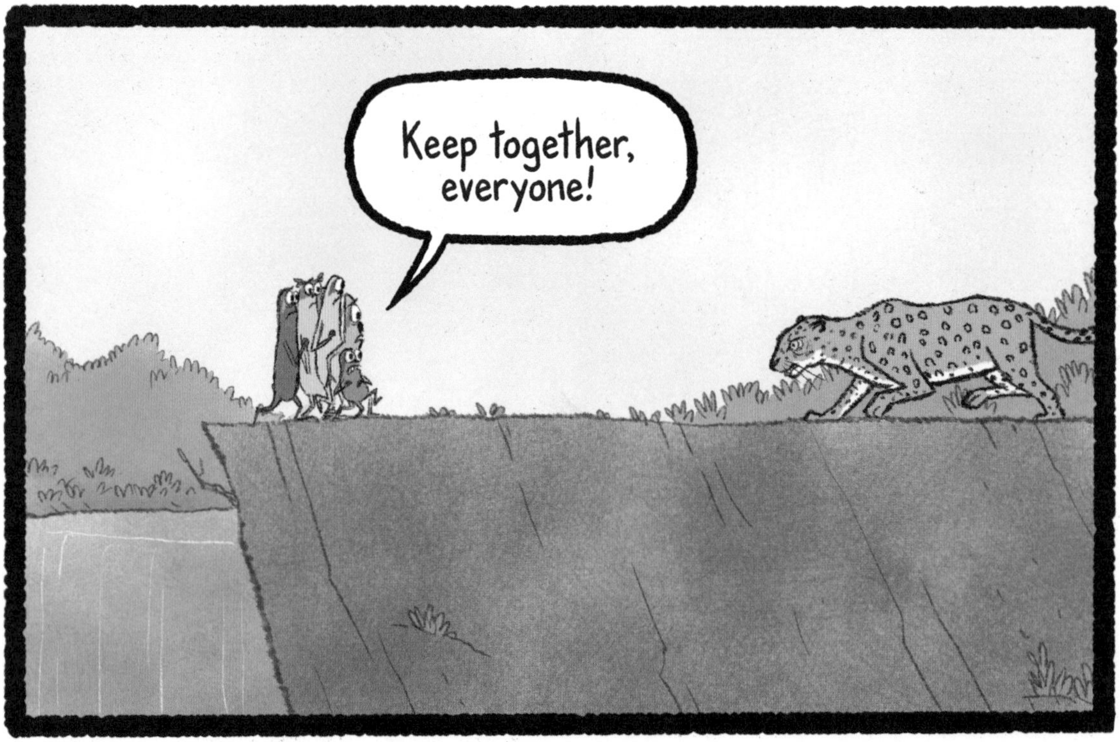
Keep together, everyone!

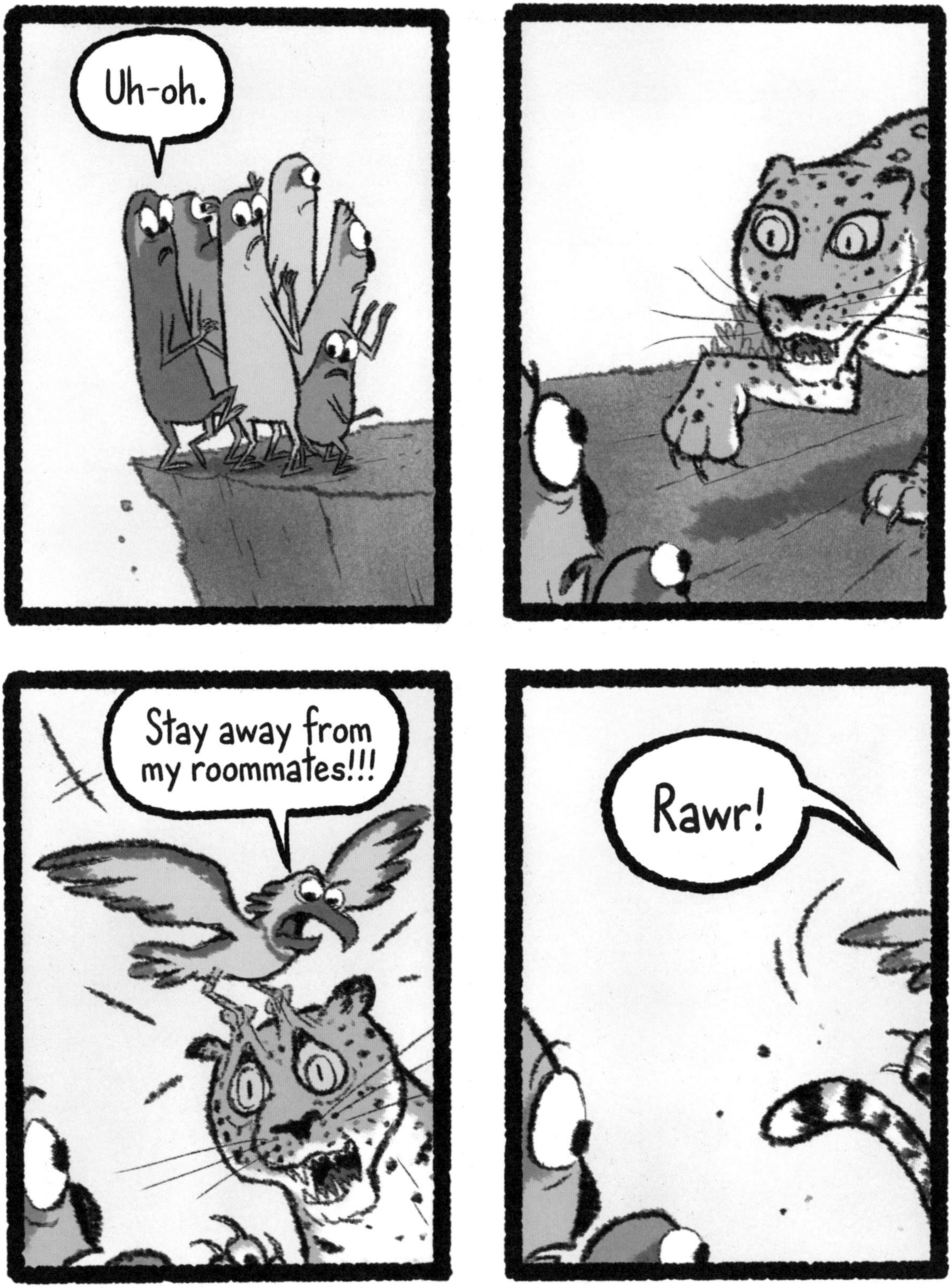
Uh-oh.
Stay away from my roommates!!!
Rawr!

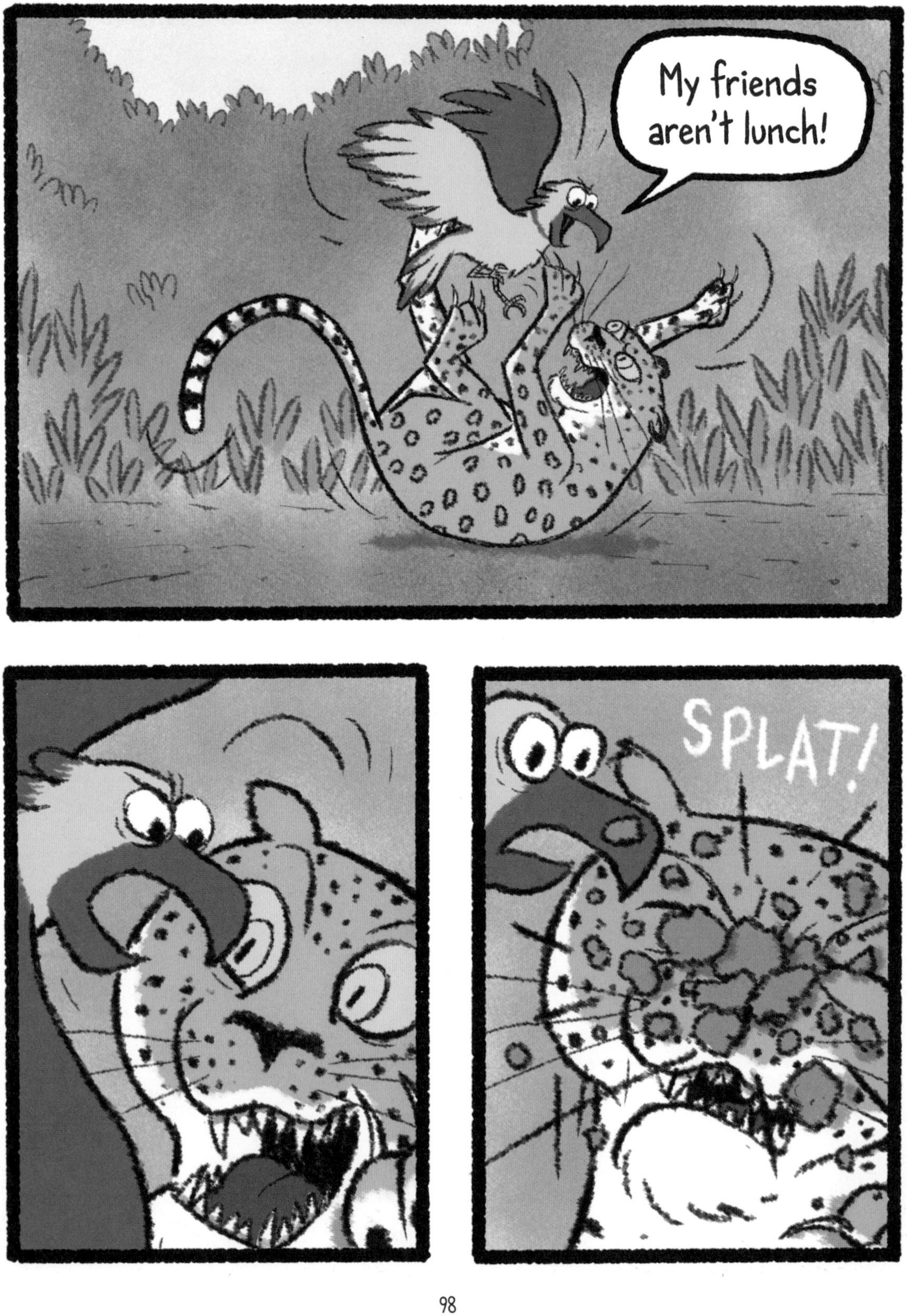
My friends aren't lunch!
SPLAT!

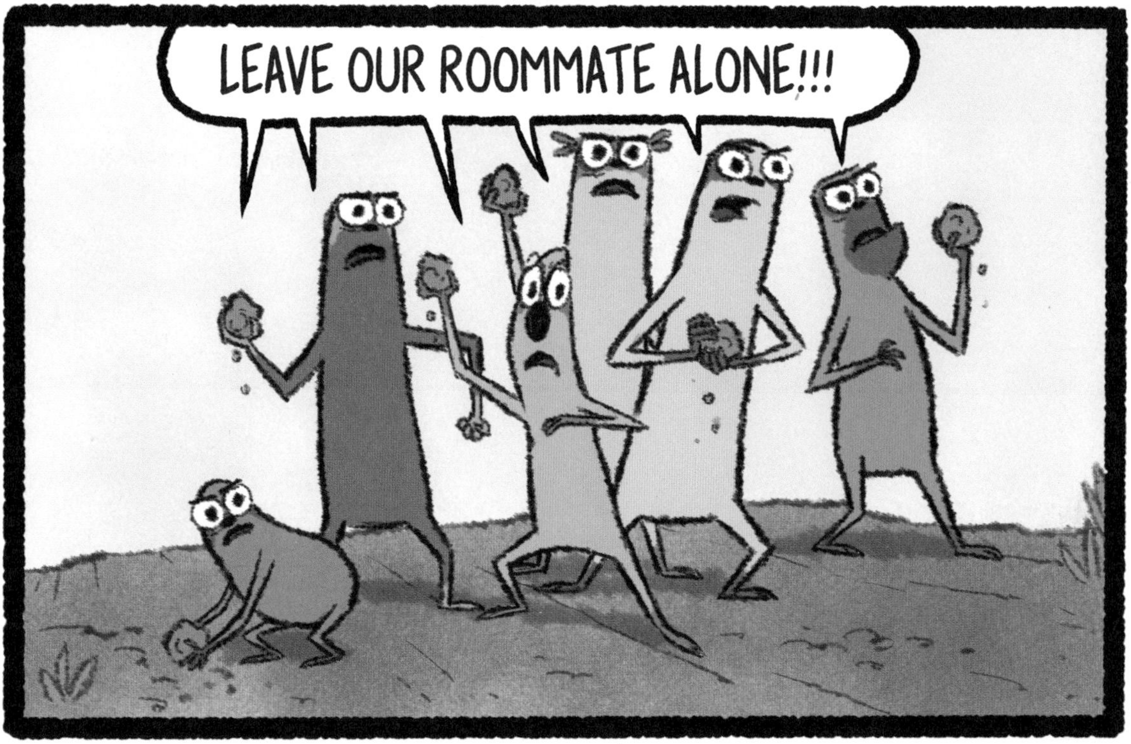
LEAVE OUR ROOMMATE ALONE!!!

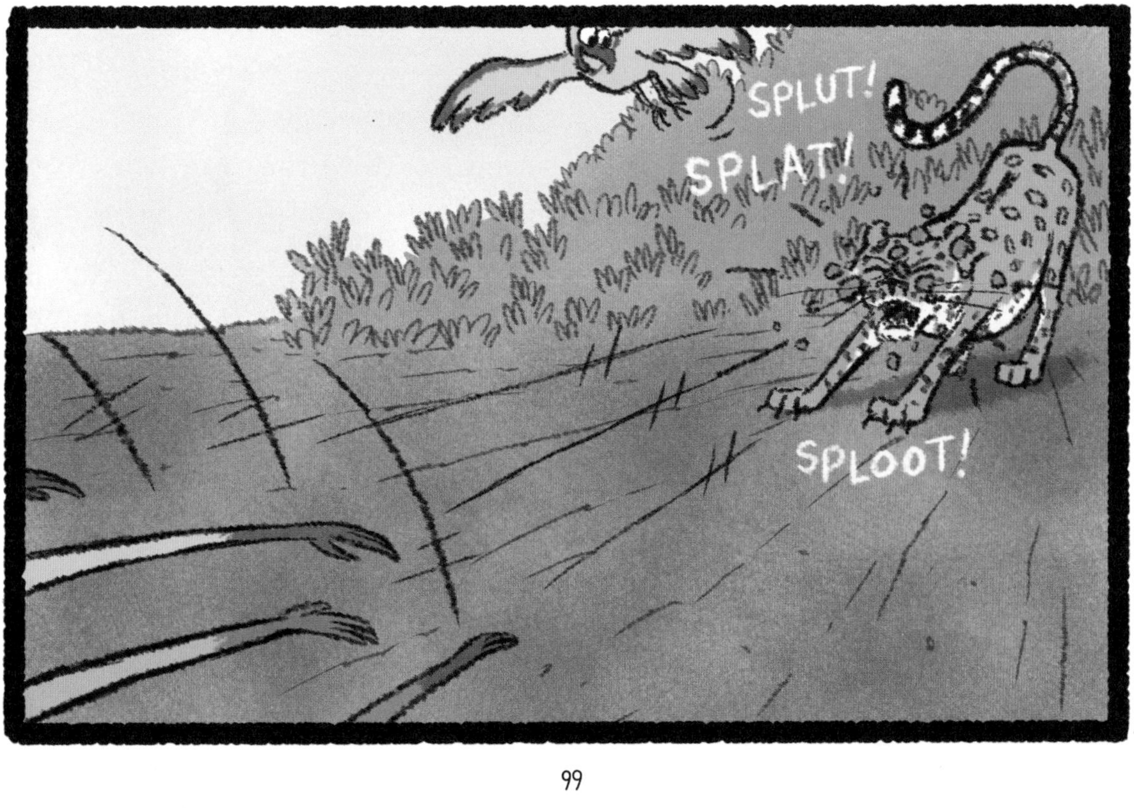
SPLUT!
SPLAT!
SPLOOT!

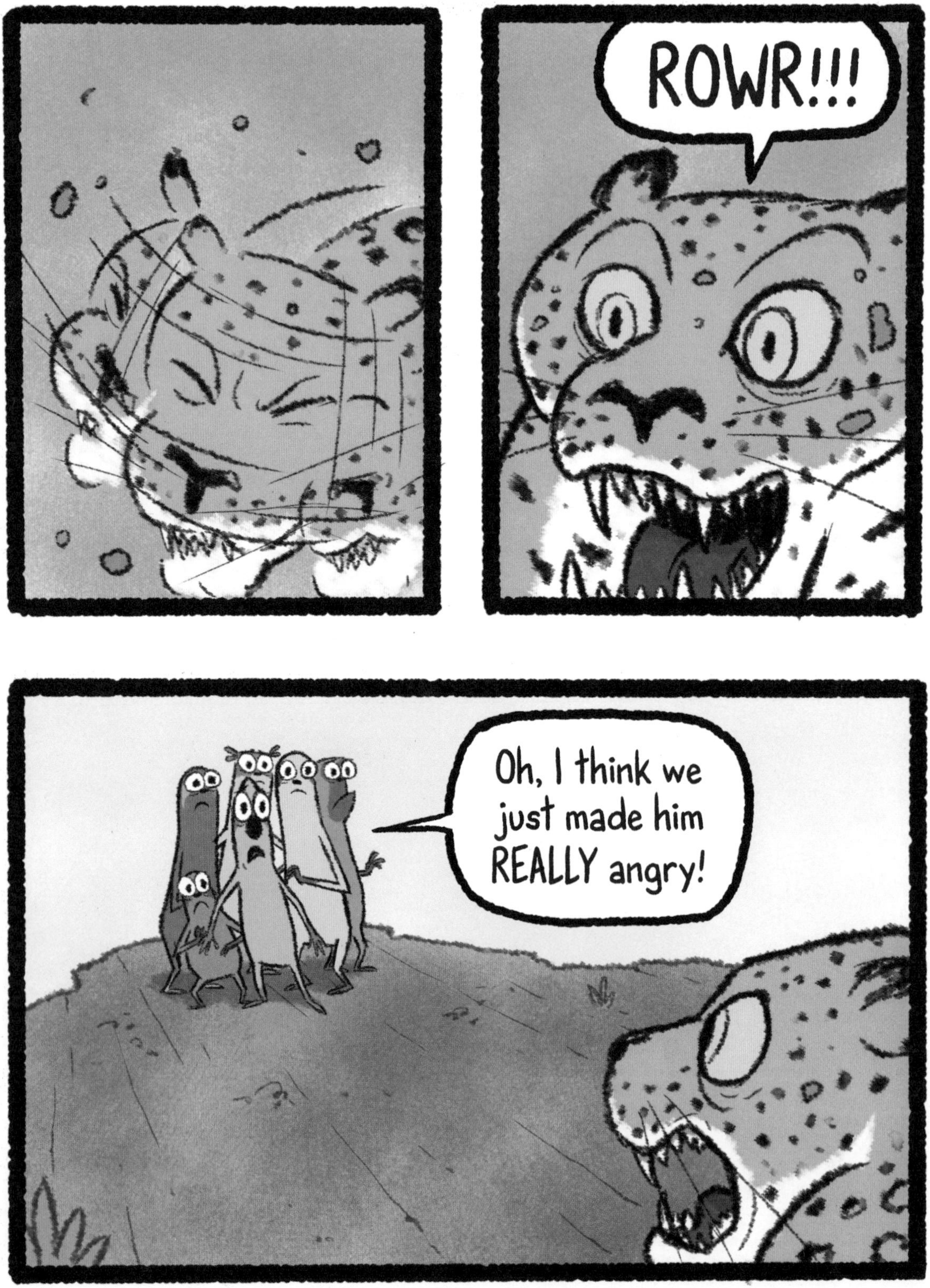
ROWR!!!
Oh, I think we just made him REALLY angry!

Well, we almost found a new home.
JAGUAR!

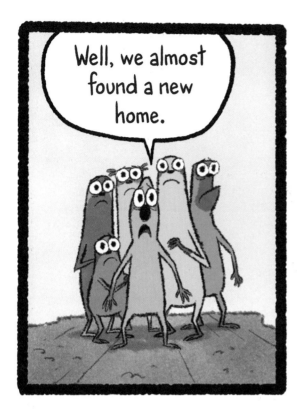

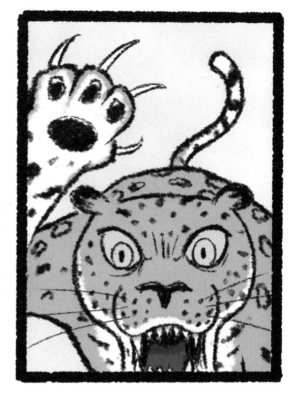

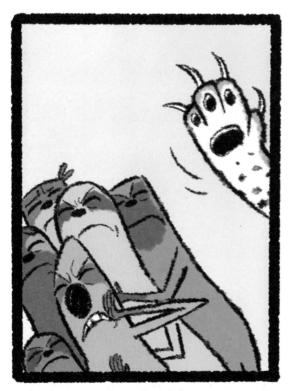

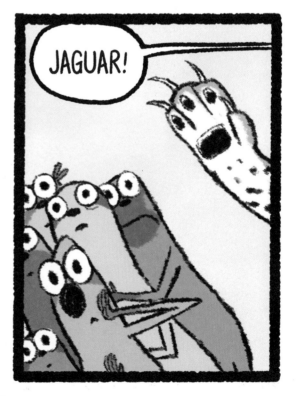

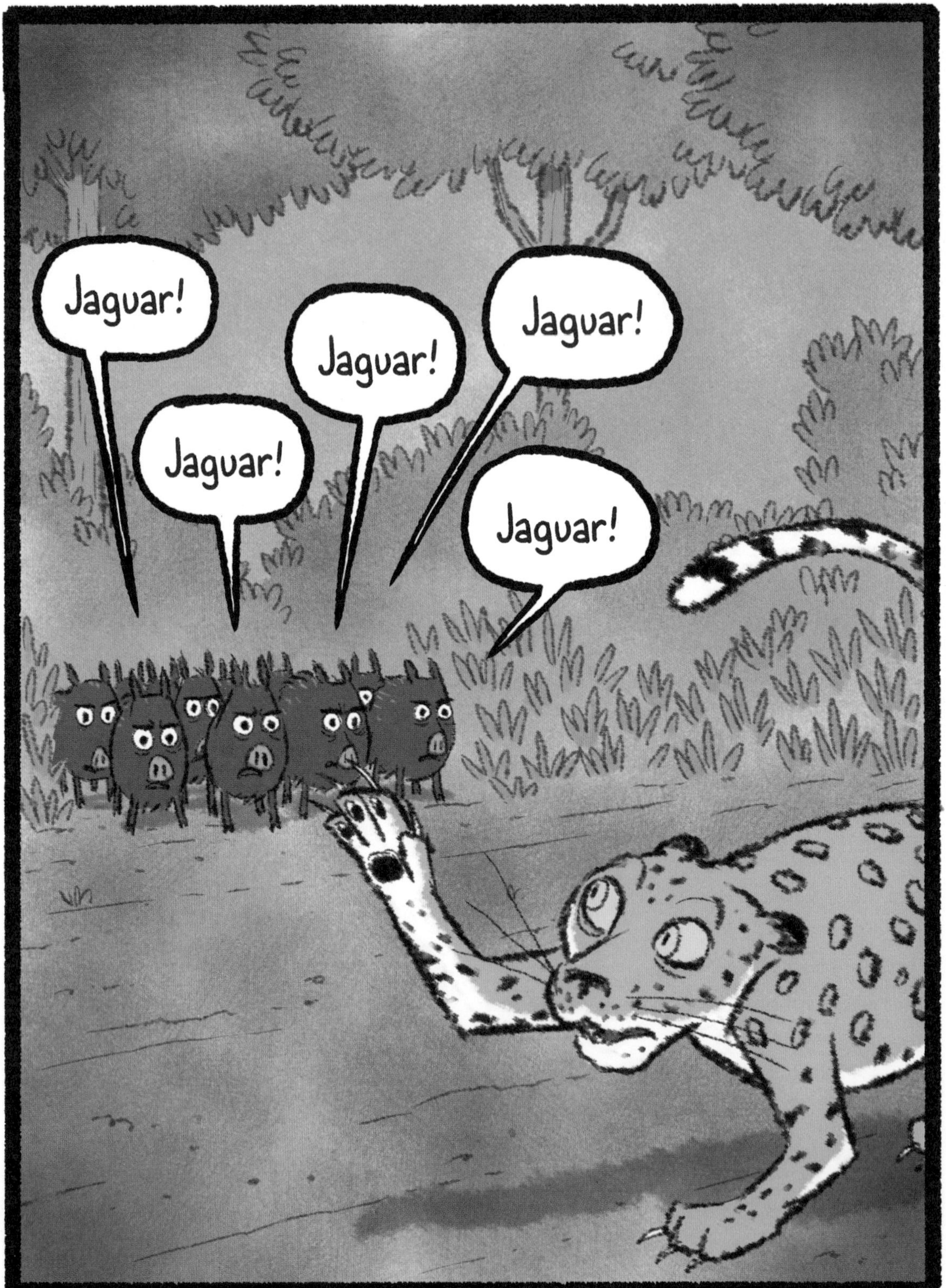
Jaguar!
Jaguar!
Jaguar!
Jaguar!
Jaguar!

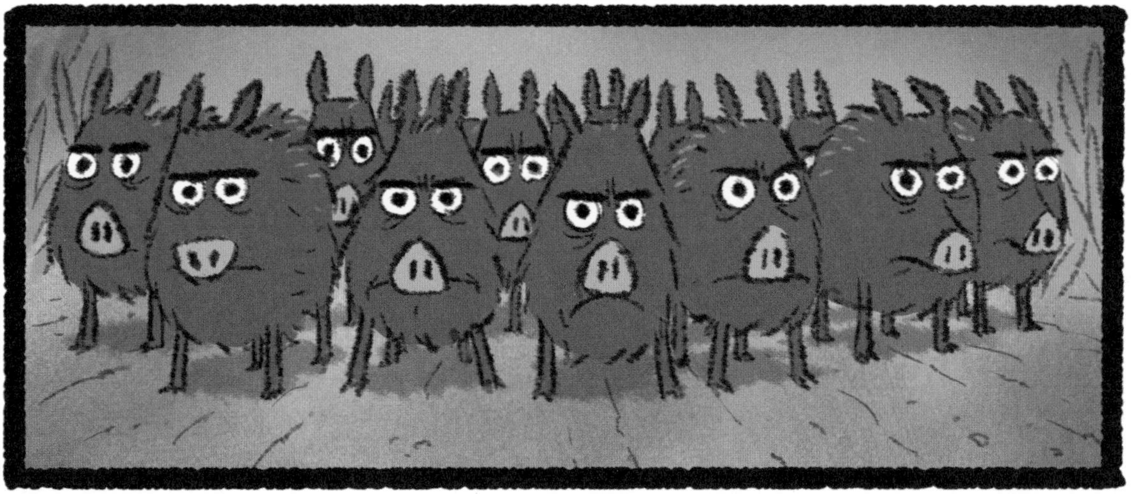

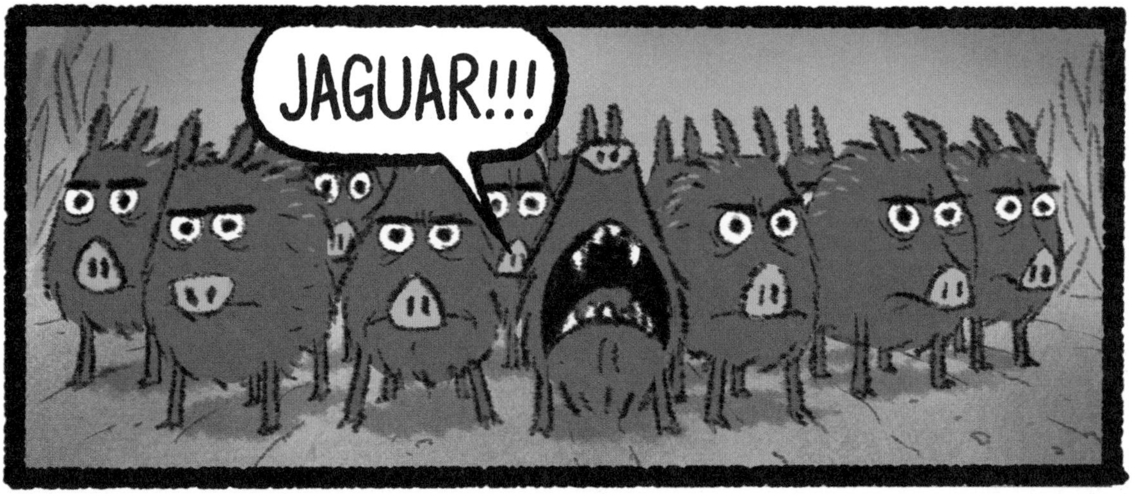
JAGUAR!!!

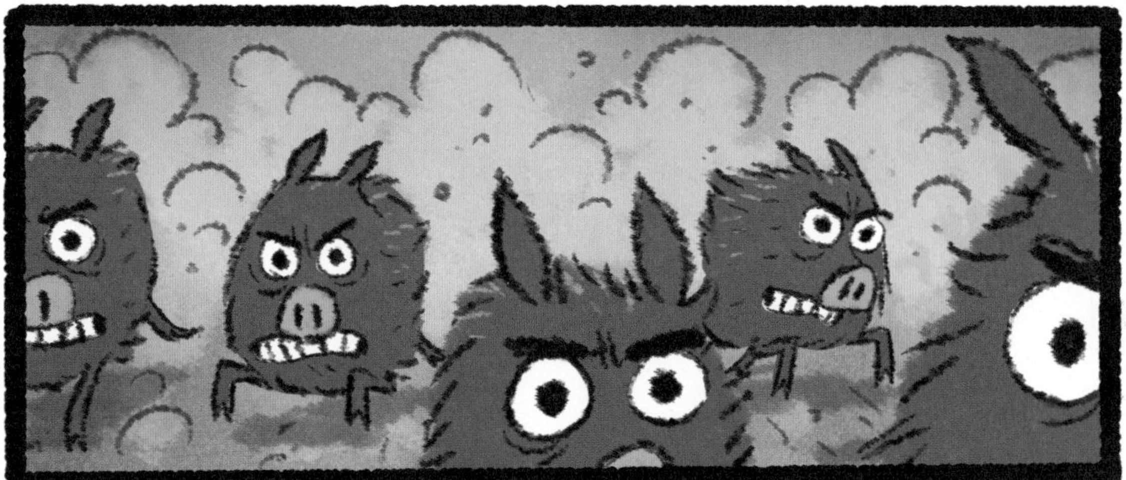

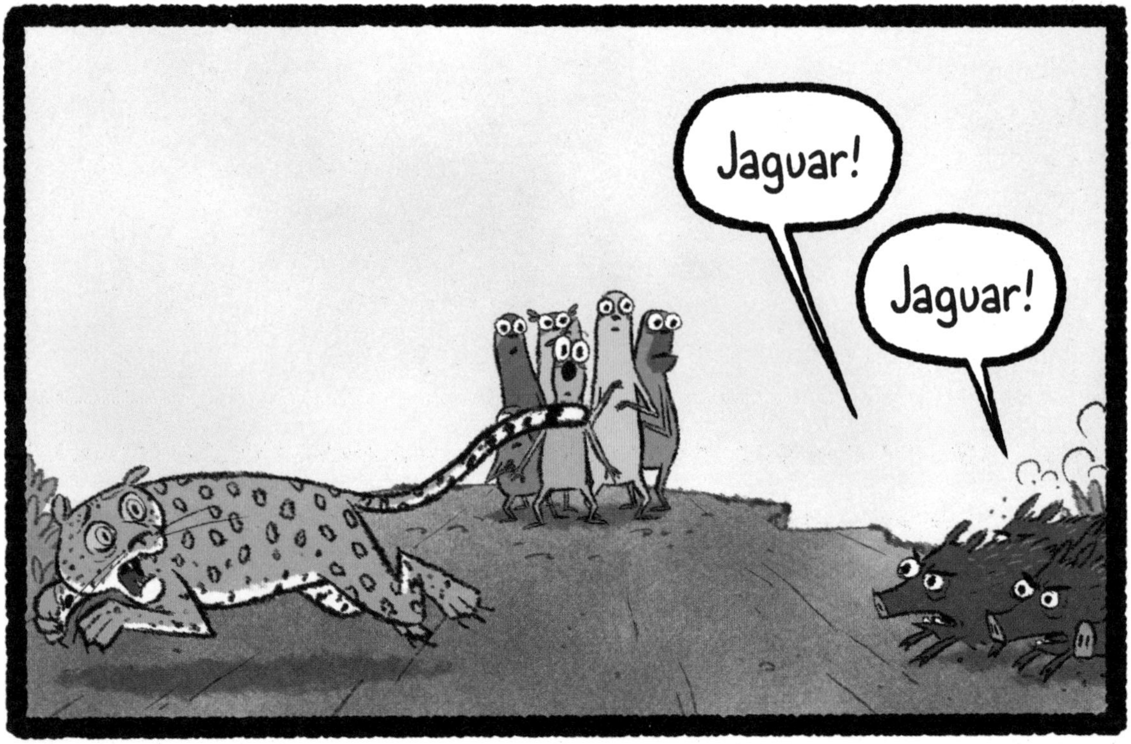
Jaguar!
Jaguar!

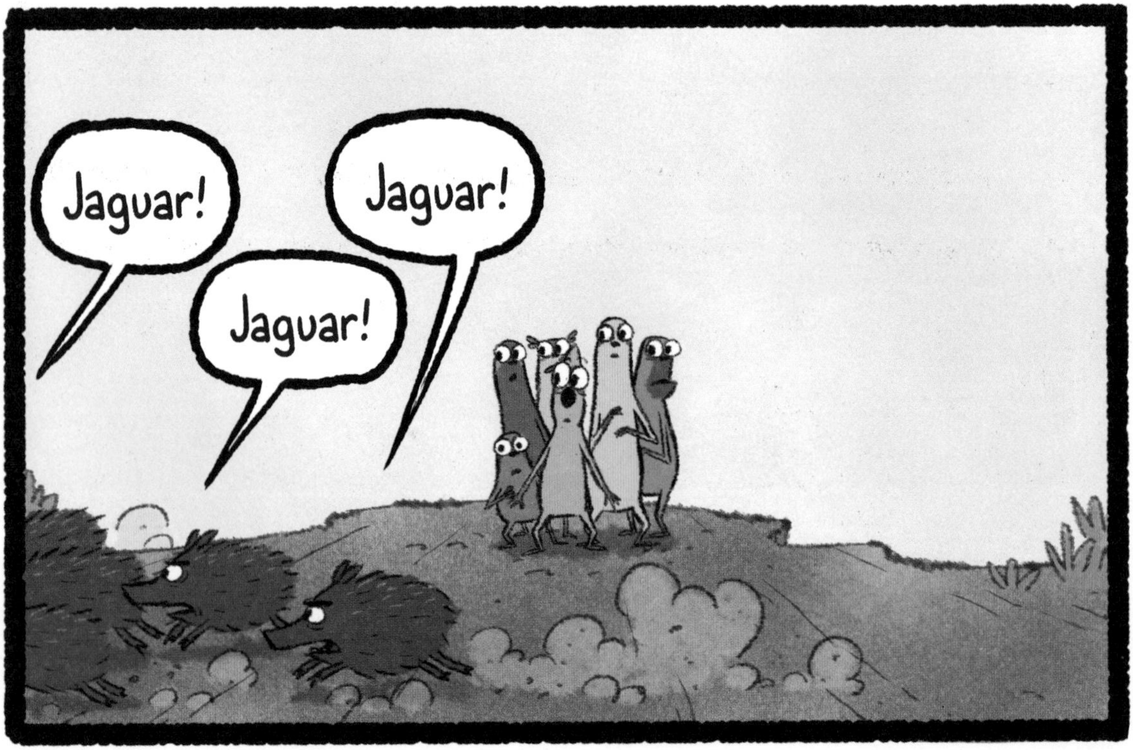
Jaguar!
Jaguar!
Jaguar!

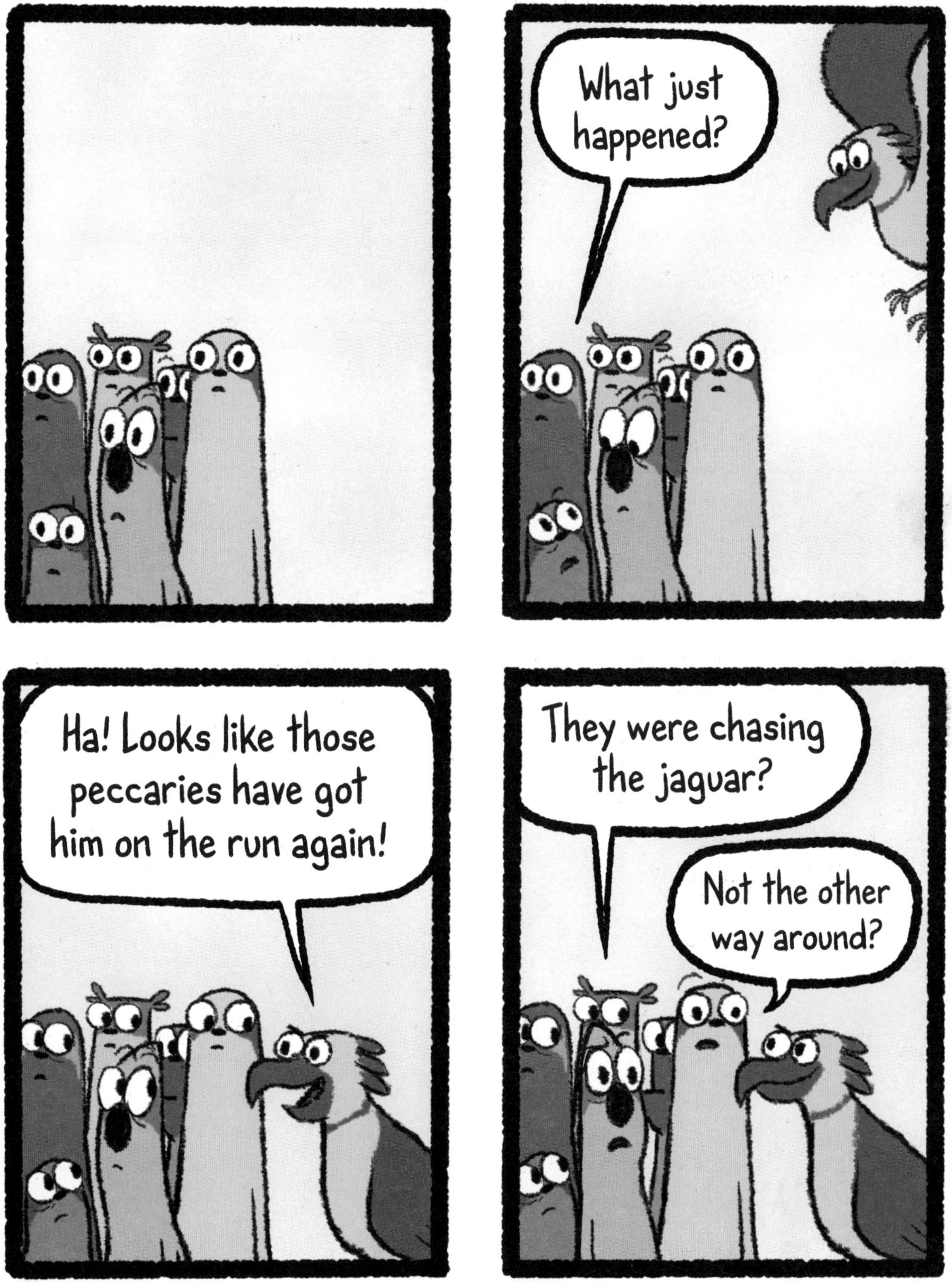
What just happened?
Ha! Looks like those peccaries have got him on the run again!
They were chasing the jaguar?
Not the other way around?

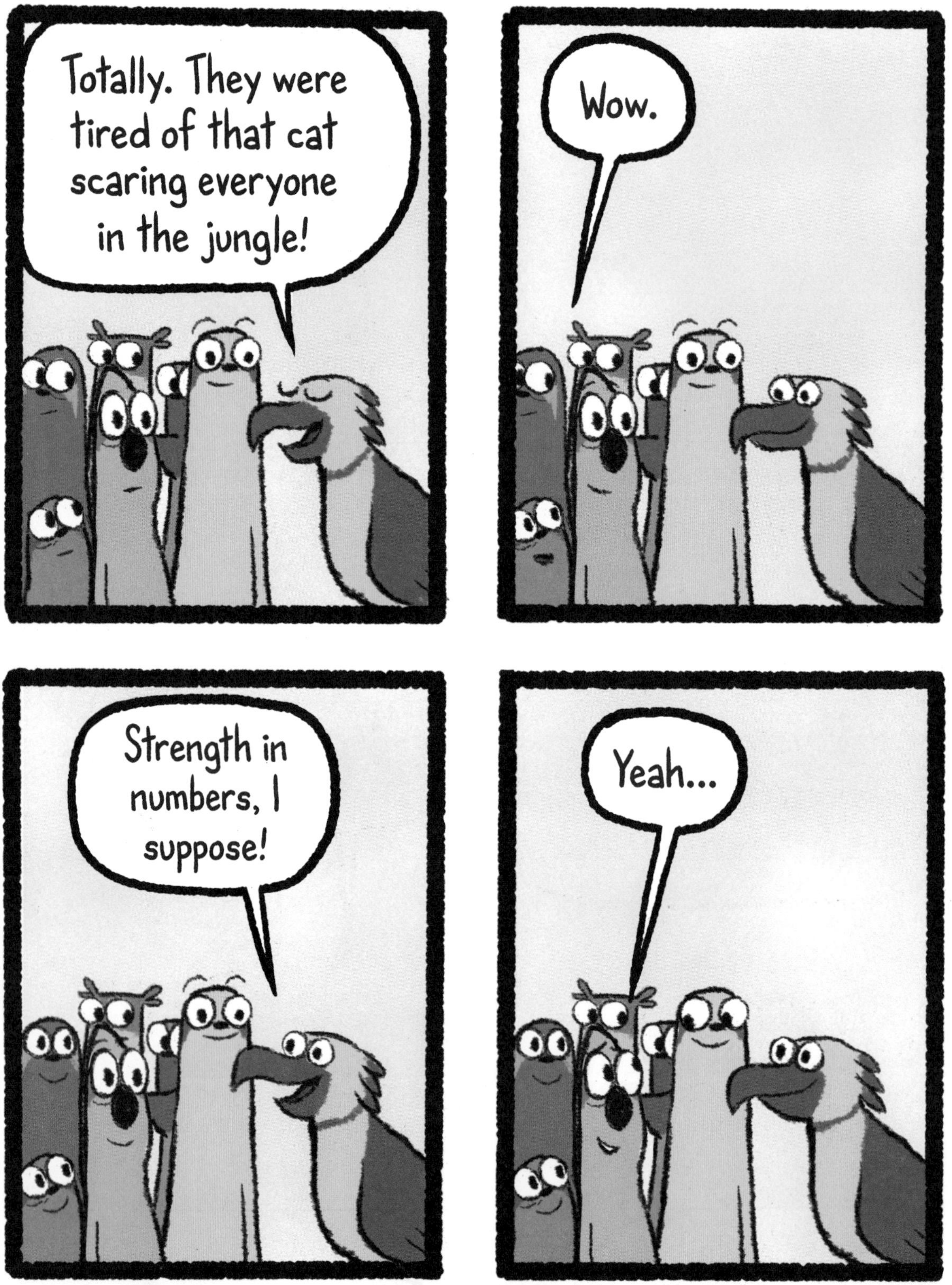
Totally. They were tired of that cat scaring everyone in the jungle!
Wow.
Strength in numbers, I suppose!
Yeah...

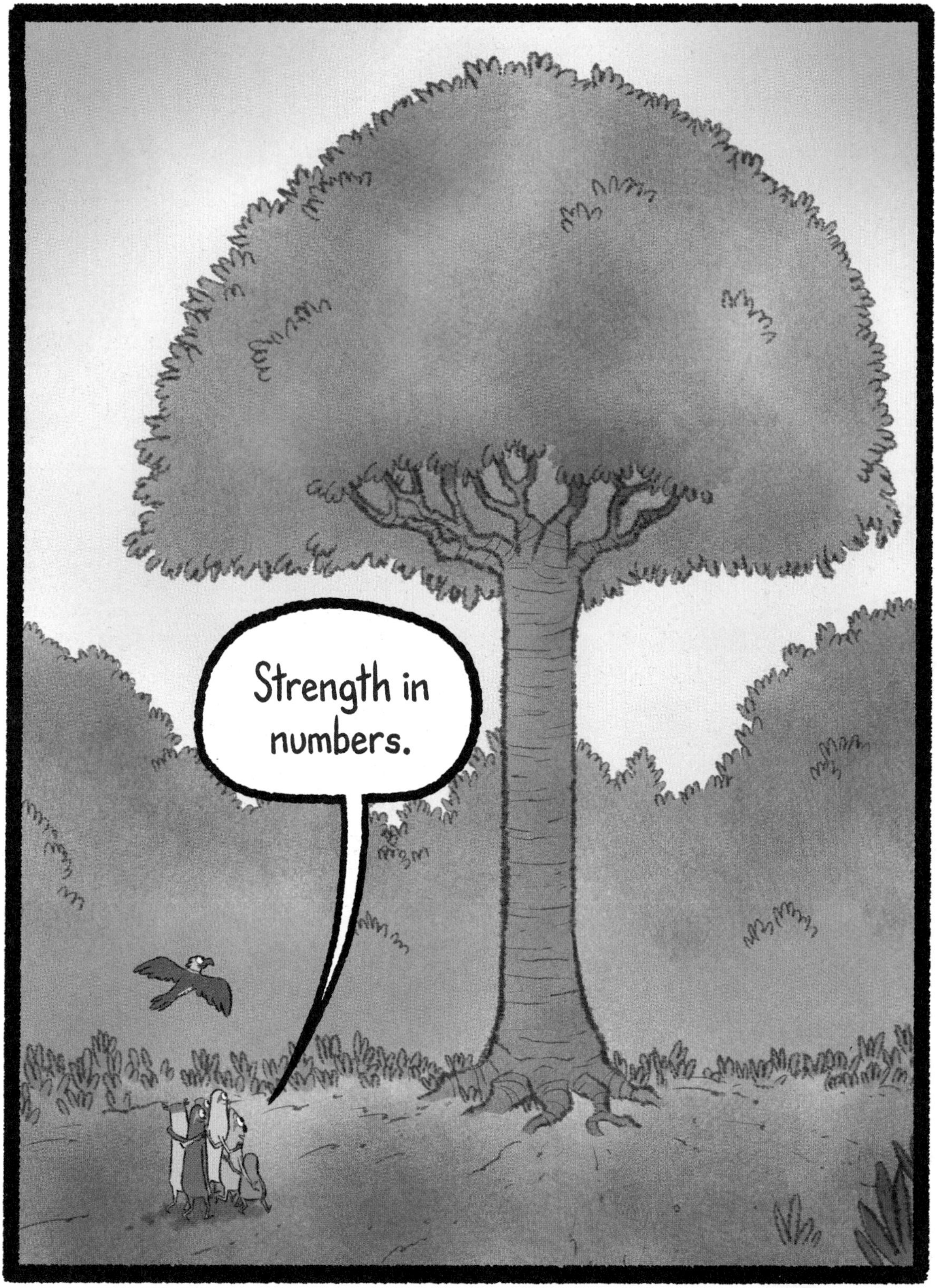
Strength in numbers.

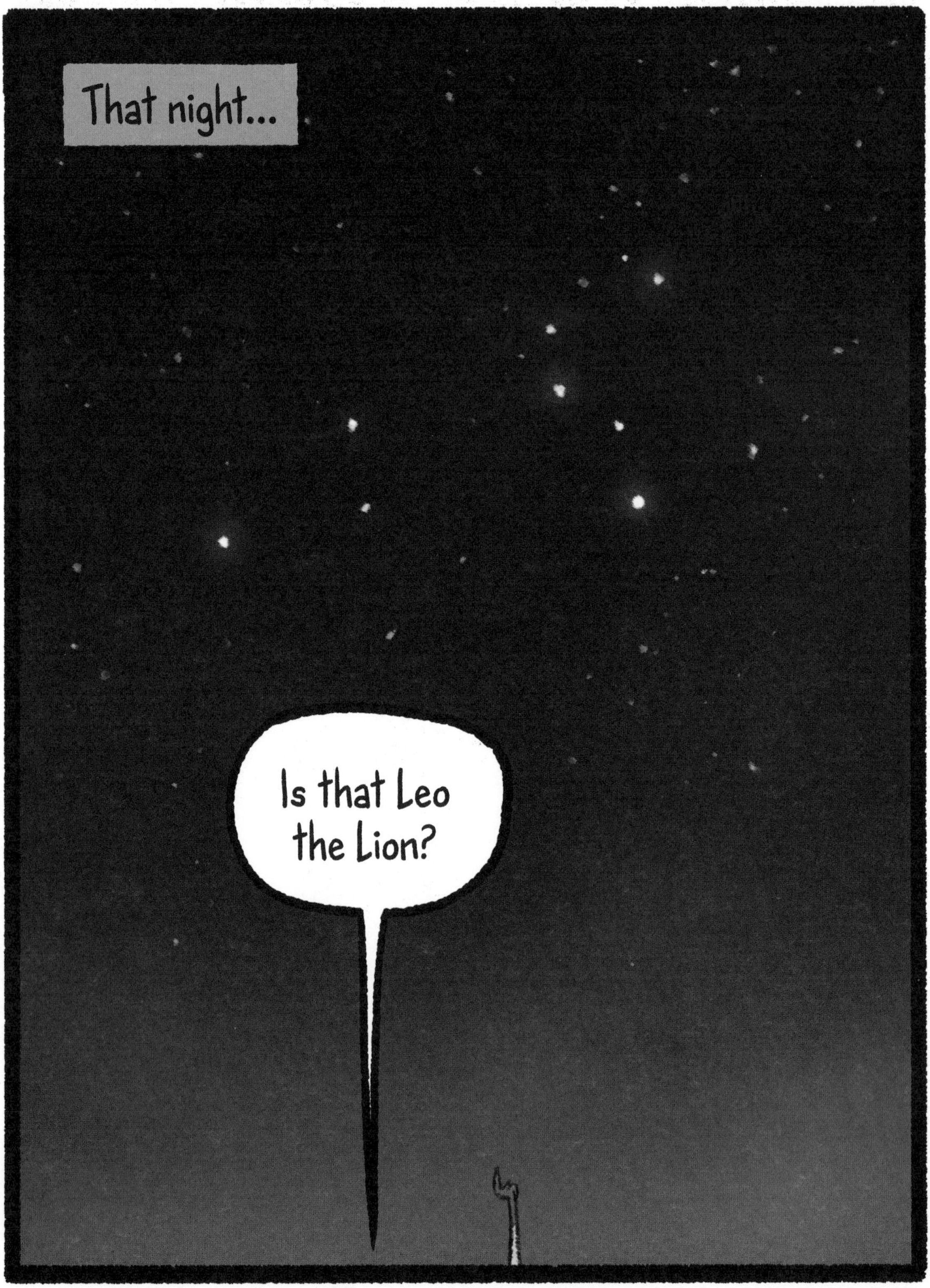
That night...
Is that Leo the Lion?

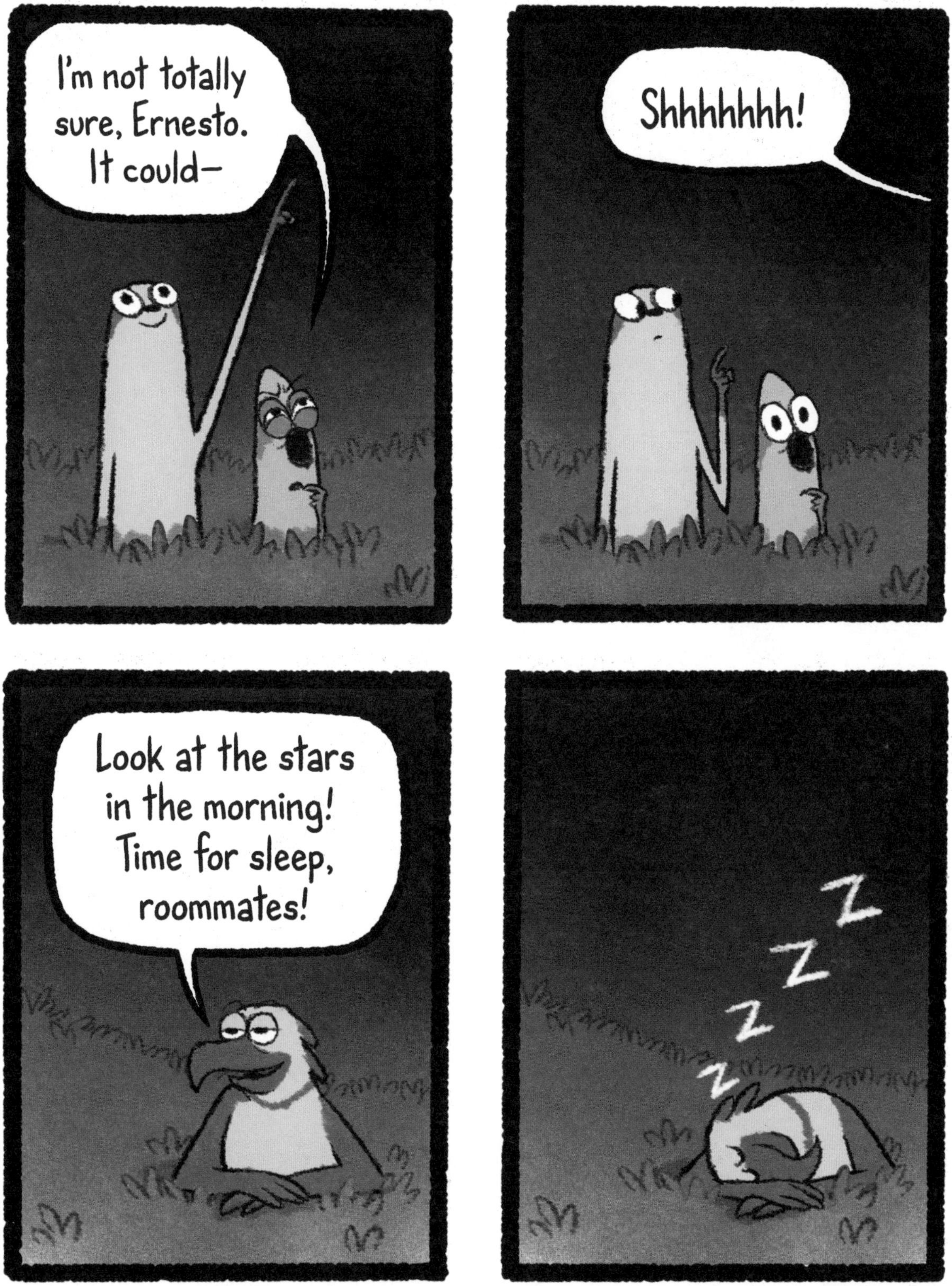
I'm not totally sure, Ernesto. It could–
Shhhhhhh!
Look at the stars in the morning! Time for sleep, roommates!
Z Z Z Z

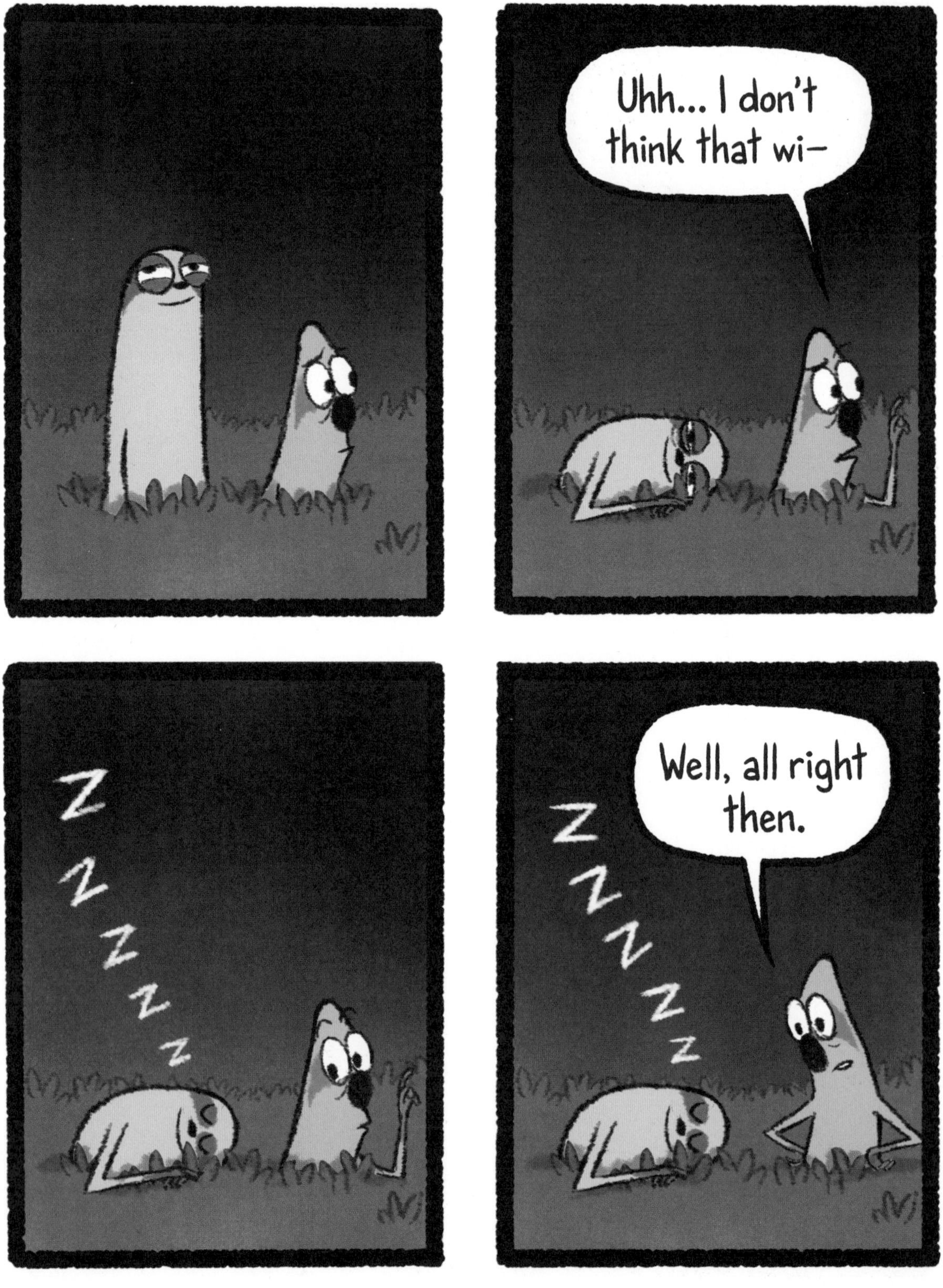
Uhh... I don't think that wi–
Z Z Z Z Z Z
Well, all right then.
Z Z Z Z Z Z

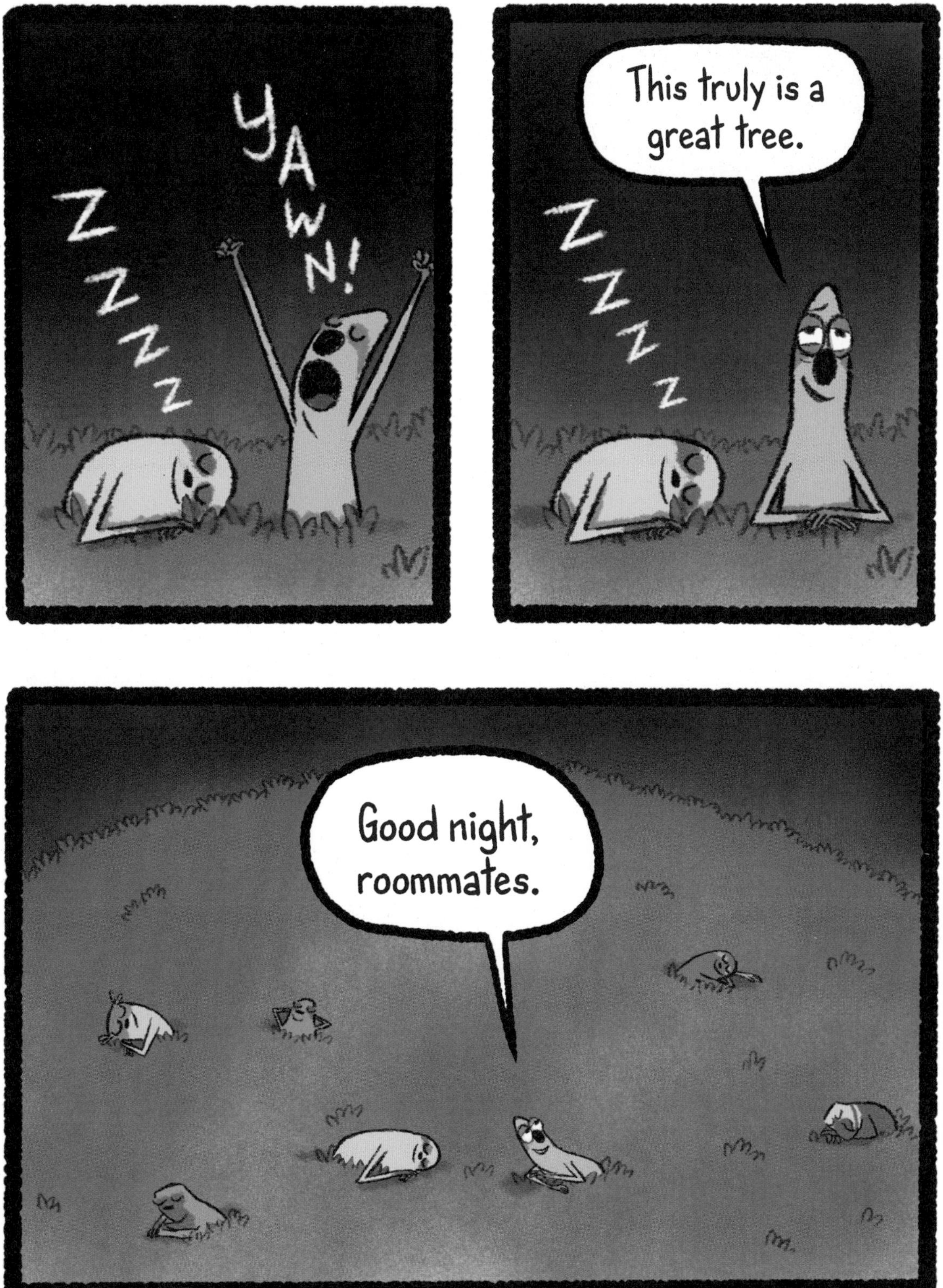
ZZZZ
YAWN!
ZZZZ
This truly is a great tree.
Good night, roommates.

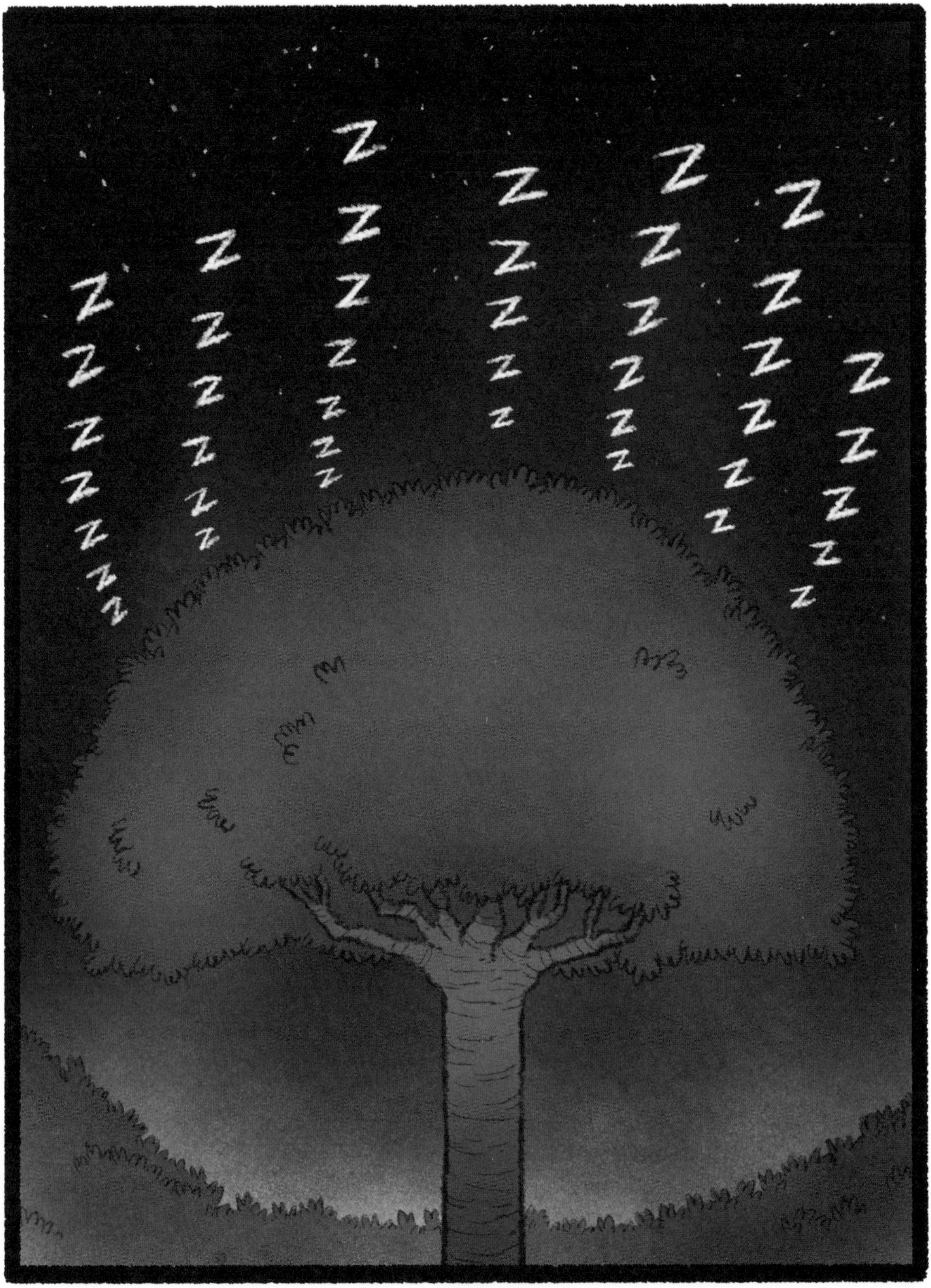

# Fun Facts about Sloths!

## Real Fact!

There are two types of sloths in the world!
Two-toed sloths and three-toed sloths!
(Although all sloths actually have three toes
on each hind leg—it's the number of
fingers on their forelimbs that differ!)

## PETER & ERNESTO Fact!

Peter first met Ernesto when they were both just three months old.

## Real Fact!

Sloths generally have poor eyesight and hearing! They depend mostly on touch and smell to find their food!

# Real Fact!

Although slow moving on land, sloths are very good swimmers!

**PETER & ERNESTO Fact!**

One time, Peter and Ernesto woke up covered in butterflies!

## Real Fact!

Sloths come down out of their trees once a week to pee
or poop because their metabolisms move so slowly.
This is when they're most vulnerable to predators such as jaguars.

# PETER & ERNESTO Fact!

Peter and Ernesto don't always hang in
the traditional way that sloths do!

First Second

Copyright © 2019 by Graham Annable

Published by First Second
First Second is an imprint of Roaring Brook Press, a division of Holtzbrinck Publishing Holdings Limited Partnership
175 Fifth Avenue, New York, NY 10010

Library of Congress Control Number: 2018938081

ISBN: 978-1-62672-572-0

Our books may be purchased in bulk for promotional, educational, or business use. Please contact your
local bookseller or the Macmillan Corporate and Premium Sales Department at (800) 221-7945 ext. 5442 or
by e-mail at MacmillanSpecialMarkets@macmillan.com.

First edition, 2019
Edited by Calista Brill and Alex Lu
Book design by Molly Johanson
Printed in China by 1010 Printing International Limited, North Point, Hong Kong

The entire story was created using customized brushes in Photoshop and hand drawn on a Cintiq monitor.

1 3 5 7 9 10 8 6 4 2

BY ART
WE LIVE